Praise for *A Carnivore's Inquiry*:

"Murray is a mesmerizing writer who uses succinct, evocative language with the precision of a pointilist."
—Rene Rodriguez, *The Miami Herald*

"Though *A Carnivore's Inquiry* has any number of scary (not to mention stomach-churning) moments, the novel's real appeal lies in Katherine's erudite, mordant humor. . . . Beneath both the humor and the horror lies a scathing indictment of American values. Katherine, with her ceaseless hunger, serves as a gorgeous, freaky metaphor for that clichéd American dream of having it all."
—Joanna Smith Rakoff, *Time Out New York*

"Compelling, maddening, hilarious . . . remarkable."
—Ron Bernas, *Detroit Free Press*

"Stylish, chilling, highly literate psychological thriller."
—*The Bookseller* (UK)

"Why is this book, full of murder, loneliness, and insanity, so darn funny? That's the genius of this oddly wonderful and engrossing second novel by Murray. . . . The plot itself is tight and fast, quirky and dangerous."
—Anne Rochell Konigsmark, *The Atlanta Journal-Constitution*

"Mesmerizing . . . Murray paces her psychological thriller with consummate control, keeping the reader enthralled through subtle suggestion and a scattering of grisly details. But the author has a darker purpose. More than the story of one deranged woman's obsession, the novel and its brilliant subtext hint at the ways American society devours the weak, while building a case for a blood hunger in human nature. . . . Readers will be hooked by Murray's classy treatment of her sexy-sinister subject matter."
—*Publishers Weekly*

Also by Sabina Murray

The Caprices
Slow Burn

Sabina Murray

A
CARNIVORE'S
INQUIRY

Grove Press
New York

Published simultaneously in Canada
Printed in the United States of America

FIRST GROVE PRESS PAPERBACK EDITION

Library of Congress Cataloging-in-Publication Data
Murray, Sabina.
A carnivore's inquiry / Sabina Murray.
p. cm.
ISBN 0-8021-4200-1 (pbk.)
1. Young women—Fiction.   2. New York (N.Y.)—Fiction.
3. Mexico—Fiction.   4. Maine—Fiction.   5. Murder—Fiction.   I. Title.
PS3563.U787C37 2004
813'.54—dc22   2003064615

Grove Press
an imprint of Grove/Atlantic, Inc.
841 Broadway
New York, NY 10003

05   06   07   08   09   10   9   8   7   6   5   4   3   2   1

For John

The inhabitants seem to live in that Golden World of which old writers speak so much, wherein men lived simply and innocently without enforcement of laws, without quarelling, judges and libels, content only to satisfy nature.

—Peter Martyr deAnghera, *Decades de Orbe Novo*

Why trembles honesty; and, like a murderer why seeks he refuge from the frowns of his immortal station?

—William Blake, *America: A Prophecy*

1

I am standing at the side of the highway, which is a good place because it is nowhere. The snow is crusted on the ground and more is falling. I drove out of the United States last night; I also drove out of spring and back into winter, which makes me feel as if I am driving into the past, although it's much cleaner than the one I left behind. Canada is a country of lumberjacks and wolves, hospitable, cold, and foreign.

Beginning is always hard, especially when one's story is not yet over. I am an only child. From my mother I inherited my dark eyes and my darker sense of humor, from my father an ability to bring things to a significant conclusion and the black Lexus S.U.V. It's a gorgeous car with a fantastic stereo, but it makes me feel as if I'm in a fast-moving coffin. I can move at ninety miles an hour without realizing it, which is why I pulled over on the side of the road. We are all hurtling into the future like so many unwilling comets. Sometimes I feel the need to stop, to look back before moving on. The snow is hissing in the wind and almost seems to be whispering my name—*Katherine, Katherine*—as if there is something great in store for me, but down the highway I see nothing but a nation plunged in darkness. As I look back to the United States I see the same thing. And why not? Our nations' histories are raveled together, all of this great American continent conquered by trappers popping their bullets into beavers and Spaniards unsheathing their swords. Our civilization is the heart that was pulled still beating out of the heaving bosom of the New World. Am I just a product, as my mother always suggested, of this violent, bloody past?

And what of the Old World?

Europe is to my right as I stand facing north. I can see a glimmer of light flattening the horizon, a pale fire of history, which, although very distant, seems enough to keep me warm.

2

—⊷ ≦◊≧ ⊶—

I remember the day of my return to the United States for its foul weather
and for my first encounter with Boris. Boris was at his editor's office
then, which took him near Penn Station. I had taken the bus from the
airport and then had retreated into the subway, because I was feeling
both tired and nervous and—like a rabbit—felt the need to go under-
ground. I suppose if I had thought of somewhere better to go, for example the Metropolitan Museum of Art, I might never have met Boris.

It was Columbus Day and somewhere in New York people were protesting the rape of America. I was informed of this phenomenon by
two sign-toting students. The young woman carried a sign that said,
COLUMBUS WAS A MURDERER, the other protestor (her boyfriend?) COLUMBUS BLOODY SUNDAY, which might have been
a reference to Irish independence, bloodshed in general, or the day of
the week on which Columbus arrived in the New World. I doubted
that either of them was American Indian—the girl was pale and blond,
the boy Jewish, Italian, Greek, Armenian, or some combination—and
had therefore benefited from the conquest of the New World. Outrage leaves little room for reason. They had to be students because they
had time and youth, signs and shabby clothes, all of which attested in
an outward way to their moral superiority. Like me, they were waiting
for a train. Unlike me, they knew where they were going.

I suppose the protestors wanted to efface Columbus's role as discoverer, leader, romantic figure and I was tempted to remind them

that the Spaniards had done that many years ago and during the explorer's lifetime. Perhaps they should consider that our country bore the name of Amerigo Vespucci and, if they were interested in a revisionist approach, Columbus Day was more of a time for recent Sicilian and Neapolitan immigrants—the large share of Italian Americans who historically had nothing to do with the Genoese—to share their sausage and meatballs with more than the usual pride.

Columbus Day was also an occasion for me to consider my return to America after time spent in Europe. Europe at the time of Columbus was a bloody, plague-ridden plot of land. Godless too, unless one counted the Inquisition, the wholesale slaughter of Hugenots, and other such phenomena. The bloodbath in the New World was not so much a definitive act of aggression, but rather an expansion of what was going on at home. Old news. Not news at all. So rather than pondering all the bloodshed that Columbus now stood for, I felt more inclined to think of his last years. His longing to return to America. His mind tormented by a grandeur that had deserted him. I thought of myself as a friend to Columbus, someone who understood the necessary violence of discovery, an enlightened peer, maybe along the lines of a fellow discoverer—Vespucci, for example—who, no doubt, felt the loss when Columbus finally crossed over into that other borderless land, a new New World, to which we are all fated. Vespucci understood Columbus's (or rather, Colón's) torments and successes, how with their caravels and galleons, Vespucci and Colón had towed the Old World out of the Dark Ages and into the brilliant light of paradise.

I had spent some time in Florence, Vespucci's home town, which added to my feelings of kinship. In Europe I'd been swept up by a sense of anachronism. While peering in the long glass window of a shoe store where the latest fashions were displayed, one could find the shoes obscured by the reflection of the Duomo. At night, alone on the terrace of the Uffizi, it was as easy to picture assassins with jeweled daggers as the actual Moroccan hash dealers. It was as if, in Florence, time performed no function, as opposed to Manhattan, where here, in the subway system, the notion of Dutch traders and foolish Indians accepting glass beads seemed not only distant but improbable. There's a saying, "time functions to prevent everything from happening at once," and although I can't remember who said it, I have a lingering suspicion that it was an American. I checked my watch to see the time, and noted, with some amusement, that it was still set to the time in Italy.

I wonder how Vespucci felt when he learned of his old friend's death. Perhaps relief, because he would no longer have to petition the king on Colón's behalf. Perhaps a certain sad pride at having known him in his prime.

I picture Vespucci going to his chair by the window with a mug of the new coffee, for which he has developed a suspicious dependence much like others for wine. No doubt Vespucci thinks the letter from his friend is full of complaints about King Ferdinand, how once again his petition to be reinstated as governor of Hispaniola has been denied. *Amerigo, set the king straight. I am the rightful governor of the Indies.* Since Colón still insists that Hispaniola is in Asia. If Hispaniola is indeed in Asia, which is a very old world, why does Colón feel the outrage of someone robbed of his discovery?

What might have been a source of antagonism between Colón and Vespucci could well have been the basis of their friendship. Wasn't Colón's childish willfulness in the face of reason endearing? Still, being Colón's friend and Pilot Major of Spain put Vespucci in a difficult position. But he would fire off a letter to the king. *Think of all Colón has done in the name of Spain.* Although the king would never reinstate Colón as governor.

The king himself had removed Colón from his post.

The king had ordered Colón shipped back to Spain in a cocoon of chains.

The king had condemned Colón to spend his final years haunting the streets of Seville, a quiet end—tragic, even—for a man who wanted to keep fighting with the Indians, digging for gold.

But Vespucci reads that the letter is not from Cristobal, but from his son, Fernando. And Vespucci sadly realizes that Fernando could only have one reason to write him.

. . . *from gout on May 20 of this year, 1506. As you were his good friend and even patron I do not need to list for you the accomplishments of his life which, although an august fifty-four years, seems brief for a man of such potential . . .*

The day is ending in a bath of golden light and birds swoop energetically close to the margin of land and sky, birds leaving trails across the blue: the coastline of the fields, the promontories of the hills, the isthmus of the solitary tower, the delta of the pine-choked valley. In his mind Vespucci sees the edges of the world gathered together like the corners of a sheet, he and Colón weaving them together. What had once been the broad, virginal Pacific is now threaded over by the paths of a dozen caravels crossing and crossing, so that the spume of one vessel is soon laced over by the wake of another. The world is now round. The world is now small. Vespucci had looked through a telescope, Colón down the length of a musket, but they had worked together—partners in a grand enterprise.

I was startled then by the high-pitched screech of a train on the track behind me. The two protesters were involved in a deep, tongue-probing kiss. Protest was, I suppose, sexy. They might have missed their train, but they didn't seem to care. Did they care about anything, Columbus included? Columbus had willed Hispaniola into being, planting Europeans into the New World like saplings, leaving a bristling forest. Although he was old when he arrived at court—forty-two, his once red hair already drained of color—people believed in him. Hadn't Isabella given him three ships? Hadn't Vespucci used his ties with the Medici to finance part of his venture? Columbus's faith in himself, in his dreams, was unshakable. Four days before the sighting of Hispaniola there was a rebellion. The men were terrified that they would go sailing off the edge of the earth. But Columbus had asked them to be patient, probably with a loaded musket, and they struck land. Who cared where it was—what it was—as long as it wasn't populated by dragons, as long as it didn't terminate in a bottomless, frothing waterfall?

Shouldn't this be what we consider on Columbus Day?

A year before Colón's death, he met with Vespucci and they shared a meal. This must have been an awkward dinner, because it followed yet another failed petition for the governorship of Hispaniola. This was the last time the two explorers met. I imagine that Colón did not look well. He had been suffering from gout for the past seven years. Perhaps Vespucci saw the end coming. Perhaps he saw it in Colón's eyes, in his crumbling strength.

I imagine Colón eyeing Vespucci in a petulant way. He envies Vespucci's position. "What have you been doing?" he asks.

"You know what I have been doing."

"Maps and stars," says Colón.

"Cosmography and astronomy," corrects Vespucci.

"You bumped into the Indies because you were looking up at the sky. You didn't see where you were going. You think, 'What's this doing here? Must be something new.'"

"The world is too large for that to be Asia," says Vespucci.

"Because of your stars, you say that. But I say that the Indians make it clear that we have reached Asia."

Then maybe Vespucci stops. He does not know what is kindness now. Should he argue to show that he still values what Colón has to say? Should he accept the explorer's opinion out of respect? "I trust my equations," says Vespucci. "You trust your eyes."

"Who cares what is true?" says Colón. "You have the king's ear."

The two friends have differences that run deep. Vespucci, a Florentine, is a nobleman. Educated. Privileged. Urbane. Colón springs from Genoa, the son of a weaver. He is a self-made merchant from the city of commerce.

"You like paintings. You like poems. You like the stars. But I . . ."
Here Colón thumps his chest with his fingers, "I sailed in the name
of Spain."

Vespucci looks at his friend, at the gravy on his shirt. "Cristóbal,
I sailed in the name of Spain."

"No, you sailed for yourself."

"To learn. That's not for myself. That's for everyone." Vespucci
cannot understand Colón's stubbornness. Cosmography is exploration. Knowledge isn't any colder or deader than the stars burning and
spitting in the black fabric of the night sky. Vespucci is a romantic
himself. How could one not be in thrall to the progression of degrees,
the web of longitude and latitude, the brief embrace of planet and
star? His life is lived in fifteen degrees per hour, his interest in the
ink divining land from water, the equatorial circumference of the
earth. Circumference. At least both men believe in that, even though
claiming that the new continent was the Indies meant the earth was
sucked in at the waist, like a peanut.

"I didn't sail for Spain," says Colón. He laughs with Vespucci.
"I sailed for me. To be the first."

But what had they sailed for? Had they sailed to kill off the Indians? Had they sailed to make way for European-style commerce? From
where I stood—subway platform, twenty-first century—it was not clear.

"We sailed for spices," says Vespucci. "For money. We sailed because the Queen with her crazy Inquisition has driven all the Jews
out of Spain and there are no more merchants. We sailed because
the Turks slaughter our knights and we cannot go east by land."
Vespucci looks disdainfully at his friend's pork. At the pigeon, which
he has ordered but not touched. "We sailed because the meat we eat
is rotten and we must mask this with cinnamon from Ceylon, pepper
from India, and clove from Zanzibar."

"Are you saying we sailed in the name of rotten meat?"

"Perhaps." Vespucci smiles. "Rather than spice, let there be fresh
meat in your Indies."

And here I thought of an Indian skirted in leaves, a full head
shorter than Vespucci, shown in neatly delineated (and anatomically
impossible) profile offering the explorer a hot dog. Or perhaps a knish.

Or a falafel. Some honeyed peanuts. A pretzel. Or perhaps a neon-colored bag of cotton candy. Because if nothing else, the New World was full of food. I could see the people in the train station shoving handfuls of the convenient fodder into their mouths. And I realized that this was one of the many definitions of American: one who can achieve the needs of his or her appetite. This is what exploration had opened up the door to. Not only widespread slaughter, but the necessary accompaniment of gorging. Of course there were no hot dogs at the time of Columbus and Vespucci, not on Hispaniola, not in Brazil, nowhere. In fact, the explorers brought famine along with them—the hunger of the Old World into seemingly abundant paradise.

"I ate lizards," says Colón. "I ate a dog. It didn't bark, but it was still a dog." Colón smiles wryly. "But there is a kind of fresh meat."

Vespucci laughs. "They eat their enemies. So what?"

"You told me," says Colón, "that at the mouth of that great river, you spoke to a man who had eaten three hundred men."

"He had many enemies." Vespucci thinks. "And now they have more."

"We are their enemies?" Colón waves Vespucci off. "They hate us now, but we will change their minds."

"I have little faith in that," says Vespucci. "Your Indians pepper us with their arrows. The drumsong and howling is hardly done in gratitude."

"Once the Indians are civilized, they will see what we have done for them."

"Such generosity," says Vespucci. "When I was at the court of Louis XI the Hugenots were rioting in the streets. The rebellion was put down. And after, the bodies of the Huguenots were butchered and sold as meat." Vespucci thinks for a moment and then smiles. "Maybe you should go civilize the Parisians."

"Maybe I should," Colón laughs. "But there is nothing noble in that."

"Noble?" questions Vespucci.

"We are helping the Indians," says Colón. "We are their saviors. They have no faith. We give them our God. We give them medicine."

"We give them disease. It is our duty to cure it."

As usual, Colón noted, Vespucci bordered on sacrilege.

"We give them guns," says Vespucci, "but only the barrel."

"Amerigo," Colón says in an almost fatherly way, "we give them civilization."

"There is no civilization," says Vespucci. "There is no New World."

"Then you agree that Hispaniola is in Asia?"

"No, Cristóbal." And Vespucci smiles and pats his friend's arm. "I say Hispaniola is in Europe."

Or maybe Vespucci said nothing of the sort. Maybe Christopher Columbus and Amerigo Vespucci argued and came to no agreement, or agreed that the Indians were all cannibals and worthy of condemnation, and, worse, conversion. Or maybe they ate in silence, shoveling the undistinguished food into their mouths without conversation, the hours spent waiting for an audience with the king having left them with a profound hunger.

What is the value of them arguing anyway? Vespucci and Columbus come to us as bedfellows, parts of a whole. History. Europe. Exploration. Colonization. America. The two discoverers are inseparable and we can no more divorce reasonable Vespucci from aggressive Columbus than we can live in thrall to intellect apart from appetite.

A train pulled in and the two protesting students got on with their signs. As they boarded, an old lady with gray curls was struck on the head, which I thought was a rather violent act. I might have even called the protesters' attention to it, but they were gone, barreling back into the twenty-first century, and it was time for me too to get going. I saw Boris on the platform then. I didn't recognize him at first, but thought perhaps I might have met him once, so I watched him quietly, unseen, from behind a pillar.

3

The city was shrouded in cloud and Boris was in a dark state. He stood armed with nothing but his green umbrella, battling a deep depression, which today he attributed to the rain. Boris looked up at life from the bottom of this mood as if he were trapped in a well—the view was limited and anything worthwhile seemed a remote possibility. People were belting him about the ribs with book bags; they were looking at the space on the wall behind him. He was invisible, nonexistent. Here in this tunnel there was no oxygen, only dirty light and the deep rumbling of the train. It was as though he were in a vast intestine and, beyond the tunnel's bend, was a stomach about to purge itself. He took a pack of Rolaids from his pocket and consumed five. Boris glanced around nervously. He thought he must have been waiting a quarter of an hour at least, when it had only been five minutes.

I watched him from behind the pillar. The train arrived.

Boris seated himself and I sat next to him, in the only available seat. I could have stood, but I was tired from a combination of jet lag and the six demi-bottles of Chianti, courtesy of Alitalia.

We sat shoulder to shoulder with our eyes directed forward. There was a smell on Boris like pipe tobacco, but I detected no smoke. He breathed through his nose, which was so clotted with springy hair, little tendrils escaping his nostrils, that his breath whistled. He had his legs crossed at the ankles and when the train lurched, his knee bumped mine. Every now and then he would push his glasses up his nose with his thumb.

I recognized him then.

On the airplane I had lifted a woman's *Vanity Fair* when she got up to use the restroom. On her return, she had watched me read it with an ineffectual outrage, but it could have been my magazine, so there really wasn't anything she could do about it. Boris had been in the "Night Table Reading" section. He was listed as the author of *Soulless Man*. He was reading *A Man without Qualities* in the original German, which I suppose is something like *Eine Man Ohne Qualities*.

Boris caught me eyeing him and began rummaging around in his leather bag. He took out a magazine, plain pages, and began reading it intently.

"What are you reading?" I asked.

Boris looked over, annoyed.

"It is an Author's Guild magazine. Not of interest to most people."

"You're Boris Naryshkin, aren't you?" I said.

"Yes, I am." He was surprised.

"I'm Katherine. I saw you once in a magazine."

"Which magazine was that?"

"I can't remember," I lied. "It was some time ago."

"What do you know about me?" he said.

"You write depressing books."

"Have you read any of my books?"

"No. But I can tell that they're depressing."

"How can you tell?"

"By the way you sit."

Boris smiled. "My editor says much the same thing and he has read everything."

There was an awkward pause.

"Who do you identify with, Vespucci or Columbus?" I asked.

"Today?" said Boris. "Columbus."

"Why?"

"Because I am not well-liked."

"I like you."

"You don't know me."

"It's much easier to like people you don't know."

Boris, off-guard, smiled.

"You make your money depressing people?"

Boris nodded slowly.

"What a relief," I said. "I just got back from Italy today. I spent the last year with men on vacation. Light-hearted men. Actually, they were shallow, which I suppose doesn't exclude being heavy of heart. I can't picture any of them depressed, or in a deep depression. Maybe a shallow depression."

"A dimple," said Boris.

"What?" I said.

"Dimple could be a word that means shallow depression."

"So instead of getting depressed, these people get dimples?"

"Yes," said Boris.

There was a moment of silence.

"Would you be interested in joining me for dinner?" he asked.

"I'd be delighted," I replied.

Boris took me out to his favorite restaurant for some northern Italian food. I ordered a hare ragout. It came with salted gnocchi and a salad of wilted arugula and radicchio. Boris ordered something else, I'm not sure what, but he made a great deal of noise while he ate it. The wine was a predictable Chianti. Boris made a big show of sending back a bottle. I'm sure now that the wine that followed tasted exactly the same as the wine he refused. There was no conversation for a couple of minutes. I really didn't know what to say. I was lost in my thoughts. Bored on the plane, I'd tried to picture what man my father would like to see me with least. I thought of the usual suspects: addict, musician, performance artist, his business partner. But Boris had to be the worst of them all—the European intellectual who would find my father inferior. I drank the wine down and poured myself another glass.

"You like the wine?" he asked.

"Oh yes. It's wonderful," I said. "What do you think they did with the bottle you sent back?"

"I think they drink it," said Boris.

"I'm pleased to hear that."

"It is just a theory," said Boris. "Why does it please you?"

"I'd hate to see it go to waste."

"Even if it was bad?"

"Your vinegar, another man's ambrosia," I said, startled by the words, sure I must have heard them somewhere before.

"You are a relativist."

I wasn't sure what he meant. "Yes," I said. "Is that bad?"

"Morally," said Boris, without much conviction. He smiled. "How old are you?"

I smiled. "I'm twenty-two."

"Why were you in Italy?"

"You don't need a good reason to go to Italy. Everyone should go to Italy. Why aren't you in Italy?"

"Because there is no money there, at least not for me." Boris eyed me suspiciously. "Why did you come back?"

I pushed my *ragout con lepre* around my plate. "I got sick of the food," I said and Boris smiled.

Boris had left Russia sometime in the seventies. I pictured Boris as looking much the same only slimmer, with more hair, wearing brown polyester pants. It was easy to convince the Americans—who hated the Russian government—that everyone had some pressing reason to escape. Some people did. Boris didn't. He thought his opportunities were better in America. And they were.

"I learned English quickly because I speak French," Boris said.

"Don't you miss Russia?"

"No," he said.

"Don't you miss your family?"

"Most of them are dead. Here, I have started a new life. Isn't that what America is for?"

"Sure, if you're not American."

Boris laughed again. "You make me laugh," he said, as if it were a problem. He shifted his weight in the chair and looked around the room. He seemed nervous that someone would see us, but there weren't that many people eating. It was early, around seven, too early to eat in the city. There was one large party, a family, complete with two grand-parents, three middle-aged men, brothers, who all looked alike although slightly balder, fatter, or grayer than one another. There were three anxious wives to go with the brothers, one applying lipstick, the other two with chairs turned inward, wrapped up in some gossip. The table was littered with wine bottles and two small boys were hiding under the table hatching a conspiracy. At another table a woman picked at a salad while hammering away at her laptop computer. She looked like a lawyer. The sounds were all muffled and the dim light made every table seem strangely isolated, as if we weren't really there. I wondered if the other diners felt the same way or if it was just my jet lag. I looked back at Boris and was surprised to see him there. He was done with dinner, done with the bread, and looked at me with frank suspicion.

"Tell me about Russia," I said.

"What is there to tell?"

"You're a writer," I said. "Tell me a story."

Boris regarded me closely then nodded to himself. He pushed back from the table and crossed his legs. "Once, when I was a small boy on vacation in Georgia, there was a place on the mountain," he showed me the shoulder-height mountain, "where they did experiments on monkeys and apes. I was driving with my family on the road near the mountain. I don't know how it happened, but all the animals had es-caped. There were baboons running here and there, so we stopped the car. All of a sudden there is this, what is this, the big red one . . ."

"Orangutan?"

". . . on the hood of my father's car. He got up there and we stopped and he masturbated for half an hour. My mother was in the car. She covered my eyes. My grandmother was in the car. She started to pray."

"Then what happened?"

"That's the story. After that, it is not so interesting. We drive home. We read newspapers and brush our teeth." Boris shrugged. "I grow up and come to America."

"That's it?"

"I die. I am buried and no one comes to my funeral. All my acquaintances say that I was a bastard and that they are happy now without me."

"Wow," I said, "that's a great story. Tell me another."

"First dessert." Boris said. He glanced down at the dessert menu.

"Tiramusu?" I suggested.

He shook his head. "Not here. Here, we eat *zuppa Inglese*." Boris raised his hand for no waiter in particular. "You tell me a story."

"Me? About what?"

"You."

"No," I said. "I'll tell you about her." I looked over at the woman with her laptop. "She's not really working. She's alone and doesn't want to look stupid. She's typing, 'How stupid it is to be alone. I make two hundred thousand dollars a year. You'd think I could find someone to eat dinner with me.' She types that over and over."

"That's not a story," said Boris.

"I'm not a writer. Tell me more about Russia."

"Why this interest in Russia? Russia is just like America only colder and with less money." The waiter came over and Boris ordered the *zuppa*, some coffee, some dessert wine.

"Please," I said.

He nodded again and shrugged as if defeated. He took the last of the bread and with his mouth full said, "My great uncle Alexei was covered with violent scars."

"Scars? How do you know they were violent?" I asked.

Boris smiled in a patronizing way. "Scars like this you don't get from falling off your bicycle."

"How did he get the scars?"

"From gunshots, from bayonets." Boris ran his finger around the rim of his wine glass. "He did not say where he got these wounds."

"But didn't you know?"

"He was a quiet man. We would holiday together. There was a house by a lake," said Boris. "He had strange habits."

"What strange habits?"

"Uncle Alexei," said Boris, "drank the still-warm blood drained from the necks of cows."

"Why?"

"Because of his blood sickness."

"Blood sickness? You mean hemophilia?"

"Maybe. He never said."

"Drinking cow's blood helped him?"

"Only when he drank it warm."

"That's not a story," I said.

Boris shrugged and turned his attention to dessert.

I closed my eyes and pictured Uncle Alexei wrapping his aristocratic fingers around a clay cup filled with steaming blood. He was a thin man in his late sixties. His hair was white and carefully parted. His beard was trimmed to a refined point. He wore no shirt, but long woolen underwear. His back was pocked with scars. These oval-shaped scars had edges of raised, pink skin. The centers were sunken and the effect was that the man's back was covered with two dozen unblinking eyes. His white skin had a bluish glow. His mouth was fine and his lips were thin and red. He brought the cup to his mouth and drained the blood, then fell back into his low chair. His eyes grew drowsy and one pale hand slipped to the floor, the palm tantalizingly open and upward.

"What are you thinking?" asked Boris.

"I think," I said, "that you're trying to seduce me."

Boris pondered this. "Do you want to be seduced?" he asked.

"Possibly," I said. "Do you have anything planned for this evening?"

I accepted Boris's invitation to go back to his apartment for a glass of wine. On the walk home, I was still sober. I could feel that start of fall, an edge in the warm evening air. I held Boris's arm, because he was stumbling a little, although he was unaware of it. He was talking about European philosophers, scholars, and writers, all of whom were his good friends, all of whom I was hearing of for the first time.

"You are very pretty," he said. I took the keys from his hand and quickly unlocked the door.

Boris disappeared into the bedroom. The bathroom was off it and I could hear first Boris's thundering urination and then a violent throat-clearing. I poured myself another drink and took off my shoes. I was sitting there patiently, with my feet on the sofa and my head on my knees, when Boris appeared at the threshold of the living room. He was solidly naked, which was surprising, although not that surprising. Boris was stocky and strong. He had wide feet with a high arch and an impressive spread of toes. Reddish hair sprouted from the tops of his feet and laced up his trunk-like legs, except for two or three inches of bare skin where his thighs met his groin. A street lamp through the open window illuminated a thick, blue penis lying like a robin's egg in a nest of hair. Boris's belly was round and hard, the belly of a satyr. His breasts were plump and slantwise on his chest.

"Do you mind if I finish my drink?" I said.

"No," said Boris, now self-conscious. "Take your time."

I was still weak, recovering from a flu that I'd picked up in Italy the weeks before my return to the States. I'd been in Rimini, which was on the east coast, just a short hop from Ravenna. Rimini, at the end of tourist season, had been moving into hibernation. Everything was disappearing: the noisy children, the bare-breasted grandmothers, the *frutti di mare,* and—most importantly—the vacationing men. I had struck up a relationship with a huge and handsome construction worker named Pietro, who was staying in a cheap room above the bar I frequented. Pietro returned from visiting his wife, who lived in the suburbs of Florence, to find that I had moved in. He was patient with my illness, even when I broke out in a patchy rash. I thought my skin was splitting and that some new me— although it looked remarkably like the old me—was emerging. I spent ten days in his room above the bar eating soft pasta with eggs and chicken soup, which Pietro made himself in the rooming house kitchen.

"What will you do when you are not sick?" he asked me.

"I don't know, Pietro. Maybe I can move in with you and your wife. I could be your housekeeper."

"You are not clean," he said smiling. "Your clothes on the floor, hair in the sink."

"I could be your cook," I said.

Pietro shrugged. "My wife makes good food. You don't. You don't even eat."

"You want me to leave."

"I," said Pietro, "want you to be happy, not small happy," he gestured around the room—the cot, the sink in the corner, the overflowing ashtray—"but big happy."

"Like you and your wife?"

"Yes."

I can't say that Boris made me feel "big happy," but I did feel safe. I had terrible nightmares—blood and bone dreams, where faces torn out of the walls were coming at me—but Boris's snoring always woke me up before I had to see my nightmare through to its conclusion. I slept less than I ever had, maybe four hours a night. My mother had the same sleeping habits, a result of her illness. When she'd married my father she was still all right—he said normal, although I doubted that—but once she got sick, her sleeping patterns became erratic. I remember her, in the time before the pills, always being awake. If I got up in the middle of the night to use the bathroom I'd see the light on in the living room and hear the television—sitcom laughter, muffled narration—or she'd be reading. Maybe now my mother was willing me to have the education that I'd somehow failed at or that had somehow failed me. Boris had a lot of books and I sat in the living room waiting for the sun to rise, reading and reading. *Bleak House*. *The Gulag Archipelago*. *Birth of the Modern*.

I had never been a good student, although I'd shown enough intelligence to frustrate my teachers. In literature, my papers lacked focus and I had a bad habit of referring to characters—what on earth does Anna Sergeyevna see in Gurov?—as if they were my acquaintances. In art history I was determined to pursue the course of study with no attention to dates, although a complex chronological scheme was clear to me. In history, I remembered anecdotes and family trees with surprising precision; in class I often found myself telling stories of this monarch's sexual dalliances and the odd, three-toed offspring that somehow resulted. The sciences all seemed to be scheduled in the early morning. Philosophy was populated by abstract, sincere, unattractive boys and equally unattractive, aggressive girls. I displayed great enthusiasm for the visual arts, equaled only by an absence of talent. I tried drama. People said I had a flair for the dramatic and I thought I could bring my G.P.A. up to the 2.0 necessary to continue, but I hated all the other students. I spent entire class periods in the costume room brushing the wigs affectionately. I failed and failed and failed. Packed up my things, tried elsewhere, helped a boyfriend sell coke at parties, and was asked to leave.

After all this, I still tried to nurture the fantasy that college had been wonderful for me, that I'd been part of a super group of girls, but when I tried to remember them, my imagination replaced the Bryn and Erica and Jasmine, who I had actually known, with a group of giggling, cigarette-pants-wearing coeds, who all looked like Sandra Dee. I really had no friends to speak of and I'm sure it was my fault.

My mother always told me that friends were overrated. I had never known her to have one, other than me, and despite the fact that she had a befuddled mind (diagnosed) and a slew of drugs in her blood (prescribed) I still trusted her. In fact, my mother was the only person I trusted and after a year in Italy, although I'd been safe from her illness and her slow retreat from life, I missed her. But now, back in the States, I found myself unwilling to see her. She was still in the hospital, unless some miracle of well-being had happened in my absence. In a way I liked that. I could find her. I would go and see her soon. As soon as I figured out how to get to her without involving

Boris, as soon as I could make peace with seeing my father or, more likely, find a way to my mother that did not involve going through him. I hadn't really made a success of my time in Italy and although I personally felt that success was overrated, my father did not. I was his one failed investment and I bothered him.

Italy had ostensibly been a chance for me to pursue my interest in art. I was one of those people who made up for what she lacked in talent with her father's money. And my father liked the idea of my studying art in Italy far more than my working at a local restaurant while trying to get credit at South Shore Community College. So he anted up. And I took off after the first humiliating day of life drawing, spent sketching a nude Florentine named Davido, who I managed to master in other ways.

I tried to call my mother a couple of times, struggling with pounds of *gittoni* at public phones, but had never been able to get through. The first time, the nurse had tried to put my father on, and I'd hung up. Another time the nurse didn't know who my mother was and when she was trying to figure out where she'd been moved, my stack of phone tokens ran out. Things like that will wear you down, make a country lose its charm. Also, being American was a full-time occupation, exhausting and false. America was named for an Italian, so shouldn't there have been some sort of easy sisterhood between the two countries? There was not. I wondered how Vespucci would have felt if he knew that his name would be attached not only to the wondrous new continent, but also to hamburgers, blue jeans, rock-and-roll, and loud men who videotaped themselves while walking backward up the steps of the Uffizi. I constantly found myself playing Jean Seberg to a host of unlikely Jean-Paul Belmondos and this had made me want to go home. But here, with Boris, wasn't I doing the same thing?

"Boris," I asked, "do you like Faulkner?"

"Liking is irrelevant," he said. "I know Faulkner."

Sometimes he thought he was Faulkner.

I had good days and I had bad days. Sometimes my headaches knocked me out for hours. Sometimes they kept me up. I wandered around the apartment, spent hours looking at his shelves and all his collectibles—the first editions and the special bookcase by the stereo that he reserved for the hundreds of opera librettos that, he told me, comprised the most extensive private libretto collection in the Americas. All this pacing ought to have made me stir-crazy, but I still felt under the weather. Boris—to undercut my concern—bought me some fancy iron supplements that came with an eyedropper.

He said, "Take it with orange juice." Boris was occupied with his new writing project, a novel called *The Little Vagrant*. It was best for him to assume I was in good health and so that's how it was. He actually found my pallor appealing.

He told me, "In the old days, women drank arsenic to look like that." Then he disappeared back into his study. He was there from about eight in the morning until four in the afternoon. I made him sandwiches and brought them in, but he didn't want to talk. He usually yelled at me, "Leave it. Leave it." But if I didn't bring him lunch, he'd ask me if I was trying to starve him. At night, he read.

At the time, I had a weird affection for Boris, for everything about him. Even the way he looked. The hair on his chest and shoulders was soft and gray, like cobwebs. His teeth were yellowed and crossed in the front. When he smiled, his mouth pulled downward, which made him look in pain, bothered by the possibility of happiness. The top of his head was completely bald, but the hair that stretched around it—the foothill vegetation—sprouted wildly. There were shallow, polished lines on his forehead, but his face still looked fresh and pink, like a baby's. He had soft, pudgy hands with short fingers. He gestured with these hands, stretching them into the space between us with splayed fingers, as if he were presenting me with two starfish. With these hands, he reached out to me. With these hands, he fended me off.

With a fifty-dollar bill in his hand, he was almost handsome.

We were content and amicable, although after the first month I became aware of discord—an abstracted, patient discord—that was hovering around the apartment just as the ghost of Boris's old pipe-smoking habit lurked in the rugs. To make myself useful, I had started organizing his libretto collection but soon found myself being drawn into their pages. Quick melodrama. Almost instant gratification. Boris was on the cold side, but I didn't take this personally. Boris was not even warm with himself. Joy was not elusive, it was irrelevant. Boris considered himself an Epicurean, but anything past base sensual stimulation—a good cheese, Callas singing "La Wally"— was beyond his capacity for enjoyment. He did not know how to enjoy himself. He had learned what was enjoyable by studying others and took pride in this, since it was intellectual. One Thursday night he took me to the opera—*Madame Butterfly*—which was a great three-hour opportunity for him to meditate on the discomfort of his seat. He thought he might have hemorrhoids. While the soprano was still in the "*di*" of "*Un bel di*" he turned to me and said, "She's weak in the high register."

People peered over their opera glasses at him and he scowled back. He ruffled noisily through his score, although he couldn't read music.

"Shut up, Boris," I whispered. I rested my head against the scratchy wool of his jacket and fell asleep. I didn't know how else to deal with him when he was aggravated. I didn't want to make a scene. I couldn't imagine anyone being able to sustain a relationship with Boris, then I realized that I was doing just that and it surprised me.

Boris had been involved with a woman a short time before. Ann. An artist. For fifteen years. I was seven years old when they got together. One afternoon when I'd run out for cigarettes, I returned to find Boris and Ann sitting together at the dining room table. Boris must have been in the middle of explaining our relationship because my entry caused a deep silence. At first I thought she was just a friend. But she was looking at me as a man would look at me. Her eyes kept moving to gauge the length of my legs, or just stopped on my face, even though Boris was speaking. She was looking through a man's eyes, Boris's eyes, to see what he saw in me. And I think all she was coming up with was "young-young-young," with an occasional "thin" thrown in just to make the situation intolerable. I say this because she seemed to wilt in the few minutes we sat there as if having consumed an aging potion that caused her cheeks to sag and her eyes to sink. I saw a *Night Stalker* rerun like that.

"Is Ann a good friend of yours?" I asked.

"Ann is my oldest friend," he replied. "You have to make peace with her."

"Oh. I have to make peace with her. I don't know if you noticed this, but Ann's the one who has a problem, not me."

"I will not involve myself in such pettiness," he said.

"But you are involved in it Boris. She's your ex."

"This jealousy is ugly," said Boris.

"Jealousy?"

Boris took my chin in his hand and walked me in this manner over to the mirror. "Not becoming," he said. "It mars your features."

Sometimes I thought I'd like to mar Boris's, with an ax.

Ann stopped by about once a week to check up on Boris. One day, a Wednesday, she stopped by and Boris wasn't there. He had a meeting—lawyers, editors, I don't know—so I invited her in for coffee.

Ann walked around the living room as if she were a real estate agent. She looked out the window, then at the built-in shelves, as if she'd never been in the apartment before. Ann was attractive in a stocky, Swedish peasant sort of way. She had intelligent gray eyes and thick lips and nostrils. She was dressed in a bolt of earth-toned fabric that was pinned on the shoulder by a large bronze fist. Her hands were stained vibrant primary hues and I remembered how Boris referred to her work as "Ann's finger painting."

"Ann," I said, "how do you like your coffee?"

"Black," she said. She smiled in a dismissive way. "Katherine, what do you do?"

"Day to day?" I set down Ann's mug on the table and sat catty corner to her. "I'm organizing Boris's librettos. There's a lot to read here. I just read *Moby-Dick*."

"I'm glad to hear you're not illiterate."

"Well, I have read *Moby-Dick*."

Ann smiled coldly. "Not a complete moron."

"Although very young."

Ann set down her mug. "I'm making you uncomfortable. And I'm making myself look like a fool." She stood up. "Thanks for the coffee."

"Ann," I looked at her beseechingly, "don't go. I'd like you to stay and finish your coffee, at least."

Ann stopped to look at me.

"I mean it. I have no one to talk to except Boris. And you know Boris. I just sit there . . . and I brewed that pot fresh, just for you."

Ann was momentarily stunned. "What are you doing here," she indicated the ceiling, "with Boris?"

I contemplated this. "Boris and I have a symbiotic relationship."

"You're using him."

"He's using me."

Ann regarded me thoughtfully. "Couldn't you find someone more your speed to float you?"

"I suppose I could. I don't know." I spun the mug in my hands. "I like Boris."

"Why?"

"Do you know Boris's story about the masturbating orangutan?"

"No."

"Then you wouldn't understand," I said. "Why do you come back to Boris?"

"This is it for me, honey," she said, although neither of us believed it. Ann looked deeply into her coffee as if it held the answers. She was almost pretty like this, quiet, gentle. Her immense gray eyes looked vulpine and northerly, as if I should see snowdrifts reflected in them.

"I think you're just a phase of Boris's," she said. "When you dump him or become too difficult, this will all be a dream, the thing that Boris and I fight about."

"Ann," I said, "I don't understand you at all."

I heard a clatter on the stairs followed by a dull thumping on the door. I knew this meant that Boris's hands were full and that he was knocking with his head.

"You'll stay for dinner?" I said.

"What are we having?"

"I don't know. There's an eggplant in the refrigerator. Will you stay?"

"Sure," said Ann. "I suppose you want me to cook. Unless you have something you do with eggplant?"

I shook my head, not as threatened as I should have been, then went for the door.

Outside in the hallway, Boris was embracing a large package wrapped in brown paper.

"What have you got there?" I asked.

"It's a portrait." Boris caught Ann's back disappearing into the kitchen. "So what's Ann doing here?"

"Ann," I said, stepping back from the door, "is cooking us dinner."

"That's very sporting of her."

"Yes, it is," I said.

He gave me a look, not pleased but curious, then walked over to the dining room table to set his package on the table.

"Katherine, you will love this," he said and began to tear at the crinkled brown paper.

Boris had been wandering around Little Italy in search of a reasonably priced can of extra-virgin olive oil when he was struck by a picture hanging in the window of Agnellino's Catholic Supply. According to Boris, it was a picture of me. Boris did not hesitate. He went inside and bought the print, framed, for thirty dollars.

"Where's the olive oil?" I asked.

"I couldn't carry them both," he said.

We looked at his Madonna, which was lying in the center of the dining room table in its crumpled sheath of paper, like a rosette radish on a lettuce leaf.

"It sort of looks like me," I said.

"It's a perfect likeness." Boris looked around the walls deep in concentration. He set his hands into his field of vision with the thumbs tugged down into right angles. "No," he said. He turned to another wall. "No," he said again, and then he framed the living room wall that set the kitchen off from the rest of the apartment. There was already a painting hanging there, a self-portrait of Ann. Boris held the picture with its cheery gilt plastic frame. He set the print into the space in front of him.

"Yes," he said.

Boris removed Ann's painting and set it on the floor. He hung the Madonna with great care. He stepped back to look at the print, straightened it, and then poured himself a glass of wine. Ann had wandered out from the kitchen and was standing in the doorway running her hand through her hair. She contemplated her self-portrait.

"Symbolism?" she said, gesturing to her picture.

"I don't resort to such bald statements," said Boris.

Ann stood back to study the print. "Is this new religious fervor?" she asked. She squinted over at Boris. "I remember you telling me that the only good thing about the Communists is that they torched all the Christians."

Boris didn't hear. "It's Katherine," he said. "Striking resemblance, don't you think?" He turned to me. "Madonna della Katerina, as if the artist saw her and painted her."

"Unlikely. This painting is Renaissance." Ann looked at some small print beneath the picture. "Perugino, and it's not even a Madonna. It's a Magdalena."

"What's a Magdalena?" asked Boris.

"Mary Magdalene," said Ann.

"The prostitute?"

"The saint," I said. Ann and Boris looked at me, their faces impassive. "She dried Christ's feet with her hair," I added.

"Why were they wet?" said Ann.

"Why were what wet?" asked Boris.

I said nothing.

"I like it hanging there," said Boris. "It adds a touch of humor to the apartment."

Ann was a good cook. There was only the eggplant in the house, but somehow she managed to make it suffice—with pasta— for all three of us. I'd set the table with candles, which threw long shadows up on the white walls of the apartment. I made shadow puppets with my hands, a vague rabbit, something that looked like a rottweiler, or maybe a crocodile. Ann and Boris were talking about her new manager. Her manager, as far as I could tell, was someone who managed to sell Ann's paintings to people who didn't want them.

"*Sang froid: Arctic Landscape* that I did last spring? He sold it to someone as 'Autumn Sunset.' He said they could put it in their din-ing room. He sold it because the dimensions were perfect for above the sideboard."

"Didn't that have a skull floating in the foreground?" asked Boris, half-interested.

"A skeletal hand. If you don't look that close, it's not notice-able. I have some white light on the water in another part of the painting . . ."

"How much did you get for it?"

"That's not the point, Boris. It's in someone's dining room."

"It must be nice to make a living as an artist," I said. I was think-ing this and stated it by accident.

Ann's eyes narrowed. "Does art interest you?"

"Yes, I suppose it does."

"What artists do you like?"

"Oh, I don't know. I like Goya."

"Goya," said Ann. She shook her head.

"How can you dismiss Goya?"

"I'm not dismissing Goya," she said. "What do you know about Goya?"

"I didn't say I knew Goya. I said I liked Goya." I drained my glass of wine. "That picture of the donkeyman and the eagleman and they're sitting on the shoulders of two bear-bodied donkey-headed things? I like that. It's a good illustration of human nature."

"That 'picture' is *The Caprices* of the late seventeen-hundreds, and has nothing to do with human nature. 'Fantasy without reason produces monsters; but together, they beget true artists and may give rise to wonderful things.'"

"Bonus point for Ann," I said. I poured myself more wine. "Lovely bullshit."

"It's a quote from Goya."

"Well, I think he's bullshitting. People did that, even in the late seventeen-hundreds." I looked over at Boris, who was trying not to laugh. "I think he drew them in a moment of madness, then came up with some sort of discourse to cover his artistic ass."

"You have absolutely nothing to support that theory."

"No? Goya's always depicting various forms of rage, madness. Don't you think that implies that he had some sort of inside track?"

"To insanity? No. Not at all." Ann said, inclined to disagree with anything I had to say.

"I think Goya drew his creatures in a moment of madness that frightened him, that his ability to draw such ugly creatures disturbed him. I think he felt possessed by his art. Who moved his hands if not he?" I rapped my fingers on the table. "Goya tries to make sense out of this accidental creation, the product of his madness. He still wonders whose picture it is. "

Boris chuckled and Ann glared at him. "The half-creatures are allegorical, not madness wedded to reason," she said, and then to prove this conclusively she added, "*Disasters of War*. 1810."

"Ah," I said, "The Carnivorous Vulture."

"Girls," said Boris, "this has been amusing, but my knowledge of Goya is now exhausted and the discussion has become dull."

Ann looked at me victoriously. "Forget the Carnivorous Vulture," I said. "The only thing we have to deal with is the critical vulture, just as good at going after corpses. Goya's dead and can't speak for himself." I got up from the table and went to sit by myself on the couch.

"I seem to have touched a nerve," said Ann.

"Thank God for that," I said. "I was beginning to wonder if I was still alive."

Boris cocked his head and looked at me. I smiled charmingly. My boredom was inconceivable. "But really, Ann," he said, "how much did you get for *Landscape?*"

Ann looked at me, then back at Boris. They had a lot to talk about, those two, and watching them made me want a friend, someone I could laugh with. Someone I could live this evening with over again on my terms—how annoying Boris was, what a lunatic Ann turned out to be. I closed my eyes and pretended to take a nap.

Ann's voice fell to a whisper, but I could still hear her. She said, "Really, Boris, you know nothing about her. You might catch something."

And Boris said something that I couldn't make out.

"Why isn't she in school? Where are her parents?"

And Boris said something else.

"Some benefactor you are. I don't care how old she says she is. She's still a child. Look at her."

And then Boris said something that made Ann laugh.

4

That night I pulled out a book on Romanticism off Boris's shelf. It was a huge, coffee-table book and, by the smell of the pages, had never been opened. On the front page was the inscription, *For Boris on his birthday, affectionately, Ann.* And then in cramped, insecure writing, a postscript, *Don't worry. Romanticism is not romantic.* I opened the book to the section on Goya. I had grown up in a house filled with books like this. My mother had a particular love for Goya and I was familiar with all the faces of the family of Charles IV, their squishy noses and eyes sunk like currants in leavening dough. I loved Goya in my own way. While other children frightened themselves with Dracula comics, I'd been mesmerized by *Los Caprichos* and the Black Paintings of the Quinta del Sordo.

I turned the pages eagerly, hoping that the editor was not too politically minded (massacres, civil war commentary) and had included my favorite painting, that of the god Saturn eating a child.

Saturn Consuming His Offspring took up a whole page.

I looked at the gaunt and long-limbed giant, his flowing hair. He emerged from the darkness of the canvas, his mad eyes wide, the whites arced impossibly around black pupils, as if he'd been caught in the headlights of a car. Saturn's hands gripped the body of his headless child. A gash of red dripped slantwise down the child's up-turned arm and neck; it seemed to have been devoured head first, forearm second. The child was raising its cropped arm as if to feed its father, and Saturn chewed his way down to the armpit. The legs and buttocks of the child rose up from between the thighs of Saturn. They disappeared—feet entirely obscured—into shadow, the same shadow where the genitals of the god were hidden. I looked at the twin legs bound close, the rounded buttocks. The child was actually a monstrous penis, Saturn's penis, and he was eating it.

Was Goya painting the despair of the sexual urge, how copulation—beyond mere monster coupling—begets violence? Or was it just an autofellatic fantasy, and how had I never noticed it before?

This was not what my mother had told me the painting was about. I got the standard story, that Saturn was consuming his child because an oracle had informed him that one of his children would kill him. Each time his wife, Rhea, gave birth, Saturn would eat the baby. Rhea finally managed to hide one child, Zeus. In his place, she gave Saturn a stone in swaddling clothes and Saturn swallowed it, blankets and all. Zeus would kill Saturn, but not before administering a powerful emetic that made him vomit up his other five children. I'd asked my mother about this.

"If he ate them, wouldn't they all be chewed up, like in the picture?"

My mother shrugged this off. "The Titans were very big. Maybe he swallowed them whole."

"Then why doesn't Goya paint it like that?"

"Because that would be boring."

Zeus, it is interesting to note, continued the legacy of cannibalism. When he heard that his soon-to-be-born daughter would one day supplant him, he swallowed his pregnant wife. Afterward, Zeus was tortured by an intolerable headache. To ease his pain, he called on Hephaestus to split his head open with an ax. Athene jumped out, full-grown and vibrant. She dazzled her father and Zeus loved her more than any of his other children. Athene forgave Zeus for having eaten her and her mother, and Zeus pushed Athene's possible ascendancy to the throne out of his mind. He loved his daughter, despite what she represented to him. And that she loved him back, the key to familial love, apparently, being the ability to forget.

I took one last look at Saturn. Zeus had turned Lycaon into a wolf for offering him a stew of Mollosian hostage, but he ate his own wife and daughter. They were all cannibals, all of them.

On the next page I saw Goya's etching *Disasters of War*. The Carnivorous Vulture. Ann was wrong to think that this was a simple allegory. All vultures were carnivorous but Goya's walked upright, like a man. Her shriveled wings were more like feathered arms and she stomped—an Iberian Godzilla—onto the landscape. A peasant came at her with his pitchfork and the horizon was crowded with people rising up in a solid bank, like woods or mountains in other paintings. In this picture, surprisingly, the peasants appeared to have the upper hand. The bird's wings were flung open, her eyes round with fear, her beak empty. This was the aftermath of the slaughter, what descended (vultures swinging in tightening circles) after the rampaging armies had returned to their homes, after the thunder of muskets had stilled and the last of the smoke dissipated.

This was a painting of hunger.

The last two pages in the Goya section were devoted to *Scenes of Cannibalism*, loose, vibrant sketches of the Jesuit martyrs Lallement and Brebeuf, who were slaughtered by the Iroquois in 1649. The first painting showed wild nudes preparing bodies. A corpse hung from the top of the painting, like bull carcass in a meat locker; another lay prone. The three cannibals were preparing the bodies: eviscerating, bleeding, skinning. These figures crowded the lower right-hand corner of the painting; the rest of the canvas was empty, an imposing intrusion of space. There was no actual eating in the painting, although one nude was hunched over in a very suspicious way. The other painting showed savages around a fire. A central figure (oddly bearded for an Indian) brandished a head in his left hand, a severed hand in his right and—due to the spread of his legs—his genitals. Cannibals seemed more of an opportunity for Goya to paint the nude, some in classical poses and some more natural. Cannibals offered more of an opportunity to paint the human figure than, say, the family of Charles IV. And Goya didn't seem bothered that his Indians looked no more like the Iroquois than they did like Spain's royal family.

The Iroquois were not cannibals, despite the legend of Brebeuf. Brebeuf was a Jesuit priest, a missionary to the Indians in the

Canadian wilderness, who were not interested in conversion. Brebeuf made friends with the Hurons but had less success with the Iroquois. After torturing Brebeuf for two days (pouring boiling water over his head, thrusting a hot iron down his throat, encircling his neck with burning stones) the Iroquois were impressed by his ability to withstand his trials. They continued, slashing him with knives, pulling off his nails, until they finally tied Brebeuf to a stake and lit him on fire. After the flames died down, the Iroquois warriors cut down Brebeuf's body. He was a strong man, even if he was wrong-minded, even if he was an ally to the Hurons—the Iroquois' hated enemy. The Iroquois, suitably impressed, thought they might ingest some of his might. They cut out the great man's heart and, we are told, ate it.

I traced my finger over the nude savage's figure and was about to close the book when the phone startled me by ringing. I jumped, as if I'd been asleep, and picked up the receiver. I noticed the time. It was 4 A.M.

"Hello?"

"Katherine, is that you?"

It was my mother.

"Katherine, are you there?"

"Yes. Where are you?"

"I'm where you left me. I can't talk for long."

"You sound well. Are you?"

"As well as can be expected. They changed my medication."

"I'll come see you."

"No. You should stay away. Your father's very angry."

"He's been angry for twenty years . . ."

And then Boris called from the bedroom, "Katherine, who are you talking to?"

"I'm on the phone," I said.

"I hope that's not long distance," he added.

"I have to go," said my mother.

"How did you get this number?"

But the line had gone dead.

*   *   *

Several weeks passed and I waited for my mother to call back, but she didn't. I was beginning to wonder if I'd just dreamed it. I thought of calling her at the hospital, but I didn't think she wanted me to. I thought she might be worried that my father would find out that she'd been making phone calls, or something like that, and I didn't want to inadvertently get him on the phone. Also, my mother had sounded so good that I wanted to enjoy that. I didn't want to call back and get my mother overdrugged, underanimated, somewhere in the pale.

5

Ann had a show so I took the train to Soho. Boris was working and said that we could go later, but I knew how he was and that the possibility of missing Ann's show didn't bother him. Honestly, I wanted to go. Boris had no friends so any contact with other people happened over these desperate conversations with shop folk at Zabar's (What does that mean, hand-rubbed chicken? Is it sanitary?) or gushy "thank you"s at the Korean grocers (No. Thank *you* so much.) My going to the show may seem over solicitous to Ann, who still found me difficult to tolerate, but I was eager for time away from Boris. I thought I might have a conversation with someone.

I pictured an event where legions of turtlenecked men and slick-haired women turned in tight circles before paintings, looking alternately through and then over the rims of their glasses, bending in to check price, stepping back to gauge value. And I was right about everything, except for the legions. There were five people in the whole gallery, and one of them was Ann, another the owner, who, while I stood on the sidewalk and wondered if I could nip down the block and get a real drink before entering, stepped out to have a cigarette. Ann was drinking from a large glass of wine. She accidentally met my eye, then looked away. I suppose she wanted to give me the chance to escape. But some generosity of spirit made me go in. I don't know why, but I felt that I should.

"Ann," I said. "I'm early. Boris is coming by in about a half an hour. He had something to finish up." I gestured at the something, which might have been just outside the door of the gallery.

Ann looked at me, unsmiling. "You're not early," she said. She drained the last of her wine.

"Maybe not," I said. "But some of these paintings are really wonderful."

"Really?" said Ann, not believing. "Which one do you like?"

I saw a portrait of Boris in the corner. The picture must have been a few years old, because Boris was a bit thinner around the middle and a bit thicker on top. He was sitting naked in a chair, bored. Light from somewhere lit up half his body in bold purples, blues, and yellows. "I love that," I said, pointing to it.

Ann smiled finally. "I liked it when I first did it, but now . . ." We walked over to the picture together. "I don't know. Doesn't it look like Boris is decomposing?"

"Yes," I said. "That's why I like it. You've somehow captured Boris's spiritual decomposition."

Ann looked at me and smiled. She seemed grateful for my company and, though this didn't feel altogether comfortable to me, I said nothing, scared that I would somehow wreck the mood.

"I met Boris at a show, you know," she said.

"Really?"

"Yes. At the Orbiting Spoon Art Gallery. It closed a year ago. I recognized him immediately from the picture on the back of his book. Boris walked over for a glass of wine and I caught him looking at me out of the corner of his eye."

There was a moment of silence. "He introduced himself?" I said.

"No," Ann said. "Well, sort of. He was looking at the paintings." Ann rolled her eyes. "He starts gesturing around the room and he says, 'Horrible, isn't it?'"

"No," I said, and then higher, "no."

"Yes. And then he goes on. 'No sense of depth, color juxtaposition is offensive, obviously a no-talent.'"

"I'm assuming he didn't know it was your show."

"No," said Ann. "But I told him."

"Good for you."

Ann shrugged. "I was in assertiveness therapy at the time. I don't know if I'd have the balls to do it now."

Ann and I looked at Boris, who looked unapologetically out from the canvas.

"Was he at least embarrassed?"

"No," Ann said. "I actually liked that about him." Ann paused to recall. "He said, 'I really love the show. I'm tired of conventional depth. There's something in your treatment of depth reminiscent of Manet in his *Fallen Matador*. I find your color juxtaposition innovative and I like your work. The only reason I insulted the exhibition is it was the only way I knew to start a conversation. To insult a show is a common way of breaking the ice. If I've offended you, it wasn't me, just the casualty of society's stupid dictates.'"

"And you bought it?"

"Sort of." Ann couldn't seem to remember. "I told him I'd read *The Soulless Man*. I liked the first line, 'Why would one choose to hold a hand so cold?' and the last line," here Ann paused dramatically, "'In the final closing of those eyes was the end of a personal history important to no one, except for the executor of this action.' I told him that I loved the last line so much that I read it over and over. Which is why I remember it. But I just kept reading it because it didn't make any sense."

There was a moment of quiet. Ann was deep in thought.

"And then you went out for a drink?"

Ann shook her head. "Assertiveness therapy. We dispensed with any formalities."

She slept with him that night and did his laundry the next morning.

Ann sold a painting to a wealthy couple from Oklahoma, but aside from that, the evening was pretty much a disaster. The two of us sat on the front step of the gallery with a bottle of wine, passing it back and forth. The gallery owner and Ann's manager were involved in a discussion with an interior designer from Philadelphia, who thought

Ann's work would be popular with her clientele. Neither of us had said anything about it, but I knew that Ann was waiting for Boris and I hoped to God he'd show up.

"How's *Moby-Dick*?" asked Ann.

"I've finished that," I said.

"That's right," said Ann wearily. Conversation was becoming difficult. "What'd you think?"

"I read an essay by this guy at Columbia, Crain, I think. Anyway, I knew that Melville was a big queen, but Crain has this theory that, at the time, sex between men was the greatest taboo, so every time someone's about to fuck someone else . . ."

"What?" said Ann.

"Well, instead they eat each other. There's some incidence of cannibalism. The cannibalism stands in for the fucking. It's the lesser taboo."

"Kind of like the other white meat?"

I nodded then reconsidered. "What are you talking about?"

"I don't know," said Ann. "Look, there's Boris."

Sure enough, Boris had materialized across the street. He was holding a bunch of flowers.

"Katherine," said Ann, "do you and Boris . . ."

"Do we what?"

Ann sighed. "I want to ask you about your sex life, but I'd like to think that I'm above it."

"It's all right," I said. "I mean it is Boris groaning and wriggling, smelling like an onion."

"No need to be vulgar," said Ann.

"Sex is vulgar," I said. "Vulgarity is sex's best quality. And if its too vulgar for you . . ."

"Well, I could always replace it with cannibalism," said Ann.

The traffic stopped and Boris made his way across the street. He stopped in front of us and looked past the doorway into the still gallery. "Am I too late?" he asked.

Ann and I looked at each other, than back at Boris.

"Who are the flowers for?" I asked.

"They are for Ann," he said.

"Then," I smiled, "you are just in time."

On the two-month anniversary of our meeting, Boris took me to the opera again, a production of *Salome*. It wasn't very good, although I'm no judge of operas. I tend to go from aria to aria, set change to set change. I've noticed that I like operas where the tenor is bigger than the soprano, which isn't all that often. And there were no recognizable arias in *Salome*, or any set changes. All the characters milled around a pit in the middle of the stage. From this pit would come righteous, howling baritone. Finally John the Baptist slunk onto stage, shaking his great hairy head at people. Then they decapitated him offstage and brought his head back glued to a platter. They'd done a good job with the head, the great drooping lips and meaty cheeks. The soprano sang to the head for close to half an hour. I looked over at Boris. He was tapping on the floor with his foot. His pants had ridden up and the sock on his right foot—a thin black nylon sock—had slid into his shoe. There was about a two-inch space of exposed fleshy ankle. I reached down, carefully, slowly, and pulled up Boris's sock. Boris looked over at me but didn't care, and soon—without much explanation—the opera ended.

"I'm hungry," I said. "Let's leave before the curtain call."

That night we dined at Boris's favorite restaurant. I ordered the osso buco. I ate quickly—although there was too much rosemary, which made the sauce taste metallic—and was happily sucking the marrow out of bones when I noticed Boris's eyes trained on me with more than the customary intensity.

"What?" I asked.

Boris chuckled. "You're still such a child, Katherine."

"And what does that make you?" I asked. I smiled sarcastically.

"Lucky," he said.

I'd become disillusioned with our relationship over the last week—something to do with Ann, or maybe the beguiling Perugino peering down at me while I drank my morning coffee. I was no longer satisfied and was trying to figure out how I'd managed to convince myself that I was. I had a roof over my head and food and entertainment, although it was all Boris's idea of fun—I hadn't been to a movie in months—but I was giving him the prime of my life. Maybe I even had reason to resent him. I ate my food quietly. Boris had met with his lawyer the previous week. I'd asked if it had something to do with book contracts, but he'd denied this. His agent took care of all that. He'd been smiling in an annoying, patronizing way and it occurred to me that he might have changed his will. Maybe he'd made me a beneficiary, or sole beneficiary. I didn't know how much Boris was worth, but he wasn't a big spender. *Soulless Man* had been in print for more than fifteen years, although none of his other books had done as well. One—*The Drowning Boy*—had been made into a movie.

"Boris, why did you see your lawyer last week?" I asked.

"Oh, the usual," he said.

"But you don't usually see your lawyer." The waiter appeared to refill the water glasses and Boris and I were momentarily silent.

"Why this sudden interest?"

"You worry me when you don't tell me things," I said. "People go to their lawyers to arrange wills. People arrange their wills when they're," I paused here for effect, "when they're ill, Boris."

Across the room a woman was laughing maniacally. Boris chewed in silence. He was old enough to have a heart attack, but in the two months I'd been watching him, his health seemed to have improved. I wondered if there was a cyst blocking something that was responsible for the rosy glow—a glow that we would later attribute to blood clogged up in his face.

"How's your health?" I asked him.

"I've never felt better," he replied.

"Do you ever think about death?" It had occurred to me that Boris might one day become suicidal. Maybe I could drive him to it. I'd seen *Gaslight* on cable late the night before. "Sometimes it seems easier to end it all."

Boris looked at me with a fatherly expression.

"One day you could just die, Boris," I smiled. "One day, you're working on a novel, the next you're in a casket with neatly folded hands."

Boris raised his eyes to me and tilted his head. He was studying my face. "Katherine, don't be so dramatic."

"Dramatic?"

"Are you depressed?"

"No," I said.

"I can send you to a doctor. I hear the drugs are good. People like them." He reached across the table and held my hand. "I understand that maybe I have been too busy and that you might feel neglected."

"Oh, shut up, Boris," I said, retracting my hand. "You don't understand anything."

"Is that productive?" Boris raised his eyebrows. He pursed his lips.

"You don't know me."

Boris shrugged. "Can anyone know another?" he said, which sounded like something I'd heard before, only stated in a better way.

"I know enough about you to know that I know enough about you," I said. "I can't stay here, with you, in New York, any longer. I think I'm losing my mind."

Boris started looking annoyed. "Katherine, I can't leave right now. I'm in the middle of a book."

"Fascinating." I smiled blandly. "So what's the next Nobel Laureate writing? What's *The Little Vagrant* about?"

Boris relaxed back into his chair. He seemed to think our equilibrium had just been restored. "You will like *The Little Vagrant*. It's about a young woman in Italy. She is searching for security, for warmth, for someone to really care. Instead she meets careless man upon careless man. In the end she feels desolate."

"Desolate?" I studied my hands on the tablecloth. "Boris, how could you?"

"How could I what?"

"I told you those stories in confidence."

"What stories?"

"What were you thinking?" I stared in disbelief. "I find your marketing of my life in poor taste."

"See? Childish." Boris crossed one leg over the other, which took some effort, due to the girth of his thighs. "You automatically assume that the book's about you."

I was speechless.

"Yes, yes, admit it, Katherine." He dismissed me waving his hand in the air. "There's a bit of the narcissist at work here."

I started to get dizzy. My hands were numb. I picked up my glass of wine, which I meant to drink, but I was clumsy, trying too hard to hold it. Suddenly, the glass exploded, sending shards flying. My hand was bleeding. I dropped the glass on the table. The wine had splattered all over the table. Boris was stunned, or maybe just embarrassed. The waiter came running. He stood ready to dab any stain from any fine garment, ready to apologize for the accident—however it had happened—once it was explained, but Boris and I were silent.

"Settle the bill," I said, and headed for the door.

That night we had a huge fight. Boris should have let me leave, as I'd intended. My things were easy to pack. I'd only acquired a silk shirt since I'd moved in, which crumpled into a tiny ball. He grabbed my elbow by the elevator. He got down on his knees, which was more terrifying than affecting. He begged me to stay. He told me that everything he owned was mine.

"Everything?" I shook him off.

"Yes."

I had been right about the will.

Boris collapsed onto the floor, sitting on his big backside. He was out of breath. "How can you leave me? You are all that I have. You are my family, my arms, my legs."

I was not me. I was Boris's limbs. I let my bag drop to the floor. I looked longingly at the elevator, but I realized that I was past the point of valuing freedom. I'd gotten more mature, somehow, in the past couple of months and it had made me mercenary. Boris had his hands on my calves. The top of his head was shiny and, with the light shining right above us, I could see my distorted reflection on it. "I need my own money," I said. "I don't want to ask you for ten dollars every time I want cigarettes."

"Of course."

"I need to see friends, to do things on my own."

"But you have no friends but me." Boris looked at me pleadingly.

"I'll make them."

Boris nodded down at the carpet, its pattern of a trellis strangled by wild rose.

I reached out my hand and helped him stand. "We should go inside and get a drink, toast to our new beginning."

"Maybe a celebration is in order," he said. But from the tone in his voice, I knew that Boris had nothing to celebrate and that he was deeply regretting having told me about the will. He was also consoling himself by thinking that he could change it whenever he wanted. He must have been; something kept him civil. Boris decided that we should take a vacation to blow out the bad air. We picked up his battered VW Rabbit, which he kept parked by Ann's apartment in Brooklyn, and drove north. Boris liked New England so we decided to head to Maine to see the last of the leaves.

6

Boris fell asleep right around Providence and I kept heading up I-95. The weather was glorious—cold and bright. I hadn't driven in a while so it was novel and fun. My mind wandered back to school and for a brief half hour or so I committed to the idea of going back, of making peace with my father, of springing my mother, of graduating and becoming a productive member of society. I saw the buildings and the glass windows and brass knockers of a million residences and saw myself peering out, opening the door—heard my feet thudding along the old floorboards. And maybe I'd get married. And maybe I'd have children—a gorgeous dark-haired girl who would love me, ask me what to wear when she was teenager. Or maybe I'd have a loyal dog to warm my feet. I'd take up hiking. And all this if I could just get organized, reach an epiphany, and go back to school.

I'd left the highway without thinking. I'd taken the exit to Hingham and on automatic pilot, with Boris next to me in the front seat, was driving home. I didn't even realize what I was doing until I was in the driveway of my house. I cut the engine and looked at sweep of lawns, the stacked-boulder fences, the piles of leaves that rustled in the light breeze and dusted a few leaves back across the grass. I saw that my father had finally taken the swing down from the oak tree, which I suppose was better. I'd never used the swing as much as my mother and she only really liked it during one of her episodes. I remembered once, I think I was seven, seeing her flying backward in her bathrobe, and then forward out of her bathrobe, and then in her bathrobe as she sawed through the early morning air.

A cardinal was yelling for its mate and squirrels were racing around, squabbling, but other than that the house was silent. My father would be in Boston so I wasn't worried that he'd see me. And then I saw the figure in the bushes—a white shirt, jeans, the head in a scarf. I froze. Was it my mother?

And then he stood up.

Mr. Jones, his scarf a bandana left over from the seventies. His hands wrist-deep in muck. "Can I help you?" he called out.

I started the engine and began reversing out the drive. I saw Mr. Jones studying my face and then, recognition.

"Katherine!" he yelled. But I was already driving away.

Boris woke up. "Where are we?" he said sleepily.

"I've gotten us lost," I said.

Boris peered out at the road squinting. He saw the town sign, welcoming us. "We are in Hingham," he said. He pronounced "Hingham" as "hingHAM."

"There's a gas station," I said. "I can use the restroom there." But all I really wanted to do was have Boris take over the driving.

Boris wasn't much of a vacationer. He didn't want to get away from it all. He decided we'd stay in Portland. A small city he could handle. More nature than that terrified him; uninterrupted views—skies rather than skylines—gave him panic attacks. Portland was covered in fog. It was thick and ubiquitous, as though a cloud had fallen from the sky and would blanket the city until someone could return it to the heavens. The fog put me at ease in much the same way I suspect rabbits are at ease when the visibility is poor. I liked the knotty streets and uneven cobblestones. I liked the way the brick buildings slowly came into focus out of the haze, leaning on each other as tired and crooked as old men. Spires poked out of the cloud cover. Streets turned you around until you were lost in a web of oxbows and dead ends. Bells from unknown steeples pealed in the heavy air; horns sounded balefully from the bay; the scent of fish hung in dense, salty pockets on the quays.

Boris and I arrived in the early afternoon and spent the last part of the day wandering around the Old Port. There was some excitement in town about a killer who had escaped from a lunatic asylum a few miles away in a town called Gray. Every overheard conversation buzzed with talk of the madman at large—a William Selwyn—who had already been dubbed "Bad Billy." All of this, or so I was informed by a portly woman who saw my newspaper as an invitation to conversation, was a tragedy as they had only apprehended Bad Billy three years previously, after his sixth murder. His last victim, a woman of twenty-two, had been caught unaware at the bathroom mirror. When they found her body, her left eyebrow was significantly thinner than the right, her hands fisted around a pair of tweezers.

This was all very interesting, of course, but the woman proved difficult to get rid of. I folded my newspaper into my lap. Wasn't it unfortunate, she said, that her own safety should be so compromised? No single woman would be safe, because single women were, after all, what William Selwyn was after. She raised her trim eyebrows expressively.

"It excites you, doesn't it?" I said. And she left.

Boris finally returned from the bathroom and announced that he was hungry. There would be, he assured me, on one of those dark and salty jetties, a fish shack where we could "sup" with the locals. Boris was now sporting a floppy Gilligan hat that he thought made him look like a fisherman. He found his seaman's dive with the help of some neon arrows and a sign that depicted a lobster in a beard and yellow raincoat.

Boris and I were seated immediately. The restaurant was not a haunt for fishermen, but rather—judging from accents—people from New Jersey. Our waitress wore a hat, as did the entire wait staff, that had two foam lobster claws sticking out at the sides. Boris studied the menu. "What's the house specialty?" he asked.

The lobster-cracking paraphernalia delighted Boris. He looped the plastic bib around his neck and tied it in a firm knot. He clacked the crackers menacingly at his dinner—a ruby lobster at rest on a bed of lettuce. "This is what I love about Maine," he said. He waved around the restaurant and I regarded all the things included in his embrace: portrait of moose, papier mâché anchor, "Lord Give Me Patience, and I Want It Now" framed in wooden blueberries. "Why aren't you having the lobster?" he asked.

I regarded Boris's dinner, which looked back at me, its black, stemmed eyes fixed in the final instant of the boiling pot. "I prefer eating closer to my species," I replied. I had ordered the steak.

Boris went to work on the lobster with surgeonlike intensity, although his bib made him look like a baby. He lifted the creature in his two meaty hands and in one expert, juicy crack split the tail from the torso. "They say the best meat's the tail, but I prefer these little morsels up in the body."

I leaned to take a closer look and nodded politely. I felt one of my headaches coming on.

"Katherine, what's wrong?" asked Boris.

"Migraine," I said. "I'm going out for some air."

I left the dining room and let the door slam behind me. Something about the lobster had set me off. Maybe I felt sorry for it, but that seemed unlikely. Even had it lived, its days of scraping about the ocean floor, occasionally raising a massive claw to menace a passing halibut, were not worth romanticizing. But I still felt sick. As I'd watched Boris and his generous jowls, the thought had occurred to me that Boris, like grilled fish, might offer the best eating in his cheek.

The day was closing. At five, the sun had sunk low and banks of purple cloud were stacked, one upon the other, on the thin, black line of the horizon. The air was heavy with fog and salt and quickly penetrated my wool sweater. There was no one around. I looked out at the waves. A stiff wind blew the water to a beaten metal sheet of regulated dimples and shallow depressions. It whistled through the riggings. The cold air had settled my head a little. I wasn't really hungry. Boris was at work on his lobster, reading the newspaper that he had flat on the table beside him. I thought I should get some sinus medicine. Somewhere, in among the kite shops and hand-knit sweater stores, there had to be a drugstore.

I crossed a busy street and headed away from the water. Half-way up Exchange Street—where the majority of the quaint, tourist-oriented shops were located—a musician had set up with his violin. I always liked violin music and I stopped to watch him for a minute. The musician was tall and thin, and his hair stood in a fuzzy shock around his head. He had a long, lean face and he was smiling to himself, with his eyes closed. He smiled through the difficult parts. He was listening to the violin almost passively. I looked at the buildings, the long glass faces of the storefronts, the swinging wooden signs, the old-fashioned streetlights. All these things were painted over by the music and somehow made more beautiful.

The only others watching were an eager mother with her uninterested children—two boys—one overweight, the other thin. The mother smiled at me, then blinked her caulked lashes in rapid succession, batting them like butterfly wings.

"Lovely," she said. Her fat son cowered; the thin one poked an expressive finger down his throat. She reached into her purse and produced a quarter, which she held up for me to see, then dropped the coin with a muffled clink into the violin case. She shook her head in delight and squeezed her soft, white hands together. Her fuchsia lipstick had adhered thickly to her two front teeth. She exuded an aura of perfume aged in wool.

One of Boris's librettos was for *Les Mohicans,* a French opera loosely based on the Fenimore Cooper book. In the opera Indians kidnap the girl, her colonel father, her lover and—of all things—her dancing instructor, Jonathas. In the pivotal scene of the opera, Jonathas plays his violin and the Indians begin dancing, hypnotized by the music. It is thought that if the Indians were not dancing around they would be preparing to eat them all, and that once Jonathas stops playing, the Indians will indeed do just that. So Jonathas plays and plays, never taking a break, until English troops arrive and save them. This scene had seemed particularly silly to me when I read it, but now, in thrall to the music, it seemed possible. Even likely. I opened my purse and took out a hundred-dollar bill. I held it up for the mother and the gaping children, then placed it carefully in the case.

The music came to a close and I ducked into a doorway to view the musician. He stood holding the bill in his right hand, looking street end to street end for an explanation, the stilled violin held loosely in his left. He put the bill in his pocket and raised his bow again, but after the first whine of the strings, he changed his mind. He packed up his violin and left with his whistling of Massenet's *Meditation* straining through the fog, impossibly close, lost in a screech of a car's tires, and then gone.

I took my time getting back to the restaurant, even though my headache was long gone. Boris was going to be angry. I had the money only because he'd given it to me to buy lunch, decided to charge the meal, then forgotten about it. Boris had honored my request to have cigarette money by meting out exactly ten dollars at a time. I decided to tell Boris that the hundred dollars was lost—blown or stolen out of my purse. A gust of wind, a petty thief, it didn't matter to Boris as long as his precious money hadn't fallen victim to generosity. I rounded the end of the pier.

Boris was done with his lobster and nearly half my steak by the time I returned.

That night I couldn't sleep. Boris was snoring away, but I got bored lying there, despite the comfort of the bed. I was hungry and didn't know where I could get any food. I went downstairs to the living room of the bed-and-breakfast. The door to the kitchen was locked, but I remembered there being a crystal dish with peppermints in the living room. I entered the living room through a narrow door. The bustle and cheer was gone, replaced by silent gloom. The only sound was the ticking of the grandfather clock that stood guard in the corner. A pair of bookcases flanked the fireplace. The majority of the volumes were vellum bound and lettered in gold, and had, I suspected, been purchased by the yard.

I ate a peppermint. That done, there was no more to do in the living room than there had been in the bedroom, except now I wasn't menaced by Boris's snoring. What was there to do in Maine? The young violin player had been very attractive. I surprised myself with a little fantasy of him playing for me alone, and then for me naked. I wondered where he was. The moon was shining through the window and light pooled on the floor close to my chair. Out in the cold night, I heard a cat at first calling and then attacked. There was a distant crash of trash cans. A draft had worked its way into the room and a stack of pamphlets left on the mantel slid to the floor. The grandfather clock shuddered to the hour—midnight—and after a labored click let loose its cacophony of bongs. Then rain blew in with a patter and I felt the power of a dark patron moving over the city, as if the raindrops were fringe sewn to the edge of his cloak.

I wanted some fresh air. From the street I had noticed a small cupola at the top of the bed-and-breakfast, which must have been a widow's walk in an older, saltier time. Boris and I had a room on the third floor. I had noticed a narrow door to the left of the bathroom. This had to open to a set of stairs and at the top of these, I thought, I would find the cupola.

The door was unlocked but jammed shut, and I had a hard time opening it. I'm sure the door was seldom used. The stairs bowed in the centers and in some places were splintered beyond wear—the work of insects. I heard the scurrying of rats in the wainscoting. The dust was thick, which made my footsteps quiet. I was blanketed in darkness, ascending unsteadily. The steps must have been built for people whose feet were six inches long. The banister rattled in my hand. Finally, the stairs ended and I found myself on level ground. I took one slow step after the other, until I felt something brush against my face. After a moment of panic, I realized that I had reached a string and when I pulled it a dusty bulb came on, glowing softly.

I was in an attic where, piled against the yellowed walls, were several generations' worth of junk. The toys of a dozen childhoods had been kept, as though the adults thought they might one day return, one day find themselves again entertained by roller skates or wanting to read *The Secret Garden*. There was a pair of wooden skis leaning in the corner, a box of paperback books—thrillers from the seventies—the recent aged and somehow the more tragic for it. A weeviled Persian rug covered some space of floor, exquisite in parts, but now food for moths. A veil of dust lay over all the objects and tinted every surface a shade of blue. I felt sad for these things and for people, who die one object at a time.

In the north corner was a tiny cane-backed wheelchair. It gave me the shivers. Why did people keep such things? Surely they weren't so pessimistic as to think that another family member might need it. Why were the steel crutches and thick-soled shoes for housing leg braces still here, along with the hospital bed and child-height commode? I thought of physical torment, twisted limbs, and an early, painful death. But how could one let go of any of it? I walked over to the wheelchair and pushed it. The wheels moved noiselessly, leaving a six-inch trail on the dusty floor.

Maybe the parents couldn't face a time when their little one would no longer need to be wheeled into the sun or lowered onto the toilet. Perhaps there would never be an appropriate time to junk that bed, which had been the site of so many sleepless nights and some of peace, where the mother rested her hand on the child's brow wondering how she would not always be afforded this luxury. The thick-soled shoes implied steps shuffling along the uneven cobbles outside. How could anyone ever admit that the time for these shoes had passed?

I thought of my mother, who had regarded me throughout my childhood as a daily miracle, our time always too special. But it was she who was sick. It was her pain that made every second count. And in the end, it was she who left, faded away, like a photograph slowly becoming overexposed, until she existed only in the tubes and pumps of her hospital machinery.

Across the room, another staircase, small and spiraling, rose to a trap door and through this hole I climbed into the cupola. It was a black, boiling night full of menace. The air was thick and salty, the moon hidden behind a cape of dark cloud. Bats flew around squeaking to each other. A sweeping arm of light lit the harbor briefly and then withdrew. On the sidewalk below a couple, arm in arm, stumbled from a bar. She was laughing a fat laugh and he returned it with a

grumble full of lust. She threw her arms around him and they groped
and sweated on the path below. I thought of clinking glasses, of thick
embracing smoke, of the creased brows and grinning faces one found
in bars. Boris was dead to the world and I had at least an hour till last
call.

I dressed quickly and left the bed-and-breakfast through the living room. I had a key to the front door, one to our room, and another, smaller key, but its purpose had not been explained to me. Fore
Street, where the bars were lined up for easy comparison, was only a
couple of blocks from where we were staying. I could soon hear laughter and the slurred haranguing that goes with heavy drinking.

Lines snaked out of bars and people smoked on the sidewalk. I
could hear them laughing as they waited for the first pint or tumbler
to float them out of Friday and into the weekend. The line moved
quickly and I was soon at the door. The door swung open, releasing
gusts of laughter and cigarette smoke into the street. People exited
and entered, body for body. I could feel men's eyes pass over me, then
move on. The bar was full of smoke and hillbilly rock. I felt instantly
better. A red-haired man peered over his Scotch at me with glazed
eyes. A woman with a shelf of crimped bangs swayed him back to
her by his elbow. Her mouth narrowed and she looked at me disap-
provingly, but I really wasn't interested. I nodded to the bartender.

"I'll have a Guinness," I said.

"This is a brew pub."

"Whatever stout you're serving."

There was nowhere to sit, just rows of sweaty backs. I wrestled
my way to the bar and took a stool recently vacated by a man who
had left in such a hurry that I knew he was throwing up. I had hardly
wiped the first froth from my upper lip when someone tapped my
shoulder. There was a young guy standing behind me. He smiled
pleasantly.

"Can I get that for you?" he asked.

"Thanks, but I've already paid for it."

His face fell.

"You can get my next one."

He was wearing a big sweater and had shoulder-length, dirty-blond hair. He raised his drink and I returned the gesture. I found him good-looking, in an angular, Scandinavian way. I was sure he had an athletic hobby like mountain biking or extreme skiing. If he smoked, he only smoked pot. He had a big, easy smile and perfect teeth. I looked down at his shoes, brown leather hiking boots.

"Were you planning any climbing tonight?"

"What?" He was shouting, we both were, because the bar was so loud.

"The boots. Those are for climbing, aren't they?"

"No. These are trekking boots. I use shoes for climbing."

"Shoes?"

"Yeah. They kind of look like bowling shoes, except with thin rubber soles? You don't wear socks with them?"

I didn't know. "Do you work around here?"

"Freeport," he said. "L.L. Bean?"

"Ah," I said. "Duck boots."

"Duck boots."

I raised my glass and in four long gulps downed the remaining beer. "You can get me that pint now," I said.

He smiled and threw himself onto the bar. He had mastered the art of beer purchase. He seemed to know the bartender, who shot him a knowing look, implying that I was dangerous. He, in turn, smiled, implying that he could handle me.

He handed me my beer and I thanked him.

"Do you live in Portland?"

"No," I said. "I'm on vacation. I live in New York."

"Cool," he said.

I smiled and looked patiently around the bar. Aside from the girls who clung to their boyfriends, the bar seemed overrun with men. "Where are all the girls?" I asked.

The guy shook his head. "It's Bad Billy. They won't come out."

"Ah yes. William Selwyn. Have that many people died?"

"No. But it's still a problem." He lowered his eyebrows. He was concerned.

"What's your name?" I asked.

"Malley."

"Malley?" It sounded like a dog's name. "How original," I said. "My name is Katherine." I extended my right hand. Malley wiped his hand on pants and shook it. Clearly he seldom shook hands, or maybe not with women.

"I like the name Katherine," he said.

"Really?"

"Yeah."

"I've always found it unbearably boring."

"Are you named after someone?"

"No. You ask a lot of questions, Malley."

"Do I?"

"I think it's compulsive."

The windows of the bar were steamed over and I felt safe. Portland was a fun place with young people. New York seemed far away, at least Boris's apartment did. Malley had once worked at the bar and convinced the bartender to let him go downstairs to make me some fish and chips, even though the kitchen was closed. The fish and chips came in a little basket. There was ketchup, but Malley hadn't been able to find any tartar sauce. I lied and said that I didn't like it anyway.

"Can I call you Kathy?" he asked.

"No one else does. Never Kathy. Never Kate. 'Katherine' is solid and respectable." I was momentarily thoughtful. "That's what my father says."

"Any brothers and sisters?"

"I'm an only child." I smiled, as if this explained something. "My mother wanted to call me Marion, after her great-aunt."

"Did you like Aunt Marion?"

"Yes, but my father didn't. Aunt Marion liked to tell dirty jokes." Aunt Marion had died shortly after I turned eight. I could still conjure up her scent: Youth Dew struggling beneath a cloud of Silk Cut.

"She sounds cool."

"She was, but she didn't like her name. According to Aunt Marion, everyone born in 1903 was named Marion; 1903 was the Marion Year, dedicated to Mary."

"Why weren't they all named Mary?"

I thought for a moment. "I don't really know."

I pushed away my basket, which was now empty except for wax paper and grease.

"Let's get out of here," said Malley.

We escaped the bar and stood on the sidewalk.

"Where should we go?" asked Malley.

"I don't know." The temperature was dropping and I could see my breath. "Let's go look at the boats."

We were quiet. I couldn't stop thinking about Aunt Marion, but Malley wasn't bothered by the silence. I guess that's what people who spend their time with rocks and trees are like.

Aunt Marion always reminded me that she knew how to have a good time. I think she said this because she was worried about my mother, who, even if she'd been in good health, still lived with my father and hadn't had fun since 1968. She told me stories of riding in cars with boys (I think they were all from Georgetown, except for one football player from Boston College who had huge hands and went by "Honey") and smuggling liquor into dance halls strapped to her legs by her garters. She said, "I carried it way up there and boy did it tickle." Women knew how to dress then because they wore hats. Women did not know how to dress now because they did not wear hats. Women didn't know how to have fun now, because sex was seen as "liberation" instead of "fun." She said women were now liberated, but were no longer fun.

I wondered if I was fun, if anyone had been fun since 1928.

"Malley," I said. He was rolling a joint. "Do you think I'm any fun?"

He thought about this for a minute. "Sure." He lit up.

He offered me a drag and I waved him off. "I think I'm having an existential crisis," I said.

He was puffed up like a dying a fish, but he nodded sympathetically. Finally, he exhaled. "It's Bad Billy," he said.

"Really. Why?"

"Everything gets more important when there's a serial killer on the loose."

I thought about this. He could be right.

"I mean," said Malley thoughtfully. "Why does he have to go around killing people? You can be really mad without killing people."

"Isn't it usually something in one's childhood?" I suggested.

"Like in *Psycho*?"

"Yeah. Like that."

Malley nodded thoughtfully. "It doesn't seem right."

"Some people kill for love." I got up and looked at the water, the way the moon reflected up out of the pooling grease and fish guts.

"It's still not right," said Malley. He had a fine sense of morality, of right and wrong, like most people who weren't bright enough to think independently. "You can only kill something because you need to eat."

"Does that extend to other people?" I asked.

Malley had his lungs full. He shook his head vehemently. "Of course not," he said, his teeth clenched, the air stuck in his throat.

I sat on a lobster trap and looked into the harbor.

"What if you kill for love?"

"Nah," said Malley. "Who kills for love?"

"There's a story, someone called the Monster of Montluel. His real name was Martin Dummolard. He was in love with his landlady."

"So?" said Malley.

"The two of them terrorized Lyon at the end of the nineteenth century."

"What did they do?"

"They killed people and ate them."

"Are you sure?"

"Yes."

Malley shook his head. "That's fucked up."

I nodded.

"Why'd they do it?"

"For each other?" I pictured young Martin, a country boy com-ing to Lyon lured by the possibilities of city life. He longed for a place where the people outnumbered the cows, where conversation intro-duced more than the possibility of arthritis, labor, and the thick taste of onion grass in the last batch of cheese. His hobnailed boots ring on the cobbles of Lyon and he is overjoyed to have finally left the squelching kiss of mud. "Martin killed for love of Justine," I said.

"How did he meet Justine?"

"I told you that," I said. "She was his landlady."

Martin stands at the door of a boarding house. Everything he owns is in a canvas sack. A knock on the door is met with a loud and harsh order to wait. And he waits. And he waits, not knowing the effort being made up from the chair, through the door, along the hallway in som-ber thumping effort. Because Justine is a massive woman, a behemoth of her kind, and the power it takes to raise her bulk and propel it, heav-ing and grunting, from the armchair by the mantel, to the parlor door, to the darkly lit hallway, where the paper sloughs from the walls hang-ing in limp tendrils like kelp in the Sargasso Sea, is an awesome force, as is she, a woman who is seldom pricked with denials. A woman like this, round and pocked like the moon, pulls others—as if they are water in thrall to tides—in her wake.

"And he was in love with her?"

"It happens," I said. "Haven't you ever been in love?"

I thought of Martin listening to the awesome groan of wood down the hallway, his anxiety as the door swung open.

Martin's breath catches in his throat.

Justine Lafayette stuns him in that first and fatal moment. His eyes trace over the breadth of her generous, drooping lips. Her eyes, round in loose, wrinkled sockets, are a winsome shade of green. Per-haps, once, these eyes were sunk deep in flesh, but as if strained by the very heft of her face, a tremendous sighing effort has given up and the flesh, rather than pushing—like leavening bread—beneath the skin, is loose and dimpled, hanging in pouches from her large skull. She has taken effort with her makeup. Her eyes are kohled and her cheeks rouged in outrageous diagonal slashes. This, with the thickly applied lipstick, makes her appear ready for war. She thrusts this great head out at Martin.

"*Quoi?*"

"*Une chambre?*"

She retracts her head and nestles her great jowls into the stiff, grimy lace of her collar.

"*Nom?*"

"Dummolard."

"*Premier nom?*"

"Martin."

She nods as if she has expected this, the name, and the man. She turns and Martin holds his breath as she executes a perfect 180-degree turn within the confines of the hallway. The stiff fabric rustles as she moves and deep within the folds of her skirt, Martin hears another rustle, which must be the inner legs of her linen bloomers rubbing together, pressed and crumpled by her thighs. He follows her down the darkened hallway (as she blocks most of the light that struggles through it) and sighs in joy. He will follow her to this room. He will follow her anywhere.

"And they killed for love?" said Malley.

"Martin liked blood and Justine had a passion for human flesh."

"She was a cannibas?"

"Cannibal, Malley."

Who knows when Justine and Martin first realized the form of their symbiotic desire? Who knows when Martin first prowled the streets for the first of the eighty young girls he would murder, or when he first returned home smiling with the package of meat, bled with his own lips? What went into the stew, other than the flesh of those poor virgins and prostitutes who were unfortunate enough to encounter Martin on their way back from chapel or the champagne parties of light-hearted, well-shod men?

"Well, how did they figure it out?"

"Figure what out?"

"That she was a cannibal, and that he liked drinking blood."
Malley pondered the much-diminished joint. "I mean, you just don't
ask someone, 'Are you a cannibal?'"

"No you don't," I said. "But when you're in love, you find
someone's faults more interesting than their virtues."

I plotted the whole thing mentally in my terrible French:

Justine: *Je suis une cannibale. Je voudrais manger les hommes.*

Martin: *Non! Ce n'est pas vrai? C'est bon! Je suis un vampire!*

Malley was still contemplating the last smoky effort of his joint.
He finally threw it into the water. "Martin and Justine," he said.
"That's intense."

"They killed almost a hundred people before they were caught."

"What happened to them?"

"Martin died in a lunatic asylum. Justine was guillotined."

"How do you know all of this?"

"Marty Neuberg. I dated him in the eighth grade. He thought
he was a vampire and so he read all about them."

"Was he?"

"Was he what?"

"A vampire?"

"God, no. He was more into comic books than blood."

We were quiet for a moment. Malley got up and came to sit
beside me. The damp had gotten into his sweater and he smelled a
bit like a wet dog. "I got back from Belize a week ago," he said. "I
lived in a hut with this guy named Salvador. He grew his own and
we smoked a lot. He showed me how to spear fish. I learned to stand
in the water so still that the fish didn't notice me, then I'd spear it.
We'd grill it." Malley sighed.

"Why are you telling me this?" I asked.

"Because I didn't feel bad about killing the fish because I ate it."
Malley seemed very proud. "I was living in nature, you know."

7

I woke up on the pier. I'd been in a deep sleep and the shock of being awake brought me quickly to my feet. The sun was still cold, so I knew it was early. The air smelled fishy and I realized I had slept on a pile of nets sheltered on one side by a stack of lobster traps, on the other by the rotting boards of a building. I could hear the waves splashing beneath me. I stood up and looked around. There was a seal bobbing in the water, its large eyes questioning, and then it dove. I checked my reflection in a dirty windowpane. I looked all right. I didn't see Malley anywhere. My shirt was gone. I still had my bra on. The cold air swept upward and under my jacket.

I felt remarkably well-rested.

I had to get back to the bed-and-breakfast before Boris woke up. Lucky for me, it wasn't far—only a few blocks. I found the last of my cigarettes flattened into my back pocket yet somehow not broken and the matches, which were damp but after some effort flared into life. I inhaled deeply. Portland was still asleep, although the fishermen were up. One, missing teeth, smiled at me broadly and I guessed he'd seen me sleeping. I smiled back and zipped my jacket up all the way up to my chin.

The bed-and-breakfast lights were still out, but as I entered the dining room, I could hear noises in the kitchen—cooking noises—the slam of bread dough and the whir of a coffee grinder. Although I had left the door unlocked, someone—Boris—had bolted it. The television was on and strains of the local news were coming through the door. I knocked in a state of dread.

"Who's there?" Boris called.

"Boris," I said. "It's just me."

The bolt slid and the door swung open. Boris was wrapped in a towel. His anxiety was impressive. "Oh my God!" he said, and wrapped me in a suffocating hug.

"How long have you been up?" I inquired over his fleshy shoulder.

"An hour."

"That's funny," I replied. "I could have sworn I'd only been gone forty-five minutes. What's the big deal?"

Boris pushed me back and looked at me at arm's distance. "What were you doing?"

"I went for a walk. I wanted to see the sunrise." I tilted my head to better gauge Boris's mood. "It was spectacular. What on earth is wrong?"

Boris's eyebrows descended. "It's not safe."

"Portland?"

"I have been horribly worried about you. He's struck again."

"Who?"

"William Selwyn. They are still looking for him, and now . . ." Boris sat down.

"And now what?"

"Just two blocks from here, he attacked and killed a young man. He killed him . . ." Boris was pale, sick. "He bit him. Tore a huge chunk of flesh right out of his throat. The man went into shock. He bled to death."

"I thought Bad Billy was into women."

"He was," said Boris nodding thoughtfully. I noticed that Boris's hand was on his throat.

"Do they know who it is?"

"Not yet. They think the victim was heading back to his car at closing time." Boris pushed me back. "What are you wearing?"

"My jacket," I said. "I didn't want to wake you up and I couldn't find a shirt."

Boris shook his head then brought his hands to his temples.

"Boris," I said, "are you all right?"

Boris thought for a moment. He shook his head. "I feel mortal," he said.

Had he felt immortal before that? A long moment passed. "I'm going to wash my face," I said.

I suppose I should have felt lucky but instead I felt a lingering, smoldering dread. Boris felt it too. Even though the weather had turned, no more rain, the brilliant sun seemed to find fault in everything. The charming buildings seemed more decrepit and the cheery store signs tacky and false. I was happy that Boris wanted to get out of Portland. He'd suggested we do some exploring and I agreed.

Boris and I spent Saturday driving up the coast. I was smoking like a fiend, something I'd not been able to do in a while, because Boris didn't let me smoke in the apartment.

"You seem upset," said Boris.

"Not at all," I said. "Deliriously happy. It's so beautiful." I gestured to my right with a cigarette, indicating a bombed-out Sunoco.

"How about we go off this beaten path?"

Boris veered right dangerously—I felt sure we balanced on two wheels—and headed down a dirt road that was actually a private drive. I could smell salt and knew that had it not been for the dense forest, I would have been able to see the water. The road offered two options, one chained off, so Boris and I continued to the right. At the end, on what seemed to be a narrow point, was a small cottage. The windows were boarded over for the fall, but the last of the sunflowers and a dried-out bed of assorted petunias told me that it had recently been occupied. There was a sign out front—for rent—and a phone number.

Boris smiled at the cottage. The house itself was not impressive, but the views from all sides were stunning. There was a creek on one side and a shallow bite on the other. The property came to a point, then dropped sharply to the water. The tide was going out, leaving mudflats. A heron, its wings beating in reverse, gingerly set its feet in the mud.

"I bet there are clams there. I could make us clam chowder," I said, as if clams were the only ingredient.

"Interesting," said Boris.

"Funny how you just drove down here." I took Boris's hand in mine and leaned against his shoulder. "Seems like fate."

"Fate?"

"Oh, I don't know. This house, it being for rent and all." I began leading Boris down the point. "Is that a dock? How wonderful."

"I suppose no one will mind us looking, since this property is available to rent," he said.

Boris was having fun walking around, but I was beyond that. I had already imagined the layout of the house, pictured myself on a blanket on the lawn reading a book. I wondered where the nearest store was, how much the rent could be, and what kind of heat—if any—the house used. Strategically, what I needed was alcohol, something to smooth Boris's edges. Something to numb his intelligence. "Let's go have lunch," I said.

"All right."

"But I want to come back here."

I ate a good burger at a restaurant set on the muddy inlet. Boris had another lobster. I'd ordered Bloody Marys for us both. When Boris was on his fourth, I introduced the idea of renting the cottage. He had the money, after all. He'd lived in the same apartment since 1972 and each month paid a mere five hundred dollars of the three thousand it was worth.

"But who will live there?"

"It's for the weekends," I said. "For you."

"That's what you want?"

"No." I rested my head on the table. "I thought maybe I could stay here, to keep it up."

Even through the vodka, Boris was suspicious. "Out of the question," he said.

"Why?"

"Because I don't want you living here."

"What you're saying is that you can't let me out of your sight."

"Don't be so outraged, Katherine. You can't expect me to pay for this, for you, to stay here, away from me . . ."

"You could move here with me." I only said this because I knew Boris couldn't. His rent-controlled apartment had become an obsession with the building committee and any time he spent away—even a long weekend—would result in various letters shuttling between the lawyers.

"Katherine, why that cottage? Maine is nice on a weekend, but I'm sure there is nothing here for daily life. There's no culture, only restaurants like this—burger, Bloody Mary, chicken finger," he said, consulting the menu. "How will you live?"

"How indeed." I regarded Boris with my head tilted to the right. "I don't know. But I tell you this. I'm not going back to New York."

"Katherine . . ."

The situation was getting desperate. I decided to gamble. "Maybe I don't need time on my own," I said, smiling as sweetly as possible. I reached across the table and arranged one of his curls behind his right ear. "Maybe we need to spend more time together. You work all day. You could spend more time at home. We could do things together. You said you wanted to improve your Italian. We could take a class. And maybe sign up at a gym, get some of your extra pounds off. I've always wanted to do a yoga class, but not on my own." I nodded to myself, a person making peace with a new situation. "Maybe you're right. Maybe I don't need time to think. Maybe I just need more time with you."

After some thought and another drink, Boris decided that it probably was better for both of us if we spent some time apart. He made me promise that I'd get a job, nothing too involved, maybe some bookstore work. He'd noticed that I read a good deal. I must have played the situation right because Boris thought that renting the house had been his idea. This sounds like an amazing piece of luck, but I was benefiting from good timing. Boris had not written in a couple of days, which made him jittery. Soon, my move made perfect sense. He could visit on weekends; he could finish his book in peace.

Also, the thought of having a vacation home appealed to Boris, although he preferred staying in hotels. A vacation home would bounce well off other people ("It's just a cottage really, but it's my castle"), would make a charming segue in cocktail conversations ("The Hamptons are nice, but if you really want to escape, I have a place in Maine"), would allow him to achieve the beleaguered, moneyed stance that he liked to cultivate ("I like to chop my own wood"). The house had recently installed heat. We could lease it as long as we vacated in June, when the place went from nine hundred dollars a month to nine hundred a week.

We met the owner late that afternoon. She had grown up vacationing in the cottage. Her home was in Boston. She was in a hurry to get back to Massachusetts. She liked me, although she kept giving Boris funny looks. He was drunk and kept grabbing me in casual, sexual ways.

"The deposit's one month's rent," she said. Boris had slung his arm across my shoulders and his hand had come to rest on my breast. "You can move in whenever you want." She looked away. "I haven't had a chance to turn off the water and electric."

I handed her a check. She handed me the keys. As simple as that.

The house had a little floating dock and a red canoe. I could barely picture myself on the dock and the idea of me in the canoe seemed a distant possibility, but Boris instantly assumed everything. He was still wearing city rayon and Italian loafers, but his mind's eye had already set him on the dock, khakis rolled, bare feet pressed to cold wet wood.

Boris let me keep the car. He had accumulated just enough parking tickets to introduce the risk of towing and I think he was trying to distance himself from Ann, who gave him almost daily car reports.

I drove him south to Portland so he could catch an evening flight back to New York.

"Be careful," said Boris. "This William Selwyn . . . he is no joke."

"Oh, Boris. How many people get killed every day in New York?"

"I don't know," he said.

"Lots," I nodded confidently. "I'll be very careful."

A stiff wind was blowing outside the terminal. Flaming leaves scraped along the sidewalk. Clouds of cedar smoke billowed out of chimneys and pumpkins set their handsome bellies on every doorstep. There were cornstalks lashed to pillars and doorjambs, cheery reminders of fall's riot and summer's repose, the harvest and the winter chill to come. Flickering candlelight licked at the teeth of a few jack-o'-lanterns. In a tree, a linen-closet ghoul floated in the evening breeze.

I stopped at the drive-through at KFC for a bucket of chicken, got a six-pack of Harpoon, a newspaper, and some gas at the 7-Eleven, and headed back to the house. I needed some time to think. The moon was full over the bay. A dappled path of light extended to the water's edge and night things cawed and whistled. I sat on the dock with my chicken bucket and Harpoon. This was the last of the warm weather. Soon everyone would be bundled up in wool, leather, and thermal drawers. Soon, only faces would peer up from the bundles, exposed and wizened, dried and windburned. Other animals were already done lining their dens. Other animals were already cozy in layers of blubber and thick fur, their sharp teeth retired for winter's approaching deprivations, while in the dark alleys of Portland Bad Billy was searching for his next victim. People did not hibernate. The winter gave them no respite from their hunting.

The light from the kitchen window shed just enough light for me to make out the headlines. I hastily ate another piece of chicken then looked cautiously at the paper.

I was unable to move, staring at the paper, then realized I had stopped breathing. There, on the front page of the *Portland Press Herald,* was a picture of Malley. The photograph must have been taken for Malley's college yearbook. I remembered him telling me that he'd just graduated the year before. He was wearing a tie and some kind of tweedy jacket. Poor Malley. People didn't generally look that full of promise or excited about being alive. Pictures were false chronicles in that way, but Malley was genuinely excited by life. I thought of all those unclimbed rocks.

But then I began to worry. How many people had seen us together? Did I want to be involved in this? Would the bartender remember me? Of course he would. The police were looking for more information. I threw down the newspaper and took a big mouthful of beer. I was going to have to make a statement. But what would I say? The whole thing was a monumental, frightening, pain in the ass.

I had one beer left and no one to talk to. I missed Boris, which appalled me. I was dangerously low. Mosquitos sang a measured coloratura around my head. I waved them off and they reassembled. I picked up the rest of the chicken and made my way back to the house.

I must have been drunk to call Ann, although not drunk enough to call Boris. I did have an excuse—I couldn't find the proof of insurance and Ann knew where all that stuff was—but I was really just looking for another voice to put on the end of the receiver. I could hear the phone purring in another dimension, New York. I felt as if everything in New York were happening in the previous week.

"Yes," said Ann, picking up.

"I haven't asked you anything yet."

"Who is this?"

"It's me."

"Katherine?"

"Is it too late to call?"

"No. It's eleven, but I'm up late. Where are you?"

I explained to Ann about the house.

"And Boris went for that?"

"You'll convince him it was the right thing to do."

"I might even visit," said Ann. "What was the question?"

"Question?"

"You had something to ask me?"

"The proof of insurance. I can't find it."

"It's in the glove compartment in a FedEx envelope. There's an itemized receipt in there from a garage in Connecticut. I had some work done on the car in June. And the registration." She paused. "Did Boris leave the car with you?"

I hadn't even thought that Ann might want the car. "Are you mad?"

"Mad as in angry, or mad as in crazy?"

I wasn't sure. I could hear the television loud in the background and the sound made me sorry for Ann, who shouldn't have been alone.

"Is that all?" she said.

"I met this guy at a bar. Nothing happened."

"Why are you telling me this?"

"I don't know. I suppose because he's dead."

"Dead?"

"It's in the paper. In the picture, he looks so happy and now he's dead. He bled to death. Someone bit him, they think. There's this crazy guy who escaped from a lunatic asylum." I paused. Why was I telling Ann this? I put down my beer.

"What does this have to do with me?" said Ann. "What does it have to do with you?"

"Lunatic asylums are just like cages, aren't they? They're not an asylum for the crazies, they're an asylum for everyone else."

"I suppose that's valid."

"Can you imagine being locked up, day after day?"

"I saw One Flew Over the Cuckoo's Nest."

"Doesn't it scare you, Ann, to be locked up like an animal in a zoo, looked at, fed, maintained but not loved at all, not understood? To always be separated from humanity by bars?"

"We're all alone anyway."

"And that doesn't scare you?"

"Katherine, are you on drugs?"

"No," I said. "Just drinking."

"Good," said Ann. "Go to bed."

*   *   *

The next morning I woke to the maddening caws of some perverse crows. I'd been having some dream about the Tower of London and it took a minute for me to figure out where I was. I found some coffee, sugar, tea, and flour—colonial supplies—in the cabinet. The coffee was bitter and I'd forgotten to buy cream. I dressed to go for a walk to check out the property, but then felt dragged down by guilt— a vague wariness, so after a time spent searching for keys, which I'd left on the back of the toilet, I drove to Portland. Ostensibly, this was to make a statement to the police, but I was rapidly talking myself out of it. It was a beautiful day. I had the top down and my sunglasses on. If I cut my hair into a bob and put in some highlights, I'd be harder to recognize and bartenders saw so many people that they might not make the connection. I'd been thinking of changing my look anyway. Cutting my hair would no doubt annoy Boris and this made it more attractive. The police could wait. If they found me, I'd make up some excuse. How did I know they needed me to make a statement? But I didn't have to decide just then. There were other things to do in town. I had to apply for a job, even if none too enthusiastically. I had noticed some bookstores in the Old Port that looked fully staffed, one which seemed to be run by lesbians and where they probably wouldn't hire me. I decided to apply there first.

I parked my car by the pub, which was the only place in town I knew. I bought the paper. Bad Billy was still at large. A photograph of the murderer was on the front page. William Selwyn looked like a classic killer. He had pronounced yet fine features and black hair that he wore slicked back. He had a broad forehead, which gave him the appearance of being intelligent, and fine, arched eyebrows. I tucked the paper under my arm. It was unseasonably warm, in the seventies, and the sky was a brilliant, garish blue. The buildings left sharp shadows on the ground, pockets of cold in an otherwise sunlit day. Shop doors opened onto the street and greeted me with the scent of coffee, then pizza, then steak, then garlic and soy, then coffee once again.

I had grown selfish in the last few hours, not so nagged with thoughts of Malley's unfinished days and distraught parents, more concerned with my own life. I went into the bookstore to fill out an application, but for some reason couldn't bring myself to admit this to myself or anyone else. I spent close to forty-five anxious minutes assembling a stack of hardcover books. My search for a job had—I added in my head—already cost me ninety-seven dollars. The woman working the counter frightened me. She had fierce iron-gray hair that stood straight up and short fingers, muscled hands. She could have worked in a coal mine, but was instead punching numbers brutally into a cash register.

"What have you got there?" she said. She regarded the books in turn. "Ah, Richard Noll, *Vampires, Werewolves, and Demons*. And *The Lais of Marie de France*. You're into werewolves."

"I also have *The Little Prince*," I said. "Does that mean I'm into little boys?"

She tried to stare me down, but soon gave up, and handed me my change. "Is that all?" she said.

"I was wondering if I could fill out an application."

"We're not hiring."

"Did I ask if you were hiring?"

She reached under the counter for a pad of generic application forms. "Do you want a pen?"

"No thanks. I'll fill this out at home." I smiled and picked up the bag with my books.

Outside the window, under the arcing, backward letters of "bookstore," was the violin player, who had apparently been watching me for some time. He had stopped in front of the bookstore to check his hair in the window's reflection. His hands were cupped around his face to cut the reflection, which made him look like a winged *putti*. We looked at each other through the glass until finally I broke into a wide smile.

He was waiting for me on the step.

"I know you," I said. "You play the violin like an angel."

"And you tip like you're loaded."

"Oh," I said, "that. How did you know it was me?"

"I didn't have a very big audience." He smiled. "I'm Arthur," he said. "I'd like to take you to lunch."

"I'd like to go to lunch," I said.

"The seafood place across the street?"

"Sure."

The restaurant was in the basement. We paused at the door. Hanging above was a life-size fiberglass sculpture of a giant clam consuming a man. Only the man's trouser legs and shoes remained, protruding from the clam's mouth. In the window was a sign advertising the featured beer—Sam Adams Oktoberfest, and the special—oysters.

"Do you like oysters?" I asked.

"I've never had oysters," he replied.

I pushed open the door. Inside there was darkness and chill. I heard the clink of glass as the bartender sorted clean wineglasses above the bar. There was the subtle smell of smoke and behind the hiss of grilling steak, I could hear the cooks laughing. We sat at a booth. Above our heads we could see the feet of passersby—feet coming together in conversation; feet rushing off. The waiter brought us drinks. Arthur had long fingers, muscled hands. He rolled his pint glass in his hands.

"There's a storm rolling in," he said.

"Tonight?"

"Late this afternoon."

"What do you do during storms?" Our oysters arrived and I squeezed lemon over the lot. "Do you still play?"

"I sit in a bar, usually." Arthur smiled. His teeth were crooked.

"You don't go home."

"I live in my van."

"That's awful."

"You get used to it," he said, stoically. "One good thing about living in your van is that you don't have to drive home."

"Any drawbacks?"

"It's freezing."

"Why do you live in your van?"

"Guess," he said.

He had beautiful, squinty green eyes. "Bad breakup?" I suggested.

"Very good."

"Want to talk about it?"

"Most of my friends have suggested I find another topic of conversation."

I smiled, but with some prodding and three beers, Arthur was a little more forthcoming. Arthur had moved into his van two weeks earlier after leaving his girlfriend of six years, her heroin addiction, and incidentally, his heroin addiction, in a collapsing house at the foot of Munjoy Hill. Much of Munjoy Hill offered a stunning view of Portland; however, Arthur's room looked out at a vulcanizing shop. The house was flanked by a burned-out building and the Nissen bakery, which filled the air with bread fumes at strange hours but offered the advantage of selling day-old bread at ten cents a loaf. Arthur had also recently vacated his position as drummer for Intravenous, a metal band whose songs were indistinguishable from one another. The band had a loyal following and Arthur's departure was seen as bizarre and ill-advised. Of course, many thought the same of his cleaning-up, particularly his girlfriend, who felt betrayed. In her eyes, Arthur had aged inexplicably; his conversion made him as alien as a stockbroker.

Arthur hadn't played the violin in ten years, not since he was sixteen. But he had always been an exceptional player whose talent had tortured those around him, particularly when he disappeared into Boston at the age of seventeen and resurfaced two weeks later as a frightening punk rocker. Arthur was once again reinventing himself. He still had his studded leather jacket and bleached white hair (which, from the back, made him look like an old man) but playing the violin made him genuinely happy. Also, now that he'd quit heroin, he couldn't talk to any of his old crowd. There were some people, for example Intravenous's front man Bob Bob, for whom he still felt genuine affection, but talking to Bob Bob made him feel both self-conscious and bored. So he was strangely alone.

"How long do you plan to live in your car?" I asked.

"Van," corrected Arthur. We laughed. Arthur took one of my cigarettes and lit it. He put his feet up on the seat of the booth and watched the smoke escaping from his mouth. "Someone has to need a roommate." He shook his head wearily. "I know I'm getting old because the notion of living in my van depresses me."

"Once," I said, "that might have been romantic."

"Once," he repeated. "I've been kind of degenerate for the last six years. I told myself that I was living, being young. But now I just feel six years older."

"There's nothing embarrassing about getting old," I said.

"It's nothing to be proud of either," Arthur replied. He looked at me slyly. "What are you doing this afternoon?"

"Me?" I laughed. "I don't know. I have a new house—more of a shack—that I'm renting north of here. There's a fireplace. It's not really cold enough, but if there's a storm blowing in I thought I might try it out." I had no plans. "I have to fill out this application," I said, holding up the piece of paper.

"Need any company?"

"You want to come home with me?"

Arthur turned deep red and I saw him checking his reflection in the mirror behind the bar.

I thought for a moment. Boris was two states away and he'd promised me I could have friends. "I think you should."

"Really?"

"Can you bring your violin?" I asked.

"I bring everything I own everywhere I go," he said.

Arthur followed me up the coast. We stopped at the Mobil and got some beer, a half-dozen Duraflame logs, and a box of candles.

"We should get a movie," said Arthur.

"Something creepy," I said.

One good thing about the house is that it was fully furnished, complete with monster-sized TV and VCR and DVD, among other things—microwave, electric can opener, dishwasher—American necessities, things required by the folk willing to pay the high summer rates.

At the video store I picked out *Silence of the Lambs*.

We pulled into the driveway at around three. Gray clouds were rolling up the sky in a wall, shutting out the sun. The tide was completely out and birds were shouting warnings—coarse and sweet—in the wooded areas and scrubby pines. The air was heavy and electric. Arthur stood a comfortable distance away with his hands in his pockets. I looked over my shoulder at him, then back down at the bay. Suddenly, a gray coyote scooted across the point, disappearing over the drop into the woods.

"Did you see that?" I asked.

"Yes, I did." He seemed very peaceful.

A sudden gust blew in a cloud of rain than clattered over the roof in handful-sized drops. There was another spell of no rain, then lightning split the clouds open and it began to pour. Arthur and I ran into the house. I kicked my shoes off inside the door and Arthur did the same, although it took him a minute to loosen the laces of his boots. The water was sheeting against the windowpanes. I flicked on all the lights. While Arthur went to the bathroom, I opened the flue. The chimney looked fine, although the number of birds around the property made nests a possibility. I cheeped up the chimney, thinking that if indeed one had made its home there, it might reply.

Arthur came back from the bathroom. "You're cheeping," he said.

"Yes, I am," I replied.

"There's a leak," he said, "right over the toilet." He began laughing.

"Oh my God."

"How long have you lived here?"

"About twenty-four hours." I shook my head. "I was wondering why there was an umbrella in the bathroom."

"On the bright side, the water goes right into the bowl. It's kind of like a self-flushing unit."

I nodded wearily. "Why don't you light one of these logs? I'll try the VCR."

Arthur began flicking his lighter against the log's wrapper. I held the remote and aimed with both hands. There was a sharp crack and the house went dark.

"What the hell did I do?"

"Power's off," Arthur arranged the log, which was burning well, although some smoke was coming in. "Do you know where your fuse box is?"

"The boiler's in a closet, door after the bathroom. Maybe it's in there." I opened the box of candles. "Take one of these."

I lit a cigarette and puffed aggressively. Arthur came back down the hall. His candle suffused him with angelic light. "You couldn't find the fuse box?"

"It's not the fuses. The power must be out."

"Oh fuck me."

"Call the power company."

Power was out all over the coast. I looked out the window, where afternoon had been blown away and night now stood with no street lamps and no stars, only the occasional swoop and blur of headlights across the bay. The electricity would be restored as soon as possible, but lines were down everywhere and we were advised to stay put.

"Do you want a beer?" I said.

"Thanks."

"I have some leftover chicken, if you're hungry."

"Not right now, but it sounds good for later."

"I want to apologize to you."

"For what?"

"For the storm. For dragging you out here."

"The storm isn't your fault and you didn't drag me out here," said Arthur.

"Maybe I'm just apologizing in advance."

"For what?"

"I usually manage to piss people off." I smiled. "What are we going to do?"

"We can tell stories. Do you know any good stories?"

"I know tons of them," I said.

I took the couch and he sat in the armchair. He put his socked feet on the coffee table.

"Do you mind?" he asked.

"No, not at all. Please make yourself comfortable."

"Tell me something about yourself," said Arthur.

"You might not like me."

"That is a possibility," he said, smiling. He shook a cigarette out of the pack on the table and lit it.

"There's nothing to me," I said. "I grew up south of Boston. My father's a businessman."

"What does your mother do?"

"Not very much," I smiled stiffly. "She's in the hospital."

"Is it bad?"

"I don't think she's ever getting out." We were quiet.

"I'm sorry," said Arthur.

"Don't be." I began shaking my head as if I could shake loose the thoughts of my mother.

"What's wrong with her."

"I'm not sure. She has lupus. It's kind of affected her brain, nerve damage."

Arthur watched me intently. "How long has she been sick?"

"Oh, she's always been sick. My father thinks she's safer in the hospital," I raised my eyebrows in a relaxed way, to make it seem that all this was acceptable. "My mother was always getting lost. She was always late picking me up from school. She'd leave the house and forget why and find herself doing the grocery shopping at four P.M. I'd be waiting for her on the steps of the gym. All the other children would be gone."

Arthur nodded. "You haven't come to terms with her illness?"

"Terms. What terms? Yes. You're right. One day, no doubt, I'll wake up and be fine with it, but now . . . She's always been so distracted that sometimes I think she's just forgotten how to function. One day she'll remember how to behave and come back. She'll be very apologetic."

There was a comforting silence.

"Do you see her much?" he asked.

I shook my head. "What about your family?"

Arthur put a cigarette into my mouth and lit it. He was silent for a moment. He leaned back into his chair and I took a long drag from the cigarette. He pushed the ashtray across the table. "My father died," he said finally, "when I was very small. He was a good man."

"That must make you sad."

"When I remember," Arthur rubbed his temples. "But sometimes I think it's all right. I haven't come to much."

I shrugged my shoulders.

"At six years old, I was a tremendous success."

I pictured the little Arthur looking much like the Little Prince at the edge of the stage in his high-collared coat and knee boots. He was holding his violin and out past the orchestra a sea of applauding hands created a deafening sound, as if a thousand birds had all taken wing. Arthur closed his eyes tight willing all memories away. "Do you know any stories with happy endings?"

"No, not really. Fairy tales."

"Know any fairy tales?"

"Sure," I said. "How about *Hansel and Gretel?*"

"I know that one."

"I could tell you another."

"No. Let's hear *Hansel and Gretel.* I always liked it."

Outside the house the trees were bowing rhythmically. The wind rose shrieking and then silenced itself. The doors shook in their casings, as if a hundred angry spirits were demanding to be let in.

Arthur knew the story, so I had to innovate here and there. I tried to convince him that the cottage in the story was actually the house we were in. "Try to imagine this place, only with fewer appliances and more period detail."

"What period?" asked Arthur.

"Carpenter gothic," I said. "Try to imagine that you are Hansel. There nestled between the aged trees and dripping vines is a tiny house, barely a plaything, but so perfect that you feel you must be dreaming."

"Wouldn't I be suspicious?"

"Yes, But before you can think it through, Gretel has broken off a piece of shingle and is eating it."

Arthur closed his eyes. He was imagining the windowpanes, clear slabs of crystalline sugar, the candy cane doorjambs and fixtures of marzipan and boiled sweets. Loops of icing decorated the eaves and blocks of licorice formed the foundation and steps. He approached, his hand extended nervously. This was the work of an enchantress, but he was hungry and the smell of ginger, coriander, nutmeg, vanilla, mint, and cinnamon clouded his reason. He snapped off a piece of the window box: his favorite, white chocolate.

Arthur was smiling. "Remember," I warned him, "this story is not all candy and gingerbread."

"I know that much," he said.

Because ultimately *Hansel and Gretel* is a story of evil grownups and the persevering children who manage to survive. It's a story of abstract greed translated into unmistakable hunger—that of the stepmother, who says she'll starve if the woodcutter doesn't kill his children, and the witch, whose hunger is known and understood by all. Hunger is the catalyst to every element of the story—crumb-eating birds, house-eating children, children-eating witches. Hansel eats everything put near him and finds himself knocked down the food chain. The once-malnourished boy now has a triple chin and enormous, straining buttocks; his large and somber eyes are reduced to small black pits, like cloves pressed into a Christmas ham.

I find it hard to feel bad for Hansel. It's the witch I feel for.

The witch, if she had not been blind, would have seen the air about the oven quivering in the heat. She would have noticed the burners glowing red hot and the flush of warmth over Gretel's cheeks. But she didn't. She didn't feel the heat prickle across her skin, or her hand begin to roast as she reached into the oven with her stick, tapping for the problem flue. This is her last moment, this search and the thought of Hansel's fine rump with Yorkshire pudding. She is desiccated by her years and when Gretel pushes her into the oven she catches fire as if she were kindling.

There is a brief flare.

One long tongue of flame licks out of the oven, touching Gretel's apron. Gretel beats it out with a wet rag. She hears a loud crackle and a heated snap, and that is all there is of the witch. No slow roast. No dripping juices. No intoxicating smell. Within minutes, the witch is reduced to ash and bone.

And Hansel and Gretel are returned to their father, who is free of his wife. She has mysteriously died, apparently consumed in the same fire as the witch. How has this happened? The father wonders about this. He is glad the woman is gone, but her departure is strange. Finally he asks his children. And maybe it is Gretel who answers him—girls are quicker than boys at that age—and she will say, "Why, father, don't waste your time thinking about it. People vanish every day."

8

——•—— ⋈⬩≣ ——•——

My childhood was a quiet place, my home so silent that books seemed to be the only place to find words. I slunk about the house with my black hair braided to my waist, Mary Janes scuffing on the floor, book in hand. There were many places I could read. The house offered small chance of interruption. The living room had comfortable chairs and natural light, but I preferred my father's study with its broad wooden beams hewn by pilgrims, the shelves of scented wood, the oriental rug whose weft and pile made me think of generations of Chinese women, one after the other, losing their sight, although in retrospect the rug was Persian. I, in deference to my family's code, was silent to the point of being invisible. I'd watch my father balancing the massive checkbook, scratching missives back and forth from his company (Park, Shea and Dunn) to other investment corporations that spun money out of paper. He pounded stamps and from this ink and rubber came gold. Sometimes I'd watch him for close to an hour before he noticed me sitting in the chair. I sat with my book, wide eyes focused on him, silent and stiff as a rag doll.

For my sixth birthday my father brought home the usual elegantly wrapped children's book. The bow was cloth, wire-edged, deep red with gold trim. The paper was heavy and printed in matte flowers with whorls of silver and gilt-edged leaves. When I tore the package open, the rip made the low, shredding noise that is made only by paper of the highest quality. The book was *Hansel and Gretel.*

If I hadn't been sure that my father's gift had actually been purchased by my father's secretary, I might have thought he was sending me a message by giving me this tale of thwarted infanticide. I know that I disturbed him. I looked like a miniature of my mother, the same dark beauty, but where she fluttered around like the daintiest of moths, I crouched in the corners like a spider. The translation that turned my mother's fragile beauty into my gloom was exactly equal to my father's failure. His inability to make her happy and his complete disregard for anything to do with me—perhaps out of his love for her and knowledge of her slow withdrawal from health—had created this discrepancy between the females in his life.

Hansel and Gretel looked like a promising read. I knew I had heard the story before, but couldn't remember the exact sequence of events. The witch was frightening, the gingerbread cottage delicious. Hansel and Gretel stared out innocently, but I recalled some variety of wiliness that saved them in the end. I gave them both a grudging respect, even Gretel whose blond pigtails and apple cheeks reminded me of my first grade nemesis, Penelope Cornwall. I nodded a solemn thank-you to my father. He gruffly acknowledged this and left for his office.

My mother had bought me close to thirty gifts, all brightly colored and expensive. There was a china tea set with twenty place settings, in case I had planned a banquet for the variety of stuffed animals and dolls she had also purchased. She made me open all the packages while she watched, and with each tear of cardboard and split of plastic I managed a small "oh" of wonder, which I knew pleased her. I even played with the things, sitting "Teddy" and "Dolly" up against the furniture, as my mother instructed me. I offered them invisible cake and tea, which they consumed without chewing and, although this gesture meal was an ordeal for me, I could see that my mother was pleased. She wiped little happy tears and hugged me close to her, finally sobbing at the tremendous accomplishment of having made it to yet another of my birthdays.

All the while I was longing to escape. I had dug up our recently departed tabby, Claude, and had been spending evenings with him in the backyard behind the compost heap, where I thought his compelling odor might not be noticed. I don't know why I did this. It didn't give me any comfort. I think I was trying to prepare for (or anesthetize myself against) death—mine, my mother's, anyone's— and although Claude presented a fearful sight, with the worms and grimace and leathery sides, I got used to him soon enough. Claude, who had little to say in life and less in death, was soon discovered by Mr. Jones, who disposed of him with the other garden trash. Mr. Jones, forgivably, had assumed that the carcass (almost a skeleton at this point) was not Claude but some other unfortunate cat whose ninth life had finally quit on our property.

After Claude was gone, I began reading *Hansel and Gretel* over and over. I don't know why. Soon I had committed the entire text to memory, but still found myself drawn to the pictures and the rich smell of the paper, which somehow lingered despite my constant reading. I thought of what might happen should my mother finally succumb. Would my father take up with another woman? Would my father kill me with an ax in order to make her happy? This seemed unlikely, as my father was unconcerned with anyone's happiness, even his own.

I'd like to think that the reason I loved the story—although love is a strange word choice, strange in nearly all its applications—was because of the triumph of good in the end. But in retrospect I think it was probably the child-eating witch that kept tempting me back to its pages.

I woke up on the couch. It took me a minute to figure out where I was, that the screaming outside was the crows. I remembered that Arthur had been there, but he wasn't in sight. I got up and went to the door. His van was still parked in the drive. I pushed open the door. The clouds were all gone, the sky an even blue. I walked out in my bare feet and knocked on the back of his van.

"Come in," said Arthur. I could tell from his voice that I'd woken him up.

I swung open the door. He was lying on a platform of boxes in a sleeping bag. I climbed inside and sat on a speaker.

"When did I fall asleep?"

"Not long after the power came back on. The first fifteen minutes of *Silence of the Lambs*."

I picked up a framed photo that was at the top of a box—a man in squatting in catcher's gear, poised as in a baseball card. "Who's this?"

"My father."

I put the picture back in the box. "I'm starving."

"Me too."

"There's no food in the house," I said. Boris would have had food, fried eggs, sausage, cheese.

"Let's go into town. What do you feel like eating?"

"Grease," I said. "And look, how convenient, we're both dressed." It was true.

Arthur took me to a diner right on one of the wharves, a place that actually did cater to fishermen. The tables were full, so we sat side by side at the counter on swiveling stools. I ordered steak and eggs and Arthur ordered something of his own concocting, which involved hash, eggs over easy, an English muffin, and melted cheese. While we were waiting for the food, I drank my coffee and Arthur went to find the paper. The fisherman beside me hunched grimly over his eggs and toast. A slick deposit of egg yolk rimmed his beard and moustache. His face was wrinkled like an elephant's backside. Lobster traps were stacked outside the door and gulls scuffled on the boards. I sipped my coffee, which was somehow better burned than it would have been otherwise.

Arthur sat beside me, slapping the paper down on the counter. "He's still at large," he said.

"Bad Billy?" I leaned over and read the headline. He must have altered his appearance. There were several photos of Bad Billy with different hair styles and mustaches and beards. "Which one do you like best?"

Arthur took a look. "He makes a good blond," he said.

The food arrived with a pot of jelly and the waitress topped up the coffee and dumped out some creamers that she had in the pocket of her apron.

"You shouldn't sleep in your van," I said. "It's too dangerous."

"Bad Billy's not into guys."

"What about that Borden guy?" I said.

"Ah, Borden." Arthur shook the paper out and folded it back.

"You should be careful." I poured an extra creamer into my coffee, which turned it a dreary gray. "Sometimes it's hard to know how to be careful."

Arthur lowered his eyebrows dramatically. "I could be Bad Billy."

I sighed and sipped my coffee. "You make a good blond," I said.

After breakfast, Arthur set up on Fore Street. Soon it would be lunchtime and the businesspeople would be stalking the streets in suits. He started tuning his violin. I lit a cigarette. I'd actually filled out the application for the bookstore.

"I could get you a waitressing job," offered Arthur, "at a Mexican restaurant. I know the owner."

"I don't want a job," I said. "But thank you."

He finished tuning his violin and adjusted the case. I put in a dollar. "For good luck," I said. I began to leave.

"Can I see you later?"

"When are you off?"

"It doesn't really matter. I'd like to be here when the offices let out, but it's Monday night so there's no point waiting for the bar crowd."

"How about seven?" I said. "That'll give me a chance to get some stuff done."

Arthur nodded. He looked happy.

The bookstore was busy at lunch hour. There was a line at the register, which was manned by my old friend. I went past the line and stood smiling until she looked up at me. She glared in a way that was calculated to make me feel insignificant.

"Can I drop this off?" I asked.

"Go ahead," she said. "But we're not hiring."

The phone was ringing when I got home. I thought I'd missed it, but then it just started ringing again. I knew it was Boris.

"Where were you?" he said, instead of hello.

"In Portland. I had to drop off an application at a bookstore." There was a moment of silence. "Boris," I said, "what's wrong?"

Boris was having a bad time of things. His last novel, *Rupert on the Beach*, had been rejected by his old publishing house. Apparently, they had been sitting on it for close to a year before finally deciding against it. I hadn't even realized that *Rupert* was under consideration. Boris was such a literary fixture that I'd assumed, as had Boris, that the book would automatically be accepted.

"There's a new editor," said Boris, despairingly, his voice surprisingly clear on the phone.

"Oh, Boris." I was genuinely sympathetic, although glad for the distance between us.

"He says he can't identify with Rupert. Maybe, just maybe, it's because he is TWENTY-FIVE YEARS OLD and has never done a DAMNED THING except go to COLLEGE and read the COMIC BOOKS."

Boris was so upset that he was misplacing articles. "What are you going to do?"

"What can I do? I am almost done with the first draft of *The Little Vagrant*. This little PUNK seems interested in that."

"But they've already given you the *Rupert* advance."

"I know," said Boris. For the first time he sounded truly old and defeated.

Boris was under so much pressure that he had no time to visit me. In fact, Ann had agreed to move in with him temporarily just to cook and clean and keep an eye on things, while Boris shifted from desk to coffee maker to bathroom in his socks and boxers, reddish tufts of hair now matted to his skull, a strong odor of despair surrounding him that smelled much like gamy stew.

Boris had decided to return to *Rupert on the Beach* because the thought that it might not be of interest was truly terrifying, since Rupert was actually Boris, thinly disguised, and the plot was a clunky stringing together of Rupert's musings as he stood solidly on the beach staring out at the waves. Sometimes Rupert thought of childhood experiences—his mother peeling potatoes and how hungry Rupert felt. Sometimes Rupert defined things in a new way—love grips you like a vise, then caresses you like a silk scarf, then bangs you on the head like an anvil. Sometimes Rupert recalled his coming to America— there was a scene where he, a young boy in a gray wool cap with a dirty face, stood at the prow of a ship filled with babushkaed women and mustached men, and how they cheered as they sailed past the Statue of Liberty. This last scene was not from Boris's life (he actually stepped off a plane in Dallas/Fort Worth in 1972) but rather purloined from Hollywood. No, this young editor was not a raging philistine—despite his having gone to college—but was probably just a careful editor who, most importantly, had bothered to read the book.

I spent the day exploring the unexplored corners around the house with a sponge and Lysol. In the cabinet beneath the sink I had uncovered an unsprung trap, the bait gone. The trap was the usual spring-locked mouse variety, but was so large that it seemed intended for possums. I closed the cabinet and looked around, but I was quite alone. Later, when I was on my knees scrubbing the baseboard by the front door, I saw something—a dark shadow—slipping like a bead of mercury along the kitchen counter. The shadow disappeared behind the microwave. I took the broom and used the handle to edge the microwave away from the wall. There was a crack in the wall there. I don't know how something large enough to occasion the trap could slide through the crack, but it must have had rubber bones or the ability to turn into mist like a vampire. I shuddered. It was only six o'clock. I'd be early to pick Arthur up, but there was nothing left to do but unload the last of the groceries that were sitting on the counter. The kitchen cabinets were still airing out, filling the kitchen with a lemon odor that smelled nothing like a lemon and more like a hospital.

I parked up on Middle Street, a few blocks from where Arthur had set up. The temperature had dropped considerably and the cold air excited me. I bought a pair of gloves at a store specializing in South American goods. The gloves cost five dollars and made my hands look like Muppets. The cold air pricked my nostrils and I clumsily pulled at the lapels of my jacket. By the time I reached Fore Street—where the bars were—my eyes were tearing.

I stopped at the corner of Exchange Street. I couldn't navigate my handbag with the crazy gloves and needed a Kleenex. When I looked around the corner of the building, Arthur was standing in the same spot I'd left him in, violin hanging casually in one hand, bow in the other. He was talking to a woman. She could have been any-one, a friend or some interested fan, but something in me knew bet-ter. And then she walked right past me. For one short moment I was presented with her profile, and then her back, which I studied until she disappeared down Milk Street. Arthur had described his girl-friend—her long blond hair and thin face—but he hadn't mentioned her striking cheekbones, her heavy lips, and her swagger that clearly announced that she knew men wanted her. He hadn't mentioned the fact that she was almost six feet tall, that her confidence projected all around her in an intrusive, sexual aura. He hadn't mentioned the fact that she must have been at least ten years older than he was, that she was one of those people who was not ravaged by drugs but rather seemed to have been preserved by them, as if the various chemicals had leached into her internal organs, pickling them, rendering them immune to the attacks of free radical cells and aging.

She was wearing well-worn jeans with white paint splashed in a few places. Somehow, her jeans were uniformly loose, but fitted, despite her wide hips and slim thighs. The jacket she wore was leather with tassels and silver, a jacket that would have been hopelessly out-dated, a recent relic and definitely not retro, on someone else. On her, however, it looked hip and dangerous, as if she had weathered so much fashion that she was now impervious to it. Her hair hung straight down her back, and from the way it swung, seemed to weigh twenty pounds. She was making fists, clenching tight then spreading her fingers wide apart, and then she was gone.

I almost admired her.

I watched her go and struggled with the urge to follow her. I had been wondering about Arthur all day, what he was like, why he didn't talk about his family, why he liked me. Men usually told me everything in a hurry, as if they hoped to control me by burying me under a mountain of useless personal information, as if—once I knew all about their childhood friends, former jobs, maudlin desires—I'd be so weighted down by all this knowledge that I would be unable to leave. But Arthur was as reticent as I was. Seeing her made me feel more in control. I had at least seen whom he had loved—what had once been enough for him—and, at the time, that was all the information I wanted.

Arthur was despondent, looking into his violin case as if it held some answers. I stood casting my shadow there for a second before he looked up.

"Oh," he said smiling, "it's you."

"I dropped you off this morning," I said. "I had to pick you up."

He nodded. He clearly hadn't thought about it.

"Was that your girlfriend?" I asked. I smiled mischievously. It was uncontrollable.

"Ex-girlfriend."

"She's very beautiful."

"That is true." He scratched his head.

"What's her name?"

"Why?"

"You might want to talk about her sometime."

"Eva. Her name is Eva." He took a deep breath.

"Does she miss you?" I don't know why I thought this was so funny, but I started laughing.

"She wanted money," he said. "Therefore she does miss me."

"Did you give her any?"

"I gave her a twenty." He nodded at me, still smiling.

"That was very kind of you," I said.

"What is so damned funny?" asked Arthur. He was kneeling now, counting up the money, lots of quarters, enough dollar bills to make it look like a reasonable day.

"I don't know. I have no idea. I must be happy."

"Do you want to get a burger? It's my treat."

"That sounds wonderful," I said.

Arthur needed a beer and so did I. We went to Gritty's. Bob Bob (Robert Robertson on his driver's license) was behind the bar, a happy surprise for Arthur, because he was always happy to see Bob Bob, especially when he didn't have to talk to him, as in this situation where Bob Bob was working. Bob Bob was a part of the Munjoy Hill household and was still housemates with Eva. He didn't work full-time at the bar, but he knew the owner, who liked him and gave him shifts every now and then when his money was running low. Bob Bob must have been in his late thirties at this point. He wore his hair in a thick, brown ponytail that had a few silver strands racing through it. His eyes were glassy and his skin had an unnatural, paste-pink hue, but I could tell that he had once been handsome. Arthur told me that that was enough for a number of women.

We sat at the bar side by side.

"This is Katherine," said Arthur. He spoke with a forced casualness.

Bob Bob smiled warmly and shook my hand. "I feel like I should say something witty and charming," he said.

"So you're Arthur's new lady friend," offered Arthur. "I'd be careful of this one."

Bob Bob thought about this and then nodded. He smiled at me, as if he had actually said it. I ordered a burger and a Black Fly, which was one of the offered brews, despite the fact I had no idea what it was. Arthur had the fish and chips. I could see Bob Bob eyeing us while we ate. I thought he might be checking me out, but he seemed more interested in Arthur. I wasn't surprised when he came over at the end of the meal and with great purpose, rested a heavy, veined hand on Arthur's arm.

"You look great, man. You're the shit."

"Thanks," said Arthur.

"You look . . ." said Bob Bob.

Arthur waited.

"You look fucking great." Bob Bob smiled nervously.

Arthur raised his eyebrows in amused suspicion. "I like you too, but just as a friend." They both started laughing.

"No," said Bob Bob, "but I do have a favor to ask you."

Arthur angled in to Bob. "I can't say no until you ask me."

"We're playing at the Hole in the Wall next Friday. Can you play?"

The smile didn't leave Arthur's face, or even shift perceptibly. "No," he said.

"We're taking the door and it's five bucks a person."

"You could find someone else."

"I could," Bob Bob paused, "but someone's coming out from Edge Records . . ."

"I think I've heard that before," said Arthur.

"Well this time it's true. He's one of Park's college buddies."

"I don't know."

"Talk him into it," said Bob Bob, turning to me.

"Why?"

Bob Bob thought about this for a minute. "I'll owe you one," he said.

Arthur was quiet on the way home. His hands gripped each other in his lap. He was shadowed by a grim, foreboding cloud that I should have known cast its shadow over us both.

"You think I did the right thing?"

"Clearly, I'm missing something."

"I don't know if it's really good for me to be around those people."

"Is this a drug thing?"

"Yeah," Arthur drummed nervously on the dashboard with his forefingers. "I guess it is."

"Don't hang out. Leave right after you're done."

"Will you come?"

"Sure." I gave Arthur a cautious look. "I know nothing is as simple as you want it to be."

"What do you mean?"

"Sometimes you want to stop doing something, but it's not enough to want to stop. Something else has to happen."

"But what does?"

"What?"

"What happens?" Arthur resumed drumming. "Nothing ever happens."

We pulled into the driveway. I got out of the car and started heading to the house. Arthur paused by the car. He didn't want to be presumptuous. I turned and looked at him for a minute.

"Red Sox are on tonight," I said.

"I'm a Yankees fan."

"They're playing the Yankees."

Arthur smiled and followed me, hands in his pockets.

I unlocked the door, which swung open quietly. The house had filled with darkness in my absence. The air was cold and damp. I felt around the wall for the light switch, because I couldn't remember where the switches were located. Much of the wiring in the house seemed to be of the handyman/husband variety. Sometimes the light switches were even upside down. Arthur stepped inside. He still had his hands deep in his pockets. I could just make out his profile—the hook of his nose and his high forehead. He took a deep breath and looked at me, angling his head to one side.

"Just a minute," I said.

Suddenly, from the kitchen, I heard a scuttle of something—claws?—a weighty thud—a jump?—and then a crash, as if a whole bag of groceries had been knocked off the counter.

"Jesus Christ," I said.

"What the hell was that?" asked Arthur.

I flipped on the light. There was a metal flashlight hanging on a hook by the door and I picked it up.

The kitchen was still but a bag of rice was emptying itself onto the floor. "I think we have a rodent visitor," I said. I picked up a box of Cheerios and a stream poured out of the bottom of the box. "There's a trap under the sink."

"Doesn't look like it's working." Arthur looked at the sink then back at me. I stood behind him while he opened the cabinet door. Arthur was squatting down to get a better look when the rat sprang out. There was a moment of complete stillness where I could see the rat—legs extended, teeth bared—suspended in the air. Then it landed on Arthur's legs. Arthur yelled and so did I, but I still had the flashlight. I batted the rat into the cabinet door. It fell to the floor, momentarily stunned, and before it could come to I had beaten its head in, crushing the skull that fragmented with an audible crunch.

I was out of breath. It couldn't have taken more that two seconds. "Kill it," I said. "Kill it."

Arthur looked at me. He was awed. The rat was beginning to ooze onto the linoleum. "Go sit down. Have a cigarette. I'll clean this up."

Arthur put the rat in a plastic bag and knotted it. The front door slammed and I heard the metal cover clang shut on the trash can. I was still trying to light my cigarette when he came back in, flicking and flicking a dead lighter. I didn't notice him watching me.

"Are you all right?" he asked.

"I'm fine," I said. "Do you have a light?" Arthur took the lighter from my hand and shook it, then the thing flared into life.

"You're shaking," he said. I was. Trembling. Outside a stiff wind had started and the panes were rattling in the casing. Arthur sat down on the couch next to me. He picked up my left hand and held it.

"It's cold in here," I said. "Why don't you light a fire?"

He didn't move, just looked out the window for inspiration. A tree was losing its leaves. The tide was blowing in. The phone started ringing. It bleated and bleated, but I just sat there feeling the blood draining from my hand wondering what I should do. My heart was still pounding from the rat-slaying high. I pictured myself waging a battle against evil (rats) armed with the truth (the metal flashlight) in the name of virtue. I had no idea how to translate virtue to my life, but seeing Arthur there, feeling his warm hand—all of his warmth—projecting out to me, I felt that he was virtuous and somehow good. The phone stopped ringing. I thought of moving closer to him, resting against his chest, or some similar gesture that would have pushed the tension along, gear by gear, to who knows where, but I didn't. I let the moment pass until the very gesture of holding hands seemed odd, as if our arms were a clothesline strung between two unfeeling trees.

"What are you thinking?" Arthur finally asked.

"I'm thinking about you," I said. "What are you thinking?"

"I'm thinking that it's been five days since I've bathed." He raised his eyebrows apologetically. "It's making me self-conscious."

"Then you should have a bath," I said.

The rain had started up again. I turned the tap off when the tub was full and steaming, and Arthur undressed. Water was coming through the ceiling and into the toilet in a constant trickle that made it seem as if the bathroom were subterranean, as if minerals were depositing themselves on the walls and curtain rod, creating slick, calcified sculptures. Arthur sank deep into the water and groaned happily. His face disappeared beneath the surface. He stayed submerged for a few seconds and I lit us cigarettes. I turned the light off so that our faces were only illuminated by their burning ends. I sat on the floor on the bathmat and leaned against the wall so we were side by side, divided only by the ceramic wall of the tub. I'd brought a bottle of wine in and I opened it and took a swig.

"This," said Arthur, "is heaven."

"Is it?"

"Yes. I'm sure it is." He sighed and leaned back against the wall and closed his eyes.

The wind beat against the walls. Outside, the shed door had worked loose and slammed and slammed in the wind. "Have some wine," I said.

Arthur slid up and took the bottle.

"Join me," he said.

I stood up and undressed at a leisurely pace, then sank into the water at the opposite end of the tub.

Arthur and I had sex that night, which didn't really surprise me. I knew Boris would be mad if he found out, but he knew I needed to make friends and meeting women was next to impossible if you weren't doing something normal (work, school) and meeting men was next to impossible if you weren't destined to fuck. Why would a man speak to me if he wasn't trying to have sex with me unless he was gay and liked my clothes? Of course, this may sound as if I'm trying to justify my actions. No. Not really. I never felt any guilt about Boris. In fact, when I sat around and thought of monogamy as a concept, the whole thing seemed bizarre.

As a small child I had a game of repeating the same word over and over until it made no sense, until it became an unhinged sound and contemplating monogamy had much the same effect on me. I'd made peace with the fact that I had a hard time saying no to myself. If I desired it and it was in reach, I had it. And—strangely enough— the fact that Boris didn't know that I was incapable of being faithful made me think he didn't care to know me well, and this was a bit hurtful.

9

I remember that Friday for a number of reasons. First, it was the day that Intravenous was to play at Hole in the Wall with Arthur as drummer. Second, it was the day that my father found me.

My father had been tracking me for months, ever since I had disappeared into the north of Italy sometime in March. His money transfer had sat in the bank in Florence untouched, which had caused him enough worry to send someone to look for me. My mother was not well and the daughter whom he'd fathered specifically to fulfill such needs as looking after her had disappeared. For once in his life, he was at a loss about how to best proceed. So as my mother slowly drifted into her own lonely world, I was being pursued across Europe. I knew this from my old lover Silvano, who had been contacted by the detective in Florence. The detective had knocked on Silvano's door on a Monday morning and Silvano had sent him flying into the street with one swipe of his mighty Fascist paw.

I can picture Silvano in his socks, underwear, and golden bathrobe—more reminiscent of the Medici than Montecatini, standing on the steps of his urban Oltrano villa bellowing the hair off the detective's head. I could have told Silvano that anything to do with my father had nothing to do with love, but the detective was young and handsome, had come asking for me, and as far as Silvano was concerned (he hated the English since a bad experience in North Africa in 1940 and refused to learn their language) any young man asking for me was best communicated to with unmistakable physical violence.

After Italy I had headed into Amsterdam, where I purchased a fake U.S. passport from a nineteen-year-old Canadian. I traveled as Sarah Lowenstein until my return to the United States in the early fall. And for a while, my trail had gone cold and the detective had returned to New York. When he finally tracked me down, I was living three blocks from his apartment. In all likelihood, we had been using the same subway stop.

My father said he had a pressing need to get in touch with me. He also knew that my avoidance of him was intentional and so he decided that the matter was best handled by his lawyer and Boris, whose address was the one discovered by the detective.

As far as I could tell, my father, who had power of attorney for my mother, had decided that it was time to liquidate some assets. Or maybe my mother had insisted that he give me my inheritance while she still could. At any rate, my father was sending me the deed for the Hidalgo Ranch, a property my mother had purchased in New Mexico when, in a brief and expensive fit of optimism, she had thought a Zuni shaman held the key to a miraculous recovery.

Boris was so excited by the upcoming publication of *The Little Vagrant* that he had trouble mustering the required solemnity to deal with this delicate matter. I had never spoken of my family (he had never asked) so he remained crisp and businesslike, then added,

"I am so sorry, my dear."

I too was having a terrible time finding the right key of emotion. "What?"

"I am sorry about your mother."

"How does her illness affect you?"

"You are upset."

"I've been upset for years."

"Come to New York," said Boris. "I will take care of you."

"I think my being alone is better for both of us right now."

"Perhaps. Others might recommend a distraction."

I didn't want to tell Boris that I was distracted, very, with all kinds of wonderful feelings for Arthur, so I half-listened to his odd attempts at nurturing and was probably more agreeable than I would have been otherwise.

Boris was having a party for *The Little Vagrant*. This was very premature, since the book wasn't due out until the following summer, but Boris was of the opinion that every member of the New York literati was aware of the problems *Rupert* had faced. They thought he was washed up and he would prove—with an all-out, catered, open-bar gala—otherwise. I didn't understand his reasoning, but the logic was vaguely familiar and I could picture something like that happening in a Russian novel. I could also picture Boris overextending himself and spending every penny he owned convincing an uncaring (and probably innocent) public that he knew no financial struggle. There was something desperate in his voice. I didn't want to go, but the party wasn't for another week and Boris was a financial interest of mine, like a stock—I thought— that I should monitor carefully.

"I will be there. Is that all, Boris?"

It was not all. Boris was in possession of an envelope of things that my mother wanted to me to have.

"The lawyer sent them to you?"

"Yes. This is after all your home."

"And you went through them?"

"Katherine, we have no secrets."

I demanded that Boris send the things immediately, FedEx, for morning delivery.

"Is that necessary?"

"If you ever want to see me again that envelope better be here by noon." I set the phone on the receiver.

Arthur was standing in the doorway buttoning up his shirt. I was surprised to see him standing there. He'd just moved his clothes into the house the day before and I had yet to make the adjustment. "Who were you talking to?" he asked.

"A friend."

"What friend?"

"Boris."

Arthur nodded. I could tell he was disappointed and this made me angry.

"When are we leaving?" I asked.

"At eight. It's just seven-thirty now."

I took a quick shower. My mother had bought the ranch in New Mexico with money that she had inherited from Aunt Marion. She was in an advanced stage of her illness at that point, but there was still hope. I think my father had let her out of his sight because my mother seemed too weak to be of much danger to anyone, except maybe herself, and he felt indulgent and possibly guilty. A ranch in New Mexico had to be worth quite a bit of money. There were hundreds of turquoise-wearing, silver-clinking, Indian-loving New Yorkers who no doubt would cash in the time-share in Florida, forfeit the yearly ski trip, for this far more spiritual retreat. I wondered if my mother wanted me to sell it and get some money of my own. That was really all she'd ever wanted for me: autonomy, independence.

And I would escape Boris. I would, and as I showered and shampooed, I thought that he would be free of me. Boris would go back to Ann. Arthur and I would stay together for some impossible amount of time. After a few hurdles, my life would achieve a stunning, appealing normalcy.

I drove at eighty-five miles an hour down the highway into Portland. Arthur rested his hand on my knee, which made shifting the gears awkward, but I didn't mind. He had put an Intravenous cassette on and the music came out in one stream of sound. I couldn't hear where it went or make out any of the words. Arthur drummed on the dashboard with his forefingers, not particularly inspired, but very competent.

"I'm going away," I said. I had just decided.

"Why?"

"I have some business I have to settle."

"Where?" Arthur had stopped drumming. He was studying the side of my face.

"New Mexico."

"Can I come?"

I shook my head.

"How long will you be gone?"

I hadn't really figured this out. "My mother's given me her ranch. I want to sell it."

"Maybe you should keep it. We can become farmers."

"I think it's in the desert."

"Or miners." Arthur thought for a minute. "We can become Indians."

Intravenous's reunion gig had a good turnout. I was so busy planning my future—our future—that I spent much of the time zoned out in visions of New Mexican prosperity, or in yellow clogs in my mind's flower garden, kneeling with a trowel, planting bulbs. Intravenous's music was antimelodic and loud, interrupted by occasional guitar solos. Bob Bob was terrifying on stage. He must have fashioned himself after Iggy Pop, only Bob Bob was much larger and pinker. He looked like a violent, head-banging ham. During the break, the guitarist introduced himself. He was Mark Park.

"Let me get you a drink," he said. He had a strange smile on his face, as if he wanted something. "It's on the house."

I looked out at the dance floor, girls swinging arms and hair, and it occurred to me that I might be too old for this, which was a strangely comforting feeling.

"Do you live with the Munjoy Hill gang?" I asked politely.

"Lord no. I have a condo on the Western Promenade. It has a lovely view. You should come visit some time." Mark Park leaned across the bar. "Two Long Island ice teas," he said. "Katherine, right?"

I nodded.

"I know you," he added.

I looked closely at his face. There was something familiar there. "Are you sure we've met?" I could have known him at any of the three colleges I'd attended. He looked like everyone, down to his Mexican shirt with lengthwise embroidered panels.

"My father is Lawton Park," he said.

I looked into his eyes and nodded to myself. He did know me.

Lawton Park was a business associate of my father's, the "Park" in Park, Shea, and Dunn. Since my father had no friends, his business associates gained undue significance in my life. I hadn't seen Mark since high school, but I remembered parties at the Park residence in Hyannis. Mark was a skinny kid with the latest stereo equipment. He'd used his various Discmans and components in place of foreplay, on his way to tempting you into the closet. I usually got stalled at the graphic equalizer. He had been very optimistic as a boy and I could see the same optimism now at play.

"Do you want to see my bass?" he said.

I hadn't remembered him having a sense of humor. Arthur was nowhere in sight. I wasn't sure what this meant, or if it meant anything. I saw Eva come stalking out of the downstairs, where the bathrooms were located. She gave Mark a peace sign and he nodded. The room was hot, but she wore her jacket, impervious to temperature along with age. She went up behind Bob Bob and wrapped her arms around his neck. She ignored me in an easy way, which made me regret having come out that night. I felt that I was wearing too much makeup, that my leather pants (a gift from Silvano) were too stylish.

"Let's go outside and have a cigar," Mark suggested.

"Sure," I said.

Outside, the underage crowd guzzled bottles wrapped in brown paper. They groped each other beneath the bright lights of the street lamps where clouds of moths floated, as if they'd vaporized out of the couple's heads. Mark had a silver cigar case with his initials engraved on it in curling script.

"Cigar?"

I shook my head.

"They're Cuban."

"I prefer Costa Rican," I said.

"No wonder you drive your father crazy," said Mark.

I laughed. I didn't like Mark, I never had, but I was finding the familiar good, despite myself.

"What are you doing in Portland? There's absolutely nothing here," he said.

One of the teens threw a bottle onto the street. It shattered prompting a chorus of retarded laughter. I really didn't know what I was doing in Portland. "I'm slumming it," I said finally. "So are you."

Mark regarded me closely. He was bouncing to some tune playing in his mind. He shook his head. "No," said Mark. "I am slumming it. You are insane."

I had trouble sleeping that night. The wind blew, shivering the leaves and somewhere, two branches sawed against each other, creaking and groaning into the night air. There was some nocturnal thing out there, lost and alone, calling from the woods. It sounded like a cat. Arthur was sleeping deeply, snoring into the crook of my neck. He smelled like shampoo and cigarette smoke. Something about Arthur made me feel indescribably sad. I liked him in the pit of my stomach. I knew he was going to go bald young and he already had a bit of a potbelly, but picturing him aged ten years made me laugh. I wanted to be there for it, but felt that this was unlikely. I got out of bed. All this thinking had made me want a cigarette.

I stood out on the back deck. The tide was in and the bay a gorgeous glossy black. The moon was almost full and shone a full path straight into the open sea, or maybe all the way to Spain, then that thing called again, a lonely scream, and before I really understood what I was doing, I found myself walking in my bare feet out toward the woods.

The grass was freezing the soles of my feet and making my toes ache. I paused at the edge of the greenery and took a last drag off my cigarette before throwing the butt onto the damp grass. The scream sounded again and then was silent. I began to get scared. There was something unnatural about that scream. I wondered if that's what banshees sounded like, if otherworldly creatures lured people out with similar pathetic, helpless cries. I stood still listening to my own breathing, feeling my pulse in my finger tips. Something made me look quickly over my shoulder, but there was nothing there. I turned back to the woods and saw it—a light—moving deep in the trees. The light disappeared and I was just about to convince myself that there had been nothing, when the round, hovering glow swung sharply to the left and became a beam. There was someone lurking in the woods. Someone with a flashlight. I turned and ran back to the house.

I was completely out of breath when I reached the deck. I'd left the sliding glass doors wide open. I put the planks in place to lock the sliders shut, then crossed the living room to bolt the front door.

"Katherine?"

I spun around. "Jesus Christ."

Arthur was standing there with his hands in his armpits. "Did I scare you?"

"You almost killed me. What are you doing up?"

"I had to go to the bathroom. What are you doing up?"

"I'm always up," I said. "Go to bed. I'll be right in."

I don't know why I didn't tell him about the light.

Maybe because I thought it was Bad Billy, safe in the woods. And I wanted to keep him out there, loose in the woods, a part of Maine's untamed beauty. Maybe Bad Billy was necessary for culling the herds of people, something natural, as wolves were necessary to keep the deer population in check. I tried to argue that he wasn't doing any harm, there were lots of people after all. But murdering helpless individuals pretty much defined "harm." But what about helpless? What made these people helpless? Why didn't they defend themselves, and if they did, why were they so ineffective?

I found it hard to sympathize with people like that.

When I could hear Arthur's snoring again, I packed a trash bag with a blanket, a candle, matches, two cans of beans, three apples, half a loaf of sliced bread, a can opener, and, in a generous moment, a canister of Planter's cheese twists. I brought these out to the edge of trees, whistled (because that's how you call wild things) and then left running back to the house. I locked the door with my heart pounding in my chest. I settled onto the couch with *Frankenstein*, which my mother had read to me when I was a child but couldn't remember well, knowing that the next morning my monster Bad Billy—who I was sure was hiding in the woods—would have taken the bag, taken the beans, and returned to his lair. I would take care of my monster and he would keep me free.

10

The next morning, I was awakened by a banging on the door. I had no idea who it was. My guilt (or whatever corresponding mechanism I had) suggested Boris. Arthur was sound asleep. I got up and tiptoed along the hallway. There was more banging. I went into to the bathroom, which gave a good view of the driveway. To my delight, there was a FedEx truck parked up against Arthur's van. I ran to the front door. The man was walking away.

"Hello," I called. "Sorry I took so long. I was asleep."

"That's okay," the man said. He took a pen from behind his ear and handed it to me. "Just this envelope, but I need a signature."

The envelope was light. I shook it. Something rattled inside. I signed my name in the correct box. "Thanks," I said.

I made a pot of coffee before opening the envelope. I sat sipping the coffee, looking at the envelope, which I had leaned up against the carton of half-and-half. I don't know how long I was sitting there, but it was long enough for Arthur to get up and take a quick shower. He came into the kitchen wrapped in his towel and took the chair across from me.

"Is that the envelope from your mother?" he asked.

"From my father. My mother's stuff from my father."

We sat still. "Aren't you going to open it?"

I nodded. I took the envelope and tore the strip at the top. Inside was a photograph taken on the front steps of our house. My mother looked particularly glamorous in the picture, fierce round bob, Lilly Pulitzer dress, long legs, kooky sunglasses. I held her hand absentmindedly, staring with ill humor at the camera. My father smiled out with perfect teeth. I handed the picture to Arthur.

"Where's this taken?" he asked.

"Hingham," I said.

"Is this your house?"

I nodded.

"Wow. It looks like a bank."

"The pillars are gone now," I said. "My mother always hated them. Made her feel like she was living in a mortuary." The next thing I pulled out of the envelope was a safe-deposit key. A paper tag hung from it, yellowed, and on this was a long number in fading, feathery ink written in my mother's hand—exotic-looking "1"s and the French sevens, cut off at the waist. "Safe-deposit box," I said to Arthur. "This must be the jewelry."

There was a wadded-up linen handkerchief in the envelope, which was clean and empty. I knew my mother kept her less expensive jewelry folded up in handkerchiefs, so I checked the corners of the envelope. As expected, I found a pair of earrings. They were simple dogwood earrings with twisting clasps, not for pierced ears. The gold was of high quality and the workmanship on the enamel exquisite, but to the untrained eye they looked gaudy, cheap, almost drugstore. I had loved these earrings as a child. I looked at them in my hand, remembered how they'd looked on my mother.

"Try them on," said Arthur.

"I'll never wear these," I said. "They're not for wearing." I wadded them back up in the linen handkerchief and pulled an old envelope out of the FedEx packet. The envelope was a return billing envelope with a yellowed cellophane window. Inside were curling locks of black hair. I set this down. Arthur was quiet for some time.

"Is that your mother's hair?"

I shook my head. "It's mine. She must have kept it with her." I inhaled deeply. "My father had to have thought it was her hair too." I pushed the envelope across the table. The hair, my hair, made me inexplicably sad. I felt so stalled by it that I thought I might fall asleep sitting at the table.

"Are you okay?" said Arthur.

I thought for a moment, then nodded. "Look here," I said. I held up a piece of computer-generated paper. "This must be the deed to the ranch."

Arthur was silent for a moment, but I could tell something was bothering him.

"What?" I said.

"Nothing," he said politely.

"Just say it, Arthur. It won't bother me."

"All right." He cocked his head to one side. "You should go see her."

"Now?"

"Why do you think she's sending you all this stuff? She misses you. Even if she is all fucked up on drugs, she's thinking of you."

"What do you know about any of this?"

"I know how it is to wish you'd done something differently. You'll never forgive yourself if you don't see her." Arthur lowered his head and looked at me with such honesty that I felt my heart quiver. "Is she dying? Because it sounds like she is. You never talk about her leaving the hospital . . ."

"I never talk about her!"

"But you think about her every day. I can see when you're thinking about her. You look so sad."

The last thing in the envelope was a picture postcard, *The Raft of the Medusa*. I picked it up and looked closely at it.

"What's that?" asked Arthur.

"Maybe you're right," I said. "I think she is trying to tell me something."

11

I think my mother loved the paintings of Géricault because the possibility of death seemed remote, despite the fact that it was always suggested in his work. True mortality is morbid and abstract, the opposite of artificial and concrete, and therefore difficult to represent. Similarly, my mother filled her days with artifice, laughter, and plans for the future, because impending mortality was abstract and didn't pass the time.

As a child, I knew death was present in our house, the bogeyman beneath my bed not threatening me, but menacing my mother with his long, bony fingers. I was aware of death; she was not. I wouldn't go so far as to say there was hope in her life, or that she had a cheery attitude; rather she had a certain gay abandon that one might have after losing everything in a hand at poker.

She was awash in her life, precariously balanced on a raft that threatened to sink at any moment. Appropriately, she had on her dresser the postcard of *The Raft of the Medusa,* which she had purchased at the Louvre on her honeymoon. I find this ironic since her honeymoon—a send-off into married life—was the start of what proved to be a journey destined to end in tragedy. The painting depicts a moment of hope. Two passengers wave billowing scarves in the air, presumably to alert an approaching ship to the survivors' presence. The tiny raft has floated to a purpose and the divine hand of God, poised just beyond the picture frame, is about to snatch this small band of pioneers—eighteen people in all—out of water and away from certain death.

The actual raft of the Medusa was a makeshift floating vessel made of planks tied with rope and was intended to keep close to 150 people afloat—French settlers and soldiers—who were shipwrecked off the coast of West Africa on the way to Senegal. The senior officers, who were to tow the raft and its passengers to safety, commandeered the rowboats. After a short stint of rowing and towing, however, the officers decided to cut short their labor—and the ropes—and took off into the sea.

The raft and its inhabitants, knee-deep in water, were left to the seas and skies and menace of sharks. There were three kegs of wine; this was their only sustenance. One hundred fifty people floated in the searing heat with no food, some wine, and not even the space to comfortably sit.

On the first night, most people panicked or despaired. The people looking out to sea, moaning at the sky, et cetera, were despairing. The people plotting against each other, bouncing up and down in a dangerous manner, and challenging others to duels, were panicking. All, even those deeply in prayer (which is neither panic nor despair) were appreciating their situation.

Everyone was hungry.

The following morning, the death toll was at twenty. Some people had been dragged from the edges of the raft by the sea's salty hands. Others had drowned, their feet tangled in the coils of rope while still on board, their bloated bodies floating in the well of the raft's center. The following night, in the intense darkness, the people at the peripheries of the raft pushed toward the center to escape the encroaching sea. There was hysteria. Some of the sailors broke open casks of wine and driven by hunger, fear, and alcohol, became mad. One man took a hatchet and slashed at the ropes; the raft would sink and all would drown. He was overcome by other passengers still hoping to survive. In the escalating skirmish sixty-five people died.

On the third day—after some futile attempts at fishing—the living began to butcher and eat the dead. This gave the passengers strength and hope. Some considered the bodies manna from heaven, the presence of this new food an act of God.

On the fourth day, a tinderbox was discovered; the flesh could now be roasted. People found stealing wine or afflicted with hysteria were cut down by appointed executioners. Nothing was wasted.

On the sixth day the sick were thrown to sea, to preserve provisions (wine and flesh) for the others. Bones tossed into the ocean's yawning mouth were already stripped of flesh and cartilage.

On the seventh day, the *Argus* sailed into view. The survivors, fifteen in all, were saved, although five died before reaching land.

Little of this makes it onto the canvas of *The Raft of the Medusa*. There is no mayhem, disorganization, hysteria. Movement. Instead, the passengers are posed in such a way as to suggest classical statuary, although here it might be interesting to note that Géricault used the severed limbs of dead criminals as models for his work. This accidental nod to the truth of the story interests me. I am not saying that Géricault was unaware of the sensationalistic subject matter of his work. In fact, that was Géricault's great innovation, which ushered in the Romantic age: Géricault took the bizarre and sensational as inspiration for his monumental works of art.

This is the job of the romantic.

There is a story that Géricault set up a small studio devoted to the painting of this great picture. His young friend, the painter Eugène Delacroix, came to visit. We are told that on seeing the great canvas, Delacroix was so affected that he took off running down the street. I ask this question: Was it the canvas that sent him running, or the numerous severed limbs that littered Géricault's studio? While Géricault's memories of Michelangelo's statuary were fresh (the painter had just returned from Rome), the various limbs from which he drew had started to decay. Critics have even suggested that the atmosphere of decomposition in Géricault's studio is evidenced in the blotching, greenish patchiness of the canvas's sky.

While on the subject of meat, I wonder how the raft of the Medusa would be treated if, perhaps, it had been painted by Goya. Would Goya have created fantastic creatures instead of recycling corpses? Would his creatures have managed the flesh-tearing accuracy of *Saturn Devouring His Children?*

One Halloween (which my mother revered, much as hat-wearing Episcopalians love Easter) my mother decided that I should go as an Algerian. I didn't know what an Algerian was, but it looked much like a genie and I liked my belly bare (despite the autumn chill) and that my face was obscured with a silk veil. The veil was deep red, one of my mother's favorites, and smelled of Arpège perfume. To dress me, my mother had opened up one of the art books in the house and studied a painting by Delacroix. In the painting, the women's faces were bare, but my mother assured me that this was the choice of the artist who wanted to catch all their beauty, not just their eyes. I remember this Halloween in particular because I didn't go trick-or-treating. My father had arranged for some parent to pick me up at five and supervise my door-to-door collections, but my mother sensed a hesitancy on my part—the other children liked to make fun of me—and called them up and said I had a cold.

"What will I do?" I asked, relieved.

"Well," she said, "we'll just have to wait for the children to come here."

"We don't have any candy."

"That's true," said my mother.

"We could go buy some," I suggested.

"We could," she smiled and I felt the hair on my arms stand up, "but that would be boring."

She opened the kitchen cupboard and pulled out a box of brownie mix. She nodded to herself.

"Why don't we just get candy?" I said again.

"Shut up, Katherine," she said. "I'm thinking."

She took her bottle of pills off the refrigerator (she'd been de-pressed, sleeping a lot for the last month, and I think the pills were meant to counteract that behavior) and shook it festively. I was only nine at the time and hadn't really developed as a person, but I did have that unquestioning morality, which is the way of children. I said, "We can't give the children pills."

"Haven't they been making fun of you?"

"They make fun of everyone," I argued. "Besides, Miss Wood-house says it's only because I'm smarter than they are."

"What a lovely woman," my mother said genuinely, but she had already dumped the contents of the brownie mix into the bowl and I knew the neighborhood children were doomed.

The first child to show up was Parker Burnham from across the street.

Parker—who must have been six—was wearing a Winnie-the-Pooh outfit with the hood pushed off his head. He rang the doorbell just as the last of the brownies was being placed on the plate. Parker had perpetual allergies. His eyes were runny and his nostrils red-rimmed. He breathed through his open mouth and looked so pathetic that for a moment I thought I would do the noble thing and knock the brownies off the plate.

My mother opened the door.

"Drick or dreat," said Parker Burnham.

"Trick," said my mother, and offered him the plate. Parker didn't know what to make of this and looked down the path at his mother, who was chatting with some other parent and not really paying at-tention. "Go on," said my mother, "have one."

"But it's not wrapped."

"Which is why you should eat it now, before your mother sees."

And Parker gobbled it down.

By the end of the next hour, my mother's dosed brownies had been ingested by a significant amount of children, who were exhib-iting some bizarre behavior—specifically, the hyperactivity and hal-lucinating warned of on the bottle of pills. Randy Gertstein leaped off the roof of his front porch, forgetting that—even on TV—Batman didn't fly. There was some candy dumping and a lot of mask-inspired hysteria. My mother was a dangerous woman.

When all the children had finally been rounded up and brought home, my mother made popcorn and we put on the TV, *Doctor Jekyll and Mister Hyde* with Spencer Tracy. I found it hysterically funny, especially the way he showed his evil transformation by swinging his eyeballs and pulling his lips off his teeth. After that, we watched *The Wolf Man*. It must have been close to eleven when it ended (my father showed up in the last fifteen minutes) and I remember weeping at Lon Chaney Jr.'s demise as my father listened to the messages on the answering machine, mother after uncomprehending mother, wanting to speak with him as soon as possible.

12

I left for New Mexico the day after the Intravenous gig. I knew the drive would probably push the old VW Rabbit to its very limit, but I needed a long drive. Roads were the best thing about America—how it was possible to go and go for impossibly long periods of time without ever getting anywhere.

Arthur hugged me by the car. "This is your last chance," he said.

"My last chance for what?"

"To take me with you," he said.

I kissed him in a friendly way. "I have a couple of personal issues. I think a road trip will be good for me. And that will be good for us."

Arthur nodded. He gave me fifty dollars so I wouldn't have to rely solely on Boris's credit card. I hoped Boris wouldn't get the bill until I was already in New York. But the thought of Boris getting so pissed off that he dumped me really wasn't that frightening, particularly not when tempered with the possibility of a mortgage-free property sale. This was not much of a plan and if I'd stayed around to think about it, I might have talked myself into something better. But I didn't. Escape was too inviting, although all that time alone with a broken cassette player left me far too much time to think.

I thought of my mother's pale hands and the expert way she could twist her unruly hair into one perfect, symmetrical bun. I thought of the soles of her shoes upturned as she gardened, the calculated way she must walk to wear such even treads. When she prepared vegetables, she held the knife lightly in her hand, her movements so fast that they were indistinguishable, and the rinds and peels fell away in perfect coils and petals. Her slices and juliennes were miraculously exact, products not of nature, but of my mother's exquisite workmanship. My mother showed me how to apply makeup, how base was not a uniform mask, but rather stippled over dark spots, swept lightly across the smooth forehead and cheeks, how unevenness in application resulted in a regular, unblemished complexion. How was this woman, so capable of controlling nature, at the mercy of her body? Was there no way to save her?

I pulled into a truck stop some time after six. That day I had consumed two packs of Camel Lights, a dusty box of Oreos, and some Funyuns, which had blown out the window somewhere in Pennsylvania and were probably poisoning birds. I think I was in Indiana at that point, although I'm not sure if I'd managed to drive that far. All truck stops are the same to me. In the waning light, the land spread beyond the building and gas pumps in promising flatness. Even the sunset-lit clouds were strewn in horizontal shreds. I saw some low trees crouching beneath the weight of the sky. Against this, a blinding "Stuckey's" sign outshone the sun, which—despite its gorgeous hot yellow—was slipping into the land with the hopelessness of an egg yolk flung against a glass pane.

I parked in the assigned area and walked through the diesel gas pumps to get to the restaurant. Trucks pulled in and stopped with great, creaking brakes. Trucks pulled out with tremendous chuffs, like steam engines. Gnomelike men and heavy trolls with straining bellies jumped down from their vehicles that exuded heat, dust, and smoke. I walked quickly to the restaurant.

The restaurant was brightly lit and flooded with instrumentalized country standards that, without their words, were almost sinister. I took a stool at the counter and ordered a senior special grilled liver and onion dinner.

"Honey, you all right?" asked the waitress. She wasn't old, maybe only thirty, but had the mannerisms, makeup, and hair of someone much older.

"Why?"

"You look pale."

"Oh," I said. "I probably am pale. Nothing that liver won't fix."
I smiled and pushed my menu back across the counter. I was arguing
with myself in my head. Everywhere I looked there were men eating
alone, eyeing me in various degrees of subtlety all the way up to open
staring. I wanted to protect my solitude, but at the same time this
solitude was giving me anxiety. I was halfway through dinner when
I noticed a dirty hand on the counter out of the corner of my eye.
The nails were outlined in black. This was a hand that never came
clean. I smelled gasoline and oil. I turned my head. The man sitting
next to me must have been close to fifty. His face was deep and lined.
In contrast, his body was lean and youthful. His jeans were narrow
but ample for his small hips. His forearms were muscled in an exag-
gerated way, like Popeye. He was drinking a cup of coffee and smoking a cigarette. I finished my dinner and he left me alone. I had a
headache coming on—a bad one—and needed a cigarette, but I'd
forgotten mine in the car. I looked back over at the weasely guy and
caught him straight in the eyes. His pack of Raleighs was on the
counter.

"Can I have one of those?"

"Didn't know folks like you smoked anymore."

"And what kind of folks are those?" I took the pack off the
counter and shook a smoke out. He lit a match and held it for me.

"I meant it as a compliment. You look like quality people."

"No offense taken, but you really shouldn't be so quick with your
pronouncements." The cigarette tasted like pure tar, almost liquid.
"You have no idea what kind of person I am."

He was intrigued. He looked straight at me and I held his look.
"I'd like to get your dinner for you."

"No," I said. "But you can get me a drink."

"Don't drink anything but coffee anymore."

"I love coffee."

He nodded to the waitress and she topped us both off. He
watched me stirring creamer into my coffee. I watched him drumming his fingers on the counter.

"Do you like country music?" he asked.

"Sure," I replied.

His truck was parked out on the edge of the truck stop, which was a small concrete island in an expanse of endless, hissing grass. The parking area was lit by street lamps that made the light dim and far, as if the lamps were a part of a man-made constellation glowing for some other, skybound life form. The concrete out beyond the dull pooling of those lights was cracked—thrown up in some areas and eroded in others. Where the ground showed through, more grass thrust itself skyward. A smell of moist soil soaked the night air. The silence was briefly interrupted by the hooting of a distant owl, and then—by contrast—increased. I followed the man across the uneven tarmac to the truck. He leaped up to the cab with ease and I was close behind him, although without the same grace. He was a primitive with no need for conversation. He placed his oil-tainted hands on my face and pulled me to him. My stomach churned and for one moment—with his tongue inside my throat—I thought I would be ill.

I pushed him off, which he seemed to like. "Why don't you put on some music?" I said. I pulled my feet up on the seat.

"There's some tapes in the glove compartment. Put on anything you want."

I dropped the glove compartment open and a straining light came on inside. Willy Nelson, *Red-Headed Stranger*. Lynyrd Skynyrd, *The Best of*. There were some other tapes—Johnny Cash, James McMurtry, John Prine—in among the papers and empty cigarette packs. I dug around. My fingers found a long, leather sheath. At first I thought it might be a flashlight and brought it out. It was a knife with a handle inlaid with antler, a big knife. The blade had to have been six inches long. I pulled the knife out of the sheath. There was a hook at the end, a serrated edge, a smooth edge. The knife was clean, recently oiled. I could see my reflection lit by an outside fluorescent light, distorted through the center, where the blade rose to a low spine.

"What do you use this for?"

"It's a deer knife."

"Do you kill the deer with it?"

"Hell no. That's for gutting. You can use it to skin a deer too. Or a rabbit."

I held the knife, mesmerized, envious.

"You should put that knife down," he said.

"Why?"

"Blade's sharp. We wouldn't want an accident."

"An accident?"

"You wouldn't want to cut yourself." I saw fear flicker in his eyes and then his hand reached across to me, reached to reclaim the knife.

I remember that I didn't want to give it up.

I've never fully accepted the idea of accidents. Rudimentary knowledge of Latin demands that we recognize that "accident" comes from "accidere," to happen, and that "accidere" comes from "cadere," to fall. I, however, would like to point out the "dent" (although an accident itself) in the word—teeth—because accidents are the teeth of life. Occasionally man finds himself in the jaws of existence, chewed over, and when there is no reason that makes sense, the happening is an accident. This occasion for onion-peeling comes about because of the years I spent mulling over the word. Every now and then a car hits a patch of ice and terminates the lives of all the churchgoing folk within it, and maybe that is accidental, but growing up with my mother I found that a ponderous number of accidents were always happening.

When I was thirteen, my father found himself in the desirable position of making a business deal. To cement the goodwill between him and his future ally, he decided to have a dinner party. My mother referred to such moves as "prostituting one's family." She referred to the people invited to these parties as "the living dead." Business parties at our house acquired the acronym N.P.s, which sounded antiseptic and proper, but actually stood for "necrophiliac prostitution."

My job was to entertain the son of the future ally—someone named Tim, who was twenty years old, and happened to be home that weekend from Bowdoin. I had no idea what Tim and I were supposed to talk about (I was in the eighth grade) and as I greeted the guests at the door, standing with a bland smile between my father and mother, pictured the evening as a complete loss. Tim, however, turned out to be attractive in a boyish, uncultivated way that must have appealed to me in my youth. He had a cut on his forehead, misbehaving hair, and a crumpled jacket. His father was clearly disappointed in him and I felt the blood surging into my hand as I shook his. The adults went to sit in the living room and I waylaid Tim, placing my hand boldly on his arm.

"How'd you get the cut?"

"This?" Tim's hand flew up to his forehead. "Hockey puck."

"I don't believe you," I said and smiled. "Do you smoke?"

"Do you?"

I gestered to the door with my head. As we were leaving, my father—aware of my precocity—called after me. "Where are you going?"

I rolled my eyes. "Tom, I mean Tim, wants to see your golf clubs. Apparently, he's heard all about them." My father's golf clubs were legendary. I smiled my best pissed-off-teen smile, and my father turned back to his group, eager to get the attention away from me. I caught Tim looking longingly at the fridge. "There's beer on the porch," I said. It was winter and we usually left the extra beer there to stay cool and leave room for other things.

The night air was cold, but with no wind I found it pleasant, even in my light sweater. I pulled two beers out from the stack of six-packs and Tim opened them with a well-worn bottle opener he had on his key chain.

"How old are you?" he asked.

"Sixteen."

"I thought you were younger."

I grabbed his face and kissed him. A moment later I asked, "How old do you think I am now?"

"Eighteen," he said. "Definitely eighteen."

I began walking to the garage. His eyes were following me. "Do you want to see those golf clubs?" I asked.

We returned to the party forty-five minutes later. My father was annoyed. He'd been waiting to seat everyone for dinner and the servers, hired for the evening, were peering around the doorway to the kitchen with eager, anxious faces. I stood beside him, aware of the smoke that must have been rising off my clothes.

"Where were you?" he whispered.

"Just doing my part for the family business."

My father looked back to the front door where Tim was rebuttoning his jacket, this time correctly. My mother, who was twirling an empty champagne flute in her fingers, snorted a laugh and then coughed to cover it up. I could see her smiling at me over my father's shoulder.

The party broke up around midnight. Tim managed some sort of awkward, groping kiss behind someone's minivan as his parents were leaving. I remember entertaining a fantasy of visiting him at college, but the visit was unlikely, given my age. I stayed out late drinking beers by myself, smoking. My parents had gone to bed, or so I thought. I was just coming inside when I saw my father rushing down the stairs. He was grimacing and he had his hand cupped over his neck. I could see he was bleeding. I knew he was going for the first-aid kit, which we kept in a kitchen cabinet.

"Dad," I said, alarmed, "what happened?"

"Nothing."

"But your neck . . ."

"An accident."

I raced up the stairs, leaving my father to minister to himself. My mother was sitting at her dresser wrapped in a towel. I watched her reflection in the mirror. She was putting on a face mask that was clay green. Her hair was held back in a headband that made her hair fan out around her face. She looked like a marmoset.

"Mom," I said cautiously, "what happened?"

"Do I sense disapproval?" she said, uncaring.

"His neck is bleeding."

"Oh that," she said. "An accident."

I stood in the doorway. My father's profanity echoed faintly from the downstairs bathroom. I shook my head. "What were you fighting about?"

My mother turned and looked at me squarely, her glossy green face and sharp black eyes expressionless and calm. "Katherine, what makes you think we were fighting?"

And then she smiled.

13

I awoke in my car. On the passenger seat were two packs of Raleighs and the *Best of Lynyrd Skynyrd*. The ghost of a headache still lurked; light bothered me and my mouth was dry. I got out of the car and stretched. The night before, I had taken my keys—which were digging into my leg—out of the front pocket of my jeans and set them on the dash of the truck, something I now regretted. Things had gotten out of hand and I'd left in a hurry. And the keys were forgotten. The Rabbit didn't lock anymore, so I hadn't thought about them at all.

I was going to have to go back.

The sun was barely up but already the chug and grind of trucks could be heard from the pumps as well as the steady rise and fall of vehicles soaring by on the highway. I flipped down the sun visor and took a look in the mirror. My hair was matted to my skull, showing that my head came to a bit of a point. I was shockingly white. I looked like I needed a shower and a pint of blood. I lit a cigarette and got up.

The truck was parked out on the cracked concrete, far from the rush of things, but visible from the pumps and the passenger car lot. I began to walk. I was just going to get my keys and leave. What was so difficult about that? I stopped to stub my cigarette onto the concrete, then stalled. From where I was standing, I could see a cowboy boot sticking out in front of the truck, visible just beyond the front left tire.

I squatted and lit another cigarette. The boot was not moving.

Maybe the boot was just a boot. Then I saw the boot begin to jerk a bit, then it was still, then it jerked a couple of times again. I was try-

ing to figure out what a person might do to have that kind of movement—a violent dream? masturbation? epilepsy?—when I saw a small,
ill-defined shadow extend beyond the tire. Behind the shadow, pushing it along through the gray morning light, I saw the thin snout and
hopelessly delicate paws of a coyote. Our eyes met and she bared her
teeth. I smoked. Her jaws were dripping with fresh blood.

I headed down east on Route 70. Indianapolis—according to the
atlas—was a three-hour drive. At around ten that morning the high-
ways began to transform from the eternal ribbon to the dip and swoop
of broad, urban concrete. I desperately needed a break and decided
to take the turnoff for the zoo. If I sat on a bench there, no one would
bother me.

An infant giraffe had just been born the week before and there
were signs celebrating the new addition, pointing in exuberant zoo
ways to the giraffe corral. I had a headache, just a small one, so I
bought a cup of searing hot coffee and walked in the white sunlight
wherever the arrows pointed. Once my father had brought me to the
zoo. We were in Chicago—some odd combination of business trip/
mother sees a new specialist/family vacation—where I had spent the
days ignored either on the smooth blue vinyl of a hospital couch, or
in the waiting room of the doctor, where I remember one reanimated
woman coughing and coughing into a roll of paper towels. She did
not rip the towels off, but merely crumpled the tar- and fluid-soaked
sections into a paper bag, coughing through the whole roll and re-
garding me with her rheumy eyes all the while. She was challenging
me to say something, but I looked away. In an issue of *Family Circle*
I read how to make a cake that looked like a jack-o'-lantern or a ghoul
or Dracula's castle. You could make fangs for your child's costume
out of marshmallows. Mother must have been in the office for close
to two hours, because my father showed up—hassled and unamused—
to take me to the zoo.

He had his briefcase with him and found a bench to sit on, telling
me to meet him in an hour. We would have lunch then. (Actually

he looked at his watch and said, "You have sixty minutes. After that, I suppose I will have to feed you.") I headed for the big cats. There was a long hallway, the cats' inner sanctum—where they assembled together for meetings, I supposed. They were separated in their rooms and protected by bars that were clear and almost invisible. All of these rooms led to larger pens where the cats, exposed to the elements, could entertain the usual horde of popcorn-chomping children with their antics—leaping off rocks, licking their paws, swimming gracefully through a pool, or lounging in the low branches of a tree. All of these, except for the swimming, I'd seen Claude perform around the yard (Claude was still alive then) but without the menace. The menace intrigued me. I was down the food chain. My big eyes were the eyes of a mouse, or maybe something more exotic. A monkey or a lemur. I was dinner. The cats' inner sanctum was as a quiet as a church, because the weather was mild and most of the cats were displaying themselves out of doors. I stood in front of the lion house, where a mural of an African plain had been rendered, although none too convincingly. Perhaps they were scared the lions would try to escape into it and bump their heads. I was considering this when I heard a low rumble that sounded like someone running their thumb down the teeth of an enormous comb. I was leaning over the barrier (in my recollection my face was quite close to the bars) when an enormous lion with a head the size of a dishwasher came strolling out to meet me. He smelled of fresh meat and flicked his tail in a casually inquisitive way. I could see, even in his slow gait, the sinking of his massive weight into his muscles, the pull of gravity about his sides, the luxury of his fur. His mane was long, tousled, and wavy. I could see myself reflected in his deep brown eyes—the whole of me—my distorted big head, diminishing pigtails, shiny Mary Janes poking through the bars of the barrier. He took me in without a blink and I stood returning the gesture. And then he roared.

That roar sounded like the ocean breaking in a storm and I'm sure it moved every hair on my head and dried out my corneas. That roar put me in a warm cloud of half-digested meat and sticky fangs. That roar was a biblical wind, a calculated reminder of God's omnipotence and my futility. That roar seemed to last for ten minutes until I forgot where I was and then remembered, only to find myself running as fast as I could away from it, past a nanny who was clucking into a stroller, past a little boy scraping gum from his shoe, past a group of muttering Japanese consulting a map, and into the all-cleansing sunlight.

Here, at the Indianapolis Zoo, I watched the baby giraffe dancing first to the right and then forward, then rushing back to its mother, as if on bamboo stilts. My bench was shaded by a tree and the cold air, through my nostrils, was soothing my headache. The coffee was almost gone. A group of schoolchildren in uniform were lined in two perfect queues waiting to be marched somewhere. An indignant African bird called loudly from a netted enclosure, furious to find itself in the Midwest. My left leg was falling asleep and the cold metal of the bench had worked its way through my jeans, chilling my rear. I thought, perhaps, I should look for the wolves.

The wolf pen was a ten-minute walk from the giraffes. I suppose wolves make giraffes nervous and the distance was a form of courtesy. The wolf pen was a depressing affair. Perhaps because wolves were native to Indiana, the zoo did not feel the need to comfort them with a jutting ledge of rock or aggressive foliage. It was enough to just mark out a square of the fertile, unremarkable Indiana soil and to say that this was home. As if in response to this, a large male wolf lay panting in the sunshine, overcome with ennui. His side collapsed and expanded, collapsed and expanded, with surprising drama and as he breathed I could see his impressive fangs, which struck me as right out of Red Riding Hood, although other than that, he looked just like a large, lanky dog. There was a reek to the pen—urine, musk, despair—that quickly made me low. I was once again confronted with the horror of being imprisoned. I was jittery, too much coffee and too little sleep, but I decided to free that wolf. There was no one around and I thought if I could only slip behind the building, I could make my way in. There had to be some sort of opening for feeding the beasts. I would let him out and soon, loping through the valleys and piny forests, his howl would call the moon into the sky. His brethren would join him in a lupine circle and a chorus of throaty song would shiver the pine needles and cause the coursing spring-melt streams to glitter magically in their beds . . .

All this was the result of a willful, aggressive, romantic denial. It wasn't even spring, only fall. And, most importantly, I was in the heart of a large city. My freed wolf would probably knock down some garbage cans, go after a cat, and then get hit by a truck while trying to navigate the freeway. But this was far from my mind when I found the door to the feeding area ajar and stepped inside. Inside was dark. I stood still, waiting for my eyes to adjust, overwhelmed by the stink and somewhere, to my left, alerted by the shuffling of something nearby. The light was coming from down the room, which was slowly revealing itself to be a narrow hallway flanked by doors on either side. Something was scraping its nails along the floor. I thought it might be a rat, but it was too large. Also, the gait was awkward, unbalanced. I froze in place, my hands flexing nervously at my sides. And then I felt a cold, wet nub press into the back of my hand.

"Aahh," I screamed. Someone flipped a light switch and soon the shivering neon bars lit up the whole room. A zookeeper was running toward me.

"Shut the door. He'll get out," he yelled.

"What?" I said. I saw a young wolf sitting beside me; it must have bumped my hand with its nose. I went quickly to the door and shut it.

"What are you doing in here anyway?" The zookeeper was about forty, overweight, with an odd fringe of soft red hair that made him look tonsured.

"I was looking for the restroom," I said. I looked down at the young wolf, who was still sitting. Then he got up and began to limp over and I saw that the wolf only had one hind leg. He could still move quite quickly and hopped over with agility and speed. "Is he friendly?" I asked.

"That depends on your definition of friendly," said the zookeeper.

The wolf's hind leg seemed to grow right out the middle of his hindquarters, but at closer inspection, I could see the nub of a missing leg and the twisted angle that the other leg had grown in to accommodate the wolf's weight.

"My definition of friendly is that he won't bite," I said.

"I think you're safe," said the zookeeper. He was full of bravado and had a superior, nerdy manner. I guessed that he had no friends and probably frequented Renaissance festivals. "His name's Leto."

"That's an interesting name," I said.

The zookeeper gave me a condescending harrumph. "It's from *Dune*."

"Yes?"

"Haven't you read it?"

"*Dune*, no." In my mind, I had already changed the wolf's name to Quequeg.

"*Dune* is the greatest book ever written."

"Have you read every book?"

"I've read enough."

I smiled coldly and returned my gaze to the tripedal wolf. "What happened to him?"

"Actually, a tiger got him."

"A tiger? How did that happen?"

"We had the cubs out for some school thing and Leto got away. We found him near the big cats. He'd already lost the leg."

I looked into his gorgeous gray eyes. Something yellow glittered there, a memory of evil. "Why isn't he with the other wolves?"

"The public doesn't want to see a three-legged wolf. And the other wolves probably won't like him at this point. I've kept him back here with me for the last three months, but he's getting too big . . ."

"Are you going to adopt him?"

"Leto? He looks cute, but I know too much about wolves to keep him in my house. Besides, the zoo would never allow that."

"So what will happen to him?"

"I'm going to have to put him down." Yeah, this guy was a real man, unsentimental, tough.

"You can't do that." I had the urge to pat the wolf, but something made me think better of it.

"You better go," said the zookeeper. "The public aren't allowed back here, and this chitchat is nice and all, but I have to feed the hyenas."

"All right."

"I hope you don't mind showing yourself out," he said, too busy (or at least he wanted me to believe so) to bother with me. "And don't let Leto out."

"Righto!" I said, surprising myself with the chipper tone of my voice. Also with the anglicism, which had come from some heroic quarter, a childhood Kiplingesque programming that encouraged cavorting with wild animals.

Of course, I had no intention of leaving Leto in the zoo to be lethally injected, three legs or not. I had a blueberry muffin in my pocket, which I had been meaning to eat, but a truer, higher purpose for the humble pastry had suddenly revealed itself to me.

It wasn't hard to convince that wolf to come into the light, and he did, blinking, and soon was bouncing along behind me at a good clip. Luckily for me, the exit was not far from the wolf pen and I was soon skirting the edge of the parking lot, having given the wolf half the blueberry muffin while displaying the other half, which would be his should he make it into the car. When I reached the car, I had a moment's hesitation. The wolf was large despite its age and had to weigh close to sixty pounds. As he panted in the bright sunlight, I could see his shining teeth and the wall of wild, which shielded all but the surface of his eyes from me. Still, I opened the door of the car, pushed down the passenger seat, and threw the other half of the muffin onto the back seat.

Soon we were making a right and then another right. I'd decided to stay off the highway. I suppose I was looking for something slightly rural. Of course, the logical thing would have been to take the highway for a half hour or so—urban Indiana does not take long to thin out—but I was also nervous to be driving with an unfamiliar wolf at high speeds. So we wove through a few streets until I found myself driving along a wealthy, suburban street, which would no doubt turn into a cul-de-sac from which I would never escape. I regarded my friend in the mirror. The wolf sat much like any canine, rolling back on his haunches, front feet planted, in the center of the seat. He was whining in a high-pitched way, as if he was controlling himself from barking. He was cute. He didn't smell at all. His eyes were lovely and that coat of fur very impressive. Maybe he'd look good in a red leather collar—or even better, some sort of punk chic black-studded thing.

"Quequeg," I said in the rear view mirror. "Good boy, Quequeg."

I was actually more focused on the rear view mirror than the road in front of me, when I saw in my peripheral vision a fortyish man walking what—to my limited view—was a well-groomed West Highland terrier. I think I was in the process of editing out that man and his pet and replacing them with me and mine when the wolf let out a fierce growl and jumped over the back seat and into my lap. I know I was screaming, screaming and driving. I slowed down then swung into the high curb and hit my brakes. The man walking the dog looked up with momentary surprise. The wolf's claws scrabbled against the glass. I suppose he thought (as did I briefly) that I was being attacked by my dog. Growl growl growl, went the wolf. I grabbed the handle and started winding down the window. I saw the West Highland terrier's eyes get very round. The dog was trying to get away, running as fast as his two-inch legs would take him. He was on one of those retractable leashes (a misnomer because they only extend, never re-tract, particularly at critical junctures) that was reeling out to its full capacity.

"Astro! Astro!" yelled the owner. But Astro was running, wrap-ping himself in tighter circles around his owner's legs until finally his spiraling orbit came to a stop. I got the window down and Quequeg leaped into the suburban wilderness. I think he made his first kill. I suppose it was the terrier, but in his hunting Quequeg managed to knock down both beast and master. As all mammals have the same kind of blood when looked at with the naked eye, I've never been sure whose was spilling onto that immaculate sidewalk as I reversed away.

Did I feel bad? Sort of, but I had more important things to think about. The Midwest had developed these bizarre, sinister associations and I needed to get out. I saw the first sign indicating the direction to the highway and ground the car into fourth gear. Soon I was speeding at upwards of eighty miles an hour. I felt the speed was necessary, even though this made the car shudder in a way that caused my hands gripping the steering wheel to go numb. I'd never been further west than Chicago and the prospect was exciting. As a child, I remembered my classmates coming back from California burned up by the sun, full of stories of Disneyland. But my California—my West—was not a place soaked in sun, inhabited by giant mice and equally enormous dwarves. I had formed my opinions at an early age and these opinions had somehow made it, unquestioned, into my adulthood. In the same way, Captain Cook and Captain Hook had been conflated in my mind until a course in Australian history made it clear that Peter Pan and Captain Cook had never known each other. Similarly, my West was still populated by pioneers and their oxen, and their dreams being carted into impassible mountains, covered with snow. Somehow the lure of gold still existed for me. Unsophisticated, perhaps, but the West had been of no interest for many years. I'd been looking to Europe. To me the West was still undiscovered.

In the old days, before maps (I was rather good at reading maps) one would have had to engage a guide to get west of the Rockies. Into the hands of that guide one would entrust one's life and the lives of one's family. The Donner Party did that. They asked Lansford W. Hastings where they should go, and he directed them to the fatal, legendary cutoff that now bears his name—the Hastings Cutoff. I suppose many of the guides were good, which is why they've vanished into history. Good seldom is interesting and bad usually is. Among the guides that I remember well is Alfred Packer. Alfred Packer was an adventurer and guide, but he wasn't particularly good at finding his way. Or maybe he was. Maybe the paths he took are just strange to the majority of people and make sense only if they are viewed as accidental.

Alfred Packer was born in Allegheny, Pennsylvania, in 1842. He went west in 1862 and enlisted in the Eighth Regiment of the Iowa Cavalry in 1863; however, due to his epilepsy, he was mustered out of service. The winter of 1873 finds Alfred Packer in Provo, Utah, offering his services as guide to a group of twenty hopeful prospectors headed to the San Juan Mountains of Colorado. In truth, Alfred Packer knew little of this region. In January 1874, the group stops off at the village of Chief Ouray, who warns them not to attempt a crossing until spring. Packer and five of the men decide to continue into the mountainous region. Apparently, the call of gold has stifled that of reason.

Packer and five prospectors step boldly into the windy, white San Juan Mountain range.

In the early spring, the remaining fifteen prospectors, who had wisely heeded the advice of Chief Ouray, embarked on their own tiring, but nonetheless uneventful, passage through the mountains. Upon emerging on the other side, they inquire about their fellow prospectors. Fellow prospectors? No one knew of their friends and former companions. Could it be that they had not yet emerged from the mountains? Could it be that these fifteen men who had cautiously chosen a spring passage had actually passed them, been the first to reach the destination? Were they all dead, victims of cold, hunger, and blindness? Had the hissing snow and brutal wind buried their landmarks, their paths, and then their frostbitten, hungry bodies?

Alfred Packer? One minute. They knew him. Black hair? Broad cheekbones? Deep, penetrating gaze? Ah, yes. But he had not come out of the mountains in winter, not him, not with the meat on his bones like that; he would have been emaciated. And he had no companions. He traveled alone, yes he did. He bought no food when he appeared (miraculously?) at the Los Pinos Indian Agency, but just whisky. People still remembered that plump roll of money, the flutter of bills, Packer's cavalier dispensing of cash.

Packer's first explanation states that he has been left behind due to a leg injury. This callousness on the part of his companions is responsible for his survival. However, in August 1874, when the bodies of the other men are found, they are not strung along the trail, as would be expected if the hand of God had smote them leisurely, in turn—the typical scenario for small groups of starving, frostbitten, lost prospectors/pioneers crossing mountain ranges. Instead, the men are all grouped together. In addition to this, they all seem to have met some variety of violent death. Packer changes his story. The food was gone. This is true. In fact, all the men were surviving on a diet of rosebuds and pinesap. Packer is chosen to scout for food, leaving the other five prospectors together. Upon returning, Packer finds that a certain Shannon Bell—in a crazed state—has slaughtered the other four men. Packer, in an act of self-defense, shoots him.

Then an Indian guide finds strips of meat—man meat—strung out along the trail. On the Colorado side of the trail.

On the survivors' side of the mountains.

Packer is forced to reconstruct his story again: they were all dead anyway. Why not make meat of the others? Since when have dead men been concerned for the mortal body when faced with the fate of their immortal souls?

Shortly after this last retelling, Packer is sentenced to death by hanging for cannibalism. Packer escapes from jail and changes his name to Schwartz. He moves from Arizona to Missouri to Colorado to Wyoming, where (or so the legend goes) his laugh is recognized in a bar in Fort Fetterman. For reasons unknown to me, his predicament attracts the sympathy of a Denver journalist whose championing of Packer's plight—the plight of a cannibal—results in the reduction of the sentence from five counts of murder to mere manslaughter. Packer dies a free man of natural causes in 1907. He is sixty-five years old.

I would like to return to April sixth, 1874, when Packer emerges from the snowy belt of mountains, his cheeks full and flushed, his roll of cash heavy in his hand. How jolly that man appears. A whisky is all he needs, no, make that a full flask. No salt meat for me. No flour. I have my provisions right here, in my satchel. Keep your chalky bread, your tainted beef, your pickled ham. I carry my own meat and am in no need of provisions.

This would be the last time he stanched his hunger.

The only picture of Alfred Packer that I have seen shows him in the long hair, floppy mustache, and goatee of the period. He is perched on the edge of a chair, blanketed in a black coat that obscures his figure, the long lines of his bones. His hands are gently fisted. His eyebrows descend to the cliff of brow. His eyes are deep in his face. Most notable are his cheekbones, the broad cantilever of bone protruding from each side of the face. The cheeks beneath are caverns, sails of skin pulled taught with no flesh beneath. He looks to be a man eternally starved, emaciated, deprived. His sentence is to be always hungry. Never satisfied. To be constantly in the presence of food and never allowed to eat.

14

Gallup was on another level of the earth. I'd heard the town had the highest percentage of alcoholics in the nation, which appealed to me. I thought I could get a drink there, and I needed a drink. I was happy to be in New Mexico. In New Mexico the birds sang all year long. My mother had driven down this very highway. I wondered how far I was from the Hidalgo Ranch.

I pulled over on a dusty road trimmed on either side by barbed wire. The sun was strong and buzzards swung lazy circles beneath the few tendrils of cloud. They projected their shadows onto the ground, perfect beams of darkness. On the far side of a ridge of red rock something must have been cut down, because their circles grew smaller and finally became one and slowly the great birds swung in lower and tighter, as if all those vultures were being sucked down an enormous, invisible drain. They were gone now, hidden behind the ridge, and all that was left was the sweet after-smell of death.

The signs for the Navajo reservation confirmed my approach into Gallup. I needed a shower and a meal. There was so much nothing between the towns in this part of America. All the people were spread thinly through the plains. It reminded me of molecules. In the east, we were solid, and here out in the flatter, bigger part, they were liquid. I pulled into a parking lot where a sign, lit in spasms by a malfunctioning bulb, announced that rooms were a mere twelve dollars a night. I was getting my bag from the trunk when the light bulb suddenly fizzled and died. I wasn't really paying attention to my bag and let it drop. Change spilled out everywhere.

The guy working in the office saw it happen and thought he should give me a hand. He got up from the reception desk and came out. I could feel him looking over my shoulder.

"Hi, I'm Johnny," he said.

"Hello," I said.

"Can I help?"

"That's not necessary."

He picked up *The Best of Lynyrd Skynyrd,* which had fallen on the ground. "Lynyrd Skynyrd," said Johnny.

"Free Bird," I replied. I zipped my bag up and dusted my knees. "I am assuming you have an available room."

"Take as many as you like."

"What about a place to eat?"

"I was on my way across the street to get a burger. Want to come?"

"Sure," I said.

We headed across the street. Johnny rested his hand on my shoulder and said, "You look like you need a drink."

"Very perceptive," I said.

The restaurant was smoky and dim. Johnny and I ordered burgers and beers. The burgers came smothered in green chili in a basket of heavily salted fries, which I am sure had been cooked in lard. This was the best burger meal I've ever had. There were only a few people in the room. I could make out an old man in a booth near ours hunched over a plate of food and along the bar shadowy, rounded figures had lined themselves up like a row of boulders; occasionally, when you had forgotten they were people, one of them would move.

I'm not sure how many beers I drank. At one point, I called Arthur from the pay phone. I used a secret ring, hanging up a couple of times. We'd figured this out before I left so he wouldn't accidentally find himself in conversation with Boris. Arthur was concerned.

"I wish you'd call me more often, Katherine."

"I will," I said. "Do you miss me?"

"Yes," said Arthur.

"I miss you," I said. "I think I lack judgment."

"That is probably true."

"I have to go now."

"Call again soon," he said. And we both hung up.

Back in the booth, Johnny had decided he needed me. He said, "I need you, Elizabeth."

"Katherine."

"I need you, Katherine. You're really beautiful. You're so . . ."

"Exquisite?"

"No. Different."

"Different from what?" I said. I waved over at the old woman who was waiting tables and she turned and headed back to the bar for more beer. "What do you know about me?"

"I know you listen to Lynyrd Skynyrd," he said.

I laughed and shook my head.

"I know you're hiding something," he added.

I drank some beer and when I put my glass down, Johnny was nodding and smiling at me. "Why do you think I'm hiding something?" I asked.

"You don't ask me anything," he said, "so I won't ask you anything."

"Maybe I'm just not interested."

Johnny laughed a big laugh, the laugh of a much older man. He looked around to see if other people were enjoying themselves as much as he was. They weren't. He nodded to me approvingly. And I, despite myself, began to have a good time.

I led him back across the street. He was drunk and unsteady, but something in his eyes had stayed awake. "Do you have a boyfriend?" he asked.

"I have two." I smiled. "And you, do you have a girlfriend?"

"No," he said. "Sometimes I sleep with a lady up the street. She's okay, but she's married. There's a widow on the reservation."

"You're into older women."

"The widow's my age, twenty-seven."

"That's young to be called a widow."

"She has four children."

"I didn't know that widowhood was a function of having children."

"She's not looking to get married."

"And neither are you?"

"I wouldn't be any good."

"Why not?" I asked. Johnny pushed open the door to the motel, which wasn't locked.

"I don't know," he said.

"Well, what do you do?"

"What do you mean?"

"What do you do?"

"I work in a motel."

"No one just works in a motel."

"I," he said, "just work in a motel."

Johnny waited at the reception desk while I took a shower. He had a bottle of Wild Turkey in one of the drawers and I saw him pour himself a glass. I took a long time. I had three days of dirt and oil coating me. Also, the salty smell of that trucker was somewhere in my hair and at odd times, I'd get a whiff of it, as if his spirit had been disturbed. When I finally got out of the shower and reappeared in the paneled lobby, Johnny had fallen asleep with his head on the counter, his hand sprawled around a set of keys. I took the glass of bourbon to my room and was soon asleep myself.

The following morning Johnny and I set off together to find the Hidalgo Ranch. The landscape around Gallup was both calculated and unreal. Rocky outcrops interrupted the horizon here and there and sometimes I thought I could see the curvature of the earth, feel the car engine straining on the incline. To me, the whole thing looked surreal—denying the rational—demanding that I meld my subconscious onto the landscape in order to have it come together as a whole.

Or maybe the sparseness just reminded me of Dali, a blank Iberian plain interrupted by a rotting carcass and crows, which, when viewed at high speed in one's peripheral vision, acquired some suspicious details—a bust of Voltaire, pronged twigs, infamous wilting clocks.

I knew something of Dali from a modern art course I'd taken in college. I'd come up with a topic for the final paper that my professor, Consuela Smith, thought had much promise. I'd decided to compare Dali's and Goya's treatments of war. It would have been a good paper, but the course was taught in the spring and just as I was sitting down at the computer to compose my thoughts, the weather turned. The sun came out. The temperature nudged past eighty and I knew that my paper and I were both doomed. I could never work in good weather and so the paper was never actually written. But I had read some good books in its pursuit. Driving out in the desert, I remembered that I'd never given up writing the paper, even though I'd failed the course, and that "F" had been the final straw of the final semester of my college career.

My favorite Dali painting was *Autumn Cannibalism*. Dali painted *Autumn Cannibalism* at the end of 1936, at which point he had already alienated himself from the surrealist movement, although the break would not be complete until 1939. Dali's embrace of traditional Spanish values—Catholicism, penitence, and classicism—put him at odds with the founders of the movement, Calas, Breton, and others, who in the late thirties were still passionately political and had little time for Dali's frivolous nature or his pursuit of money, which earned him the anagrammatical nickname "Avida Dollars." Dali was not political at all and did not view things through the revolutionary lens essential to surrealist values. Writing on *Autumn Cannibalism*, which is inspired by the Spanish Civil War, Dali states: "These Iberian beings eating each other in autumn, express the pathos of the Civil War considered (by me) as a phenomenon of natural history as opposed to Picasso who considered it as a political phenomenon." In addition to acknowledging the legacy of Picasso, Dali also pays homage to Goya (*Soft Construction with Boiled Beans* of mid-1936 is undeniably indebted to Goya's *Colossus*), whose *Los Caprichos* takes similar inspiration. Although

where Picasso is political, Dali naturally cyclical, Goya goes person by
person, grimace by grimace, pint of blood by shed pint of blood.

And there is no blood in *Autumn Cannibalism*.

Autumn Cannibalism depicts a plastic couple in intimate embrace
in the act of eating each other. Although the features are not uniformly rendered—the hands detailed, the heads leavening into each
other like rising bread—the anthropophagy is clearly a function of
sexual intimacy. The man pinches a doughy inch from his lover's waist
while spooning cream from the breast region (although there is no
breast here, only a white enameled flatness) while the woman's left
arm dangles about his neck, her hand languidly holding a knife. The
knife cuts into the torso of the man, which presents itself as a loaf of
bread. Although perhaps my description of the anatomy is lacking,
the cyclical nature of love—one's feeding and feeding, the plastic
ability of the bodies to nourish as food, the constant flux of the forms,
the flow of man into woman, their rendering as a single, spiraling
form—should seem more familiar.

Or maybe it doesn't, this elemental desire, the lovers reduced
to ingredients and appetite.

15

My mother's ranch was north of Gallup on Route 666. The property seemed marked off at random. To my untrained, unenlightened eye, there seemed no purpose to having claimed this particular chunk at all. There was a log cabin of the prefabricated, Sun Valley type. The rough-hewn logs and wraparound deck were calculatedly rustic, just as the gleaming steel, heavily applianced kitchen was calculatedly convenient. I sat on the porch swing, which offered an endless view of uninterrupted land.

"How much do you think this place is worth?" I asked the realtor. She was Indian, but more Mexican than Navajo.

"A lot, to the right buyer," she smiled. "It may not seem like much to you, but there are some Anasazi ruins about a quarter-mile north of here."

"On the property?"

"Just inside the property lines."

"Are we going to have problems selling it?"

"What kind of problems?" asked the realtor.

"Legal problems," I said.

"The Anasazi are all gone, and so far there hasn't been any interest from the Navajo or Hopi, so we should be all right."

The realtor went inside to check the condition of the bathrooms. Johnny was waiting by the car talking to the handyman, a huge Indian who could have been forty or a hundred years old. When he saw that the realtor was gone, he came up on the porch and sat with me.

"This place freaks me out," he said.

"I thought you'd be all spiritual and one with this. I thought you'd bring out your drum, maybe set up a sweat lodge . . ."

"Here? No way. This is Anasazi. In Navajo, that means Ancient Enemy."

"No. It means Ancient Ones. Your ancestors."

"You're going to tell me who my ancestors are?"

"I'm just teasing you," I said. "So what's so scary about the Anasazi?"

"Well, they left in a hurry and no one knows where they went or why."

"A drought?"

"There was a drought, but there had been other droughts."

"War?"

"Maybe. But the Anasazi were organized. They could have put up a good fight."

"What do you think?"

"I've heard that the Anasazi ate their enemies. I think that's a Hopi thing, but there's been all kinds of digging around here, and I guess they think the same thing."

"'They' being the archeologists?"

"That's right."

"What a funny place for my mother to look for God."

"Some people," said Johnny, "think the cannibals were rebels from Mexico. They just came up here for a while and messed around. Ate a few Hopi. Ate a few Dineh. Made some good man corn. Wrecked a civilization. Headed back south."

"And who were these Mexicans?"

"I don't know. Just a bunch of people-eating freaky Mexicans."

"What do you think, Johnny?"

"I don't know for sure, but I think it came from within. I think the Anasazi were so fucking civilized that all the animal was building up, and then it bubbled over, and took the whole nation out."

"When a thing becomes its most extreme, the seeds of its opposite are planted."

"Just like that," said Johnny. "Just like that."

*   *   *

I made Johnny drive back from the Hidalgo. The light was bother-ing me again. I wore my sunglasses and had Johnny's jacket wrapped around my head, but little slivers of light—that gorgeous R. C. Gorman plague of brightness—filtered through it all. I could feel the blood vessels expanding in my head, my blood pulsing against the walls of my cranium, and knew I was in for a bone-shattering, mem-brane-splitting migraine.

"Can you pull over somewhere and get me sinus medicine and a bottle of Excedrin?"

"Katherine, there's nothing out here," said Johnny.

"When will there be something?"

"Not for another hour."

I groaned, then inched over closer to him. I rested my head against his shoulder and pulled the jacket over my head. Johnny put his arm around me.

"Try to sleep," he said.

I woke up in my motel room. Johnny had taken off my shoes and there was a sweating pitcher of water on the bedside table with a clean glass. The curtains were pulled shut and a blanket had been thrown over the curtain rod to keep the room extra dark. My head-ache was gone. I drank three glasses of water and lay back down, exhausted. I didn't have the strength to drive back to Maine.

For dinner that night Johnny opened a can of refried beans, which we ate with fresh tortillas and some spicy chicken that came wrapped in foil.

"Where'd the chicken come from?" I asked.

"Lady up the street."

"The married lady?"

Johnny nodded.

"It's very good," I said.

"That's why she has a husband."

"Her spicy chicken?"

Johnny nodded. "What are you thinking?"

"Me?" I shook my head. "I'm wondering how the hell I'm going to get back to the East Coast. I can fly, but then what do I do with my car?"

Johnny rolled himself another tortilla and was about to bite it, but handed it to me, and then began fixing himself another. "I've never seen the sea," he said.

"Do you want to see the sea?" I asked.

Johnny thought for a minute and then he nodded.

The next morning the real estate agent came by with a stack of papers for me to go over. I suggested a couple of East Coast publications where she might try advertising. The whole meeting took twenty minutes. Johnny and I went outside to see her off.

"Wait a minute," she said. "I found a box in the crawlspace. It's your mother's."

"What is it?" I asked.

"It's taped shut. Here," she said, "it's in my trunk."

The box was about the size of a microwave and heavily sealed with brown paper, postage tape, the kind you have to wet to use. I shook the box. The contents rattled.

"It's heavy."

Johnny nodded and handed me a pair of scissors.

"Do you really think I should open it now?"

Johnny shrugged. "Is it a big deal?"

"Maybe not." I set the box down on the desk. "It's the only thing she left in the house."

"Are you sure it's for you?"

"Why didn't she throw it out?"

"Maybe she forgot."

"Maybe," I said.

Johnny's eyebrows came together in an uncharacteristically thoughtful way. "Or maybe she gave the Hidalgo to you and in the attic is a sealed box, also for you."

I shook the box again. "It almost sounds like shoes."

Johnny extended the scissors.

I inhaled. "I have a bad feeling about this box."

"Then don't open it," said Johnny. He got up from his chair and headed for the door.

"Where are you going?" I asked.

"Put my stuff in the car. Check the oil. Check the tire pressure."

I picked up the scissors. "Don't you want to see what's in the box?"

Johnny thought for a moment. "No."

"Come back here," I said. "Come back here right now and sit down."

Johnny sat down across from me and broke into a wide smile. "You're weird, you know that?"

I nodded, not as amused as I should have been, and took the first tear at the seam of tape where the two lengthwise flaps of the box met. An odd musty odor wafted out of the slit. I saw Johnny pull back. I cut the tape at the cross-ends of the box. Carefully I lifted a flap. I nodded to myself, then closed it.

"Well?" said Johnny.

I laughed to myself then smiled knowingly at Johnny.

"What's in there?" he asked.

"Why don't you take a peek?"

"Just tell me."

"I'll do better than that." I reached into the box and pulled out a skull. "It's human," I said, which was obvious. "And the back's smashed in. Look."

"Fuck," said Johnny.

"Not only that," I peeked it into the box, "I think we have a complete set, not that I'm an expert . . ."

"Bring it back," said Johnny.

"Bring it back?"

"The bones. Bring them back. Or you're going to have all kinds of bad shit happening."

"The bones . . ."

"They're fucking cursed."

I dropped the skull into the box. "You think they're Anasazi?"

"No, man. I think they're Hopi."

"Well, I'm not bringing them back."

"Why not? What are you going to do with them?"

I closed the box carefully. "I think it's a message from my mother."

"Goddamn," said Johnny.

"What?"

"Couldn't she write you a fucking letter?"

"I should call her," I said. I closed the box over.

"Damn straight," said Johnny.

I dialed directory assistance. "The Quincy Home in Quincy, Massachusetts," I said. I let the operator connect me for the additional charge and waited on the line. My heart quickened and for a moment I thought I'd hang up, but Johnny was looking at me in a supportive way and before I knew it there was someone on the line.

"Hi. I was wondering if I could speak to Alice Shea." Saying my mother's name was almost eerie.

"Alice? There's a Margaret O'Shea."

"No," I said, annoyed. "Alice. Alice Shea."

"Is she a relative?"

"My mother," I said. I heard the clicking of a computer keyboard.

"She's not here now. I think she was discharged."

"Discharged?"

"Or transferred. Her record hasn't been updated for quite some time."

"Where would she go?"

"I don't know, Ma'am. I've only been working here for two weeks. I still haven't quite got the hang of it."

I was silent.

"This is your mother?"

"Yes," I said, annoyed by the tone of her voice. "Is there someone there who knows what she's doing?"

"Maybe you could call back at two? That's when Nancy comes on. She's been here for a long time. She should know."

I remembered Nancy. I remembered her gratuitous hand-squeezing. I always suspected her of eating all the chocolates I brought for my mother.

"All right. I'll call back," I said.

I had a hard time convincing Johnny that it was okay to drive with the bones in the car. Perhaps I didn't manage to convince him of that. I think what I said was that we had the bones, we had to deal with them. We had to find out whose (and who) they were. We had to give them a proper burial. Anything short of that would be sure to anger someone's ancestors, was sure to bring on a plague of sores and drought and woe. I also wasn't convinced that my mother would have an answer for me. I didn't doubt that she knew where the bones came from, but she was not very forthcoming on a number of things. I was beginning to wonder if the bones had been left there by her because she had nowhere to take them, no place to bring them out to. I didn't voice any of this to Johnny. I was still trying to make it seem normal.

Nurse Nancy would lead me to my mother, but what if she had nothing to do with the bones? At least I would know that and knowing, at that time, was more important to me than anything, including what dim room my father had chosen to deposit the living remains of my mother.

At the second of my colleges, Simpson, a women's college, I had taken a pre-Columbian art course with a man named Barry Buster Parkinson. Barry Buster thought I had a real gift when it came to writing about art. He appreciated my jargon-free papers, the "pop" aspect of my approach to art history. For my final project, I made a hundred-fifty-pound replica of a monumental Olmec head out of aluminum foil, and received an A for the term. I was sleeping with Barry Buster at the time; but I don't think this influenced the grade. I was also sleeping with Lou Walsh, the geology instructor, and I barely managed a C.

Barry Buster and I had parted on good terms. He found my departure from the school mind-boggling and seemed to hold himself personally responsible. He was a very moral guy, other than the occasional sexual dalliance at his wife's expense. He told me that if I ever needed him, I should feel free to call him and he would be glad to assist. He probably meant letters of recommendation, but I'd never needed any of those. I called the Simpson art history department from the motel desk while Johnny watched on, keeping a good six feet between him and the box of bones.

The secretary's voice rang through the receiver.

"Gail," I said. "It's Katherine Shea."

"Katherine! How are you?"

"I'm actually in a bit of a bind."

"How can I help you?"

"Well it's really not that big of a deal. I just need to speak to Mr. Parkinson."

"Barry's in Mexico."

"What's he doing there?"

"He's putting together a show. It's going to travel around." Gail made it sound like he was a producer for *Lost in Yonkers*. "He's at the Anthropological Museum in Mexico City."

"Really?"

"He's taking pictures of pots, those cute little pots that look like animals and stuff."

"Do you have a number for him there?"

"I have a home number for him. You can talk to Gaia."

Gaia was Barry Buster's wife.

"Okay. Give me the number." I pretended to write it down. "Thanks so much, Gail. Listen. I'm hoping to be in Pritchardville in the next few months, and I promise I'll stop in and see you and the rest of the Simpson gang." The Simpson Gang. I had no idea who they were, nor did I have any intention of ever setting foot in Pritchardville again.

"Well?" said Johnny.

"I don't know." I shrugged. "Let's get going. I'm sure I'll think of something."

* * *

Within the hour we were driving down to Albuquerque. It was two in the afternoon by the time we got there. Johnny drove over to the University Quarter and parked behind the Frontier Café. I went to sit in a booth and he got lunch, cinnamon buns and fresh-squeezed orange juice. The crowd at that time was made up of college kids of the funky variety getting breakfast, all tattoos and piercings, contrived hair, and bare arms and bellies. I lit a cigarette.

"Are you sure you want to go to Maine?" I asked.

Johnny nodded. "It's not like I won't be back," he said.

After lunch we drove over to the airport. Continental had a flight to Newark that left at four. I didn't want to know how much it was. There was a long line of people at the Continental counter waiting to check in for an earlier flight to Los Angeles. At the Aeromexico counter two attractive women were gossiping in Spanish, slapping each other playfully. There was a poster of a stepped pyramid deep in jungle greenery hanging behind the counter. Also one of an immaculate powder-white beach. And another of a bowl of soup in which a coy langostino beckoned to me with a slender claw.

I returned to Johnny. I held my ticket in my hand. Johnny looked at it.

"Mexico?"

"I thought of something," I said.

"Where are the bones?"

"I checked them. I didn't want to take them through the scanners."

"You sure this is a good idea?"

"No," I said. "I'm rather convinced that it's a bad idea." I didn't even have my passport, but apparently one only needed a driver's license to go to Mexico. "There's an hour until my flight. Let's get a beer."

I ordered Carta Blanca and Johnny had a Coors Light. I gamely squeezed some lime into my beer. "You ever been to Mexico?"

"Juárez."

"Any fun?"

"I got drunk and then someone beat up my friend." Johnny laughed. "My friend said that someone was me. The margaritas were thirty cents apiece." Johnny took a cigarette out of the pack and put it in my mouth. He lit a match for me. "Why are you going?"

"Cheap margaritas."

Johnny shook his head. He looked at me long and hard. "Be careful, Katherine. I got a bad feeling about this."

Johnny gave me a rib-cracking hug at the gate. I had a moment's panic when I thought I might be doing the wrong thing by leaving him. He was so strong. Johnny fished in his pockets and found a pack of pseudoephedrine and a bottle of Tylenol. "For the headaches," he said. I don't know when he bought them.

There were about fifteen people on the entire aircraft, which could easily have transported one hundred. I thought of drug operations, covert smuggling schemes. How else could an airline survive? The flight attendant offered me some chicken enchiladas and my choice of white or red wine, or champagne. I asked her if she had any tequila. She smiled and headed back up the gangway to the cockpit. I heard a belt of hearty male laughter and the clink of glass. Then she came back my way with a half-empty, unmarked bottle of the golden liquor. She poured me a double shot into a plastic cup and smiled.

"Who do I have to thank for this?" I asked.

"The captain," she said.

We flew for a while through the clear skies and the earth peeled away beneath me in brilliant green and flat blue. I sipped my narcotic drink. The plane fell some distance, then recovered, then dipped to the left, and then recovered. We entered a toxic brown cloud. The speaker hissed to attention and after a few unintelligible nasal eruptions, went dead. My ears felt the slow ache of increased pressure and I yawned to pop them. All this I took to mean that we had begun our descent into Mexico City.

A bump, a skid, and a bump later, we had escaped the heavens and were once more bound to the soil.

16

I found a hotel within walking distance to the Zocalo, or old town square, and the Belles Artes museum. The taxi driver said the hotel was owned by his cousin. With my Italian and a few Spanish words I was able to communicate somewhat, but he'd told me the room was some price that I'd converted to a suspicious ten dollars a night. The room was, in fact, ten dollars a night. It did have its own bathroom and a TV, set on an ancient dresser, that fizzled on in black and white and offered two Mexican soap operas and a Western set in San An- tonio, which, from this particular geographic location, was actually a "northeastern." I felt significantly better than I had in the previous days and was beginning to regret having asked Johnny to take the car back. Given some rest, I probably could have driven myself.

For dinner that night I bought a half-dozen taco things from a street vendor. There was a Denny's, of all things, down on the corner that I knew I would succumb to at some point, but not just then. Mu- sicians wandered the streets in studded pants and monstrous sombreros. A few of them sang at me aggressively, then demanded money. I handed them a few bills, which it turned out (I calculated later) amounted to seventeen cents. They yelled at me and I took off running back to the hotel. I had the woman at the front desk go across the street to buy me a bottle of tequila. I was too scared to go into the bar alone, which made me feel pathetic—so pathetic that when the woman finally got back with my bottle, more cigarettes, and change, and offered to get me a glass, I refused, ready for the bottle. I hadn't had a chance to drink alone in quite a while and it was actually appealing.

The next morning I awoke feeling more jittery than hung over. My mind was working and all I needed was a little coffee to make me feel good. At a café down the street I had a thick, milky coffee and a bowl of soup with a raw egg floating in it. I thought I'd ordered a pudding, but the soup was good. Taxis were zipping by on the street. I flagged one down and was soon heading for the Anthropological Museum.

Although I'd called a number of times from the hotel desk, I'd had no luck in finding Barry Buster. The first time, someone had put me on hold for twenty minutes, and I hung up. The second time, I spoke to a person who responded to every query with a loud and then louder "yes." I said, "Do you know how I can get hold of Professor Barry Buster Parkinson?" and he said "Yes!" and I said "Great. I very much need to speak with him." And the guy said, "Yes!" "Well can you connect me?" "Yes." "Now?" "Yes." "Do you speak English?" "Yes!" "I just flew in last night and, boy, are my wings tired." "Yes." And so on. The last person I spoke to was a woman who sounded both German and Mexican. She said that if I needed to speak to him, I better come in. Parkinson was headed for Chiapas that day, she didn't know when, to track down some textile thing.

"I am not sure. Ask at the front desk," and she hung up.

I got sidetracked outside the museum. There was a crazy exhibition of a sky dance. The dancers had their ankles twisted into ropes and were spinning around on a pole far above the ground. The dance looked dangerous. There was a hamburger stand just to the right of the crowd, which also looked dangerous. I watched the dancers orbiting high above my head, blocking the sun in turn, while eating my burger. When I finally made it into the museum the combination of burger, dance, and heat had washed out my complexion. I felt all right, but looked dangerously nauseated. When I told the young, uniformed woman, "I need to speak to Barry Buster Parkinson now!" she believed me. She scuttled out from behind the desk and gestured for me to follow her, first into an elevator and then through a labyrinthine series of corridors deep below the main rooms of the museum. I chased after her, feeling much like Alice pursuing the white rabbit. The box felt a good deal heavier than it had at the front desk and I entertained the thought that some transformation had taken place, that maybe what I was carrying was no longer a disconnected assortment of bones, but a small, crouching Plains Indian from the fifth century. Finally we reached an unassuming gray door.

"Parkinson's office," she said. She swung open the door without knocking. "Mr. Parkinson. You have a visitor."

Parkinson was standing with his back to me at a tall table covered with books. "I'm sorry," he said, without turning around. "I have a journey to make before sundown and I really can't have any visitors."

"Barry Buster, I'll only take a minute of your time."

He turned quickly, then took off his glasses and placed them back on. His black hair was longer than it had been and, although I found it hard to believe, he had lost weight. Never tall at five foot six, he looked positively elfin now that he was thinner. His eyes were the same fierce blue and I realized, to my surprise, that I was very happy to see him again. "Katherine," he said.

I gave him a big hug. "You look terrible," I said. "Don't you eat?"

"Amoebic dysentery," he replied. "Hazard of the trade, and, believe it or not, a status symbol."

"I don't believe it," I said. "I just had a *hamberguesa* out in front. Do you think I'm doomed?"

"Yes. Most definitely, but nothing to do with the hamburger. What are you doing here?"

"I actually came to see you."

"And I'm leaving in a few minutes. The roads south are treacherous and best traveled in daylight. And I still haven't found the reference for an odd zigzagging border on a textile fragment, which is the whole reason for me making the trip. I think it was in a journal, but for some reason I remember the picture being in color, which doesn't really support that theory . . ."

"Barry, I need you to look at something."

"How long are you going to be in Mexico?"

I rattled the box. "It will just take a minute. I promise."

"What have you got in there?"

I pulled out a femur and waved it at him.

"Bones?" Barry shrugged.

"A complete set," I said. I pulled out the skull.

"Katherine, we are talking skeletal remains, not Limoges. I don't think 'set' is the correct term. Nor do I think that I am the right person to look at them."

"They came from New Mexico. You're not interested at all?"

"Anasazi?"

"Ruins nearby are Anasazi."

"Katherine, my specialty is pre-Columbian textiles and pottery. You know that."

"Take a look," I waved the femur seductively. "That scratch looks a bit odd to me. What causes a scratch like that?"

Barry Buster took the bone and weighed in his hands. "That scratch is nothing, but this, see?" He indicated the end of the bone. "The blunting there? That is suspicious."

"What causes that?"

"We don't know for sure, but similar blunting has been produced by using the bone as a pot stirrer." Barry Buster stirred an imaginary pot, then handed the bone back to me.

I held up the skull. "Smashed in the back," I said.

"And charred, to the naked eye. Maybe you do have something."

"What does it mean?"

"The charring? You can cook the brains right in the cranium, which makes a handy bowl." Barry Buster put the femur back in the box. He took the skull from me and looked deep into it's eye sockets. "Probably got some story to tell us, don't you," he said. "Can you leave the bones with me?"

"I would love to leave the bones with you."

"All right. After I come back from Chiapas, I have two weeks here to finalize things for the catalogue, then I'm heading to Arizona, where the exhibit's kicking off. I'll be there for a few weeks. One of my colleagues has done a good deal of work on skeletal remains from the prehistoric Southwest. I'll ask him what he thinks."

"Good enough."

"We should get together sometime," he said. "Are you back in school?"

"No," I said, apologetically.

"Will no one take you?"

"I haven't really tried." I pushed the box of bones over to him. "Think of me pursuing a course of study as an independent scholar."

Barry Buster nodded a few times. He picked up the box and put it on a shelf. "Katherine, how did you come by these bones?"

I pondered this for a moment, but the answer was fairly obvious. "Barry," I said, "I inherited them."

Barry had to rush back to his apartment, where Gaia had spent the morning packing the car. He offered to share a cab with me.

"We live near Frida Kahlo's house and Trotsky's house, and there's a museum, designed by Diego Rivera to look like a temple in the area. Very impressive in a kind of primitive, artsy, kitschy way. You must see it before you leave."

"Thanks, Barry," I said. "I will, but I haven't had a chance to look around here yet." I gestured over my shoulder back at the Anthropological Museum.

Barry gave me a big hug and an inappropriate kiss. He got into a taxi and, waving out the window, called, "Keep in touch. Maybe I'll come visit."

The museum was quiet and airy. I was excited to be there and momentarily forgot why I'd come to Mexico. Pre-Columbian art had been my favorite class, and not just because I was sleeping with Barry Buster. In fact, I think I started sleeping with him because I appreciated the course so much. I stopped in front of an enormous statue of Coatlicue, goddess of life, death, and the earth. The statue must have been fifteen feet tall. I have no idea how much it weighed. Coatlicue's head was crowned with grinning skulls. Her necklace had a large skull pendant, the chain strung together with dismembered hands and something, which at first looked like grenades—goddess of explosions?—but after closer inspection, turned out to be hearts. To the Aztecs, who saw actual human hearts with fair frequency, this must have been an easily recognized motif. At first, I found this gory, but then I changed my mind. What made the ubiquitous candy-box type heart that I saw everywhere more acceptable, other than the fact that it was anatomically incorrect? How many heart-shaped chocolates had I eaten in my time? Anything heart-shaped should remind us of our bloody muscle, tick-ticking away. I placed my hand over my own heart and felt the comfort of its drumming.

In the courtyard outside a fountain trickled appealingly. The light was dim and with all the artifacts and murals surrounding me, it was easy to imagine myself not in the museum, but in a temple. I almost felt convinced of the Aztec concept of time. To the Aztecs, time was no more abstract than anything else and was a real commodity owned and operated by the various gods. If one adopted this definition, all the subjects of the art—kings, vassals, artisans, villains, and victims—could have been running through the matter of their lives in the next room.

I stopped at the great wheel that was the sun stone. This calendar had dominated the lives of the Aztecs. It was their belief that the world ran in fifty-two-year cycles, and at the end of this cycle a great cataclysm would occur. A new phase of history of the One World would begin. I wondered what it was like for Montezuma in those last days before Aztec time—all the billions of days so carefully recorded in *katun, baktun, pictun, calabtun, kinchiltun*, stringing out from zero and chillingly accurate—suddenly and permanently ceased.

My errand in Mexico was done but my plane didn't leave for another two days. I called the real estate agent to see if she had listed the property.

"I'm listing it at one million," she said.

"Do you think it's worth that much?"

"It is if someone pays that much. The house is four thousand square feet and the lot is," I heard her rifling through papers, "over twenty acres. We could ask for more, but I think we're better off listing it at market rate."

"All right," I said. She checked my address and phone number. She'd forgotten to have me sign the agency agreement, but once that was taken care of, we could move forward. I'd had no idea the house was that valuable. All this good news ought to have made me happy, but the whole thing seemed bizarre, as if I was watching my life unfold on TV, so I found it hard to celebrate. Also, the hotel room was beginning to make me feel uncomfortable.

I never liked hotel rooms, a leftover from a childhood trauma. When I was five, after some terrible fight between my parents, my mother had run away with me. I'm not sure where we went. I remember us driving for hours. She was screaming and crying on and off. We pulled into a motel parking lot and my mother got us a room. It was late at this point and I was hungry. I think my mother left to get food, but she was gone a long time. I brushed my teeth, put on my pajamas and waited. I fell asleep on the bedcovers. The next morning, she still wasn't there. I didn't know what to do. When the cleaning woman came in at eleven, she found me crying. She took me to the office and she and the office manager, an Indian man with children of his own, listened to my story with the appropriate concern. His wife made a big lunch for me—pan-fried Spam and rice—then sat with me on the couch in her odd-smelling living room. We watched a video that was all in Hindi, a romance with men in turbans spying on gorgeous saried women from behind trees. She translated each exchange,

"He says she is very, very beautiful."

"She says he is very, very handsome."

"Now they are singing about love."

And then my father showed up with a wad of bills (I remember them refusing the money, citing my good behavior) and drove me home.

My mother went into the hospital after that and was gone a long time.

Years later, I asked my mother about it. She was surprised that I remembered the motel incident, because no one ever mentioned it at home. "I should have left him then," she said. "I wanted to."

"Why didn't you?"

My mother looked at me, surprised that I didn't already know. "Because of you," she said. "And he puts up with me because he thinks that a child should have her mother. Children always love their mothers. Even Romulus and Remus loved their mother, and she was a wolf."

This was an odd moment of tenderness for us so I didn't point out—even though I thought it at the time—that Romulus and Remus were adopted.

I thought I should get out of town. I wanted to go to Teotihuacan to see the Toltec pyramids, so armed with a map, I took the subway to the bus station. Once there, I discovered that I was at the wrong bus station, that the one I needed was the northern station—a good two hours from where I was.

"Well, what's south?" I asked.

The ticket vendor looked at a bus schedule. His eyebrows came together in the same way as I imagined a doctor's would had he discovered a grapefruit-size tumor in my cranium. "There is one bus for Tepochtlan in fifteen minutes."

"What's in Tepochtlan?"

"They make the wooden spoon."

"For what?"

"For the chocolate."

"Can I look at that?" I asked, gesturing at the schedule.

"Yes," he said, pushing the schedule across with the same solemnity, "but it is incorrect."

I nodded to myself. I looked around the train station. A group of religious kids—or so I assumed from their matching "Jesus Lives" T-shirts—were massing around their suitcases. "Where are they going?" I asked, pointing.

"They are going to Cuernavaca."

"Why are they going to Cuernavaca?"

"Because it is a very nice place with nice restaurants and beautiful food. There is a palace also of Cortes."

Cuernavaca. I remembered Malcolm Lowry's doomed British consul. "And when does the bus to Cuernavaca leave?"

"It leaves forty-five minutes ago."

I considered this. "Can I have a ticket to Cuernavaca?"

Cuernavaca seemed to be the least sinister place on earth, no death stalking the streets. Vendors strolled by with straining bunches of balloons. The sky was a brilliant blue, as if the beige tarp of the city had been rolled back. The volcanoes, Popocatepetl and Ixtaccihuatl, loomed up in monumental profile. Beyond their peaks the brilliant sky was full of promise and mystery. The plaza was clean and well laid out. I was aware of the heat, but a clean breeze was blowing, resulting in an unidentified tinkling of glass, making everything seem enchanted. I bought a pack of Chiclets from a small, barefoot boy in exchange for directions to Cortes's palace. He volunteered to walk me over for ten pesos, which seemed like a good deal to me and exorbitant to him, so we were both happy. He even gave me some extra gum to cement the goodwill between us.

Cortes's palace was made of stones, a maze of rooms that led into one another in a seemingly accidental way, as if each room were giving birth to the next as I passed through it. The light was filtered and alien, shining here and there, but every room had a pocket of darkness, a cold spot of gloom. I thought of the palaces I'd seen in Europe: the Pitti Palace in Florence, the Residenz in Munich, the Schoenbrun in Vienna. There was none of that lightness, frivolity, excess here, rather the feeling that adobe walls—the very ceiling—had calcified out of crushed bone, been cemented with thickened blood. Glass cases were arranged on the walls displaying pens and inkwells, woven goods from the Philippines, leather-covered bibles from Spain, the junk of colonization. Small clusters of people moved from case to case reverentially, arranging the occasional strand of hair or probing a rogue zit, when they thought no one would notice. I was studying my own reflection—wondering if the odd light and the angle of the glass had made me look so deathly pale—when the businessman entered the room. He was wearing a suit, which I guessed was made of tropical wool. He wore yards of the stuff because of his size. The businessman was sweating profusely, mopping away the rivulets of sweat with an inadequate handkerchief. He had a tour guide who, for the sum of fifty pesos, was impersonating an English speaker with some knowledge of Cuernavacan history.

"Please to look here," said the guide.

The businessman complied, peering myopically into a glass case that held a few fragments of Aztec jewelry against a background of reproduced pen-and-ink illustrations from the time of the friars.

"Yes," said the guide, "and then the Aztecs . . ."

"Were wiped out by Cortes?" said the businessman.

"There was a woman called Marina. She was, how do you say . . ."

"Cortes's mistress?"

And so on. I noticed that the businessman was reading the informative plaques and although they were in Spanish it was hard to misunderstand certain famous events followed by a date.

"It happened in 1519?" asked the businessman.

"Yes," said the guide.

I caught the businessman's eye and he smiled back. His mouth was covered with a pink, powdery film that looked out of place and childlike, like candy that had not been wiped away. He held his gut, ran his hanky over the smooth hairless part of his head, then turned back to his guide.

I progressed through the museum at my usual pace. There was one of the ubiquitous Diego Rivera murals splashed up on the terrace that I spent close to an hour studying. I imagined myself inserted here and there, beside the skeleton figure, in yellow pumps with hefty calves, with my profile pressed hard against the brilliant blue of a Mexican sky.

I liked Rivera a good deal. I liked the populations of his pictures, the storytelling, the death chase—a real pursuit of scuttle and conquest. Rivera was rumored to have eaten human flesh. I'd read somewhere that he thought eating people enhanced his ability to render the human form. Apparently, a friend of his who was a furrier had told him that minks were fed mink flesh to enhance the quality of the fur. Rivera thought some life force was trapped in dead flesh. Of course, I found this all a bit hard to believe. That Diego Rivera was governed by a number of appetites seemed highly plausible, but the idea of Rivera actually tracking someone down was hard to picture, unless the quarry was very slow.

Diego Rivera's unconventional belief alongside Aztec history seemed to suggest that cannibalism was a Mexican thing, up there with the Hat Dance and tequila. But I didn't believe it still applied. You needed cannibals to be labeled that way, and it had been a while since Mexico had given us any. Papua New Guinea was supposed to have cannibals. I'd read about Michael Rockefeller's disappearance. He was on an art-scouting mission skirting the coast, where most of the natives had never seen a white man. The story goes that his canoe capsized and he began to swim for shore. Maybe the Asmat got the pot boiling as soon as he hit the water. The natives most likely had been watching him for days, hidden behind the jungle shrubbery, still as trees. The whiteness of his skin might have been appealing—white looks misleadingly tender—even if the hair was off-putting. Perhaps the Asmat had heard that Michael was an American prince, that his was the flesh of royalty.

When I thought about it, I never pictured Michael flayed and boiled. He was in the water doing an elegant crawl, a stroke perfected in the Hamptons, a stroke useful for reaching floating decks and girls whose bare shoulders were slick with coconut oil. I saw his head bobbing in and out of the waves, his breath rasping with the effort. His mind conjured up the images of hungry sharks, but the shore was near and just a few short pool-lengths away.

Michael, in the water, with salt stinging his eyes and small fish nibbling his feet.

New Guinea had also given us the primitive brain-eating Fore (Aunt Marion, as I eat my first lobster: "Don't eat the brain. It's poisonous.") and the Fore had given us kuru, "laughing sickness," similar to mad cow disease, always fatal and an exotic plume in the cap of Western civilization. William Arens—an anti-cannibal, whom I had had to read in Anthropology 210—pointed out that no one had actually seen the Fore eating human flesh. And it hadn't been proved conclusively that kuru was a direct result of cannibalism. So, although the kuru of the Fore turned out to be the stuff of a Nobel prize, it was not necessarily that of reality. I imagined a Fore chief talking to his "first contact" anthropologist.

Anthropologist: Are you sure you've never eaten human flesh?
Chief: No. I'm pretty sure I haven't.
Anthropologist: Never?
Chief: No. I'd remember something like that.
Anthropologist: Not even after the death of loved one, to make them live on in you?
Chief: Well, it is an interesting thought . . .
Anthropologist: How about after slaying an enemy, to insult his remains?
Chief: I haven't slain an enemy, but I have insulted one. Is this of any help?
Anthropologist: How about to satisfy protein deficiency?
Chief: We do lack protein. Other than the occasional pig, meat is hard to come by.
Anthropologist: And there is the gustatory aspect.
Chief: Gustatory?
Anthropologist: Interesting. You wouldn't have any cultural head revulsions?
Chief: I don't think so.
Anthropologist: Any interest in the brain?

(long pause)

Chief: Sure. Brains are great. We love brains.

Anthropologist: Ever eat one?

Chief: A brain? Yes. Just last year. I don't know how that slipped my
    mind.

Anthropologist: Just one brain?

Chief: Maybe it was two?

Of course, anthropologists were usually better than that, but in
our culture there was a weird enthusiasm for cannibalism. Cannibalism was a big thrill as long as we weren't doing it. Cannibalism also,
for the most part, was embraced with little supporting data as if in
Western culture, as our faith in God failed, we still were able to believe in cannibals—their cauldrons and drums, savory stews and pit
roasts—feasting at the edges of the world.

"Do you like Diego Rivera?"

I turned to see the businessman, who was smiling at me. I looked
back at the mural, aware of the businessman's hot breath near the
side of my face. "Rivera's a hack," I said. "This is not the work of an
artist, but a testament to the power of his personality."

"It's very colorful," said the businessman.

"As is Cuernavaca," I smiled.

The businessman smiled a salubrious smile and ran his hanky
across his head again. "Is this your first time?"

"In Cuernavaca? Yes."

"That's too bad."

"Why?"

"Oh, I don't know. I was hoping you might tell me what's to see
here, where I should go next, now that I've seen the palace. Just beautiful, I thought. Didn't you?"

"Pocked with gloom," I replied. "Why don't we head back to
the Zocalo?"

"Get a snack?"

"Or a drink."

He worked in the petroleum industry and lived with his wife (shell-shocked) and two children (porcine) on three floors of a sprawling house (white, flat, with whimsical windows) in a (treeless, sun-blind) suburb outside Houston. I handed him back the photo. I was vaguely aware that I was maintaining conversation with the man. A few pleasant nods here, a laugh there (which surprised me because I had no idea what he had just said) were charming enough, apparently. This man and I had the same motivation: he wanted to get me drunk and I wanted to get me drunk. The businessman was drinking too: beer, Dos Equis, no lime, from the bottle whose mouth he wiped vigorously before bringing it to his succulent lips.

"What are you doing in Mexico?" I asked.

"Me?"

I nodded. He laughed as if it were a very personal question. He leaned into me. "I'm a headhunter."

"You are?"

"I met with the guy in Mexico City yesterday. Made him an offer."

"Do you think he'll take it?"

"I would." The businessman took a bottle of Pepto-Bismol out of his pocket and shook two of the chalky pink tablets onto his hand. He took them both, washing it all back with a mouthful of beer.

"Why do you keep taking those?" I asked. "Don't you feel well?"

"I take them to keep the stomach bugs away." He nodded meaningfully. "Montezuma's revenge, you know."

"Clever boy," I said.

"Do you want some?" He offered me the bottle. I waved him off.

"No thanks." I grabbed my cigarettes and lighter and put them in my handbag. "I wish I was a headhunter."

"You do?"

I nodded. We asked the waiter where we could go dancing and he gave us some simple directions. I was imagining what I would do with the businessman's head if it were in my possession. I'd have to shrink it and that would take some time, because his head was the size of Christmas ham. His cheeks hung down, weight and counterweight slabs of flesh. His small, upturned nose poked up through his face like a meat thermometer. His eyes were blue, watery, probably dripping with mucus from all the allergens in the thick Mexican air, but maybe clouded with fat, the same kind that congeals on the surface of cooling broth. A head like that would have to be smoked for weeks—months even—before it was suitable for wearing around one's waist. I'd seen shrunken heads in a museum, little pieces of demonic fruit with bitter mouths and sockets of crumpled vacancy, eye sockets where the sudden vacuum of death softly imploded upon itself.

Despite his weight, the businessman was a fluid dancer. He had a buoyancy that I would have thought impossible out of the water, but he seemed at home at the disco, favoring seventies standards over the techno and house, switching from beer to shots of tequila. My body—because of the amount of alcohol consumed—was beginning to rebel in not-so-subtle ways. I could still dance, but walking was proving difficult. I had to struggle to keep my torso over my legs as my feet seemed overeager to shorten whatever distances needed to be shortened: the distance from dance floor to bar, from bar to bathroom, from bathroom to table (smoke break) from table back to dance floor. Whatever visual compensating my brain usually performed seemed to have shorted out and the whole evening was being presented to me as if I was viewing it through the lens of a handheld camera. I suggested we get a taxi back to his hotel even though it was less than a mile away. And I probably suggested everything else, even though I can't remember what everything was, and think this one of the kinder sides of overdrinking, even though the next morning my head felt that it was pumped full of frozen air with my skull threatening to fracture along its original sutures.

I was lying on the floor when I woke up. This was no surprise. That businessmen was girthy and what might have been a double bed for another couple was no double bed for us. I moved my head slowly upward as I came to a sitting position, allowing for the liquids contained to find their level. The businessman's hand hung off the bed, palms the color of pork loin, relaxed sausage fingers and the University of Texas ring that bound around his pinky (although it must have once belonged to another finger) squeezing deep into the flesh in what must have been a most uncomfortable way. My stomach had sent a warning signal. I breathed heavily through my nose, hoping to calm my stomach, but ended up scuttling to my feet and racing for the toilet. I tell you, I felt very sorry for myself as my stomach purged itself clean. I had skipped dinner the night before, somehow smoked and drank my way through the businessman's beefsteak, although I'd considered the *lengua*. But my stomach was full. Three rounds later, I'd emptied myself out. I wasn't prepared for what I saw floating in the basin. Digestion had not run its course. I saw chunks of something floating in clouds of yellow bile, worn at the edges by my stomach's futile effort, a stomach unable to match the need of appetite. I felt a cold sweat in my pores, an intestinal shudder, then slowly looked back to the bed.

The businessman's feet were bare. The toes pointed down, off the end of the bed. He didn't move. My violent retching had not disturbed him. I had a choice. I could go over to him, bid some sort of farewell, or I could leave. There really was nothing left for me to say. I got up and brushed my teeth using his toothbrush. This disgusted me, but I found my delicacy hypocritical. I washed my face using his soap, dried my face and hands using his towel. And when I purchased my bus ticket back to Mexico City, I used his money, which he had left in an impressive stack of bills on the bedside table.

17

My plane left for New York early on a Monday morning. I had the woman at the hotel desk call for a cab. She seemed suspicious of me and kept trying in Spanish to come up with some sort of explanation.

"*Maleta*," she said. "*Maleta. Maleta.*" She mimicked carrying a suitcase by curling her arm up against her side and grimacing.

"No *maleta*," I said. I held up my backpack.

"*Su caja*," she said, and with the skill of Marcel Marceau created a box in front of her.

"Oh, that? No. No." I smiled. "Just me. *Solamente mio e la bolsa mia.*" I thought "bolsa" meant bag, but might have meant something else. Bolster? Bolo? Who cared? These last few minutes were hardly the time to learn Spanish, although I had some regrets at not knowing more. I stood on the street to smoke a cigarette and wait for the taxi. I could see the woman staring at me still, through the dirty glass. Up and down the street trucks were parked delivering chickens, thousands of them, plucked and pink. I had never seen so many dead chickens and I wondered at the number of people required to eat that much poultry. The sky was hazy and gray and somewhere, from one of the trucks, Mexican pop music was blasting away. The men worked quickly unloading the open crates and there was a festivity in the scene that I knew I would miss once back in the States.

My taxi arrived and soon I was speeding off to the airport. I wondered how Barry Buster was doing down in Chiapas. I pictured him pulled over on the side of the road ambushed by rebels, gorgeous Gaia smoking a cigarette by the side of their SUV, kicking the dirt with the toe of her boot, interceding in bored, Castilian Spanish. I wondered what the bones would tell.

Seeing Barry Buster made me think about finishing college, but I was too high-minded for an education. Most classes were mental weight-lifting, intended more to tighten the brain muscle than to expand the mind. Why go back? I nearly had enough credits to graduate, which was good enough. I knew an awful lot: parabolas, kinship systems, geographic strata, irregular declensions, parts of the stage, and orbiting electrons. A fine understanding of art. A good grasp of literature.

What I knew of Dante I knew from college. In one of my literature classes we had taken a quick pass at *The Inferno*. Dante first introduced me to Italy and although *The Inferno* was squeezed in with *The Canterbury Tales, Paradise Lost,* and the Bible in a course that lasted eleven weeks, I did manage to retain some of it. My teacher was an earnest woman just out of graduate school, who did not speak English, or at least not a dialect I recognized. All of her arguments were "two-pronged," everything was a "lens" for something else and "informed" an event that usually happened two centuries earlier. Her hair was frizzy in an intellectual way. Her shoes seemed to have been cobbled by elves. I have no doubt she published in many unread journals and has gone on to be a great success. Her name was Lynn something-or-other and she liked smacking her fist into her palm as if she were FDR. Most things made sense before she explained them to us, and a couple even after her efforts. One concept that fascinated me was the notion that there were two kinds of paternity.

The two kinds of paternity were the Abraham/Isaac variety and the Oedipus/Laius variety. Abraham/Isaac paternity relied on thwarted sacrifice—although the son will sacrifice for the father, in the end this is deemed unnecessary. In fact, the son's and father's survival were raveled together like two loving strands of DNA. Israel was founded when God intervened in Isaac's sacrifice. Father and son were bound in a covenant, which came to be symbolized by—of all things—circumcision.

And then there was the other kind of paternity, the Oedipal variety, wherein the son's survival was dependent on the father's death. To this I add the reverse—a mirror image and therefore the same thing—a Saturnine paternity, inspirational to Goya in *Saturn Devouring His Children,* and that of Count Ugolino, which is the subject matter of the Thirty-Third Canto of *The Inferno.*

Dante meets Count Ugolino in the Pit of the Ninth Circle. Ugolino is frozen into the ice with another spirit. Only their heads break the surface and despite all he has seen at this point, Dante is stunned. Ugolino is eating his companion, Archbishop Ruggieri, as the "starving gnaw their bread." Ugolino's teeth tear wildly at that part where "the brain meets the nape," which may not seem anatomically correct, but given Ugolino's hunger, seems possible.

Ugolino was a Pisan aristocrat who lived in the twelfth century. He was Dante's contemporary and Ugolino's grandson, Nino Visconte, was a friend to the poet. Ugolino is exiled from Pisa in 1275 for conspiring with the Guelphs against the ruling Ghibellines. In 1284 the Guelphs return Ugolino to Pisa and to political power, but shortly after that Ugolino betrays the Guelphs and somewhere down the road yields three Ghibelline-controlled castles to the enemy—the Guelphs?—and then conspires with Archbishop Ruggieri, in 1284, and prominent Ghibelline families (Gualandi, Sismondi, Lanfranchi) to oust Nino Visconte from Pisan political power. Nino heads to Florence to escape his grandfather and becomes friends with Dante.

Nino whispers in Dante's ear and thousands read of Count Ugolino, dizzying traitor turned filiacidal cannibal.

I find it hard to believe that Ugolino could be so one-dimensionally bad, but none of the count's admirable traits have made it into history or literature. Archbishop Ruggieri betrays Ugolino—for having yielded the three Ghibelline castles—and Ugolino is locked in a tower with two sons and two grandsons. He will never again gamble at politics, move the castles, soldiers, and noblemen as carved game pieces. Now his only concern is hunger.

Dante gives us the death-knell thud of each hammer-fall as the door to his cell is nailed shut.

Over the course of the next six days, all but the count starve. He is left groping blindly over the bodies. He hears their words echoing in the dark corners of the Tower of Hunger. "Father, you clothed us in this wretched flesh. We beg you to strip it away." And strip it away he does, surviving in this manner until all the flesh is gone except his own.

His first night in the tower, Ugolino has a remarkable dream. He sees a wolf with whelps being pursued up a slope by hounds and hunters, and when he wakes up and hears his children whimpering, realizes that the wolf is him. This is not the first wolf that Dante gives us. In the first Canto, Dante pursues a coy leopard with festive skin. Then for one heart-pounding moment a hungry lion rushes him, which is scary, but done with in a matter of three lines. In fact, Dante seems to be doing quite well on his own, not needing Virgil's or anyone else's assistance, until he encounters the horrifying she-wolf. He says that "her leanness seemed to compress all of the world's cravings," and her image, slinking about the slopes, fills him with such despair that he calls out to, of all things, a ghost—Virgil may be Virgil, but he's still dead—to help him out.

And I thought Italians were supposed to like she-wolves, or maybe that's just Romans. Dante was, after all, Florentine.

18

Boris was not pleased with me. I pointed out the fact that the whole Mexico adventure, including plane ticket, had come in under seven hundred dollars and that he should have been glad that I'd decided to go for a trip rather than twelve months of therapy, which would have cost considerably more.

"It's not the money," said Boris.

"Then what is it?"

"You're out of control. You're like an animal." Boris took an appraising look at me. "You're not a child anymore."

"Then stop treating me like one."

"You're uncivilized."

"Oh, how awful," I said with all the sarcasm I could muster.

"Why this wild behavior? Why this running off to New Mexico? Why do you need a vacation in Mexico? Isn't Maine for vacation?"

"You're right, Boris," I said. "It was you. I was coming to terms with my feelings for you." I smiled, proud of myself for having come up with it.

"So you think of me and run away?"

"No," I said. "I think of you and come back."

I wrapped my arms around his shoulders—Boris didn't really have a neck—and kissed him. Boris believed me because if I'd been in love with him, I probably would have done something like that. And people believe what they want to. He needed some tidy ending to our argument, because people were coming over that night. More importantly, Ann was hanging around a lot—party planning and all that—and the last thing he wanted was for Ann to be right about me because that would mean that he was wrong.

The morning of the event Ann had me dusting the tops of picture frames. She wasn't really doing anything but standing around with that realtor's pose—weight heavily over one foot, the other pointed outward, hand curled with the wrist resting on her hip—watching me and the caterer, who was in the midst of the longest anxiety attack I'd ever witnessed.

"Let the man do his job," I said. I was on a dining room chair armed with a can of Pledge and a chamois.

Ann looked at me in disbelief. "I'm helping him."

"Helping him on his way to an early grave."

The caterer smiled nervously.

"You can't set up the bar there," she said, ignoring me. "People will want to look out the window."

"No, they won't," I said.

"This," she said, indicating the window, "is the highlight of the apartment."

"It looks onto a building exactly like this one. It's like a mirror. And down on the street there's nothing, not even a good restaurant."

"Set the bar up against the shelves."

"You can't do that, Ann," I said. "There's no plug there, and if the caterers have to get anything from the kitchen, they'll have to walk through all the guests."

I didn't really care where the bar was, but the morning had been tedious with nothing to do except Pledge my dust and bother Ann.

Ann looked at me with exasperating patience. "I hope you're not wearing that to the party," she said.

I had on my leather pants, which I thought were perfect, and a white men's shirt, which was a bit worn here and there, and had a faded and not really noticeable coffee stain near the hem. It was the most appropriate outfit I had with me.

"Oh, grow up, Ann." I got off the dining room chair and began casting my eyes around the room in search of cigarettes. Ann had put them on the bookshelf. I took one and stuck another in the caterer's mouth. I wasn't supposed to smoke in the apartment but I didn't care. I lit a match. "It's the dressiest thing I have."

Ann looked me up and down. "You look like a junkie," she said.

I took the train downtown. I had all afternoon to find an outfit. I think Boris gave me the green light to go shopping to get me and Ann apart. It was cold and sunny, somehow shiny and clean on the street. I was happy to be in New York, happy to see the dog walkers with their canine bouquets, happy to be ignored by everyone. I didn't really want to go into a store. Downtown stores always made me nervous. The clothes were invariably hung on neat wooden hangers, set against walls in rows, as if you had walked into someone's closet. I would not be able to browse without assistance and this bothered me. I lit a cigarette in front of a store front that had what looked like a calfskin kilt hanging in the window. The leather was a rich butter-scotch. I guessed it would be about seven hundred dollars, about the same as my Mexico venture. I'd top it off with a sleeveless, cowl-neck cashmere thing in off-white—I had no idea how much that would cost—and then the shoes. Boots? Could you mix and match leather? Maybe I could pull off suede, black suede, calf-height boots with laces running up the middle, the kind of boots that took you twenty minutes to get on.

I was beginning to need the leather kilt. I looked inside. A bored salesgirl, with her hair pulled back so tightly that it looked like her head was painted black, was steaming a shirt. A young man with floppy bangs and large cuffs was talking on the phone. I could probably sneak in, see how much the skirt cost, and get away without being assisted. I walked in as quickly as I could and made straight for the skirt. But the price was not visible. I stopped before touching the thing and looked over at the sales people. They were both watching. Neither of them was smiling.

I rolled my eyes. "So how much is it?"

"Seven hundred and fifty dollars," they said, in unison.

I nodded.

"Try it on," said the girl.

I smiled.

"No, really. I tried it on, but I'm not as tall as you are. It hit me two inches below the knee." She shuddered recalling this. "Not a good length for pleats."

"Is there a special occasion?" asked the young man.

"Literary party."

"Writers are all slobs," he said. "Don't bother." He studied my face. "Do I know you?"

"I don't think so."

"Yes I do," he said. "Chocolate croissant, latte, no sugar."

"Dean and Deluca?"

"Mornings on the weekends." He smiled. "I remember the pants. You always wear the same pants. It's so, I don't know, Angelina Jolie."

"They're good pants," I said. "I got them in Italy."

"Try on the skirt," he said. "Go on. You know you want to."

At that point, I wanted nothing less than to try on the skirt, but it would have seemed unfriendly.

I went into the dressing room and put the skirt on. It did look good, but it wasn't going to break my heart to leave it.

"Come out and show us," said the girl.

I pulled the curtains and walked out and padded out in my socks. I lifted up my sweater so they could see how the waist fit and turned around a couple of times.

"See," she said, "On the knee just barely. Perfect." The other sales clerk nodded in agreement.

"And if I had seven hundred and fifty dollars, you'd have made a sale," I said. I returned to the dressing room. The skirt took me a couple of minutes to get off. It was the buckles, the kilt-type things, that went around the sides. The leather didn't slide easily and I was scared I'd scratch it. While I was fumbling with the buckles, I heard the door to the store swing open and someone's whisper matched with the salesgirl's incredulous, "Really?" and then the guy's enthusiastic, "oh my God." When I came back out, they were both smiling at me.

"What?" I said. I handed the skirt to the girl, which I had considerately put back on the hanger.

"Let me wrap that for you," she said.

"I'm not sure I want it."

"The skirt's yours. I've already rung it up." She closed the drawer of the cash register. "While you were in the dressing room this old man walks in. I think he was Spanish. Nice shoes. Anyway, he says he wants to buy you the skirt."

"That's a little strange, don't you think?"

"Don't argue," said the guy. "I wouldn't."

"So what's his name?"

"He wouldn't say," said the girl. "He paid in cash." She handed me the bag.

I shrugged and took the bag. "Did he want anything?" I asked.

The sales clerks looked at each other and shook their heads. "I think he knew you," said the guy.

"Why?"

"The way he bought it for you. He seemed to know what he was doing."

"Spanish?"

"I don't know if he was Spanish," he said, "but he was definitely Euro."

I picked up the bag and wandered out of the store. I looked up the street and down the street. There were people everywhere and somehow, every one of them looked familiar.

I called Arthur from a pay phone. I couldn't remember if I'd told him I was heading to New York or that Johnny was on his way to Maine. The last time we'd talked, I'd been in Mexico City, keeping company with a bottle of tequila in my hotel room.

"What's up?" said Arthur. He sounded cheerful.

"I'm in New York."

"Your friend Johnny's here. He got here at five this morning."

"How are you two getting along?"

"Fine." Arthur sounded relaxed. "He seems like a nice guy. He's asleep on the couch."

"How's the car?"

"He said he had a bit of trouble after dropping you off in Albuquerque, but some relative of his owns a garage, so he replaced, I don't know, an alternator? Does that sound right?"

"Sure."

"So he got a late start. Says he quit his job."

"Sounds like you two hit it off."

"We had a drink when he arrived. When are you coming home?"

"Day after tomorrow. I already booked a flight."

"Is Boris cool with that?"

"I haven't told him yet."

Ann was drinking a glass of whiskey at the dining room table when I arrived. She seemed softer somehow, younger. She was already dressed for the party—a claret-colored bolt of cloth with a crazy faux fur scarf. She had lipstick on her teeth.

"What'd you get?" she asked.

"You'll see in a minute."

Ann took a sip of the whiskey, then another.

"You should pace yourself," I said. "It's going to be a long evening."

"Yes it is," she said. "I don't like going to parties and I don't like throwing parties."

"Neither do I."

"Does anyone?"

"Sorry for being so annoying this morning, Ann. Sometimes you're an easy target."

Ann smiled. "Sometimes I'm a real bitch."

I looked over at Ann's drink. "I'm going to get one of those," I said. I got up from the table and went over to the bar. "Where's Boris?"

"He's at my place," she said. "He said he couldn't take all the activity here."

"Whose party is it?"

"Mine. I had to invite a lot of my crowd. Boris wanted a hundred people and he just doesn't have that many friends."

"That's so sad," I said, without much conviction. "Anyone I know?"

"No," said Ann, "Wait. Do you remember my friend Julia?"

"Julia . . ."

"She's a buyer for Cygnet, downtown."

"Leather goods?"

"Mostly. Her supplier from Florence, Silvano, says he knows you."

"Silvano?" I was horrified. I looked at the paper bag with my leather skirt and suddenly everything began to make awful sense. I started laughing, took a drink, and laughed some more. "Ann, this could be the worst party that Boris has ever thrown."

"That would be hard."

"I think it has a good chance."

By ten, when the guests started arriving, Ann was blasted. I envied her. I'd managed a good buzz by eight, which is when Boris showed up with a bag full of Chinese takeout. He had an odd manner about him, as if he were play-acting at having fun. I appreciated his fakery, but his tension sliced through my fog, leaving me antsy and bored.

"Cut her off," he said, gesturing to Ann.

"You cut her off."

We both looked at her. She was straightening a framed picture of Boris with tangled, long hair (the top of his head was still bald) standing on a beach. Was this Rupert? Maybe Ann was wondering the same thing. She knocked the frame over, then straightened it in a way that left it precariously close to the shelf edge.

"Boris," I added, "maybe she isn't drunk. Maybe we're just sober."

I headed for the bar. "I had a Pernod earlier, then a vodka tonic. I did a shot of Jagermeister, some Drambuie. I don't know. Another Pernod?"

"Pernod is revolting," said the dark-haired bartender. "The only people who drink it are college students vacationing in Europe."

"Right," I said and smiled. "What do you suggest?"

"He's got some really good Chianti back here. I've been drinking it all evening," he said.

"How about a whiskey sour?" asked the blond waiter. "Everyone's drinking martinis, but a whiskey sour is the real Rat Pack."

"Sounds great." I watched as he smashed a lemon.

"So this Boris," said the blond pouring a heavy dose of whiskey, "is he your old man?"

"By old man, do you mean husband, boyfriend, or father?"

The bartenders looked at each other and shrugged simultaneously.

"Well, let me just say," I said grabbing my drink, "that he is indeed my old man and we'll leave it at that."

Silvano arrived shortly afterward. I don't know how I managed to avoid eye contact with him, Boris's apartment being rather small, but I did. I knew that Silvano would not confront me in public; public confrontations were not *bella figura.* At the same time, I didn't want Silvano to see me with Boris because Boris was embarrassing to me; Boris was not *bella figura.* I stood with my drink in an awkward conversation with Boris's lawyer, a young guy named Rand Randley, who was into climbing mountains. He belonged to the Adirondack Club, or something like it. It meant that he had climbed all the Adirondacks.

"How many Adirondacks are there?" I asked.

And he answered me, but the information never made it into my head. I saw his mouth moving. I saw the number floating in the air and then it evaporated. I also saw, from Rand Randley's overly friendly expression, that he was as tortured as I was by the conversation, but neither of us could seem to stop.

"That's a lot of mountains," I said. "Can you excuse me for a minute?"

"Absolutely," said the lawyer.

I escaped into the bathroom. There was a young man in there, midstream. He was wearing tight blue jeans, ironed and starched, with fade lines down the front.

"Excuse me," he said, "but I'm urinating."

"That's all right," I assured him. "Everyone does." He had some kind of southern accent and I wondered how Ann knew him.

He waited for me to go. "Can I have some privacy?" he asked.

"I'm afraid not." I lit a cigarette. "You're going to have to leave." It took him a minute to understand what I meant by this, which struck me as odd. He zipped up and took off, and I began to feel very annoyed at my life.

A part of me wanted to talk to Silvano. I missed him on some level, but I didn't know what to say. I'd gone down the street to buy an orange soda and never come back. Silvano didn't expect me to stay anyway; he couldn't have. But I was going to have to face him, him or Boris. There was also a small angry crowd of people knocking on the door, so I left the safety of the bathroom. And when I saw Boris navigating across in my direction, rather than run, I merely drained my drink and leaned back against the wall, crossing one leg over the other in complete resignation.

"What's the matter with you tonight?" he asked.

"Must be love," I replied.

"Very funny. I have to speak to you in private." Boris glanced around the room. "Maybe we could stand in the corridor?" he suggested.

I sighted Silvano, who was looking at me with pained and fatherly concern.

"The corridor?" I said, making for the door, "is not very private. Isn't there anywhere else?"

"We could go up to the roof," said Boris.

"The roof would be wonderful."

Boris and I walked to the elevator in silence. He was drunk. Boris was like that. Dead sober one minute, non compos mentis the next, although he was pretty articulate no matter what. Sometimes what he was articulating would have been better off unsaid. No, Boris never really got a buzz or was pleasantly tipsy. The thought occurred to me that I was being lured out for some quick sex, which would at least be easy to accomplish and might pass a few minutes of a party that was fathomably, palpably boring. We got into the elevator and Boris pressed the button for the top floor. He smiled at me, toying with something in his pocket as the elevator ground its way skyward. I smiled stiffly in return. We made our way up a narrow staircase then, after some trouble and bilingual profanity, Boris managed to unlock the door. Finally we were out.

"I have something important to say," said Boris.

"Really?" What I should have said was that I couldn't bear to listen to anything important because I was too drunk. But I was too drunk to think of this. I decided I should just keep talking until Boris forgot what he was trying to say. "How beautiful!" I made for the edge of the building. "What could be more glorious than a sky studded with stars? Nothing but wide open air and concrete. I often thought, when I was a little girl, that I'd like to live in a place like this. I'd pitch a tent in one part, have a little camp stove close by, and do nothing all day long but feed pigeons and watch people crawl like ants down the street. That's all they'd look like, ants, so small down there. Of course, there would be the bathroom problem, but I never thought of that, just the sky and isolation. Sky and isolation. Sky and isolation."

"Katherine, what are you talking about?"

"I don't know. You make me nervous when you're serious."

"I will ignore that," said Boris, smiling to himself. "Katherine," he said, "you have changed my life."

"I have?" This really wasn't that hard to do. Changing his brand of coffee was—to Boris—life-altering.

"I am the luckiest man in the world."

"You are?" I watched Boris shortening the distance between us. "Well, I suppose you are. You have your health and a rent-controlled apartment . . ."

"Katherine! Shut up please!" Boris composed himself. "What I have to say is simple."

I was silent.

"I must have you with me," he said. "I can't be parted from you any longer. It is too sad for me to be waiting, eating alone, not having anyone to talking." Ibid. Boris was very drunk, but the fact that the whole thing seemed premeditated was eroding my confidence. "No more time apart," he said.

I began to panic. "You're moving to Maine?"

"No, no, no," said Boris, smiling.

I was greatly relieved.

"I want you to marry me."

I pulled my hands from his and took a few steps back. Boris went down on bended knee. He produced a felt-covered box from his pocket and opened it. The box held a ring, a gold one with an impressive diamond that leered out from its setting.

"Will you marry me?" asked Boris.

"Marry you? My God, Boris. You know I love you, but I just can't marry you."

"Marry me," Boris coaxed, holding out the ring.

"Boris . . ."

"Marry me!"

"You see, Boris, it's not that I don't want to marry you. I can't marry you."

Boris got up. "You have some explaining?"

"Well, yes."

"Why? Why can't you marry me?"

"Because," I said fidgeting with my skirt buckles, "because I'm already married."

"Married?"

"Yeah." I looked up at the sky. I didn't want to see Boris's face.

"Married?" Boris repeated. "To who?"

"Well, actually," I looked at Boris out of the side of my face, "I'm married to Silvano."

"You are married . . ."

". . . to Silvano Falconi."

"Who is that?"

"Oh, someone I knew in Italy."

"And who is this man?"

"Well, he's in leather."

"Leather."

"Yes, and, oddly enough, he's in your apartment."

"Now?"

I was beginning to feel cavalier.

"This is not the truth," said Boris.

"Why would I lie?"

Boris looked deep into my eyes, hoping for a lie, but I was feeling decidedly unsophisticated and I'm sure it showed. "The old leather guy?"

"He's not exactly leather . . . Well, I suppose we're all leather, aren't we?"

"Shut up," said Boris. "Is that legal?"

I nodded again.

"How? When?"

"It just kind of happened. I was in Italy and then I was married to Silvano."

"For how long?"

"I guess it will be a year in another, oh wow, a year at the end of the month. Yeah."

Boris wasn't taking it very well. His hands went up to the sides of his head. I think his blood was all rushing up there, making his complexion blotchy and pink. "You are, you are evil," he said.

I considered this and lit a cigarette. Alcohol had made me frank, which was good. If I'd had my wits about me, I might have accepted Boris's proposal and become a bigamist. Were bigamists ever women? I took a long drag, hazarding a peek at Boris, who was pacing in an agitated yet drunken manner. "Boris, where's your sense of humor?" I said.

"Sense of humor is when you see the funny thing and you say 'That's the funny thing.' Sense of humor is not for this. This is for the grotesque."

"Grotesque?" Despite myself, I was getting a little offended.

"That leather-peddling, pedphile, Guido . . ."

"You mean pedophile. A pedphile is a lover of feet." I didn't think there was any such thing as a pedphile and I didn't care. Boris was hardly a youngster. And he had no business calling Silvano a Guido when he would have gladly traded his so-called Romanov roots to be Italian. Boris stomped around for five minutes. He paused looking onto the street. He was snorting like a bull, then he came back. "How long were you with this guy?" he asked.

"Before or after we were married?"

Boris said nothing.

"Well, I guess about a month and a half."

"But you're married to him?"

"Yes."

"He's your husband?"

"Yes."

Boris looked at the ring, then shut the box with a snap. He began massaging his head. "I hate this," he said. "Is there anything else I should know about you?"

I considered this. "No."

"Anything that I should not know?"

"Look, Boris," I took his wrist. "I need a drink. Let's go downstairs, all right?" I led him over to the stair well. It was a mild evening, the kind of weather that makes even the weirdest, most difficult things seem funny. "It's really nice up here," I said. "Maybe the next time you have a party, you should throw it on the roof."

Back in the apartment, the party continued. Full swing would have been nice, but that evening lacked any kind of fulcrum. Ann was seated by herself, her legs splayed out in complete relaxation. She had a drink resting on the arm of the chair. When she saw Boris and me walk in, she made as if to get up, but then gave up. Boris went stomping off to the bathroom. I went to rescue Ann's drink before she knocked it over.

"Ann, are you all right?" I asked.

"What if I'm not?"

I squatted down beside her partially to show support, but also because in that little corner, ducked down beside the chair, I was hard to spot.

"I think I've lost my mind," Ann said. "Let me tell you a story."

"What's the story about?"

"It's about me, a Great Dane, and some carbonara."

Ann had been in her apartment fixing dinner. She was disturbed from her cooking by an incessant howling coming from the street. Peering out her window, she caught sight of a Great Dane, leg raised, who had been bound by an electric current while in the process of urinating on a lamppost. Ann banged on the window with a wooden spoon, leaving white globs of carbonara on the glass, desperate to save the dog but too far away to be of any real help.

"I felt like I was having a bad dream, screaming like fuck-all, but no one could hear me."

Finally, a man armed with a two-by-four had walked up the sidewalk. He struck the dog hard, disengaging him from the current. The dog whimpered on the ground for a short while, then got up and started limping down the street.

"That's what I need," said Ann. "I need a man with a two-by-four to hit me and hit me hard."

"I'm going to get you a glass of water," I said. "And then I'll help you get a cab. You should go home."

But I didn't help Ann. Too drunk myself. I got another drink and pursued the evening, forgetting all about her until the following day.

19

I had the kind of hangover that presented vision after vision alternating with void after void, and the visions presented the sort of stuff that makes one grateful—although worried—about the voids. I had this vague and painful recollection of Silvano weeping into his wine glass. I might have been sympathetic but was probably embarrassed, or maybe neither of these. I remembered catching my head a few times as it lolled around on my neck, pulling it back upright as if it might fall off. And I remembered that I'd arranged to have lunch with Silvano at one. Currently, it was eleven and I was flooded with waves of dread, which at least cut the waves of anxiety that seized me after every recall of the previous evening. I remembered Boris saying,

"There is the issue of divorce."

Which seemed very odd because I'd never really accepted that I'd been married.

"How do you say divorce in Italian?" Boris had asked me. I looked over at Silvano and managed a silent burp.

"*Piu vino,*" I said.

"Piooveeenoh?" asked Boris.

"*Si,*" I replied.

Boris walked over to Silvano, pointed to me and stated his word. Silvano responded by returning with a bottle of wine and pouring me a glass. Next thing I knew, Boris and Silvano were having one of those conversations where people talk to each other, but are both looking at a third party. Silvano was smiling, nodding happily. Boris was pensive. He kept making these firm hand gestures as if his idea was something tangible that floated a foot in front of him and was something to be held. Somewhere in the course of this conversation I realized I had to sleep, no, I would be asleep in five minutes regardless of where I was. I passed out on Boris's bed, fully clothed. People must have been going in and out of the bedroom to use the bathroom, but I had slept through that. I didn't wake up until four A.M., when my raging thirst sent me running to the nearest faucet. I'd fallen back asleep, even with Boris's snoring sawing magnificently through the air. He was still snoring now. I watched him—his eyelids fluttering, the corners of his mouth tightening—for a couple of painful moments of recall, before I finally got up from the bed. My eyes were itchy from makeup and my skin felt dry as paper.

Ann was asleep on the couch. I had hoped she'd be up making some greasy food. What I really needed was a fried egg and some toast.

"Ann," I said, tugging her foot.

Ann opened her eyes and squinted at me. "You were right," she said.

"What do you mean?"

"That was the worst party that Boris has ever thrown." Then she rolled over so that her face was smashed into the back of the couch and went back to sleep.

In the fridge, I found a tray full of leftover hors d'oeuvres, tiny quiches, and other treats, all perfectly miniature, from the night before. I felt like a giant. I arranged some of these on a plate and went into the dining room. I sat down and had just finished my third quiche when I heard a noise coming from the coat closet. There was a scuttle, and then it stopped. I picked up a tiny spanakopita and was about to eat that, when I heard a scuttle again, the noise of something slamming against the wall, and an audible, "Ow."

I got up and went to the closet. I waited a moment. Everything was quiet, then I opened the door.

It was the guy I'd interrupted in the bathroom. He didn't seem to know where he was. He looked around the room with amazement, then back at me.

"Howdy," he said. "I'm Travis."

"I'm Katherine," I responded.

"Where am I?" he said.

"Boris's apartment."

He scratched his head. "I could have sworn that I left last night, but I don't guess that I did."

"What were you doing in the closet?"

"Sleeping." He laughed again. "Goddamn. I guess I thought I was leaving the party."

"You have a hell of a bruise on your head." It was right in the center of his forehead and was long and narrow, reddened and slightly swollen. "I have a theory. You were leaving the party, accidentally walked into the closet, and hit your head on the bar."

"What bar?"

"The bar you hang things on."

Travis walked back into the closet. "Bar's about the right height."

"I wonder if you knocked yourself out?"

"Who can say? Maybe I just gave up."

I extended a gesture of welcome, inviting him out of the closet and into the living room. "Can I get you anything?" I said.

"Sure would appreciate some coffee."

"Coffee it is."

After I got him a cup of coffee and some ice for his head, we sat at the table. There was silence. I listened to him slurp at his coffee, heard the rattle of ice in the dishcloth. He was slowly achieving consciousness with the help of caffeine. I put my feet up on the chair next to me.

"This coffee's real good," he said.

I nodded. "Travis, where are you from?"

"Ralston Falls, Texas."

"Where is that?"

"Outside of Dallas."

"Near Fort Worth?"

"Hell no. It's about a hundred and fifty miles outside of Dallas, to the west."

"What are you doing in New York?"

Travis fancied himself a writer, which was his wording, not mine. He had finished his great tome, eight hundred pages of it, that he had spent the last two years of college and the last four years of every job imaginable, writing. Apparently, there was an editor in New York whom he knew from when he'd been a student in Austin. He'd worked at a liquor store and the editor came in every night and bought a pint of gin. At the time, this man was working for a university press, or something like that, but was now in New York with one of the larger houses. So when Travis finished his magnum opus, he'd gotten hold of this editor and the editor said sure, send the manuscript in to us and we'll take a look at it.

So Travis did. He waited a couple of weeks and called. They hadn't read it. He waited a couple of more weeks and called. They were really busy. He tried again. Eventually, all people that were in any way aware of the novel's existence were out of town. They were out of town for weeks.

"I am in New York following my dream," he said.

Apparently, when Travis showed up at the editor's office, the man made a good show of trying to find the manuscript. For the whole two years that Travis had sold him his daily pint of gin, the editor had said, every day in the same way, "Don't give up. Just keep writing. Perseverance is everything."

"Damn good that perseverance is everything," said Travis, "'cause perseverance is all I've got."

The editor, not knowing how to handle this ghost from the past, agreed to meet Travis at a bar at six that evening, where he gave the young writer four glasses of bourbon and no answers.

"Maker's Mark straight up, the only straight thing I got out of the guy," said Travis, and he set the dish towel down on the table with an air of finality.

Then the two went out.

"I guess he felt so bad, he didn't know how to get rid of me," said Travis, "so he took me to this party. I went to get a drink, then I swear the guy was gone. He was just waiting for me to turn my back."

There was a moment's silence, where I looked at Travis with sympathy and he appreciated it.

"What are you going to do?" I said.

"Try and get my damned book back."

"Don't you have a copy?"

"No." He slurped some more coffee. Hell. Eight hundred pages is a lot to copy."

"Don't you have it on disk?"

"I don't use a computer." He nodded at me sagely.

"Why not?"

"Joyce didn't use a computer. Neither did Hemingway, nor Fitzgerald. What's good enough for them is good enough for me." He wiped some water off his face and looked over at me with a look of comprehension. "You think I'm ignorant, don't you?"

"Naïve. And maybe a little ignorant."

"Name one person that isn't or wasn't ignorant."

"Plato?"

"Yeah, but he was born in 500 B.C."

"What does that have to do with it?"

Travis laughed. "There wasn't that much to know then."

Travis only had four hundred dollars left. He'd spent most of his money getting out to New York; the rest was being whittled away by food and accommodations.

"I have no idea how I'm getting back to Texas," he said.

"Come up to Maine. It's cheaper to get there."

"What's in Maine?"

"I live there. We kind of have a little artist's colony. One guy's a musician. The other's a philosopher." I don't know where I got philosopher, but Johnny was short on words and it had occurred to me that perhaps his mind was working overtime. It had also occurred to me that he might not be that bright, but I kept this to myself.

"What do you do?"

"That's a secret," I said in a husky monotone. Secret even to me, I thought.

"Who funds the thing?"

"Boris," I said. "But that's a secret too."

"But you just told me."

"But I haven't told Boris."

No doubt the whole thing sounded suspicious and Travis was not a stupid guy, but I sensed that he felt his adventure on the east coast was just starting and he wanted to make the trip count for something. A guy like Travis would rather become destitute than return home without a good story. I could satisfy that need. I wrote the address down for him. I told him to wait a couple of days and he nodded and thanked me "kindly."

Silvano's apartment was only four blocks from Boris's. I wondered if he'd been able to find any daffodils. He was the only person who knew that they were my favorite flowers—cheap in the spring, then gone. I liked the way they bowed their heads, their lack of posture, their drunken wagging in the breeze. I liked the way the two green leaves were always raised in a shrug, questioning and futile. I remembered that my apartment with Silvano had always been full of daffodils.

That apartment was in the Oltrano, just west of the Ponte Vecchio, which made everything smell moldy, but I loved it. Perhaps we were together for only six weeks, but my memory had logged it as an eon. In the afternoons I walked around the neighborhoods with the sole purpose of losing myself, always disappointed to find that I recognized that certain angle of alleyway or the conglomeration of pots and flowers on a particular set of steps. Sometimes I'd buy shoes or go into one of the old churches just to feel the silence, which I had once thought was God and now recognized as history and large amounts of stone and stained glass. One time when I came home, Silvano had filled the house with roses. I thanked him politely, but Silvano saw that the flowers made me uneasy.

"They're beautiful," I said, "but I feel like I'm in a hospital. I feel I am sick."

The next day the roses were gone and in their place were vase of vase after vase of lilies. These too were beautiful, but after some uneasy silence I confessed.

"I feel I am dead."

"What do you want?" he asked, hands on temples.

"I like daffodils."

"Why daffodils?"

It was some Wordsworth-inspired melancholy "bliss of solitude" thing that had lodged in my head in high school and was yet to be displaced with some more sophisticated poetry/flower association. I looked at Silvano, while trying to find the necessary Italian for the explanation. After a significant silence I said,

"They're yellow."

Silvano accepted this, as he accepted all my simple, present tense, declarative Italian. The truth of the matter is that Silvano had not fallen in love with me, but rather with a much simpler person. And this because I was only capable of expressing myself to him in the most basic, unadorned ways. To his credit, I did always sound like a lovable moron, a contented idiot who possessed some variety of pure soul. I was aware of this at the time, but not capable of explaining it to him. I respected Silvano and wanted him to know why we—despite our marriage—were not going to last. I managed,

"You love me because I like daffodils because daffodils are yellow. But I do not like daffodils because they are yellow."

And this was the last thing I said to him before I disappeared. Until I saw him in Boris's living room. I hit the buzzer.

"*Silvano, ecco Katerina,*" I said. He buzzed me in.

I walked down the hallway looking for apartment 5L. It wasn't hard to find. *Rigoletto* was blasting out the door, something Silvano always played when he felt tragic or deformed by his years. I knocked on the door, but he couldn't hear me. The door swung open under my rapping. Cosimo, Silvano's Italian greyhound—a five-pound dog with tiny paws and the delicate snout of a rodent—sniffed my hand and wagged his tail aggressively, unbelieving. Had it been so long? Silvano was seated at the end of the table smoking a cigar. On the table was a vase with a half-dozen daffodils in it. Silvano picked up the remote and turned down the music.

"Just when Gilda was about to do her aria," I said in English.

"Yes, but unlike you, the story is more to me," he said in Italian. He never used even isolated English words, offended by the sound of it, the lack of forced meter. He smoothed his mustache and I wondered why I'd come. "For you coffee or wine?"

"Wine," I said. I sat down at the furthest chair, hidden by the daffodils, and moved in such a way that the vase obscured Silvano's head. His head was the vase. Silvano gracefully pushed the vase aside with a walking stick that I'd noticed him carrying the night before.

"Where to begin?" said Silvano.

I searched around for words. Funny how quickly languages deserted me. Even my English seemed worse after being on the road trip and in Mexico. My Italian was almost gone.

"Wine immediately. After, talking," I said.

"Do you remember *Rigoletto?*" he asked. He poured me a glass of wine and brought it over.

"We take the train to Milan. We eat at Wendy's."

"Like a child, you wanted to eat there." Silvano's mood was fluctuating between sentimentality and complete bitterness. "And later we went back to the hotel. You were crying because you felt bad for Rigoletto, that he was destroyed and had lost everything. I comforted you and asked you to marry me. And what did you say?"

I winced. "I say yes."

"Was it because of *Rigoletto?*"

"I don't know." Why did I do anything? I remember feeling bad for deserting my father and wanting to make Silvano happy because of this. I looked at him, his long silver bob, his perfect mustache, his cashmere turtleneck. "Maybe. *Rigoletto* is a good opera."

Silvano sighed and whistled through his teeth. "You want to marry this Boris?"

"No."

Silvano laughed. "He says that you do. He says that it is essential to your happiness."

"Is his Italian good?"

Silvano shrugged. "Better than yours."

I knew that.

"But he speaks like a communist."

I had no idea what that meant. "That's very true," I said, but only because I'd remembered how to say it.

"Are you hungry?" he asked.

I shook my head.

"No? I have *prosciutto chingiale*. I carried it in my bag. And melon, which I bought here. Like all American fruit it is very large and probably has no flavor."

"I like that," I said. "I drink more wine now. It is good."

I drank a lot of wine. Italy had seemed so far away but now, in Silvano's apartment, I felt like I was back there, as if apartment 5L was in Florence. As if 5L were the Florentine embassy, a sacred square of concrete somehow beyond the reach of corporate, industrious, disposable, amiable America. How to tell this man that I had left on impulse, gone down the street to buy a can of orange soda and one of those little custard tarts from the Café Mingo, then found myself at Piazza Maria Novella and the trains? Trains going everywhere: Lugano, Rome, Trieste, Belgrade, Amsterdam, Paris, Istanbul. How could I stand there and not take one? How could I go back? I didn't have enough cash on me to go very far. I'd wanted to go to Venice for the day maybe, but I'd just missed a train. There was another in an hour, which gave me enough time to go outside and have a number of cigarettes before deciding. But I'd left my cigarettes at home. I'd only planned to be gone for ten minutes after all. Then I saw two young men with their map spread over the hood of their car. They were arguing in French. They were both smoking. As I walked over I saw them both lift their eyes from the map, that look of startled interest. Soon I was heading eastward, threading through the mountains at gear-grinding speeds through the brushy pines and ear-popping drops, hairpin curves and cerulean skies. I was heading to heaven and who knew—or cared—what lay on the other side.

Silvano's eyes narrowed. "You went to buy an Aranciata and somehow, you're not sure how, ended up in Rimini?"

"I am sorry," I said. "I go to Rimini and not call. Now I am in New York. I do not tell you. I am bad."

"What has happened to you?" he asked. Silvano was now sitting on a couch, more comfortable for him. I got up from the table and sat on his lap, wrapping my arms around his neck. He smelled of oily tobacco and lavender soap. His hair was slick with pomade.

"No talking now," I said. "I have tired. I sleep now."

Silvano's breathing was raspy, heavy. He inhaled and exhaled in great drafts and I rose and fell on his chest as if I were floating on a raft at sea. I had a headache, just a small one, that I attributed to last night's heavy drinking. Soft blue clouds were exploding against the inside of my eyelids and as my breathing slowed, I thought I heard the voices of children calling me, "Katherine, Katherine," and soon I was in a deep sleep, dreaming that I was on the beach and children were swimming in the waves. *Vieni, Vieni. Join us, Katherine.* But in the dream I could not swim. I stayed on the shore because I didn't want to drown.

I'd hitchhiked across Italy with the two French boys—Ludo and Olivier. Ludo had a new Fiat Seiscento, a graduation gift from his parents, and he and Olivier were off to see the world. I remember them sitting in the car drinking a bottle of red wine, arguing in French. They were probably arguing about me. I'd already had enough to drink at that point and had actually hallucinated my mother, who I thought was standing knee-deep in the water in her favorite houndstooth suit.

Then she disappeared.

I went down the beach and into the water. I wasn't wearing shoes, but my skirt was long and quickly tangled around my legs. I parted the reflecting surfaces, half expecting to see my mother's pale face peering up, her hair pulled by currents. Instead all I saw were my own wide eyes again and again, mirrored back from every section of the sea. My heart pumped loudly, but as I calmed down I realized that the thumping wasn't me, but rather some immense pounding machinery involved in the nearby construction.

I came up the beach, exhausted.

"Are you okay," the French boys asked. "Were you drowning?"

"*Je suis ça va*," I said. "And no, I wasn't drowning."

"Then why this?" said Ludo and he gestured up and down my body, indicating my suspicious disarray.

I wrung my skirt out and sat down on the sand. The sea was gray, cold, and blank—not beautiful at all. I pushed my hair off my face and said, "I'm not really sure."

That night I went out with Ludo and Olivier and drank myself into a coma. The bar was not much of a bar, rather the downstairs of the rooming house. The booze was cheap and the beer cold and that's all I really cared about at the time. There were white Formica tables and fluorescent lights that fizzled, at times lit you up like an X ray. Up the street, they were tearing down an old house and all the construction workers were lodged in the rooms upstairs. This is where Pietro, my handsome construction worker, normally stayed, but he had left that afternoon to visit his wife. And all that was left for me were the Frenchmen: Ludo with his blond hair and annoying laugh, Olivier with his freckles.

I had fallen into a profound misery and was having a hard time explaining this to the Frenchmen. I was having a hard time explaining this to myself.

"Sweet baby," I remember Olivier saying. "I help you. I help you." And I remember Ludo's milky eyes staring at me as he lay with his head rested on the table.

Ludo and Olivier were not very amused when I was still morose the next day. We were ostensibly driving to Paris, because their money had run out and I had nothing better to do. I could see them giving me disapproving looks in the rearview mirror. A hangover was one thing, but American girls were supposed to be fun. Something was making me throw up. Alcohol was a possible cause, but I thought it was food poisoning coupled with fear and a threatening depression, which was hovering around like an opportunistic thundercloud. At any rate, while I was vomiting out behind the Fina, they left me.

20

Throughout the whole plane trip to Portland, I thought of Arthur. A part of me had wanted Arthur to save me, for this to be the one special relationship. He was my angel. But a number of things had happened over the course of the last couple of weeks, a number of things I was going to have to keep from him. The relationship, despite all my optimism, had already failed and Arthur had become a mirror, reflecting all my deviancy back at me. I considered being frank with him, but quickly changed my mind. Arthur would be happier that way. Wasn't the truth usually the most ugly thing in life? If truth wasn't inherently ugly, than why was truthfulness so laudable?

I called Arthur from the airport.

"Are you at Newark?" he asked.

"No. Surprise, surprise. I'm in Portland."

"Great. I can't wait to see you," he said. "I'll be there in half an hour."

"Let me take a cab," I said. "It's no big deal. Make sure there's something to drink in the house."

Hearing his voice on the phone had a calming effect on me. I missed him, his easy manner, the damaged quality that made him warm and sensitive.

I'd been away for only two weeks, but it felt much longer and also somehow much shorter. The leaves were all gone and the sky an even steel color. I could smell snow in the air. Boris and I had a big fight just as I was leaving. I'd hoped that I would be able to sneak away without a blow-up and all the signs were promising. We'd made it out of the apartment in peace. Boris had whistled "Lily Marlene" all the way down in the elevator. We'd waved to the doorman, who was negotiating some packages for Mrs. Mingus while her Pomeranian was trying to eat his leg. The cab had been waiting right where it was supposed to be and there was no traffic in any direction. The avenue of sky blocked out by the buildings was a lovely blue. Boris kissed the top of my head and put me in the cab.

"And don't worry about the divorce. I'll take care of it. I'm sure there's no reason for you to be involved."

"What?"

"I'll talk to Silvano. I think we understand each other."

Boris shut the car door and waved for the driver to leave.

"Don't go anywhere," I said. I rolled down the window. "I don't want you talking to Silvano."

"Is that your choice?"

"And what's this about me not being involved in my own divorce?"

"Katherine, I am only protecting you."

"From what?"

"From yourself."

"Oh. From myself." I lit a cigarette, despite the no smoking sign. The driver took a quick look at me in the rear view mirror and lit one too. "Maybe you're right. Maybe I should stop being involved in everything about me. In fact, I would go so far as to say that the only thing wrong with me is me. Maybe you should take care of that too."

"You are not making sense." Boris looked down at his gray felt slippers and shook his head. "Can't we part civilly?"

"Go. Go, go, go," I said to the driver. I looked at Boris briefly through the rear view window. He had already turned to go back into the building. "Can you believe that guy?" I asked the cab driver.

"He is really an asshole, that man."

"Yes he is."

"You are with him for money?"

"God, I wish it was that simple."

"Isn't it that simple?"

The cab driver was African and reminded me of one of the wise kings from the Little Drummer Boy. He looked like that and had the same reassuring, supremely civilized voice. I gave him a twenty-dollar tip when we got to Newark.

"Merry Christmas for you and your family," he said.

"The same to you," I replied and meant it.

It *was* getting near Christmas. I'd somehow missed Thanksgiving while in Mexico, which was no big deal, even though I liked Thanksgiving. How could one not like a holiday devoted to food? But Christmas was fun too. Johnny would be back in New Mexico by then. Arthur and I could get a tree, decorate it. We could wrap socks and scarves and hats in gold paper, fill stockings with Baci and biscuits and fancy coffee in little tins. There would be lights blink-blinking away. For the holidays we'd drink bourbon in egg-nog and Zinfandel, smoke Export A's and Nat Shermans, eat and eat and eat, then sleep in sweet sweaty lumps beneath the covers. Many houses already had their wreaths on the door and more than one illuminable, unmeltable Frosty waved, broom in hand, from the front lawn. A few pillars on the larger houses had spruce garlands snaking up in a spiral. It was good to be back in Maine, good to be— dare I say it?—home.

Christmas was the highlight of my year when I was growing up. I attended a Catholic grade school and Advent pretty much brought a stop to any scholarly pursuits. We were herded every morning into the school hall and drilled through a number of Christmas carols. And there was the yearly Christmas play. In the first grade, I played a narrating angel, not because I was particularly angelic, far from it, but I could memorize lines and that was rare in a six-year-old. In the second grade, I again held a starring role—that of Noah's wife. I'm not exactly sure what Noah had to do with Christmas, but there was some musical based on Noah's life and as Noah's wife I had a song all to myself and much time standing at the center of the stage flanked by pairs of animals. When the dove sent to scout for dry land returned, I had the line, "Look, an olive branch! We are saved!" The dove was played by Penelope Cornwall, whose costume was outrageous, rows of feathers sewn painstakingly onto wings that really flapped and a pair of yellow bird feet. But her only line was a steady *croo, croo, croo* that didn't project very well and was hardly heard by the audience. In the third grade, I somehow fell from grace and found myself standing two rows back from the manger, as a sheep. I was bitterly disappointed by this and blamed my teacher, Ms. Balfour, who was in thrall to the Cornwall family. I remember my Christmas gift—a scented candle—sitting on the classroom piano next to Penelope's gift—fancy looking skin-products in a large basket bound up in red cellophane and gold ribbon. Penelope was the angel Gabriel—who should have been a boy anyway—but Penelope got the role and as I watched her lisp her way through her lines, her sweet manner and ineptitude eliciting all sorts of ooh's and ahh's from parents in the audience, I felt a rare and precious anger rising within me. Penelope was wearing her first communion dress, a gorgeous satin thing, pure white (my first communion dress had been pale blue because my mother thought that dressing little girls like brides was an act of unmistakable perversion) and her wings—wings again—were huge cardboard appendages stuck all over with crumpled opalescent cellophane, dusted with gold glitter. I, however, was wearing an old fleece car seat cover, belted at the waist, and pair of ears made from my father's gym socks. On leaving the house, my mother had said, "Don't you look cute."

The play was performed in the dimly lit hall. All the parents had been given candles with little paper collars and the little flames winked and failed and were relit deep into the darker recesses of the building. My mother was up near the front. I could see her face lit up by the candle and the expression which had gone from a settled bored look to a deeper, pure malice.

Penelope sang, "Do you thee what I thee?"

And I sang in response (and to the same tune) "Baa baa baa baa baa baa."

After the song was finally over, we were to file out of the hall past the parents and reassemble outside, then we were to go back in for cider, donuts, and cookies. Penelope led the way. We were all singing. I saw her pass my mother and my mother's tilting candle, and then whoosh! Penelope transformed from Gabriel to Lucifer.

Penelope wasn't injured. My father pulled the wings off rather quickly, burning his hand. He stamped out the flames while Penelope looked on, her big blue eyes blinking in an unintelligent, uncomprehending way. My father was a hero. As various parents massed around him and Penelope, I sneaked outside. My mother was illumined by a much smaller flame, her cigarette, and seemed quiet enough. I went up to her and held her hand.

"Are you mad at me?" she said. And I could see that she was genuinely worried, that somehow she felt she had failed me.

"No, Mommy, no," I said. And I felt more love for her at that moment than I'd felt for anyone before. More love than I thought was possible. I was grateful that she'd made it out of the hospital for the play, but as I held her hand in mine, I had a surging sadness: the hospital would always be there, threatening her, threatening me, and all our moments of joy were just brief flares of light in an otherwise uninterrupted gloom.

As the cab pulled up to the cottage, Arthur and Johnny came running out of the house. Johnny was in a T-shirt and Arthur in his socks, despite the fact that it was twenty degrees outside. The driver slammed on the brakes. Johnny rolled onto the hood of the car, as if he'd been hit, and Arthur pulled me out of the car. He hugged and kissed me warmly and Johnny came over and hugged us both. It was eleven A.M., the guys were already wasted, and I was so happy I thought I might start crying.

"Come inside," said Arthur. Johnny was paying the driver. "We have a surprise for you."

The house was decorated, but not for Christmas. There were streamers everywhere, balloons on the floor, taped to the beams. I could see a cake on the table, and most surprisingly of all, a white dog lying on the couch wearing a foil party hat.

"What is this?" I asked. "Whose dog is that?"

"It's your dog," said Arthur.

"My dog?"

The dog came over wagging his tail. He looked a bit concerned, but seemed eager to please. I took off the party hat and scratched his head.

"You don't know, do you?" said Arthur.

"Know what?"

Johnny and Arthur looked at each other and started laughing.

"Katherine, it's your birthday."

"Oh Jesus," I said. "What's the date today?"

"December sixth."

"Right. It's my birthday." I looked around the room—balloons, crepe streamers, cake. I was twenty-three. "Get me a drink."

"You like the dog?" asked Johnny.

"I love the dog."

"What you going to name him?"

I looked at the dog's face. "I'll name him Kevin."

"Kevin?" yelled Arthur from the kitchen.

"He looks like a Kevin. Where'd you get him from?"

"I," said Johnny, "rescued him."

"From where?"

Arthur came in with a bourbon and ice for me. "He rescued him from some guy's back porch and nearly got shot in the process."

"Kevin was not happy. He had no water. He had no food. Is that any kind of life for a dog like this?"

"No," I said. "But some would term your rescue a theft. This is a hunting dog. A lot of people around here keep them chained up outside."

"What do you hunt with a dog like that?" asked Johnny.

"Birds mostly. Maybe rabbits. They point." I cupped the dog's head in my hands. "I'm pretty sure Kevin's an English setter. And what a beauty. Look at that big square head, those jowls. Has he tried to go back?"

"To that trailer? No way," said Johnny.

"It's hard enough to get him off the couch." Arthur squatted down and patted the dog. "He likes eggnog. He likes asparagus."

"But what he really wants is some meat, isn't it, Kevin, a nice marbled rib-eye with onions."

Johnny closed his eyes tight then opened them wide. "I better have another drink," he said, "before I start seeing things."

"I think that's the definition of a real drinker," I said to Arthur. "A drinker is someone who drinks to keep from hallucinating."

Johnny came in, smiling. "An alcoholic is someone who drinks more than you."

"Then there are no alcoholics," I said, draining my glass, "only people with unrealized ambition."

"Last night," said Arthur, laughing, "Johnny here tried to convince me that he drank because of his religion. He said," Arthur looked at him, "that he had to, what did you say, 'connect with your totem?' Something like that."

I smiled at Johnny, interested. "Your totem?"

"Yeah, it's like this animal, you know," he turned to Arthur, who was laughing harder. "Shut the fuck up, asshole."

"You get fucked up," said Arthur, "and next thing you know, you're a lion."

"Mountain lion," said Johnny. "Glad to know you were paying attention."

"Why do we always transform into something wild?" I asked. "Look at Kevin." Kevin raised his head and looked at us solemnly. "Couldn't we turn into Kevin? Scratch a bit, find all the warm spots, sniff some crotches."

"We already do that," Arthur said. "What's the point in transforming?"

"I," I said, lighting a cigarette, "don't sniff any crotches."

"You," said Arthur, "are not domesticated."

We began cooking shortly after that and by three-thirty had a turkey, sweet potatoes, a pot of gravy (my specialty), Pillsbury crescent rolls, and broccoli. We were also too drunk to be hungry, but still sat down at the table picking at the meat. It felt good to sit around food, even if you weren't eating it.

"Thank you," I said. "I think this is my best birthday ever." And I meant it. I picked a piece of breast meat, dredged it through the gravy, and gave it to Kevin. "I love my dog. He's perfect. This day is perfect." Then I noticed, through the window, ash floating through the air. At first it was just a few flakes, floating here and there, but then a gust blew horizontal past the window, and I saw the first cresting wave of what I knew was snow. "Snow!" I yelled. "It's snowing. Snowing now." I took my wine to the window, stunned as always by the miracle of it, hoping to buried under and buoyed up by the stuff, hoping to be saved.

21

When I was in fifth grade, I came home with a list of paper topics that my teacher, Mr. Henryon, had given us. It was for American history, one of my favorite subjects, and I remember my enthusiasm for starting the work. My mother drifted over to the kitchen table, where I was contemplating the list.

"What's that?" she said.

"Paper topics for history," I answered. She picked up the page and read down the list.

"What are you going to do?" she asked.

"I think I'm going to do Lewis and Clark."

"Why?"

"Because they were great discoverers," I said, feeling less sure about my choice.

"Don't do them. Lewis in particular is a disappointment. You know he killed himself."

"He did?" I took the page back. "Maybe I'll do Joseph Smith."

"The Mormons? I don't think so."

"What should I do?"

"The Donner Party. Now that's a good story."

"Is it?"

"Scary. And wonderful."

I researched and wrote a phenomenal paper, at least I thought so. It was from the point of view of one of the Donner children, Eliza Donner, and was filled with flesh and despair. Mr. Henryon questioned my research methods. "History," he said, sympathetically stroking his beard, "has a need for places and dates. This is all very dramatic, and, well, compelling, but I don't know about its accuracy."

"But the dates are all written about anyway. That's plagiarism, dates and places," I argued. My paper, "The Donner Disaster," was the first of my academic failures. But the story stays with me. In my mind's eye, those Donners lurk behind every snowbank. The Donner Party members are journeying to sunny California. They are escaping poverty, religious persecution, the oldness of the East—now a little Europe—with all its entitled landowners and businessmen. But hunger cannot be escaped, because hunger isn't in the Sierras. It's in every party member, that little void always threatening to overwhelm. The soul is not what defines us as people, but this bottomless hunger. This hunger is our soul. The experiences of the Donner Party are our experiences as people, abstract furies registered concrete. The snow, instead of blanketing us over, lays us bare.

Years after I wrote that paper, I found that my mother had saved it, put it in the same folder as my birth certificate, passport, and immunization record, and the envelope containing curling locks of my normally straight hair. I took the paper out. Mr. Henryon's writing, large, generous and frank, stalked the margins in jovial deprecation, but the comment that struck me was written at the bottom, in my mother's own feathery, light script. A question.

Why not write about Lewis Keseberg?

Which of course made me wonder, "Why write about Lewis Keseberg?" Keseberg was another Donner Party survivor—a middle-aged man—and not the first choice for a fifth-grade girl to focus on. I put the paper back in the folder and logged the comment as yet another of my mother's crazy compulsive missives. She had also written "take 4" over the advised dosage on the bottle of Advil. But the question would not sleep. Finally I went to the public library and checked out a book, *History of the Donner Party*, which I had checked out five years earlier. It was summer. My mother was in the hospital. I felt, despite the archery day camp (which had needed a record of immunizations, particularly tetanus) desperately alone. Somehow, I felt that by rereading the book through her eyes I was

with her, in her company, feeling her hand on my shoulder as I
turned the pages.

I imagine Keseberg with the snow howling around the corners of the
cabin, wondering if it was still April or if the winter had pushed into
May. The year, 1847, was receding into the past and taking Keseberg
with it, recording him as a monster, a man who stayed behind to
outlive the others and take their money when they could no longer
hold it. He was the only survivor at Donner Lake, perhaps the only
one of the Donner party left, but he had received no news from the
camp at Alder Creek, which was seven miles away.

Mrs. Murphy had recently died. The pot was boiling and Mrs.
Murphy's naked body was sitting in the chair. The wind set the door
to a beating rattle. The snow hissed outside, sifted through the cabin
planks, and collected in powdery drifts in the corners. Snow settled on
the cold withered legs of Mrs. Murphy, dusted her hair, filled the crev-
ices of her mutilated body. She was missing an arm. Her eyes stared
out just to the left of the door and Keseberg thought maybe he should
adjust the chair so she would be looking more at it, less at nothing.

Keseberg stirred the pot. Maybe he was wondering about Alder
Creek when he heard the moaning outside, as if the crazy Irish had
brought with them their banshee. Because a crazy Irishman would need
something like a banshee screaming to tell him death was near, when
all a German needed was to look at the amount of food divided by the
amount of people divided by the amount of days, et cetera, et cetera.

But now there was a pounding on the door and Keseberg realized,
with some bewilderment, that he had a visitor. Tamzene Donner
entered the cabin. She was soaked to the bone. Sometimes the snow
gave beneath you and you found yourself deep in water. Is that what
had happened? Maybe she had fallen in the lake.

"Mrs. Donner," said Keseberg.

"He is dead," she replied. "He is dead and he told me to go get
the children and make sure they have enough to eat. He told me to

do that." Tamzene Donner sat at the table across from Mrs. Murphy. Her skin was blue and her skirt frozen in swirls, like the drapery in Renaissance paintings. She blinked scattering snow from her eye-lashes onto her cheekbones. Keseberg gave her a cup of hot water. "He told me to give them the silver," she said.

"What silver?" asked Keseberg.

"For the children," whispered Tamzene, lowering her voice, "for them in California."

Keseberg wondered if George Donner had died. He was moved with pity. It passed quickly, which saddened him.

"A bear came into the cabin. It sat at the foot of George's bed," said Tamzene. "The bear said I should eat it. Then it took George's ax and split its head open. I ate the brain."

"A bear?" said Keseberg. He looked at Tamzene's hands and noted the blood on the cuffs of her dress, blood that even this end-less wash of snow and her near drowning had not removed.

"I came to get you so that you can bring the silver to the chil-dren." Tamzene told Keseberg where it was buried and Keseberg prom-ised to collect it for the children. The relief parties sent out were made of mercenaries. They thought more of carrying a bolt of calico back through the Sierras than a lame child. These men, these heroes, took fifty percent of all the valuables they found. But this silver Tamzene spoke of was buried back at Alder Creek, and Keseberg was lame. His foot had not healed; he had stepped on a shard of wood at Goose Lake, back when the sky was full of birds and all one had to do was poke a hole in the heavens with a shotgun to have the food raining all around. Although the spike of wood had finally worked its way through— Keseberg found it poking from the top of his foot—he was still lame. If he could walk, he would have crossed the mountains long ago.

"I will do what I can," said Keseberg.

"I saw the masts," she said, "bobbing from the ships. I saw the ships again."

"I think you saw the tops of the trees moving in the wind."

"No," she said. "These were the ships of Newburyport filled with rum and sugar and pineapples. They were rising high, high above me. They were . . ." Tamzene Donner looked deeply at Keseberg, then grew quiet. Later she screamed. Later she confessed that she had eaten her husband and when she was finally still, there was such a silence about the cabin that—despite all that Keseberg had endured—he felt the ache of loneliness.

Keseberg makes it to California, tries his hand at a few things— including a short stint as a brewer—but most often fails. In 1877 Keseberg's wife, Philippine, dies at the age of fifty-three, thirty years after she set out with the Donners. At that time, only four children, all daughters, of Keseberg's eleven children still lived. Two had married and moved away. The other two were idiots and their incessant howling made it necessary for Keseberg to live far away from his neighbors. And that's the last we hear of him: Keseberg living with Bertha, who cannot speak and "would leave her hand to roast on the fire if he did not pluck it out" and Augusta, who only stops howling to stuff her mouth, and weighs well over two hundred pounds.

In that first onslaught of winter in Maine, I thought of Keseberg, and Bad Billy, and all the toothy things leaving their prints upon the snow, their gnawing hunger and snuffling, their breathing silenced by the fierce wind flung from tree to tree—the high hiss of spruce, the low groan of oak, the final crack of a dry birch laid to rest. Keseberg was a survivor. He made it out of the mountains, out of the horrible of winter of 1847. But he never escaped his fame as the Cannibal Keseberg. I wondered why Keseberg was made out to be such a villain. He suffered as much as everyone else, maybe more. Lewis junior, only an infant, had been one of the first of the Donner Party to die. Philippine escaped the hell of Donner Lake in an early relief party, which took her and Keseberg's three-year-old daughter, Ada, with her. And Ada was still in the snow when Keseberg made his crossing weeks after. He saw the little girl's dress poking through the snow. Her face was probably well-preserved, having been packed in ice.

So why hate him? He does nothing but survive. Isn't this just another great American tale?

22

I awoke to the gentle boom of snow sliding off the roof. The wind picked up splattering raindrops against the window. Arthur and I were asleep on the couch. I was in my underwear and he wasn't wearing anything at all, huddled up against me under a tiny stadium blanket. The morning was done with. I figured it had to be close to two P.M. The dog came over, curious, needing to go out. I'd forgotten about the dog. I'd forgotten most everything, it seemed, except for a few flashing images of Johnny, stark naked, spinning on the back deck. I remembered his hair whipping around, his eyelashes crusted over with snow. He said he wasn't cold. He was alive.

My jeans were lying by the couch. I couldn't find my shirt, so I put on Arthur's and tucked the blanket around him.

Kevin gave me a desperate, high-pitched whine.

"All right. I'm hurrying."

I pulled on my duck boots, which, without socks, were clammy and far too big. I put on Arthur's Army surplus coat, which I supposed had been intended for some polar defense. Who defended the poles? In the second world war, there were a few Japanese soldiers stranded in Alaska, bravely occupying American territory. No one bothered to get rid of them. I'm not sure how they even knew they were there. I imagined the Japanese recruiting officer. "All right boys. Everyone for taking Alaska, over here. Everyone for Hawaii, over here." The coat smelled like a wet dog, which I realized was the collar that was made out of dog or some close canine relative. There were cigarettes in the left pocket, and a lighter in the right. I headed out.

I suppose I could have just let Kevin out and waited for him to scratch on the door when he was done. He didn't seem like the kind of dog who was crazy about the rain, but something made me want the fresh air—cold wet air soothing the inner walls of my cranium, getting sucked into my lungs, the burn of tobacco and its sweet, sticky resin, a cold wind blowing through my hair and chilling my scalp. I watched Kevin sprint up a low hillock, then rise up on his hind legs, then disappear into the grass. I whistled for him—strangely familiar, since I'd never had a dog—and headed down to the water's edge. On the third try, I managed to light my cigarette. A thin crust of ice had formed on the surface of the water, but the rain was quickly melting it away. The wind picked up and somewhere to my left, a branch snapped and cracked, followed by the whoosh of foliage falling to the ground. Something was wrong.

Just as this thought entered my mind, Kevin began barking and whining, whining then barking. He sounded trapped or confused. I turned around. Kevin was up by the house and he was barking at something—a tree limb? a bag of trash?—lying fallen by the base-ment door, directly below the back deck. I turned back to the bay and finished my cigarette. Then I lit another one. And another. The rain was falling heavier now and the jacket was getting heavy. My face was numbed with cold. I began walking slowly back to the house.

Johnny was lying facedown in a puddle. The soles of his feet were pointed upward, the sure sign of someone who isn't going anywhere. He was naked and on his left buttock I could the see the deep purple spiral of his tattoo, something he'd explained to me about a Bornean hag who waited at the entry to the afterlife, checking your body for spirals. If she found one, she would let you enter unscathed. But if she didn't, the hag would pluck out your eyes and you would be forced to go through eternity blind. Maybe blind was bet-ter. Kevin looked at me, then back at Johnny, whose wild hair was matted in clumps around his neck. I looked up at the deck.

There was some kind of scrape—maybe blood, but hard to tell because the rain was washing everything away—on the railing. With the snow and freezing rain, it was possible that Johnny had slipped.

The sky was dropping rain on my face, splat after splat. I wondered when it was going to stop. I looked back down at Johnny. Kevin was licking his neck.

"No!" I said. "Bad dog!" I pushed Kevin away with my foot. Then I saw the wound on Johnny's neck, a ragged tear. It started in the front and wound around his neck, not a neat incision, but a ripped section of skin and flesh—a pillow losing its feathers. I stood back up and was soon getting sick into a clump of wild sage that grew around the pillars of the deck.

"Katherine. Katherine, what's wrong?"

Arthur was standing on the deck wrapped in the blanket. He was wearing Johnny's shoes.

"Call an ambulance," I said. "Johnny's dead."

The ambulance came and with the ambulance, the police. The sun made an appearance shortly after that. The day had turned beautiful but I found it hard to appreciate with all the police crawling over the property. Some had dogs. I'm not sure why. They had found a couple of things that day—the remains of fire lit in the woods and some empty baked-bean cans. Someone had been camping out there. Bad Billy, maybe? Who knew?

Then there was the possibility, which seemed the most likely, that Johnny had fallen off the deck, knocked himself out on the way down (there was a monstrous contusion on his forehead to back this theory up), drowned facedown in a puddle, then provided an easy meal for some coyotes or skunks.

"Would skunks do that?" I asked the police officer, an Officer Browning, who was young and seemed more interested in me than Johnny.

"Skunks eat anything, Miss. I'm sorry about your friend."

"Oh, God." I shook my head. I had been crying all morning and I wasn't sure why. There was fear in with the grief. I looked at Johnny's back. A photographer was snapping away.

Arthur was talking to another police officer, an older woman who had her arm around him. Arthur seemed to be taking it worse than I was, which wasn't that surprising, because Johnny and Arthur had spent a lot of time together over the past week.

Another young cop was rooting around under the deck. "I think I found something," he said. The photographer went over and snapped a few shots. It was the snow shovel, which had been up on the deck at one point, but for some reason was now under the deck, about six feet from where Johnny was lying.

"Is that blood?" asked the young cop.

Detective Yancy, who'd been on the phone for the last half hour, came striding over. "Don't touch anything. Get that bagged."

"Don't worry about anything," said Officer Browning.

"Don't worry? What do you think that shovel's all about?"

"We'll figure this out," said Officer Browning.

"Miss," called Detective Yancy, "a few words."

I raised my eyebrows at Officer Browning. I don't know what I meant to imply by this, but he stepped back and let me pass.

"You were drinking?" said Detective Yancy.

"Just a little."

"Is that sarcasm?"

"It's understatement."

"Say things plainly, Miss. I'm not in the mood for jokes."

"We were drunk. When I came home from the airport at eleven A.M., Johnny was already drunk. I think it was close to nine o'clock at night when I remember him going out on the deck."

"Was Mr. Verhoven drinking?"

"Mr.—? Oh, Arthur, yes, a lot. We were all pathetically drunk, and now we're all pathetically remorseful, except for Johnny. The only one who remembers anything is the dog, and he's not very forthcoming."

"Miss, I must remind you that this is not a time for jokes."

"This is not funny to me, not in the slightest, and I resent your constant patronizing. I am answering your questions . . ."

Then I stopped because I saw someone walking around the side of the house, down the lawn toward me. He was wearing a cowboy hat that was strangely lacking in irony. He was bow-legged. He had a suitcase in his hand, a suitcase that seemed impossibly light, the suitcase that women carried in movies from the thirties and forties as they headed to New York, L.A., and Paris, from Minneapolis, Cherryville, and Farmington—suitcases filled with nothing but dreams. When he saw me he set down his suitcase, took his hat off in a gesture of politeness, and stood, holding his hat in both hands, as if waiting to be invited to the investigation.

Arthur came over and put his hands on my shoulders. "Who's that?" he asked.

"That," I said, "is Travis."

Travis came walking over. He nodded when he saw me. "Katherine," he said.

"Howdy," I replied.

"I would have called, but I didn't have your number."

"That's okay."

Travis looked around at the police then down at Johnny's body. "Is this a bad time?"

"I'm going to make some coffee," I said. I went inside and Travis followed with his suitcase. I was surprised to see a typewriter by the counter, an old Olympia that looked to weigh a hundred pounds.

"You don't mind, do you?" said Travis.

I shook my head. "You can stay in the room at the end of the hall." Travis was about to ask me something, but my expression made him change his mind. I could tell. I could almost hear his reasoning, "What are the chances of something like that happening to me?"

That night I slept badly. Kevin was having nightmares, whining in his sleep, his paws twitching. Arthur had fallen asleep after sharing a bottle of Maker's Mark with Travis. All of us had checked the doors at least twice before retiring. I'd seen a flashlight in the back and it was a tense couple of seconds before we made out Officer Browning with some other guy prowling around. I heard tires crunching down the gravel drive more than once. The police were keeping a close watch over the house, which made me feel both paranoid and safe. I finally passed out at around four in the morning. Next thing I knew, Arthur was shaking my arm.

"Katherine. I'm sorry. I think you should get up."

"What time is it?" I asked, still asleep. The room was bright.

"It's two. Boris has called about fifteen times."

"You didn't answer the phone, did you?"

"Of course not. He's been leaving these weird messages. I think you should listen to them."

I sat up in bed and Arthur handed me a mug of steaming coffee. I leaned against him while I drank it and he stroked my hair.

"What's Travis up to?"

"He took the dog for a walk." There was some commotion in the kitchen. I heard a chair being pushed across the floor and strange voices. "And the police are here," said Arthur. "I don't know why."

I pulled on some clothes and went into the kitchen. I recognized Officer Browning but the other guy wasn't familiar.

"Your phone's been ringing all morning. Maybe you should answer it," he said.

"And maybe you should finish that coffee and go find out who killed my friend."

The officers looked at each other then both got up. Officer Browning raked his hand through his hair and put on his hat. "We didn't mean to inconvenience you," he said.

"Good." The phone started ringing again. "Then you won't mind if I want some privacy while I'm talking on the phone. I don't think there's anything, other than coffee cake, of interest in the kitchen."

I picked up the phone. "Katherine?" It was Boris. I waited until Arthur had shut the door behind the policeman before I spoke.

"Boris, what on earth is wrong?" I asked.

"I thought it was because of you that he would not answer the phone. I thought you told him not to speak to me . . ."

"What are you talking about?"

"Because you didn't want me involved in your divorce. That is why I thought he hadn't returned my calls."

"Are you talking about Silvano?"

There was a pause on the phone. I could hear Boris's breath whistling through his nose.

"What is it?"

"Katherine, Silvano is dead."

Boris didn't like it when people didn't answer the phone. He took it very personally, even though he had one of those blocking things that didn't let caller ID announce who you were. And in Boris's case, this was probably a good idea. Boris hadn't really taken my anger seriously. Clearly, he was the correct person to oversee the divorce proceedings. As I drove off in the cab feeling at least the power of having made a scene as I left, Boris had already moved on to phase two of his plan. He probably didn't notice that our conversation had ended abruptly. He was wondering if he'd lost face because of Silvano, if people thought I was playing him. He never thought, "Is she using me?" Only, "Do other people think she's using me?"

And Ann had been trying to get him to understand that for some time. She had encouraged Boris to go confront Silvano. I don't think she meant me any harm. I believe that there was something of an admirable morality to Ann where she really did believe in the truth, even if it was ugly and didn't improve her life. I didn't understand it, but it helped me understand her.

So after Boris's eighth unanswered phone call to Silvano, Ann was on the phone with her friend who owned the Cygnet boutique, trying to get his home address. And succeeding. And Ann was at the door with Boris's coat and scarf and hat telling him that he was absolutely right, that no one had the right to treat him like that. Ann loved Boris. She probably was outraged. I'm surprised she didn't go with him.

The doorman was actually happy that Boris was looking for Silvano. The neighbors who lived beneath Silvano's apartment had complained that morning of an odd smell as they'd hurried off to work. The doorman put a call into the super and was still waiting to hear back. Boris merely looked at the doorman and cleared his throat.

"And what is the number of his apartment?" he said.

Boris took the elevator, which was nicer than the elevator in his building and this bothered him, up to the fifth floor. The door slid open and he stepped out, surprised to find the same wild rose/trellis pattern on the floor leading to Silvano's apartment as his own. He walked down the hallway at a quick step, managing to rekindle his anger. He paused at Silvano's door. There was an odd smell and Boris—to his surprise—felt the sudden desire to leave. But Boris had suffered the insult, so he raised his fist and struck the door confidently. There was no answer. He pounded again and the door, on greased hinges, swung open.

"Falconi!" shouted Boris. "Falconi! Now we will talk."

But it was not to be. Boris looked into the room. On the dining table, a vase of daffodils had been knocked over and the flowers were wilted. Boris could see a shattered wine glass on the floor to the right of the table, beneath the window, where a thin red stain colored the glass. Boris entered the room.

"Falconi?" he said. "What is the meaning of this?"

But Silvano didn't answer. As Boris was drawing nearer to the stain on the window (someone threw the glass at the window? Why? Maybe they were aiming at someone's head, about the right height) when his foot bumped something lying on the ground. It was Silvano lying eyes wide, staring upward.

"My God," said Boris, which was strange, because Boris didn't have a god.

Silvano's neck was peeled open, flaps of skin flung to right and left like a loose leather ascot. There was a deep red stain around the carpeting and on his forehead, just where his perfect silver hair met the skin in a widow's peak, a deep bruised hole. Beside Silvano was his walking stick with the falcon head, the beak now dipped in blood.

He heard a low growl coming from the kitchen and saw Cosimo, hackles raised, lips pulled, at a frightening stand-off.

"An intruder," said Boris.

"And what about the neck wound?" I asked. Arthur looked up from his coffee.

"His dog," said Boris.

"Cosimo? They think Cosimo ate him?"

"There was no food for the animal. And the dog was left like that for three days."

"Three days?"

"You were lucky, Katherine. You and the intruder just missed each other. Maybe you even saw him."

"No," I said. "I'd remember that."

Silvano was an old man who did not have long to live, but I still felt saddened by his death. I went to stand by the window. I could hear the hiss of water coming from the bathroom—Arthur taking a shower—and the accompanying groan and creak of pipes. Down the hall, Travis was arranging his things in his room. I heard the distant jangle of hangers and the slamming of a dresser drawer. The police were probing each corner of the property, searching for a killer, and despite the brightness of the sun I felt cold. There was a cold chill in the coils of my stomach. A breeze was blowing across the bay, creating line upon line of creases on the water, and I began to wish that I could just leave everything, take a ship to some forgotten place where I could disappear. But would it be better there? Or would all this darkness follow me, track me over the surface of the water, assert itself wherever I went? Was I destined to pollute each virgin land I found with the same despair that seemed to arise and then arise again with ever faster frequency? Or was each land already corrupted, each Garden of Eden just a stage for man's betrayals?

23

Arthur woke me up because I was having a nightmare. I don't know what I was saying, but I felt his hands on my arms and when I woke up and saw him crouching over me, I thought he was holding me down. I threw him off and he fell off the bed.

"Katherine," he said, "it's me."

I caught my breath. "What the fuck were you doing?"

"You were having a bad dream. Who's Nancy?"

"I don't know who Nancy is," I said.

Arthur got up and sat beside me on the bed. "You were yelling at Nancy to let you go."

I heard footsteps down the hall and then a soft voice at the door, "Is everything all right?" It was Travis.

"Katherine had a bad dream," said Arthur.

"That's understandable," said Travis. "Night, y'all." His footsteps retreated back up to his room.

I took a deep breath and got up. "What the fuck is going on?" I said. I went to the window and looked down at the point, at the water beyond, which sparkled in the moonlight.

"We're going to be all right," said Arthur.

"Get me a cigarette, will you?"

The cigarettes were in the living room and Arthur went to get them. I was watching the water, half-watching it really, the perceptive parts of my vision pointed inward, when I saw the figure on the point. At first I thought it must be a deer, or maybe a policeman prowling around, but the figure was a woman. She was wearing a skirt—

that much I could see—and she was looking up at the house. I heard Arthur coming up the hall.

"Come here," I whispered.

Arthur came beside me and looked out the window, but the figure had retreated back into the line of shadow thrown down by the trees.

"Wait," but nothing happened.

"What am I looking for?" Arthur said.

"I saw someone out there."

"Really?" Arthur stepped closer to the window and cupped his hands around his face, just like he had the first time we'd met at the bookstore. "I don't see anything," he said, "Should I call the police?"

I took a cigarette and lit it. I shook my head.

Arthur thought. "I should call the police," he decided.

"It wasn't Bad Billy," I said. "I saw a woman."

"A woman?"

"I think it was a woman. She was only there for a second."

"Should I go out and investigate?"

I shook my head.

"I should go and investigate," he said.

"No. Let's go back to sleep. I'm probably just strung out, imagining things."

Arthur accepted this and soon he was sound asleep. He was wrapped around me, hugging me close, and it was hard to extricate myself without waking him up. I crept down the hallway, waving off Kevin, who was now up and determined to follow me. I put on Arthur's coat and lit a cigarette, then, with my boots loose and clammy on my feet, went out into the night. It was bitterly cold, but with no wind. I walked as quickly as I could to the tip of the point, worried the whole time that I'd run into some patrolling officer, but there was no one. Even where the land dropped off to the tidal bay, all was quiet, not even a fox. I turned around to go to the house, when I caught a whiff of smoke. Then it was gone. I turned to the woods and said, with minimal bravery, "Hello?"

No answer.

Then, "Mother?" Because although I found this highly unlikely, I did not know where she was, and I knew that if she had escaped, she would come to find me. There was no answer. I took a step into the woods. Everything was still except for a few high branches tapping on each other and the light skittering of leaves. I was about to make my way back to the house when I noticed the print, a footprint, small, a woman's, with the unmistakable human quality of a cigarette butt pressed into its center.

As I wandered back to the house, I found myself thinking of my brief tenure at boarding school. When I was fifteen, my father packed me off to his old school, very impressive and pedigreed, conveniently coed, in the northern suburbs of Boston. I suppose my father was feeling put upon by my mother's fits. My being institutionalized coincided with her being institutionalized for the first time, although my father didn't term it as such. He said there was a new treatment for her illness—fresh air, constant care—and I imagined her bundled up in the freezing cold on the long veranda of a sanitarium, her sickness one of the lungs rather than of the soul.

My roommate, Astrid, was a pretty, pleasantly remote girl who was in some funk over her parents' divorce. She spent most of her time in bed and found me acceptable since her last roommate had been a kleptomaniac and a compulsive liar. I was reading *The Dead* for my Joyce class and when the rock hit my window, thought that I'd hallucinated it. Michael Furey and his shower of pebbles, perhaps. With the second rock, which nearly cracked the glass, I thought it must be one of Astrid's suitors—wealthy boys with floppy hair who were invariably good shots through years spent at lacrosse, squash, and baseball. Astrid didn't seem inclined to move, although she did give me one of her appealing, monumentally bored looks. Her blond hair was matted to her skull and she pulled it a little so that it covered her eyes. I got up from my bed and went over to look. Standing on the ground outside my window was my mother. There was a cab waiting on the drive behind her, headlights slashing through the dark, its low rumble barely audible because it was a windy night. Windy and cold. I opened the window and smiled.

"Katherine," she said. She was wearing a suit, but her feet were bare.

"Come up the fire escape," I answered.

"I don't have any money to pay the cab."

Astrid sat up in bed, more animated than I'd seen her in days.

"It's my mother. She's escaped from the asylum and needs money to pay the taxi."

"Take it out of my purse," said Astrid. "I should have a couple of hundred in there."

My mother spent the night curled up in bed next to me. She had a terrible cold that turned into pneumonia. I knew she was really sick, or I would have tried to hide her a bit longer. My father came to get her and found me with my bags packed. He seemed resigned to taking us both home, although he did find the strength to argue with me for the entire hour and a half it took to reach our house.

A week later, I tried to call Astrid, to thank her, but there was no answer in our room. Finally, I called the house counselor, Mrs. Grady. I wanted to pay Astrid back. I owed her seventy five dollars. But Mrs. Grady couldn't tell me where she was. She started crying and finally said that Astrid had hanged herself the week before. Did I know why?

I didn't really, but then the impulse to live was to me just as surprising as the one to stop it all. What was the pride in survival? How did we find the strength to mount each obstacle when we all knew in no uncertain way that it was not the last? I wanted to tell Mrs. Grady that the weak make way for the strong, but I felt that Astrid's was a useless death.

That night, in bed with Arthur snoring beside me, I kept seeing Astrid's pale face, the blue eyes and thin pink lips. I couldn't get my mind to relax and found myself wondering if death wasn't anything more than a side effect of time. Astrid was very much alive ten years ago. What made the present any more valuable than any other time? Why was Astrid more dead than I was, when I was bound to be dead at some future date? Wasn't the present just an arbitrary lens for viewing existence? Finally, realizing that lying there was giving me a headache and that there was no chance of falling back to sleep, I got out of bed. If I'd stayed there I might have started thinking about God, about the existence of good and evil, how my view of time left no room for the afterlife (or the present life, for that matter) and that such thoughts were silly indulgences and I'd be better off doing some laundry or taking the dog for a much-needed walk.

Usually simple tasks had a soothing effect on me, but I was finding it harder and harder to execute them in my normal, focused way. There was an anxiety gnawing at my heart—mother lost, me here. There was no place left to breathe. There were no longer wildernesses, only zoos. There was no longer an easy freedom, only guarded institutions.

The next morning when Arthur and Travis got up, they were greeted by the unusual sight of me cooking breakfast. The house was freezing cold and I realized we'd run out of oil. I'd called the oil company and they said they'd send someone over, but it was almost eleven and I was still waiting for the delivery.

"It's cold," said Travis.

"Fucking freezing," said Arthur.

"Have some coffee," I suggested. "Maybe you can put your feet in it."

I poured the coffee into mugs and handed them around. "Thinking of Texas?" I said to Travis.

"No," he said. "You know where I'd like to be right now?"

"Where?"

"Australia."

"Why?" asked Arthur.

"Because it's summer. My dad went there once."

"Vacation?" I asked. Vacations seemed a bit bourgeois for Travis.

"My father sells crop-dusting equipment. He went out there January two years ago. He said it was hot as hell." Travis sipped his coffee. "He said he hit a kangaroo out on the highway. He said people went hunting after the kangaroos. I sure would like to do that."

"I could never hunt kangaroo," I said.

"Why not?" asked Travis.

"They're too cute," I said. "But I've always wanted to go to Australia."

"Why?" asked Arthur.

"Because of the bushrangers," I said. "A country of convicts and criminals appeals to me."

"Bushrangers?" said Travis.

"Outlaws. You know, Ned Kelly, John Donahue, Michael Burke," I said. "I took a course in Australian history when I was in college. Their heroes are bushrangers. How can you not love that?"

Australia in my mind had become an idealized America, what America might have been if we as Americans were more self-reliant, more free. In Australia (or so it seemed to me) one's capacity to succeed was equal to one's ability to exist outside of society, rather than in America, where one's self-sufficient qualities were put to the test building yet another society. My bushranger heroes were largely Irish and Scottish, victims of the English. Their transport to Australia was a diaspora of Celtic pickpockets, forgers, and cattle rustlers.

"Who's your favorite?" asked Travis.

"My favorite what?"

Travis looked at me, amused that I'd already lost track of the conversation. "Your favorite bushranger."

"Oh," I said, "that." I pondered for a moment. "My favorite bushranger would be Alexander Pearce."

"What did he do?" asked Arthur.

"He stole six pairs of shoes." I sipped my coffee. "It was his first crime. He got seven years' transportation, but he never saw his home again."

"Where was home?" asked Travis.

"County Monaghan, Ireland."

"God, you have a good memory," said Arthur.

"For certain things," I said.

*   *   *

I pictured Pearce on the deck of the *Castle Forbes,* slicing through
the low waves and dense, wet air. Hell's Gate suddenly appeared,
rising out of the water—a mountain peak whose roots reached far
below the churning surface of the sea. Pearce saw the basalt flutes of
Tasmania rising out of the ocean, the sharp edges of rock cutting the
sky. He knew he had sailed not only to the edge of the world, but to
the edge of human knowledge itself. And what monsters inhabited
this hell? What rules governed this island with its woolly-headed
natives and ambitious, bitter overseers, beaten down by heat and
famine, hostile Indians and savage convicts, seeing always the golden
skies of Mother England over the edge of horizon, the sunny warmth
of her smile.

But watch as the ship slips into the antipodean realm. Her bow
rises and falls, her masts soar majestically upward and sails are flung
to right and left. How easy to picture this ship as bearing all that is
civilized England to this misted, far-flung island. How easy to dream
that belowdecks lay bundles of silk and velvet, vellum-bound books,
fragrant cheeses, heady wines, sweating hams, carved ivory combs,
corset baleen, hooked woolen rugs, and pots of ink and quills with
which to inscribe on sheaf after sheaf of ivory paper the progress of
the New World back into the Old . . .

But the ship is bearing convicts and its boards are slick with the
sweat and shit of four hundred condemned men. Some are children,
barely sixteen, some are hardened criminals, some are women, all are
exiles from civilization sent to this prison that needs no bars, because
this is Van Dieman's Land, Tasmania, prized for her resilient timber
and not much else. Here, the interior is a mystery known only to the
natives, who are tight-lipped or silly with drink, and in either state
are not trustworthy. And why would they tell? Their only refuge is
the white man's fear. In those small pockets of dark, primordial soil,
an aborigine can still wander in peace. In the interior's twisting ra-
vines and sheer cliffs, frothing rivers and barren plains, things are as
they've always been. These places are death for the white man, who

knows too much to know how to survive, whose brain is so cluttered with muskets and profits and buttons that when faced with starvation and a buck kangaroo, the white man will stand berating the animal for not offering itself up with a prized buttery sauce and glass of heated rum.

This is Alexander Pearce's Tasmania. It is 1819. Pearce is thirty years old.

Alexander Pearce is to work off his time, four years down from the seven if he buckles under and performs well. He does not. While on assignment to various locals, he manages to steal, drink, abscond, and escape. In one six-month period in 1821, the record shows him to have received 150 lashes. He is unrepentant. His behavior does not improve. During this period he escapes into the bush and learns—from some helpful natives—how to survive in the wilderness for close to three months. Of his many transgressions it is forgery (a two-pound money order) and absconding from service that finally get him sent to Macquarie Harbor, a penal colony on the distant western coast of the island reserved for hardened criminals and the hopelessly degenerate. And if Pearce wasn't when he first arrived, he certainly is now.

Macquarie is a singular place. Its iron bars are the miles of shark-infested beach and the hostile, mysterious natives that roam the interior. One in ten men escape and nearly all are recorded as having "perished in the woods." The food—what there is of it—is intentionally pickled and rebelliously rotten. All the men have scurvy, lice, and sores. Few have teeth. Lashings are routine and the sight of a man with his back looking like an ox liver, his shoes overflowed with blood, is commonplace. Fresh meat is the stuff of dreams. And so the men leave, not so concerned with what lies ahead but propelled with what is at their backs, leaping into oblivion and probably not caring. Starving. Drowning. Lying down exhausted, never to rise. Picked off by the native Tasmanians, whose spear-hurling will not save them from extinction. As the convicts draw their rasping final breaths, I would say that they all feel that dying a free man is overrated.

Only one man escapes Macquarie twice, and he is Alexander
Pearce.

Who knows how much planning went into this venture? I suspect the escape was spontaneous. On the morning of September 22,
1822, Pearce is working felling trees when out of the corner of his
eye—near the sector of his brain where thoughts of escape lurk end-
lessly—he sees a boat floating in Kelly Basin. Tantalizing. Languid.
Waves lapping seductively at her sides—*you are never at the horizon,
you are always on the horizon* . . .

Pearce makes a run for it. He jumps into the boat and before he
can gauge the magnitude of his actions, he has seven willing companions—seven men who have entwined their fate with his—seven
men leaping like fish into the safety of the boat. With the popping
of muskets and the scent of powder heavy in the air, the men quickly
row, the shouts of the overseers lost in the pounding blood of the first
moments of freedom. Soon the smoke signals wind into the sky. Men
have escaped. Hunt them down.

The convicts, now at a safe distance, sink the boat and head into
the heart of island, where the clock of time has wound and wound so
tightly that it has stopped altogether. The trees poke into the very
fabric of the sky—trees sprouted at the time of Julius Caesar. The
melancholy cawing of the magpies, the flutter of fallen leaves as a
snake slides into hiding, the rattle of gum nuts shaken high above by
a springing possum, the buzz of the great yellow sun, these are the
only sounds heard over the grunt and heave of men walking at quick
pace, walking inward, backward, nowhere.

Who are these men?

Little Brown. Robert Kennelly. William Dalton. Thomas Bodenham. John Mather. Mathew Travers. Robert Greenhill. And Alexander
Pearce. They have only one weapon, an ax, which is in Greenhill's
possession.

What is their plan?

To survive. To this end, they must travel first to the center, then
manage eastward to Hobart. There, on the good days, they will find
passage on a ship, maybe on a Dutch freighter going to the Spice Is-

lands; they will spend their years weighed down by native women, whose soft black hair smells of nutmeg and saffron. On the bad days, they will arms themselves and retreat into the bush, where the aborigines and Irishmen (after all, aren't they the same to the British?) pick off sheep at the fringe, occasionally stopping a carriage or man on horseback with a hearty, "Bail up." But the food is now gone and the terrain has shifted. Jagged toothy peaks drain their energy, bottomless gorges swallow them whole. Of the voluptuous women of the Spice Islands, all that is left is the scent of nutmeg, and wouldn't that be better coming off a plum duff?

One of the men, Little Brown, is weak with dysentery. How long will he last? How long will any of them, with no food? Robert Kennelly heaves a deep breath and looks at the land before him— wall after wall, divide after divide—and states: "I am so weak that I could eat a piece of man." Is this a joke? This is not a time for joking. Is this a thought mistakenly uttered, better left unsaid, because as the words escape his mouth he sees the eyes of all the others swing toward him. He sees the light dying in Little Brown's eyes. He sees the keen blue eyes of Alexander Pearce calmly appraising him, those icy eyes sitting in Pearce's pocked, creased face.

Someone will not survive the night.

Days later the authorities find Robert Kennelly and Little Brown trying to escape back to Macquarie. They are hysterical, babbling, doomed. "We fell back," says Kenelly. "They tried to catch us, but we hid. There was no food." "Then what is this?" asks the constable, holding forth the small sack of meat. "That is not food," says Kennelly. "That is William Dalton." William Dalton, believed to be a flogger, although the records do not bear this out. Eaten for his supposed cruelty, cut down with Greenhill's ax. They sliced off Dalton's head, eviscerated him, hung him up to bleed, and dined first on the heart and liver. In the following week Kennelly and Brown both die, unable to heal from the deprivations faced in their weeks of freedom.

The other convicts continue east to the Loddon Plains. Thomas Bodenham is the next victual. His bones are found years later, by a surveyor hoping to be the first white man to travel the region.

Four men continue onward. All are so thin that they offer little food and although each slaughter reduces the mouths by one, it is still necessary to choose a new meal every few days. Now, the men have fallen into factions: Greenhill and Travers, Pearce and Mather. The two pairs stagger on, in sight of each other, but at a distance. Pearce considers his fate. He does not want to be so far that if another meal presents itself, he cannot partake. He does not want to be so near as to present himself as a meal. He looks at Mather. Mather has more flesh to him than Pearce, and height. Pearce is only five feet four inches. Also, Pearce has had a bout of smallpox and his pitted appearance, he thinks, makes him look less appetizing. Greenhill will most likely go for Mather, because Pearce is known for his ferocity. If he was smart, Greenhill would cut down Travers, who is weak from a snakebite, even though they have some sort of friendship. What kind? Who can say? The most unholy of affections spring up around convicts and, Pearce wryly notes, cannibalism and sodomy both dwell outside the perimeters of civilization, which is exactly where they're standing. Pearce staggers onward, his mind unable to free itself of thoughts of meat and man, and man and meat, and which is what and why not.

He hears Mather suddenly, a few feet behind him, call out in pain and panic. Pearce turns to see the struggle. Where does Mather find the strength and he unarmed, and Greenhill already having cut him, the blood spewing forth from his head? Pearce and Travers manage to calm Mather down. Maybe he is weak with blood loss, because it seems strange that any words, particularly from these companions, could calm a man in such a predicament. Greenhill is feeling generous. "Give him half an hour to say his prayers."

Half an hour? thinks Pearce. *And why? I'm hungry now. If he's so anxious to have words with his maker, we could send him forthwith, and the two could have a face-to-face. How much value can thirty minutes of painful blood-loss and mental agony have for a man?* Pearce sits in the grass listening to the pained entreaties of Mather. He looks over at Travers, who's looking at him. It will be Travers next, affection or not, because Greenhill will still be shaken up over Mather's resistance.

Much like pork is what Greenhill had said about the meat, and much like pork Pearce has found it. No. Travers will be next. And after that? Greenhill has the ax. Pearce will deal with that obstacle when he comes to it.

"How much time has passed?" shouts Greenhill.

"Do I have a bloody watch?" says Pearce. "Time enough. We've got to get moving."

And Greenhill finishes the job.

Travers weakens further. He begs Greenhill and Pearce to leave him behind to die, to have his body rot unmolested. Surely they can make it to Hobart on what they've managed to cut from Mather. Travers wakens from a moment's nap to hear Greenhill and Pearce deciding his fate. The land is now lush and green, sweet little pudding-hills, a landscape not so alien, could be Ireland. Could be England, but for those little hopping beasts always out of reach, looking from side to side of their wise pointy faces, never close enough to kill. But here's Travers stretched out in final agony. No need to hunt. The only thing that would make this more convenient is if Travers could skin and dress himself. If Travers could say, "What for you, Alexander? Fancy a piece of thigh, or maybe some of the upper arm?"

Pearce. Greenhill.

Two men, feeble with their strange diet, exhausted by heat, struggle toward Hobart. The land is now flat. A blanket of tall grass whips in the steady breeze. Pearce and Greenhill, although they do not know it, are an easy two days' travel to Hobart. The immediate enemy is sleep, which is threatening them both. Their eyelids droop, then flicker up again. Greenhill's joints are stiff, his arms and legs feel deadened with fatigue. An ax is small comfort against sleep, when out there in the tall grass is Alexander Pearce, whose sharp eyes dart out across his snub nose, out across the plain, waiting. This is a contest that Pearce knows he has already won. Across the grass, Greenhill, with his eyes now closed, cradles the ax in his hands as if it is a doll.

Pearce pulls to a standing position. He squints up at the sun. He thinks about his strange hunger, which has conquered all. In the end it was this that won over sleep, that tightened bladder of a stomach folding in upon itself, gnawing and spitting acidic juice, keeping the sharp eyes of Alexander Pearce keen, alert.

A few days later Alexander Pearce is found by a farmer. He is dismembering and eating a sheep, fresh from the field. The farmer knows Pearce, recognizes him—despite his strange table manners— as Irish and arms him. To the bush with you, Pearce. No fork-and-knife-boiled-mutton life for you. Pearce stays at large with other Irishmen, looting and hunted, murderously free, until he is finally caught.

"What makes Pearce so special?" said Travis.

"Well, he escaped with seven other men, but was the only one to survive," I said.

"You admire his determination?" said Travis.

"Among other things," I replied. My coffee had grown cold, so I got up to get some more. Pearce was not tried for cannibalism, although he readily confessed. He explained with pride his small act of survival. The authorities, confusing the truth with altruism, decided he was lying in order to create a myth of death around the others, who could at this very moment be boarding a Dutch freighter bound for Indonesia. They bundled Pearce off to Macquarie Harbor and determine to keep better guard over him.

"Pearce was also the only man to escape Macquarie twice," I added.

"Why didn't they hang him the first time?" asked Arthur.

"I'm not sure," I said. "Maybe they admired him."

The second time Alexander Pearce escaped by land. Despite Pearce's history, he had a willing companion, a Thomas Cox. Who can say what Cox had heard? Pearce was legendary. The other convicts revered him. To escape and return to tell about it was an accomplishment; the substance of Pearce's stories was of little consequence. Cox and Pearce traveled together, but apparently had a falling out over the fact that Cox could not swim. This is understandable when you consider the rush the men were in and the fact that they were standing on the bank of the King's River. When the authorities caught up with Pearce (they were in a boat and sighted him by his campfire high on a cliff) they were horrified to discover that although Cox was with him, Cox was not whole, as much of his body had been eaten by Pearce, although Pearce still had bread on him, as well as salted beef. But the beef smelled rancid, the bread was peppered with mold, and here, high on the cliff, with Macquarie far enough and the city of Hobart beyond reach, Mother England—the old bitch—clinging like a barnacle to the earth's distant backside, a man like Pearce could live and breathe. A man like Pearce could eat his meat in peace. So when the arresting party interrupted his meal, Pearce had no apology and little to say. He managed the comment, "The best eating's the upper arms." Good advice for these soldiers who, despite their freedom, seemed to need a few pointers on how to use it.

Outside, the sound of a truck moving down the drive announced that we would soon have heat. But Australia was still appealing. Fifty years after Pearce, Captain Thomas Dudley, tried for cannibalism in England and found innocent, sought sanctuary in Australia. They called him "Cannibal Tom," but it didn't stop him from becoming a successful businessman. He is entered in the history books twice: first, for eating his cabin boy, and second for being the first person in Australia to die of bubonic plague. He was, I supposed, another hero of mine, but I thought it best to keep this to myself.

24

Travis was very polite and in a strange way I think both Arthur and I appreciated having him there to absorb some of the silence. He also had a take-charge quality, and it was Travis who tracked down Johnny's family (three brothers, one sister, an uncle, and his mother) and broke the news to them. He told them how the police thought the murderer was Bad Billy, that although the lab had been unable to lift any prints from the shovel, they had identified the teeth marks as human. We had all admired Johnny, Travis said, and he would be missed. But that wasn't really true. Travis had never met Johnny—at least not alive— and even I was losing my discomfort and sadness at his passing. As the police presence began to thin out I found myself saying, "Johnny's dead. Johnny's dead. Johnny's dead." But it was more out of guilt of not missing him than actual sorrow. My burgeoning fears had subsided too, as if all the uncommon events of the last few months were the work of my overactive and powerful imagination.

A couple of weeks went by. Travis was working on a novel. I wasn't sure when he was leaving, and he seemed fairly content. He seemed to think he was in an adventure, although Arthur and I weren't that exciting, as far as I could tell. Maybe Travis was embellishing us. Arthur was spending more time in town and it seemed that we had established a routine. Travis had set his old Olympia up in the end room on a sewing machine stand. I could hear the endless sputter of his keys, noted a pile of bottles in the corner of the room— no more Maker's Mark but something called Evan Williams, which made up for its taste with an aggressive cheapness. Travis never seemed drunk to me, although at times he was louder than others, and sometimes his humor was a bit off-color, but he was always funny.

He liked to walk around in his boots, even in the house. His wore his jeans tight and shaved every morning, even though there was no one around to care. He cared. He even ironed his shirts, in strict adherence to some sort of code of honor.

"Do you use starch?" I asked him one morning.

"No, Ma'am."

"What do you write about all day in your little room?"

He set down the iron. "Now why would I tell you that? Let's just wait till the damn thing sells, and then you can buy it with some of that Boris money."

"I think we've all gotten enough out of Boris," I said. "Go on, Travis, let me have a peek."

"At least wait until I have a complete draft."

"How much do you have now?"

"About a hundred pages."

"In only two weeks?"

"The question you should ask is, 'Is it any good?'"

"Is it any good?"

"Depends on the weather, the tide, and how drunk I am." Travis turned off the iron and shook out his shirt. There was no wrinkle on it and somehow he had made everything symmetrical, the sleeves, the collar. He put the shirt on over his undershirt and carefully did up the buttons.

"Do you need any help?" I asked.

"Darling," Travis said, "you must be dying of boredom."

"Not boredom," I said. "But I'm hungry. Starving. I have an idea. Why don't you go out and get some firewood and I'll make us a real breakfast. Bacon. Eggs. Gravy."

"Where's the firewood?"

"You're going to have to walk around the woods and chop some up. Should help you work up an appetite."

"Where's Arthur?"

"He's in town hunting down a violin string and a new shirt."

"Is he auditioning?"

I nodded. "An Irish band. They do weddings and have a few regular gigs, some in Boston. He thinks it could be steady money."

"I hope it works out," said Travis. "I'll go get the wood."

"Don't mess your shirt up," I said.

As soon as Travis was out the door, I set out the eggs and bacon for breakfast, then went down the corridor to his room. There was a manuscript—loose sheets neatly stacked—on the floor beside the typewriter. The title of the manuscript, stricken through but still clear, said *Angeline*.

I read the first ten pages or so, which had a flat, meandering western tone. The description was good—the landscape wide and open, foreboding and peaceful at the same time, and so far the most animated character in the story. Angeline, half Mexican, half not, makes her appearance right before a tornado hits. Her faded floral dress and long black hair blow straight out sideways; her face is inscrutable, but edging toward happy at all the destruction. Somehow, in the tornado, her house is destroyed and Roy, her abusive husband twice her age, is beheaded by a flying piece of tin roofing. Angeline rents a room at our hero, Dan's, mother's house. Angeline keeps working at the diner, as she did before the tornado. Dan develops an obsession with her, although she's five years his senior and he's still dating his high-school sweetheart, Shirla.

I flipped through reading a page here and a page there. Dan goes to war (what war?) and returns decorated and jaded. I suppose it was Vietnam, but my flipping through the manuscript made the whole thing unclear. Some unspeakable tragedy has happened in Dan's absence. Shirla is now fat, married to Dan's high-school buddy with the clubfoot (how had I missed him?) and Angeline has taken to living with some crazy Indian twenty miles from the nearest town.

I turned to the last few pages. It's a confrontation between Angeline and Dan. Dan is holding a wrench, so I suppose he's there to fix something. The blades of windmill push light then shadow through the open window, giving Angeline a flickering, noir aspect.

"What happened to Bobby Whitefoot?" Dan asks, accusingly.

"He's dead. Drowned."

"I don't think so, Angeline. I think you've been running too long."

"What do you think happened, Dan?"

"You know what I think."

"I do," says Angeline. She knots her hair into a bun and goes over the sink. She begins washing the dishes and Dan watches her slim arms dipping in and out of the suds. It's hot and her dress is clinging to the backs of her thighs. Finally, Angeline is done with the dishes. She turns and Dan is gripping his wrench, white-knuckled. She says, "I'll bet you want to know just what happened on the bridge that night, that night at Bear Creek."

And Dan says, "I think it's time you told someone."

And I hoped Angeline would because I wanted to know what had happened at Bear Creek, even though I'd missed every reference to it. I thought the big tragedy (referred to on and off) had been Shirla's impressive weight gain.

So Angeline dries her hands on her apron. (Here Travis had a note saying "apron? or just on her skirt.")

"You'd been gone about a year then, Dan. No one came to the diner anymore and Old Abner really didn't have a choice. He had to let me go. That's how I ended up with Bobby Whitefoot."

"Now Katherine, that's not nice."

I turned quickly, dropping the manuscript. Pages fluttered all around me. "Fuck you, Travis," I said. "You scared the shit out of me."

"Well, fuck you too," he said, laughing. "I don't have my pages numbered."

"I'm sorry I dropped it," I said.

"How about reading it?" he smiled.

"No. No, I'm really not sorry about that." I thought for a minute. "I should be."

"Yes, you should," said Travis. He was on the floor trying to preserve the order of his manuscript, which luckily had fanned out and could be set back in order in a few stacks with a only a handful of rogue pages.

"I'll go get the food on," I said.

"All right." Travis stood up. "I'll light a fire."

"Travis," I said. I fixed his collar, which really didn't need fixing. "What happened to Bobby Whitefoot?"

"I can't tell you that. Can I?"

"She killed him, didn't she? Angeline did."

"You'll have to wait until the book's finished."

"What happened at Bear Creek?"

"Darling . . ."

"Come on, Travis. You can tell me."

"It's a story, Katherine. I make this stuff up."

"What happens to Dan?"

"Did you like it?"

"*Angeline?*"

"Yes, Ma'am."

"I found it fascinating. Now answer the question. What happens to Dan?"

"To tell you truth, I don't know yet. But I have a hunch nothing good comes of his love for Angeline. A woman like that is trouble and that's just the way it has to be."

"Reader expectation?" I asked.

"Life," he replied.

Arthur was home by eight. He swung the door open happily. He was carrying a bunch of flowers that I knew he'd picked out himself—sunflowers, teddy-bear chrysanthemums, starburst lilies, and a huge pink English rose.

"Katherine!" he said. Kevin was jumping all over him and I had to rescue the flowers. "Why didn't you answer the phone? I've been calling since five."

"We have to get caller ID," I said. "I thought anyone who was that persistent had to be Boris."

"I wanted you to come into town and meet the band. We went out for a few drinks."

"Did you bring me something?"

"A twenty-dollar bottle of red wine."

"Well, I'm happy for you. And I hope this turns into something both fun and lucrative. And the flowers are gorgeous." I smiled.

"Are you okay?"

"I've had a headache this afternoon, but it's gone now."

Arthur put the bottle of wine on the counter. He took off his jacket and I could see the fold lines on his new shirt. There was even a pin poking out of the collar tab.

"Where'd you get the shirt?"

"Levinsky's. Sleeves are a bit short, but it was only twelve dollars."

"I am happy, and happy for you. Open that bottle and I'll perk right up."

Arthur pulled out the cork and got the glasses down from the cabinet. "Where's Travis?"

"Travis," I said, "hitchhiked into Portland and is taking the Greyhound back to Texas."

"Really? Why?"

"We had a bit of a misunderstanding," I said.

"What happened?"

"He was getting a little too interested in me and I thought it was better if he headed home. Arthur, nothing happened, but if he'd stayed here, it would have been rather awkward." I found the cigarettes in Arthur's jacket pocket and lit one. "We left on good terms. No one's angry at anyone and he said to keep in touch. I even helped him out with the bus ticket."

"Wow," said Arthur.

"Did you like Travis?"

"Travis is a trip. He's so, I don't know, cowboy."

"Yes."

"But hey," said Arthur, shaking me by the shoulders, "it's just the two of us. What a novelty."

"What a treat."

Arthur sat down to learn a couple of tunes, because he had a practice the next day and a wedding the day after that. The wedding was in Boston and the payment was a thousand dollars, to be split among four musicians. "And they play in town at Brian Boru's on Thursdays and usually somewhere else during the week. We have at least one gig every weekend into March. Even some Christmas parties. One New Year's Eve thing in town, where we're making double."

"Timely," I said. "We'll be rich."

"I needed something, after what happened to Intravenous . . ."

"What happened to Intravenous?"

"Park stopped showing up for practice," Arthur said. "You knew that. I told you when you were in Mexico."

"You did?" I said.

"He wasn't a real musician anyway."

"Just rich," I said. I brought Arthur a bowl of stew and he started eating.

"Katherine," he said, "you haven't said much about Travis."

"There's not much to say."

"I don't want you to keep things from me."

"Why would I do that?"

"Because of my good news. You might be waiting for another time."

"Don't be crazy," I said. "Your food's getting cold."

Arthur took another mouthful and looked me straight in the eyes. "Are you happy here, with me?" he asked.

"You are the one thing that makes me happy," I said.

"Good stew," he said.

I shrugged. "It needs those little onions and more tomato."

Arthur ate quickly. I watched him. I'd already eaten and I was trying to finish the bottle of wine.

"What is this anyway?" he asked.

"Veal."

"Good stuff," said Arthur. "Come here, Kevin. I even saved you a piece." Kevin came over and sniffed the meat, but he refused to eat it. "Don't you like veal?" Arthur asked.

"Maybe he's too P.C.," I said, "to eat the milk-fed stuff."

Sunday was the day Arthur had the gig in Boston. It was an evening wedding and he didn't have to be in Boston until eight. The band was leaving Portland at 4:30, but at around ten A.M. the sky turned gray, the temperature dropped, and the first of the snowflakes began to fall. I got a phone call from someone named Eamon telling Arthur to be in town in the next two hours so they could leave. The worst of the storm was supposed to hit at around two. Arthur hadn't laundered his one good shirt, so it went straight into the wash.

Arthur carefully packed up his violin. He had four extras for every string, as he had a tendency to break them when he was excited. "The weather's turning to shit. What if I get stuck in Boston?"

"I have food, candles. There's even firewood."

"It's not the storm I'm worried about."

"You're still thinking about Johnny."

"Aren't you?"

"Yes," I said. "But what are you going to do? Stay?" I rested my hands on Arthur's shoulders. "I have Kevin to keep me company and if I hear something, I'll call the police right away."

I was reading *Typee*. I'd enjoyed *Moby-Dick* a great deal in a few places (and been tortured in many others) so I'd decided to give Melville another try. Besides, the tropical climate—despite its privations—

was an indulgence, given the darkening skies and arctic temperatures. Arthur was waiting to put his shirt in the dryer. He was hovering around the washing machine, when it finally shuddered to a halt. I heard the lid to the washer clang open and the door to the dryer slam shut. Then nothing. Then Arthur was standing in the living room and he looked concerned.

"What's wrong?" I asked.

"Travis's clothes. They're in the dryer."

"We'll have to send them to him," I said, and looked back at my book.

"Katherine, don't you find this a little strange?"

I pushed my reading glasses up my nose and shrugged. "He left in a hurry."

"Katherine there are four shirts in there and two pairs of jeans." Arthur made it sound like a question.

"Why do I feel like I'm in an episode of *Scooby Doo*?"

Arthur cocked his head to one side. "Travis only had five shirts and three pairs of jeans. That's all he had with him."

"How do you know that?"

"He made such of production of washing and ironing everything. How could you miss it?"

Arthur was right. I did know all of Travis's clothes—his five shirts, his two pairs of blue jeans, one dark indigo, one slightly more faded with a noticeable crease line, one black pair.

"His underwear and socks are in the dryer too."

"Which means?"

"Which means that he left with only the clothes he was wearing. Did he bring his suitcase?"

"Yes."

"I wonder what he had in it?"

"His manuscript?"

"And no clothes?" Arthur scratched his head. "Did he take the typewriter with him?"

"I'm pretty sure he did," I said. "It's not in the room anymore."

"Do you have a phone number for him?"

"Somewhere." I took off my reading glasses, resigned and having lost my place. "When you get back, we'll call him." I looked out the window where the snow was just beginning to stick to the branches of the trees. "You're going to have to get going pretty soon."

"I'm still waiting for my shirt to dry. Do you have Travis's number handy?"

"I'm sure I could find it," I said. "But he's going all the way to Texas. He's probably still on the road."

Arthur nodded.

"I wouldn't want to get his mother on the phone." I got up from the couch and gave Arthur a big hug. "When did you become such a worrywart?"

"Maybe when Johnny was killed on the back deck?"

"I think you're just nervous about performing with a new band. And all that new material. You'll do great. If it wasn't somebody's wedding, I'd go with you."

Arthur seemed to accept this, but a part of him was still bothered. I was worried about him, really. I'm not usually one to buy into this stuff, but I thought his artistic temperament left him less able to deal with Johnny's death. I ironed Arthur's shirt for him. I wished him luck. I waved through the thickening snow as his van sputtered down the drive and disappeared at the bend in the road, where a clump of dead bittersweet was turning a beautiful, crystallized blue.

Winter had been cold until then, but that snowstorm marked the beginning of a season of such ferocious temperatures and obscene precipitation that soon all the land around was blunted and smoothed into sugary mounds. The roads and pathways became tunnels. Kevin would leap into the snow and find himself submerged, his nose poking above the surface like a periscope. He was startled everyday by this, and I was too. I began to think the snow would never melt. Shackleton must have felt this way, and Franklin. Sometimes I'd take a wrong turn and find myself, after negotiating the drive, at someone else's house. The very sameness of the landscape was disturbing. Christmas came and went. And we celebrated, burrowed in our little bungalow like merry chipmunks. Arthur's band had a following now. In this meat locker of a winter, sitting in a bar listening to Pogue's covers and drinking thick, bloody Guinness was the only soothing activity. When he wasn't at the bars, Arthur played at parties. This new band liked its beer, but they were drug-free and hard-working. Busy, busy. And as with all people who have known the ache of an impoverished life, Arthur never said no to work. For New Year's, I went to New York to visit Boris.

Boris and I were married in the courthouse. Ann, out of some masochistic need, was there to witness, as was Boris's lawyer, the mountain-climbing Rand Randley. To celebrate, the four of us went out for dinner, then back to Boris's apartment for drinks. Rand had some papers for me to look over. Apparently, Silvano had left me everything, which had been contested, successfully, by his family. I could have fought them, but felt that it would have been in bad taste. Boris and I fought, passionately, over that. But I stood my ground. Still, there was some paperwork. I would take some jewelry, I decided, and his family—represented by his sister Laura—thought it was fair (or maybe unfair) that I should get it (a necklace worked in gold with blue diamonds and matching earrings; a heavy gold cuff; an amusing, neck-wrenching tiara) so that I wouldn't start going after the other stuff: the house in the Oltrano, the leather business, a set of apartments in Sesto Fiorentino, and a villa in Fiesole that had been rented to the University of Oregon for the last thirty years. It was my wedding day, but I thought that as long as Rand was there, it was a good time to go over the papers. We sat at the dining room table, while Ann and Boris argued in the living room. I think they were arguing over whether or not her manager was doing a good job of selling her work. She thought he was. And Boris was telling her that she should expect more from her agent, from life in general. She needed to start standing her ground.

Rand brought out his briefcase all the same and with a smile and look of determination (indicative of the same attitude that allowed him to scale numerous mountains) he clicked it open and began handing me papers—some in Italian—which I was supposed to read and sign.

I spent a minute looking over each of the papers, understanding nothing, then signed and handed them back. When I was done Rand shuffled the papers together, then with a neat tap on the table, got them into a perfect stack. This stack, the last of my love with Silvano, was then put into an envelope to be sent back to Italy, which is where the love had flourished in the first place.

"Whatever happened to Cosimo?" I asked, a little sad to be losing my last ties to Italy.

"Cosimo?"

"Silvano's dog, that little Italian greyhound. Remember?"

"The dog?"

"Remember Silvano's neck?"

"Oh. That dog." Rand raised his eyebrows and nodded a couple of times. "Laura Falconi wanted to take it. She had some affection for the animal. She said it was as if Silvano lived on, a part of the dog. But in the end they had to put it down."

"Really?"

"The dog, Cosimo, had gone a bit nutty. It attacked her."

"Cosimo?"

"In fact, it attacked several people."

This was humorous, because Cosimo couldn't have weighed more than seven pounds. I imagined Cosimo flying at people's necks, their round-eyed surprise, their desperate flailing. "I guess once he tasted the forbidden flesh, there was no stopping him."

I meant that as a joke, but Rand didn't laugh. He nodded in a sincere way and I was forced to look around the corners of the room.

"The odd thing is that he only went after women. One of the police officers. Laura Falconi. Ann." Rand raised his eyebrows and nodded. "Cosimo hated women."

"Really. So they put him down." I lit a cigarette. Poor Cosimo. The world was a dangerous place. "He would never have eaten Silvano if he wasn't really hungry. I wouldn't be surprised if they just put him down because he made them uncomfortable, the cannibal-ism and all."

Rand gave it some thought. "Not that the dog really was a can-nibal, because Silvano wasn't his species. Besides, there's no law against cannibalism in New York."

"How strange."

"In fact, the only state with a law against cannibalism is Idaho, and that was only passed in 1990."

"Really."

"The last person to be tried for cannibalism was Alfred Packer."

"Alfred Packer. Wasn't he a guide or something?"

"Yes. Something. He was originally convicted of five counts of murder, but this was eventually reduced to one count of manslaugh-ter. He died a free man."

"Is that what they teach you in law school?"

"In part. Cannibalism horrifies people. In law school, we are taught to apply reason—the law—to a variety of unsavory things. The Speluncean Explorers, for example, is an invention of law school, where you look at the moral implications of cannibalism and survival."

"In what way?"

"If, hypothetically, explorers are lost in a cave and there only hope for survival is cannibalism . . . How does the law view that?"

"But it's all hypothetical, of course."

"Not necessarily. In maritime law, you have the Custom of the Sea. You're in a boat adrift in the Pacific. You draw lots. The loser gets to be dinner. That sort of thing."

"And that's legal?"

"Yes. Yes it is."

"Really." The needs of appetite justified everything.

"There's a famous case. Regina versus Dudley and Stephens. Captain Dudley was a cannibal. They ate the cabin boy, Richard Parker. Poe even wrote a story about it."

25

Rand Randley's assertion that Poe was inspired by the events of the *Mignonette* is not quite true. I read *The Narrative of Arthur Gordon Pym* as a child, a book that I devoured along with all the other writings of Poe. Edgar Allan Poe's horror appealed to me, and as I've grown older, I've reached a deeper appreciation of his torments. Poe does write of four men in a boat set adrift in the Pacific as the result of a cruel storm. The men draw lots and the loser is the cabin boy, Richard Parker. But the Poe novel, *The Narrative of Arthur Gordon Pym*, was written in 1838, whereas the sinking of the *Mignonette* (the yacht on which Captain Dudley and the unlucky Richard Parker were crew) did not happen until 1884. The fictional account precedes the reality by forty-six years—a shocking coincidence—the stuff of a Poe story itself. But, as with most things, the reality was more shocking than its fictional counterpart. Reality never has to contend, as art does, with beauty.

My mother told me the story of Thomas Dudley. He had been trying to make it to Sydney, Australia, from Falmouth on the southwest tip of England. His goal had been 120 miles a day, 120 days for the journey. A yacht was small for the distance—the feat the first of its kind. Dudley had difficulty assembling a crew and the yacht had to be refitted for racing since it had once been a fishing vessel. The *Mignonette* was twenty years old. Her timbers were suspect, although a shipwright had decided that—with a few repairs—they were adequate for the journey. An Australian, Jack Want, had paid for the *Mignonette* and her transportation. A lawyer, a politician, and now a yachtsman, Want had already angered the gentlemen yachters with his disregard for the more traditional aspects of the sport. Maybe they had conspired to have him purchase an inferior craft. Dudley was a working man who admired the audacity of Want and hoped that the *Mignonette* would win Want many prizes when it was outfitted once more in Sydney. Outfitted for speedily hugging the coastline and winning trophies, not for carving a path across the Pacific.

Ned Brooks and Edwin Stephens were not his first choices for the crew. Others had quit because of the state of the boat, but Brooks and Stephens had committed because Dudley was a fair man. Their rations were not to be the typical salt horse floating in brine, dubious food rejected by the Royal Navy, occasional meat that concealed hoofs and often an equine eyeball. No. Dudley had suffered among the lower ranks before acquiring his captain's certificate and was determined to feed his men better. Pork until it ran out, and after that tinned beef. The only privation on his boat was the absence of spirits which, in his opinion, made men wild and undermined discipline. Spirits reduced men to animals in thrall to appetite.

Richard Parker had not needed the added lure of good provisioning. He was only seventeen, although he claimed to be a year older, and found adventure enough to sign him on. He would be the cabin boy. A cabin boy on a boat so small with a crew of only four seemed a luxury or an encumbrance, depending on how you felt. But to maintain discipline Dudley believed that a hierarchy was necessary. A cabin boy gave a tautness to the pecking order. And Dudley believed in order, an order that was based on character, knowledge, and hard work, an order that once he was in Australia would serve him well. Then he would send for Phillippa and the children. Phillippa would be freed from the classroom, where the wealthy children learned their letters and numbers. Dudley had taught himself how to read. This process was such a torture that he had no admiration for it. Maybe he would teach Richard Parker to read, save him the indignity of illiteracy, save him the pain of figuring out the letters on his own. The boy reminded him of himself, growing up on the seas, filled with hunger for the unknown.

Dudley would offer the boy a job in Sydney. His heart was that generous.

Dudley was sailing not only from Falmouth to Sydney, but also out of the working class—with poverty lurking between every job, in every trough, the spirit crying out on the battering, deadly waves—and into the mercantile class.

Thomas Dudley did make it to Australia, the pioneer of plague victims. I wonder if he thought about Richard Parker when the bloody phlegm burst from his nose. Blood, precious fluid, because that's what they'd been after. And Dudley would have seen the look on the doctor's face, the face of the living looking at the damned. Dudley recognized that look.

He had seen it in Ned Stephens's face as he gazed at the pitiful Parker while he did his best to sharpen his knife on the oar housings of the boat. Parker would have been dead within the day but they needed his blood, uncongealed, to slake their thirst. They couldn't wait for this leisurely wasting—although it seemed to be God's intention. Did God really intend for Dudley's children to go to the workhouse, because if he died Phillippa's meager earnings would not be enough to save them from this fate. Stropping the knife, Dudley watched the horizon and hoped for the blurring that would alert him to a ship, but there was none. Is this how Abraham felt as he prepared his sacrifice? Or maybe . . . Who was to say that Parker was Isaac and not the lamb sent in his place? Parker was the lamb and with his sacrifice Dudley would save his children from the workhouse.

Rhetoric of a weak mind, yes, but Dudley was starved and his brain, that gorgeous wrinkled mass of reason, was shrunk to a peach pit. He could almost hear it rattling in his skull with the boat's every rise and fall.

And then his resolve had faltered. "We should draw lots."

"Draw lots?" Brooks said. "And risk murdering a man? Because surely as I am sitting here, that boy is more in death than life. Save him the suffering and save us others."

Dudley turned to Stephens. "What are your thoughts?"

"I wish to live," he said. His voice was a whisper because his tongue had fisted in his mouth.

Dudley too wished to live. Parker was somewhere in the pale. He had been drinking sea water and was now insensible. Was that a bad thing on this hour on this day? The task had fallen to Dudley, because one journey long ago had left him an experienced butcher of pigs.

As Dudley lay dying, he still heard the sounds of that moment, the wash of waves, the stropping of the knife, the rasp of Parker's breath as his eyes flew open—mostly whites—and held Dudley's gaze. I am a man, the eyes said. I am a child.

Dudley had related his story to all who cared to listen (solicitors, family members, Parker's kin) in a candid, frank manner because he believed himself to be innocent of any crime. Innocent people did not hide their actions because—no matter how vile—these were still actions and not transgressions. There was a precedent for his behavior. Was it not the custom of the sea? And in the last few decades there had been other cases much like his: the *Nancy*, the *Euxine*, the *Essex*. And although the survivors of the *Peggy* had suffered through a trial, had they not been found innocent in the end?

What the case revolved around was the fact that he and his crew did not draw lots. The issue was not that Dudley *was* a cannibal, but rather that he *was not* a gambler. Brooks, his crew member, was not involved in the suit. He lied, said that he was curled in the prow of the boat protesting all the while, and that after the vile act, he only drank a little blood. Dudley had been forced to relive the whole horror in the courtroom: the great league-high wave moving through the ocean; the keelwood springing open like a fist laid flat; the menacing snap of the shark's jaws and crack of the oar across its head; the brief sweetness of the turnips. And Richard Parker.

"He was very low," Dudley said, addressing the court, but he still remembered the feel of the boy's hair in his left fist, and the knife handle in his right.

The queen withheld pardon, even when all of England, Parker's own brother included, forgave him. How could she keep him in Holloway prison while she deliberated at leisure? And what about this cell, this isolation, was better than transportation as a convict? Dudley would have leaped at the chance to make the journey once more— successfully—to Australia, even if manacled. Anything was better than this merciless silence. Somewhere in this prison was his co-conspirator, Stephens, that poor man. He had welcomed Stephens onto his boat because of the man's sense of humor, his tremendous winking, chuckling, warm presence, the way he delivered all the off-color jokes out of the side of his mouth, the way none of the jokes made sense but how you didn't realize it until you were already laughing. In the silence of Holloway, Dudley thought he heard Stephens's low chuckle. He said,

"Regina rhymes with vagina."

He said, "Tell you what, if the Queen had been in the boat with us, we sure as heaven and hell would not have eaten Parker."

This had made Dudley smile and he wondered if his madness, these simple soothing conversations, weren't actually real. If this deep silence made it possible to hear the thoughts of other men.

But the pardon did come through and the cheering crowds returned—the same supportive, multiheaded beast that had been there every step of the trial, cheering him forward through the papers, coughing up their ha'pennies and tuppences for his defense. He was a local hero. Because didn't everybody love a cannibal? Wasn't he already half-formed at Madame Tussaud's Wax Museum?

Australia did not care if he was "Cannibal Tom." In Australia you could shake hands with a ship owner only later to learn that his first journey to the new world was in the hold, chained to his other companions. Australia was as forgiving to its transported hoodlums as it was cruel to the natives—blackies out by the pier stumbling around, their veins flowing with gin. These natives, so-called cannibals, who couldn't catch a slow-moving wombat and make a meal from it, even less a more sophisticated quarry.

*   *   *

I remember asking my mother why she thought this tale fitting—important, even—to tell me. I was ten years old at the time.

"Because he persevered. He survived tremendous odds. He made a new life for himself." I can still see her stubbing out her cigarette. "Never lose hope," she added.

I found her reasoning funny. What was I supposed to come away with? That a world where one could escape hanging for cannibalism only to die famously of bubonic plague was a place suffused with hope? Maybe not. But now, when I think of Dudley, I remember that one's story is never over, never finished, never predictable until one is absolutely dead.

26

The day the bed was delivered, Boris was nowhere to be found. He had tagged the furniture to be moved from the bedroom with yellow Post-its—the Shaker-style bed, the matching nightstands, a modern torchiere—and, most remarkably, the cedar chest that housed thousands of pages of manuscript. He said that he intended to mark his new life with new material, as if I had nothing to do with the new life at all. Ann arrived shortly before the movers, at ten in the morning.

"Where's Boris?" she said.

"Good morning, Ann."

She swept past me and into the living room. A fire was roaring in the grate, which made a convenient ashtray for her. "I suppose he didn't want to be here when the movers got here. I'll have to supervise." She marched into the bedroom, leaving me alone in my socks and Boris's T-shirt. "When's the bed arriving?"

"At noon," I said.

Ann came back out of the bedroom and took a long drag on her cigarette. "This apartment's smoky as hell. I thought Boris wasn't going to light another fire until he had the flue checked."

I shrugged.

"You should get dressed, unless you want the movers seeing you like that."

"I'll dress. You make coffee."

Boris and Ann shared a storage space in Williamsburg, and that's where the extra furniture was going. Ann had some of her larger canvases there and, of all things, life-sized ceramic figures left over from a brief and unappreciated phase in the mid-seventies. Boris had said something frightening and odd the night before about moving out to Long Island or Westchester or Connecticut, somewhere where he could have all his furniture. He'd also said something about children, which he'd quickly replaced with the possibility of owning a dog. Or maybe a cat. He was undecided; he was drinking. I pulled on a pair of jeans. Ann made very good coffee and I was looking forward to drinking it and smoking, without Boris sending me out of the building or up to the roof.

"Did Boris say when he'd be back?"

"I wasn't up when he left."

"Did he leave any money for the movers?"

"I doubt it," I said.

"Typical," Ann responded. She shook her head, but I could tell that she was pleased that she would have to take charge.

The bed was supposed to be me my wedding gift. Giving your significantly younger wife a bed seemed, if nothing else, in poor taste. In addition the bed was a monstrosity. I'm not sure what wood it was carved from, but it was a dense, grainless variety. The bed weighed close to a ton. A dark, universal stain soaked all the wood, inexplicably sticky in places; Boris said this was due to an ancient resin sealing process, which sounded plausible, although invented. The bed was almost a four-poster. Almost, because the proportions were off, and after some thought it was obvious that at one time the bed had had a canopy, now sawed off. The posts twisted around themselves in a sort of mannerist-meets-Willy-Wonka style. At the termini of these posts was more of the "ancient resin," which was now looking like a bold attempt at fakery. Was the thing an antique? Most likely. Was it what Boris hoped, an unappreciated Renaissance work of art? Not possible, although certain parts had been cobbled together from a time long gone. And, thrill of thrills, on one of the short stumpy legs there was evidence of the woodworm.

A mattress would have to be specially ordered, and until the thing arrived, we would make do with a futon that bent up at the end, too long by half a foot.

The movers were late, of course, and when the bed arrived they were still struggling with the cedar chest.

"What the hell's in here?" asked the younger one.

"A life's achievement," I said and smiled.

"What are you smirking about?" asked Ann as she stood by the window. She had been watching the sidewalk on and off for the past hour, waiting for Boris to make an appearance.

"I am not smirking, Ann. I am smiling. Happy people do this."

The bed was now filling the hallway. The movers and deliverers were in a heated discussion, first in English, then in Spanish.

"What a disaster," said Ann, pleased.

"I'm going to take a shower."

"Now?" Ann disapproved.

"Yes."

"Is that your solution for everything?"

I had no idea how she'd come to this conclusion. "No. Drinking takes care of most things." I studied her studying me, neither of us impressed. "My plane leaves in two hours. I'm already running late."

"And what about Boris?"

"What about Boris?"

"Aren't you going to wait for him?"

"He knows what time my plane leaves. I have to close up the house, pack my things." I folded my arms; I was not backing down. "If he wants to spend an entire day shopping for cheese, or whatever else it is that he's doing, that's hardly my fault, is it?"

When the car service showed up, the bed was stuck in the hall, one of its resinated posts lost in the ceiling tile, an ominous shower of electric sparks raining down from the hole. I had to crawl on my belly, dragging my bag, to get under it. Just as the elevator arrived, a cloud of smoke (defective flue) billowed into the hall and smoke detectors began to buzz from many different sectors. I think Ann was yelling at me, but I didn't listen. I felt free, more free than I had in months, and was nothing but happy to be leaving.

By the time I got to Newark the sky was a threatening purple. Huge, cottony cloud banks were piled up, giving the sky a deeper dimension—less of a blue flatness—walls of cloud that I imagined might hide an angry God: bolt-wielding, fickle Zeus, or Hephaestus (god of blacksmiths, gimps, and cuckolds) himself. Perhaps not the best day for flying, but probably better than snow. The flight was delayed a half hour, which was normal. I called Arthur first.

"Is everything all right?" I asked.

"Not exactly," he said, "but it can wait until you get here."

"What's wrong?"

Arthur paused. "The leak in the bathroom seems to be getting worse."

Which probably meant that the house was getting ready to break free from its moorings and float off to Turkey, like Noah's ark.

I still had five minutes before my flight boarded, so I decided—in a generous moment—to call Boris's apartment to see what was going on. Ann picked up the phone on the first ring.

"Boris?"

"Katherine. I guess Boris never showed up."

"I'm worried."

"He did this the day of his party. He'll be there in a couple of hours, with Chinese takeout."

"He would be here to see his bed arrive. He would be here, Katherine. I'm calling the police."

"Ann, relax. You can't call the police anyway."

"Why not?"

"Actually, you can call them, but they won't do anything for two days."

"How do you know?"

"*Law and Order.*" There was a pause here as Ann lit a cigarette and I wished I could. "Ann, I don't know why you're so worried. I really don't. Boris is fifty years old. He's been gone, for what, four and a half hours? Is that really so unusual?"

"I trust my instincts. I'm going to look for him." And she hung up.

Arthur came and got me at the airport. I'd offered to take a cab, but he wouldn't let me. His van was at the curb, engine running. He'd decided against driving my Rabbit because of the hole in the floor. Everything was flooding and the world was loud—trickling, splatting, drumming water and the thump-wump of the wipers. Kevin was nervous, whining on the seat between us, his eye whiskers twitching with concern.

"All the snow is melting," said Arthur. "A lot of places are in a state of national emergency."

"Ah, federal relief." I rubbed my head. "I'd settle for an ibuprofen."

"How was New York?"

I shrugged. "I got married."

"To Boris?"

"Are you angry?"

"No," Arthur looked in the rearview mirror and then the side mirror. He stayed in his lane. "I think it's sexy. You're a married woman. I'm your boy toy."

I started laughing. I grabbed his hand and held it. "I'm glad I'm home. Sometimes I get so . . . tired."

"From doing what?"

"I'm not really sure."

"You seem sad," he said.

"Oh I am, a bit."

"Why? Am I not enough for you?"

"Of course you are." I rested my head on the window. "Yesterday was my mother's fiftieth birthday."

"Tough day for you?"

"No, actually. I forgot. I forgot it was her birthday until this morning. I should have done something for her."

"It's not too late," Arthur said. "I'm sure she wouldn't mind."

"No, she'd understand, and that almost makes it worse."

Arthur nodded. He thought he understood, which was fine with me. "What is it with you and your mother?"

For a moment I was transported back to the hospital. I saw my mother lying in the bed surrounded by stern-faced nurses, my father's own grim face, the lights bleeping all around her. "Her illness is frightening. Sometimes I worry that I'll get it. I'll find myself in the hospital, unable to eat, starved to skin and bone. She was such a beautiful woman, but last time I saw her she just looked old."

"I thought she had lupus."

"She does."

"But you just said . . ."

"Are you listening? Because that's all I need right now. Not an inquisition."

"I'm sorry."

"Sometimes lupus attacks the nervous system. Sometimes it makes people irrational and violent. My mother hallucinates."

"Doesn't it just give her headaches and make her tired?"

"Usually," I said. "She has a rare form of the disease." I looked out the window and Arthur knew enough to keep quiet, that the conversation was over.

Boris had gone missing on a Tuesday. On Thursday, Ann called the police. And she called me. Almost hourly. I was involved in a constant battle against the rising water. The basement was flooded to my knees, the floor of the house was squishy, the bathroom one big, cold shower. I left my towel on a chair outside the door. I had to run from hot water through cold water, or use the umbrella. I wore a raincoat onto the toilet. The endless rain and endless ringing of the phone were conspiring to drive me crazy. But I was lucky. Many people in Maine had had to leave their homes. Animals too. The rising water table had brought an onslaught of displaced rodents, which Kevin, bless his canine heart, had taken on. After finding a mouse—dead— in my slipper with my naked foot, I had started checking all my shoes before putting them on. Still, the mice leaped from the cabinets, scuttled out from behind the coffee, scrabbled around in walls and at night, chewed at some beam right above the bed in the bedroom. Arthur and I were exhausted and Kevin's nerves worn raw. And this after only three days of rain. The forecast predicted more.

There was some sort of open gutter that ran by the side of the house like a seasonal brook. I thought it might be full of leaves so I put on my coat and went out, with Kevin, to see if there was something I could do. Arthur had gone to Builders Square to buy some tarps. He was going to tack them onto the roof over the bathroom. The rain had washed the snow off the bushes. Birds were flying around now—fish in the air. I pulled a few handfuls of composting vegetation from the gutter, but it didn't look like the gutter had been blocked. Then, while on my knees, I heard an ominous creaking. I looked up just in time to see a glacier-sized plate of snow sliding off the roof toward me. I jumped back just in time and the snow slid onto the ground with a massive boom. Kevin, whose anxiety had been a problem, was taken by surprise and shot off in the direction of the woods. Two hours later, he was still at large, and when Arthur came back from town with the tarps and some groceries, I was concerned. I had a bag of Doritos in one hand and the umbrella in the other.

"Kevin's gone," I said. "I've been calling him for ages."

"What are the Doritos for?"

"Kevin." I must have looked desparate.

"Go inside. Take a break," said Arthur. "I'll find him."

Inside, the phone was ringing again. I was feeling emotional and raw, and I suppose it made me generous. I might have some kind words for Ann, who was still searching passionately for Boris. I'd tell her that he might have gone to Russia. He had said something about his father being ill—this the father who had had two heart attacks in the last six months. Maybe Boris, in a fit of filial duty, had gone to visit him. Who knew?

I picked up the receiver. "Hello."

"Katherine. How are you?"

My hand went numb. It was not Ann who was calling. It was not Ann, but my father. My father, who I had managed to avoid for nearly two years.

"How are you?" I returned.

"I am quite well, thank you."

"Glad to hear it." There was silence. "Dad, why are you calling?"

"I understand you have suffered a loss."

"I have?"

"Silvano, your husband."

"I appreciate your sympathy but, really . . . This is not a good time for me to talk."

"Katherine. Katherine. You must talk to me. You see, I am very concerned."

I owed this intrusion to Rand Randley. Boris had given Rand my father's information back when the deed to the Hidalgo Ranch had passed into my hands. Now, Rand was in possession of Silvano's jewelry and he wanted to get it to me. Boris wasn't answering his phone because Boris wasn't there, so Rand, after a week had gone by, had thought to contact my father. My father had been reserved with Rand, but after getting off the phone with him, did a Google search on Silvano's name. I suppose after reading an article in *Newsday* (which went into splendid detail) he had thought he should call me. Parental support and all that.

"Dad, I'm all right. Really I am."

"I had my secretary look into the local Portland papers."

"Why?"

"Who is John Nelson?"

"I don't know. I've never heard of him."

"He died recently, in Maine."

"John Nelson? I swear I've never met him."

"Katherine, don't lie to me."

"John Nelson."

"He was from New Mexico."

"Oh, you mean Johnny. His last name was Nelson?" I'd always thought it had to be something like Runningdeer or Blackwater. I took the phone to the window and looked out at the deluge. "He drowned face down in a puddle. It was awful, but I'm all right now. I'm living with my boyfriend. He's a musician. We're very happy." I saw Arthur coming out of the woods. He had Kevin with him and was looking up at the house.

"I think maybe I should come visit."

"No." I said. "Out of the question."

"Katherine, we need to talk."

"No. Leave me alone. Why can't you just leave me alone?"

"Be reasonable."

"Reasonable? I don't give a fuck about 'reasonable.' I'm all grown up. I don't need you. I have my own money. I don't think you're really concerned about me and I don't know why you're calling."

"I think you know why I'm calling."

"No, I don't. I'm hanging up now."

"Don't hang up."

And I hung up.

Arthur came in with the dog, who seemed very happy to have been rescued. He ran up to me and put his muddy paws all over my jeans. I patted his head.

"Katherine," said Arthur, "are you all right?"

"I'm fucking fantastic."

"Did something happen?"

I shrugged my shoulders and was about to tell him when the phone rang again. Before I could tell him not to, Arthur answered. I waved an emphatic "no."

"Hello? No. She's not here right now," he said. "Can you repeat the name? Okay. Hold on a second." Arthur drew in the air with an invisible pen and I found him a pencil and an unopened bill to write on. "Okay. Yeah. I'll get this to her as soon as possible. I understand. Some urgency." Arthur shrugged at me. "Yes. I'm sure she'll call you right back." But Arthur did not know that at all. He looked at me with raised eyebrows. "Okay. Bye. Yeah. No problem. Bye."

He hung up the phone.

"That was my father," I said.

"No it wasn't," said Arthur. "That was," he looked at the envelope, "Barry Parkinson. Barry Buster Parkinson. Who's that?"

"My old professor," I said. I'd forgotten all about Barry and the bones.

"There's his number," said Arthur.

"I'll call him later," I said.

Arthur lit a cigarette and then headed for the door. "I'm going out again."

"Why?"

Arthur cocked his head to one side. "The snow's all melted now at the shoreline and I'm not sure, but I think I saw something out there. The tide's out."

"What was it?"

"Kevin was freaking out, so I couldn't get a good look. There was seaweed on it." Arthur looked at me gravely. "I think it was a typewriter."

Half an hour later Arthur had come walking up the point carrying the old Olympia. He set it in the center of the living room and we both had a drink and a smoke while looking at the damned thing. We were silent for some time and then Arthur said,

"Do you have Travis's number?"

"I can't find it," I said. "I don't even know Travis's last name."

"It's Connor," said Arthur. "His last name is Connor."

"How do you know that?"

"I asked him. I said, 'What's your last name? When you get famous, I'll buy your book.' And he said, 'Connor.'"

Arthur called directory assistance and after talking to two Connors—one a cousin of Travis—was soon on the phone with Travis's mother, who was wondering what had happened to her boy. They hadn't spoken since New York. Where the hell was he? Arthur was polite on the phone. He said he'd make inquiries on this end, dig around a bit. He'd call the Greyhound station, although a month had passed since Travis had hitchhiked his way out of our lives. If he heard anything, Mrs. Connor would be the first to know.

No one at the Greyhound station remembered him, but even if he'd passed through there, he wouldn't necessarily be remembered. Travis would have used cash and in addition to that, the turnover of

employees was high. Half the people who had worked there the previous month had moved on.

"He could be anywhere," I said.

"Why would he throw his typewriter into the bay? I don't like
it. Maybe we should call the police."

"And tell them what?"

"Tell them that he's disappeared."

"Maybe he hasn't disappeared. Maybe he's just gone somewhere
else."

"Isn't that what disappeared means? Isn't the ocean floor somewhere else?"

"I meant something more along the lines of Key West, or maybe
back to New York, wherever it is that writers go."

"He threw his typewriter in the bay. That's an act of desperation."

"You think he killed himself?"

Arthur considered. "He didn't seem like the type. He had a big
ego."

"I thought Travis was a cocky guy." I shrugged my shoulders.
"Maybe he did kill himself. He drank a lot."

The wind picked up suddenly and the doorway at the end the
hall, the doorway to what had been first Johnny's and then Travis's
room, slammed shut. Arthur was cracking his knuckles looking at the
typewriter. Perhaps if we put a piece of paper in it, Travis could type
out a message from wherever he was.

The typewriter sat in the middle of the room for a week until I
had enough of it and on a Tuesday, trash day, hauled it to the trash
can before Arthur was up.

The body washed up a few days after that. Hikers—trying to get a
good look at some juvenile osprey—found it out on Wolf's Neck,
across the bay. The police contacted us to see if we had any ideas.
They said they were calling all the people whose properties lined the
shore, but I was suspicious of this. Of course, they were calling us
because of Johnny, but didn't want us to be on the defensive. Arthur

immediately volunteered everything he knew about Travis and soon we were driving into Portland to identify the body, which had been lying in the water for quite some time.

The morgue was cold but not particularly gloomy. The place was brightly lit and clean. All the people rushing back and forth in their white coats, carrying various pruning shears and hack saws, actually seemed the embodiment of industry. I found the place rather cheering. Arthur kept taking his cigarettes out of his pocket, and then putting them back. I grabbed his hand and held it, which made him smile at me in a quick, forced way. I let him have his hand back and he started drumming on his knees with his forefingers, until they were finally ready for us. I walked bravely to the window, but Arthur hung back. Detective Yancy was there, but I didn't recognize the officer he was with. The two men stood patiently, waiting for some verdict.

"Arthur, come take a look." I turned to Detective Yancy. "That's not Travis."

Arthur looked, and turned quickly, sickened. "How can you tell?" The corpse was badly rotted.

"Arthur, look again."

Arthur took a deep breath and came back to the glass. He was thoughtful for a minute, deep in concentration. Then he nodded to me. "I've never seen that guy. He's taller than Travis by half a foot."

"And the clothes are all wrong," I added. "This isn't Travis at all."

No doubt Detective Yancy was deeply disappointed. And he was faced with having to identify the body. Maybe some other luckless soul's life had quit on his watch. But maybe, glimmer of hope to him, we were lying. However, after the autopsy was finished, the man was thought to be older than Travis, in his forties. Not only that, but he'd been in the water a long time. The coroner suspected he'd been dead since early November. An expert from the FBI was coming up from Washington to make a final assessment.

"Key West," I whispered to Arthur.

*   *   *

Maybe a week after that, on a Thursday, I was walking with Kevin in the woods when I saw a police car out on the road. I wouldn't have been able to see it, but the leaves had only just started springing out on the branches. Instinctively I knew that the car was headed for the house.

I called to Kevin, but he didn't come. I could see the plume of his white tail disappearing into a ditch. I called him again. I figured he'd gone after a rabbit. I'd get him later. I walked up the slope to the house and sure enough, the police car was rounding the gravel drive.

Detective Yancy and Officer Brown got out of the car. I feared the worst, that soon the property would be crawling with police. Officer Brown and Detective Yancy went straight to the front door but I caught up with them before they could ring the bell.

"To what do I owe this pleasure?" I asked.

"Good morning, Miss Shea. How are you?" asked Detective Yancy.

"Never been better."

"I'll be needing to have a few words with you and with Mr. Verhoven."

"He's asleep."

"At ten o'clock in the morning?"

"He works nights. He's a musician. What is this about?"

"You don't mind if I have a look around, do you?" said Detective Yancy. He had his hand on the doorknob.

"What is going on?" I turned to Officer Brown, who looked deeply embarrassed.

"Mrs. Connor, Travis Connor's mother, has filed a missing persons report," he said.

"He's not here," I said. I opened the door and the two policemen followed me in. "I'll wake Arthur up."

Detective Yancy had picked up my copy of *Typee* and was looking at the cover.

"Is that necessary?" I asked.

The detective handed the book absentmindedly to Officer Brown, who smiled at me sheepishly.

"What's it about?" he asked.

I took the book from him without answering and set it back down on the counter. "Wait here," I said.

Arthur was just waking up when I entered the room. "What's going on?" he asked.

"Our two favorite policemen are back. They're looking for Travis."

"But he's not here," said Arthur, still half asleep.

"Go tell them that. They want to look around."

"Okay," said Arthur.

"Oh, and Kevin's run off again."

"Great."

I handed Arthur his jeans, which he put on without underwear. "Cigarettes are on the fridge."

Back in the kitchen Detective Yancy was helping himself to some burned coffee. "I hope you don't mind," he said.

"Make yourself at home," I replied. I sat down at the kitchen table. "Arthur will be here as soon as he's had a chance to use the bathroom."

We didn't have much to say about Travis. Arthur told the police about the typewriter and about how Travis's clothes had been in the washer and dryer. He asked how Mrs. Connor was doing and told Detective Yancy how he hoped we'd find Travis soon, that if we heard from Travis, we'd let them know right away. Arthur had even written down the date that Travis had left, worried that he might forget. We all went to stand in the room at the end of the hall—once Johnny's, then Travis's—where Detective Yancy took note of the pile of bottles. Then Arthur asked if it was okay if he went to look for Kevin and Detective Yancy said that would be fine. He had a sly look on his face and I knew that he wanted to talk to me alone, away from Arthur. Then he would probably talk to Arthur alone, away from me. Then compare our stories. I knew what they were up to.

When Arthur had located Kevin's leash and a lighter that worked, he took off for the woods. And I sat down for my chat with Detective Yancy.

There was a tense, silent few minutes. We all looked at each other, then finally I said, "Did you ever find out whose body that was?"

"We're very close," said Detective Yancy. "We should know in a couple of days. How does that make you feel?"

"Me feel? I'm curious, but I suppose everyone is."

"Did Travis say anything to you, anything at all, the day he left?"

"He said several things, none of any importance."

"What were these things?" Detective Yancy nodded to Officer Brown, who began scribbling in his notepad.

"Well, when he got up and we ran into each other in the hall, he said 'Good morning.' Later, he asked me if we had any half-and-half. I said we'd run out, causing him to respond, 'Remind me to get some when I go out.'"

Half an hour later, I was still relating whatever inanities I could think of when the front door popped open and slammed shut. I waited for Arthur to appear, but it was only Kevin, alone and muddy. I figured that Arthur must be taking off his boots outside. Kevin's front paws were caked with mud. He looked like he was wearing a pair of galoshes.

"Look's like you've been digging for something," said Officer Brown, scratching under Kevin's chin.

Suddenly I heard the sound of Arthur's van start up, which, after a moment, I heard taking off down the drive.

"Where's your boyfriend going?" asked Detective Yancy.

I looked over at the door, then back at Yancy. I managed a smile. "Arthur," I said, "is going to the store."

27

I suppose it's in the nature of some men to take off without saying why, to romp at their leisure. Women are supposed to accept this—it's only natural, and has something to do with the need for men to inseminate wildly in order to keep the species going, while the girls stay close to home. But I knew Arthur well enough to understand that he would not take off without telling me why unless it was perfectly justified. He would return, I was sure, and make his explanations. Or maybe he wouldn't tell me what he'd been up to, and that would be better, as in the Tale of Bisclaveret. My mother always said that that the truth was not for everyone.

The Tale of Bisclaveret, from the Lays of Marie de France, is possibly, next to the tale of Lycaon, the most widely known tale of a werewolf, although there are many. Werewolves, werejackals, werefoxes, and other werebeasts (if you include American Indian lore, you end up with everything from werecougars to werecrows) crop up in literature reaching far east and far west until they are touching at the far side of the globe. We love anything that weds man to animal, our chest-beating men of the jungle, our paw-shaking dogs on the hearth.

Our tale begins in Brittany where Bisclaveret, noble baron, and his comely wife live in their imposing castle where, no doubt, the constant drafts shiver the tapestries and blazing torches cast long shadows on the sooted stone and winding stairways. Bisclaveret and his wife retire peacefully—or passionately—to their bed four nights a week. But the other three nights, the baron is at large.

"Don't ask me why," the baron tells his wife.

But of course she asks and asks and asks. She cries pitifully, plies him with wine. She lures him to their bed and kisses him sweetly until finally he divulges his secret. It is not the bar wench in the next village, which would have been acceptable to the wife—she could have demanded the end of such an affair. Bisclaveret is a werewolf. He spends those three mysterious days roaming in secret, hidden by the eternal night of the forest.

"How is such a transformation accomplished?" she asks, the horror clear on her face.

"I have no control over the wolf. It asserts itself and I must follow. I remove my robes and soon become woolly, toothy, close to the ground."

"And how do you return?" she asks, her icy fingers knitting at the edge of the blanket, her husband's naked body warm beside her.

"At the close of the third day I return to where I've placed my robes," the baron, still huffing and puffing, replies. "It is clothes that make the man."

If he should not find his clothing, he would be unable to make the transformation back.

Life in the castle does not return to normal. The hogs still snort in the yard. Young men still practice at swords and jousting. Knights on their way east still clink goblets in drunken toasts. And minstrels still make merry music as deformed jesters leap and juggle. But as the baron feared, his wife no longer wishes to share his bed. Marie de France says, "She no longer dared lie at his side, and turned over in her mind, this way and that, how best she could get her from him."

All this time her salvation has been right before her, yes, right across the table from her winking, that knight drunkenly, putting his hot, sweaty foot on her slender leg. Never before has she found this

man attractive, but now, now that her husband has revealed himself
to be a wolf, he is suddenly handsome. She smiles slyly at him over
her grizzled lamb hock and soon the two are behind the velvet curtain in the audience chamber hatching a plan.

"There's a hollow rock beside that old chapel. Check the bushes
around the side. Bisclaveret says there's an overgrown path that should
act as a marker. Bring the robes to me. Then you can have whatever
you want."

"Your bed?" says the knight.

"My castle," says the wife.

Some time in the next week we presume that the baron is left sniff-
ing and howling beside the chapel, clawing madly at the bushes by
the hollow rock. We presume he is also cursing his wife, and rightly
so, for within the next year, the knight is married to the baroness and
living in the castle, while Bisclaveret, poor trusting soul, is left dodg-
ing arrows, eating raw rabbit, and sleeping on the cold damp ground.

Shortly after this, the (enter the king) king goes on a hunting party
and—with the help of half a dozen courtiers and a pack of borzoi—
nearly slaughters Bisclaveret. Bisclaveret is panting wildly. He has managed to outrun the dogs for two miles, but now he fears his life is spent.
With his tongue lolling out the side of his mouth, he begs for his life
by placing his paws upon the king's stirrup and well-shod foot.

"I say, look at this," says the king. "That's a nifty trick."

The courtiers lower their bows and take to whistling and clapping at the beast.

"Let's take him home," says the king. "I'll make a pet of him. I'll
be the only king with a pet wolf."

Bisclaveret knows a good thing when he sees it and behaves very
well. He does not eat the queen's spaniel and urinates only on the outer
walls of the castle. He is even allowed to sleep in the king's chamber,
although he would rather not, because those marital acts between the
king (a slight man) and his wife (formidable) are very loud.

Hearken now to that which chanced.

The king decides to throw a huge feast and invite everyone. He invites all the lords and ladies, barons and baronesses, and even that knight who's come back from Turkey with a drinking problem (and, it is rumored, syphilis) who is now married to Bisclaveret's former wife.

"Whatever happened to Bisclaveret?" the king wonders out loud, and Bisclaveret sets up such a pitiful moaning, even attempting to pantomime the robbing of his clothes, that the king is once more moved to bouncing up and down in his seat and clapping; he tosses the wolf a sugared quince then turns to the tailor, who is making some last-minute adjustments to the king's ermine cuffs, which are long by half an inch.

All day long Bisclaveret follows the king. He watches as his liege presides over the hog pen, declaring with such a merry toss of his hand, "Slaughter them all."

Bisclaveret is there when the new tapestry arrives and sits patiently for nearly an hour while the king attempts to get it hung straight. "Up on the left. No, my left. I think the whole thing's too high," he says.

Bisclaveret sits by the king's side as the barber swathes the king's face in hot towels, trims his beard to a sharp point, and drains the pus from the abscess on the king's neck.

And Bisclaveret is by the king's side as he tastes the wines from the cellar until he passes out.

By evening the guests have started to arrive and the minstrels are minstreling fervently. Bisclaveret is trying to decide on how to make his predicament clear to the king. He is still turning his various ideas over in his mind, when who should arrive but the drunkard knight and the slut who has turned his life into permanent, hairy hell. Before he knows what he is doing, Bisclaveret is at the knight's throat.

"Get that thing off me," screams the knight.

And a band of courtiers pulls him off.

"Sit," shouts the king, "bad Biscuit." And Bisclaveret sits. "I'm terribly sorry," says the king, "he's never done anything like that before."

"Why," asks the wife, "do you call that beast 'Biscuit'?"

"Funny story," says the king gesturing to his servant to top up the knight's goblet, "he was drawing in the dirt with his paw. He drew something that looked like a 'B' and then an 'I' and then a squiggle much like an 'S' and then he even drew a 'C'. I could have sworn he was writing. I think he wanted me to call him 'Biscuit,' so that's his name now."

And the wife looks with fear at the wolf who meets her eyes so frankly that she knows his true identity.

"Clever Biscuit," says the king, and scratches Bisclaveret's head.

At this point Bisclaveret no longer cares if he is riddled with arrows like Saint Sebastian. He attacks the knight again.

"What is going on?" demands the king.

The courtiers and servants only manage to drag Bisclaveret off when he struggles free and once more he jumps on the knight.

"If you don't mind, Your Highness, I think I'll sit at the far end of the table," says the knight.

"What a terrible thing to have to do," the king replies, "but your lady will sit right here, next to me, so that you won't feel insulted."

The king enthusiastically pats the seat to his left (his wife was on his right and once seated, the lady found it most taxing to move) and the baroness sits down warily.

"Your Highness," whispers the king's counselor, "perhaps this wolf is trying to tell us something."

"What would he be trying to tell us?" asks the king, understandably perplexed. "Biscuit, are you trying to tell us something?"

At which point, Bisclaveret, leaps up one last time and rips the very nose out of the center of his wife's face.

"Oh, good God," says the king, "were you teasing him?"

The wife tries hard to get away from Bisclaveret, but Bisclaveret is still, having had the first satisfaction in close to a year.

"Send for a doctor," screams the wife.

"You must have been doing something."

"I was not."

"Perhaps," says the counselor, "it is some wrongdoing from the past."

"Yes," says the king. "What have you done to Biscuit?"

And finally, the baroness, due to the gaping wound in the center of her face, is disposed to tell the truth.

"Give the wolf his robe," the baroness shrieks to the knight. "Give Bisclaveret his robe back now!"

The knight returns the baron's robe. The knight and baroness are banished. The baron is restored.

"Bisclaveret" was a favorite of my mother's. Once when I was eight years old, I woke up, having thrown off my covers, to see her beautiful pale face pulling the comforter up to my chin. She was in a T-shirt from Hawaii that had palm trees and surfers on it. Her legs were bare and, I noticed, very thin. She was thin, although I don't think they'd figured out at that point what was wrong with her.

"I was lonely. Did I wake you up?"

"Yes. I'm glad you did."

She told me the story of Bisclaveret. I remember her hands moving around in the dark air and her laughing, because to her it was a funny story. I remember her reaching for my nose at the end and pretending to have captured it when I was already too old not to recognize that it was the tip of her thumb in her fist. I think my mother loved the tale of Bisclaveret because the real wolf in the story was the baroness. It's the baroness who is awakened by the existence of the unknown. She betrays the baron, warms her bed with another man. She is brutally, physically punished, forced to go through life with her face—the seat of all things human—altered.

Even though the baroness didn't win, my mother was pleased that not all wolves were men. I remember her sitting on the foot of my bed with her T-shirt stretched tight over her knees. The light from the bathroom across the hall kept the room dimly lit so I could see her profile.

"What happened next?" I asked.

"What do you mean?"

"After the baron got his castle back. Was he still a werewolf?"

"I suppose he was," said my mother. "I don't know why he wouldn't be."

"And what happened to the baroness?"

"Oh I don't know. I suppose the knight left her. Men don't like women without proper noses. She had to go live in a shack far from town. She raised goats and the goats were her only friends. During the Inquisition, she was probably burned as a witch."

"That's awful," I said.

"Well," my mother said, looking over her shoulder and into the hall light, "things often are."

28

The rain had finally stopped and now the days were bright and beautiful. A few daffodils raised their heads around the property. Even one rogue red tulip had popped up by the house, but how could I enjoy the weather when I missed Arthur? Ann called every day, sounding nuttier each time, and I felt sorry for her. Without Boris, she didn't really know what to do with her time except to look for him. Now the police were involved, but Boris remained silent and hidden. Kevin was company, but not much in the way of conversation. The nights were lonely. Because of this, I had taken to sleeping on the couch in the living room. The idea of going to bed depressed me and I started sleeping in shallow fits, wrapped up with the dog in the stadium blanket. The couch faced the sliding doors to the deck and on clear nights I could see the moon rising and a smattering of stars from where I lay. I was half-asleep with the TV muttering when I first saw her. She was on the deck, her pale face watching me. I watched, completely still, and she stepped back from the window. The TV threw up a sudden bright reflection and she disappeared from view. I jumped up and pulled the sliding door open. There was no one there.

"I know you're out there," I said. "You better come in before you freeze."

But the night was unusually warm, in the forties, and there was no answer. I lit a cigarette and was smoking heartily, massaging my head as if it would help my brain sort out this latest appearance, when I heard the front door swing open. I turned around, and there she was, wrapped up in my father's black cashmere coat, pale and wasted, her teeth chattering.

"Mother?"

"You're not happy to see me," she said.

"How did you get here?"

"Your father knows where you are," she said. "You should leave while you still can."

"Sit down," I said. I went over to her and she sat in the nearest chair waving me off. "You don't look good. You should be in the hospital."

She shook her head. "What you mean to say is that I should be dead."

"No I don't."

"Then let me stay a while. I'll be no trouble."

"That's not my point."

"Then what is your point?"

"How did you get here?"

"Taxi," she said and she smiled. "I can always get to where I want. It's you who seem to have a problem finding your way around, finding your loved ones."

She was exhausted. The act of speaking seemed too much for her.

"You should lie down," I said. I placed my hands on her shoulders and led her down the hallway to the bedroom. I took off her coat and she crawled into bed.

"I'm cold," she said. "Lie next to me."

I got in beside her, as we'd slept so many times when I was younger.

"Mom," I said. "I want to know about the bones."

"Oh, the bones. That's quite a long story."

"That's all right. We have time."

"Then I'll start at the beginning. You know about the whale ship *Essex*?"

"A whale sank it." I said. "It's the basis for *Moby-Dick*."

"*Moby-Dick* leads up to the story of the *Essex*. It's like a prequel."

"What does this have to do with the bones at the Hidalgo?"

"The survivors tried to make it to Chile in the whaleboats. They could have made it to Tahiti, which was much closer, but they were scared of cannibals. When the survivors were found, they were clutching the bones of their departed friends."

"They'd eaten them?"

"Yes, but they held the bones. When their rescuers tried to take the bones away, they cried. You see, they loved their departed comrades, they cherished their remains, and couldn't bare to let them go."

"I thought the bones at the Hidalgo were Anasazi."

"The Anasazi disappeared. No one knows where they went. Maybe the earth swallowed them up, and all we have to show they lived is their bones and a few pottery shards, some buildings crumbling in the desert."

"Oh mother, give me a straight answer."

"We all disappear, Katherine. We are all nothing but bones, briefly animated, then still."

I was still pondering this, almost relieved to see my mother's dementia alive and well, which made her animation so much more real, and was about to pursue my original line of questioning when I heard her breath slow and realized she had fallen asleep.

Later that night the phone rang. I was in the bathroom and by the time I had reached the living room, the answering machine had already picked up.

"Katherine, this is Barry. I left a message for you last week, which I presume you did not receive. It's about the bones. The Anasazi bones you found in your mother's attic? They're not Anasazi at all. Actually, the bones are only ten years old. I had to turn them over to the New Mexico police. They just called me. The bones belong to a young man who went missing in 1993. Do you have any idea what they were doing in your mother's attic? Please call me . . ." and then the machine cut him off. The phone rang again. "Katherine, this is Barry Buster Parkinson. I just left a message, but I'm not sure if it got recorded. Call me. My number is 512–555–9874. The bones are new. The bones are new."

29

My mother woke me up the following morning. She was standing by my dresser, looking at my things. She looked surprisingly well. The FedEx envelope was still there, pretty much undisturbed, and she was going through it.

"Is this all there's left of me?" she said smiling. She was holding the postcard of *The Raft of the Medusa.*

"What do you mean?" I asked. I was still half-asleep.

"The safe-deposit key, these earrings, my hair . . ."

"My hair," I corrected her. "The hair is mine."

"That's right," she said. She held the dogwood earrings out to me. "You always liked these."

"I like them on you," I said.

My mother brushed her hair back and held the earrings up to her ears, then she put them on.

Later that evening I received more unexpected visitors. My mother was napping silently down the hall and I had a cup of tea in my hands when the doorbell rang. Kevin barked from the couch, but couldn't be bothered to get up. I opened the door just a crack. It was Detective Yancy and Officer Brown.

"Good evening," I said. "What brings you here?"

"I think you know," said Detective Yancy.

But I didn't know. There was a lot going on. I opened the door. "Can I interest you in a cup of tea?"

"No thank you," said Detective Yancy. "We'd like a minute of your time."

"All right then." I went into the living room and the two men followed me. I turned off the television and gestured for them to take the couch, next to Kevin. I arranged myself in the easy chair cradling my tea in my hands. "What appears to be the problem?"

"Is there a problem?" asked Detective Yancy cryptically.

"I would assume as much. You are here and not at your policeman's ball, or whatever it is that occupies you on Friday nights."

Officer Brown smiled.

"What do you know of Mr. Connor's suitcase?" asked Detective Yancy.

"Not as much as you do," I said. "Where did you find it?"

"In Portland," said Detective Yancy. "In a dumpster."

"Portland? Are you sure it's his?"

"His manuscript was in there."

Officer Brown was about to say something when Detective Yancy raised his hand to silence him.

"I don't know," I said. "Maybe Travis did kill himself."

"I don't think he did that," said Officer Brown. Then he covered his mouth as a way of apologizing to his superior.

"Why don't you just tell me what's going on?" I asked. "I really have no idea how the suitcase got in the dumpster. None. Give me a lie detector test if you don't believe me."

"Where is Mr. Verhoven?" asked Detective Yancy.

I set my tea down on the coffee table and took up the pack of cigarettes. "Arthur's gone. He's gone." I shrugged. "If you find him, let me know."

"Did you have a fight?"

"You might say that," I said. "Why are you looking for Arthur?"

"His fingerprints were all over the suitcase," said Detective Yancy.

"The suitcase was in this house."

"His fingerprints were also on the dumpster."

"And?"

Officer Brown and Detective Yancy exchanged a look.

"So Travis's manuscript was in it. That's hardly damning."

"Mr. Connor's manuscript," said Detective Yancy. "Also Mr. Connor's head, his hands, and his feet."

I heard the water dripping in the sink. It seemed that for a moment no one breathed. "Oh my God," I said. "What happened?"

"That's what we're trying to find out."

"Did you call his mother?"

"I called Travis's mother," said Officer Brown. "She didn't take it very well."

"The poor woman," I added.

There was another moment of silence.

"I see Mr. Verhoven's van is parked out front."

"Arthur left it here. Something's wrong with the starter." I looked first at Detective Yancy, then at Officer Brown. "No," I said. "You don't think . . ."

"When was the last time you spoke with Mr. Verhoven?"

"Tuesday."

"How did he leave?"

"In a hurry," I said. "We'd had a fight."

"What did you fight about?"

I composed my thoughts. "He had a jealousy issue. It was an ongoing thing in our relationship."

"He left the van here?"

"He made a phone call. One of his friends came and picked him up."

"What was his friend's name?"

"I'm not sure. I wasn't paying attention."

"What was this friend driving?"

"I didn't look. I was sitting right here. We'd had a fight. I was mad." I looked at Officer Brown, who seemed both sympathetic and embarrassed. "Is Arthur a suspect?"

"The suitcase," said Detective Yancy, "was covered in a clay-like mud, the same kind of mud found on this property."

"Oh, for God's sake. And you think it's Arthur?"

"His fingerprints, Miss Shea, were all over the suitcase."

"Arthur is not a violent person," I said. After the third try I managed to light my cigarette. I offered a cigarette to Detective Yancy and to my surprise, he took it. "How do you know," I handed him the lighter, "that it's not Bad Billy?"

"Because," said Detective Yancy, "William Selwyn is lying on a table in the Portland morgue."

"He is?" I said, shocked.

"You saw him there yourself. It was William Selwyn's body that washed up on Wolf's Neck."

"What happened to him?"

"How did he die?" said Detective Yancy. "We think he froze to death. There was a week in early November when the temperature at night didn't get above the teens."

"I remember it was cold." I felt sorry for Bad Billy and felt that I'd somehow failed him.

"How did he get in the ocean?"

"His campsite was near the water. A combination of the tides and the recent flooding could have done it," said Detective Yancy, "But the fact that he's been dead since early November leaves us with a few nagging questions."

"And what are those?"

"Who killed John Nelson?"

I listened carefully.

"We're assuming it's the same killer who murdered Malley Borden."

"Didn't he die in early October?" I asked. "Wasn't that Bad Billy?"

"It seems unlikely. The wound to the neck. The fact that the victim is male."

"But what about Travis? His killing seems more like a Mafia slaying, with the head and feet and all."

"We don't know the connection yet," said Detective Yancy dramatically.

"We haven't found his neck," said Officer Brown.

"And you think it's Arthur?"

"A bartender at Gritty's saw you talking to Malley Borden the night he was killed."

"I remember meeting a 'Billy' at Gritty McDuff's. 'Billy.' He worked at L.L. Bean."

"Malley worked at L.L. Bean. Maybe you heard his name wrong."

"It does get loud at Gritty's," said Officer Brown.

"Are you taking this down?" asked Detective Yancy.

Officer Brown began scribbling in his notebook.

"Tell me more about Mr. Verhoven's jealousy."

"You can't be serious."

"We are serious," said Detective Yancy.

"No, I refuse to believe it," I said. I began to cry.

"If you're covering for him," said Detective Yancy, "now is the time to stop."

"Oh what's the use?" I cried out. "He went to New York. He didn't tell me why."

"Write this down," ordered Detective Yancy.

"He said he was going to his brother's in Connecticut first to get some money. I thought he'd held up a convenience store, or something like that. I had no idea . . ."

"Anything else?" said Detective Yancy.

"Yeah," I said. "He said he was going to shave his head."

30

I got up late, around eleven. I was back on the couch, having decided that my mother was welcome to my bed. Having her around was a trial for me, even though she spent most of the day sleeping, the rest strangely quiet as if she was waiting for something from me. I hadn't brought up the subject of the bones again because I knew all I wanted to.

"How did you get out of the hospital?" I asked her.

"Through the front doors," she said.

"I assumed as much. What about Dad?"

"He'll make his peace with it."

"How did you get past him?"

"The only way I could," she said.

"What's that supposed to mean?"

"You want me to leave, don't you?"

"You're not well . . ."

"You're the one who should leave. You're the one who's in trouble, yet you stay here day after day, in this little house. What are you waiting for? Arthur's gone."

After that unenlightening exchange, I'd had a monumental headache and wrestling with it and all the frightening images it conjured up left me wasted when it finally quit. I'd gone into Arthur's van with a bottle of wine—to get away from her, I suppose—and spent an hour or so looking through the pictures and albums, CDs, blankets, busted drumsticks, paperbacks of Kerouac, Denis Johnson, Vonnegut. His sleeping bag was still in there, but Arthur's scent was disappearing. I sat in the driver's seat and started the engine, for a moment wondered what it would be like to drive off the end of the point, into the water. Kevin, who was sitting in the passenger seat, looked at me accusingly and I remembered that the tide was out, that all I'd accomplish was sinking the van into the mud. And what good was that?

I made a strong pot of coffee. It looked like another glorious day and I was feeling more than a little resentful of it, the winking flowers, the shivering leaves, the cormorants set up like sentries along the pylons at the bay's entrance. The tide was in and I could hear children somewhere yelling to each other. It was Saturday, after all. I had just started to brush my teeth, which I was doing at the kitchen sink, looking up the driveway where a rabbit was squatting up on its furry haunches, when I saw the black Lexus SUV. The rabbit managed to scurry away in time, but it was too late for me, and I knew this deep in my bones. I set down my toothbrush, overcome by weariness, and, honestly, an element of relief.

A police car followed the SUV and the two vehicles pulled into the driveway. Kevin barked and ran to the door. I wondered who he thought was there. Maybe he could smell Officer Brown, who was raising his hand to the bell, who always patted Kevin when he came over. I doubt he was barking for my father, who had no use for dogs.

I went over to the door and waited for the bell to ring, which it did. I swung it open and saw Officer Brown, embarrassed as always, and my father, who was now completely gray-haired, but other than that, exactly the same. Officer Brown was in uniform, of course, and my father looked dressed for golf, which was as casual as he could manage.

"Hello, Katherine," said my father.

"Hello, Dad," I said. "I see you've contacted the police."

"Actually," said my father, "he approached me."

"Really?" I looked over to Officer Brown and stepped back so they could enter the house.

"Mr. Shea was speeding. I pulled him over, then he said he was your father. He couldn't find your house, so I thought I'd just bring him over. And I wanted to see how you were doing, Miss Shea."

I smiled tightly. "I'm doing fine," I said. I looked back at my father, who as usual, betrayed no emotion. "So what made you finally come visit me?"

"I received a phone call. Dr. Parkinson from the University of Arizona is anxious to track you down."

"As are many people," I said.

"Although they may not be aware of it," my father added. He looked pointedly at Officer Brown, who was beginning to be very uncomfortable.

"Coffee?" I asked.

"Black," said my father, which I already knew.

Officer Brown shook his head then stepping back, upset a lamp, which he quickly righted.

I brought my father his coffee and he nodded a polite thank-you.

"So, what made Barry contact you?"

"Barry?"

"Barry Buster Parkinson."

"He still had our home phone number from when you were in college. He had it in his records. I don't know why he needed your home phone number."

"You don't want to know," I said. Barry and I had rendezvoused a couple of times over vacations. I remembered one rainy spring break weekend in his house on Martha's Vineyard. "So the bones are new."

"It seems your mother had an interesting hobby."

"What was her hobby?" asked Officer Brown.

"Her hobby," I said, staring my father down, "is Native American culture."

"Certain cultures, not what most women go for."

"And what do most women go for?" I asked my father.

"Maybe I should leave," said Officer Brown.

"No," said my father. "I want you here."

Officer Brown was both confused and surprised by this. He crouched down and began scratching Kevin's ears.

"My dog really likes you," I said.

"Actually," said Officer Brown, "he's my dog. Someone stole him off my back porch three months ago."

"Oh," I said. "I'm sorry about that."

There was an uncomfortable silence. Officer Brown got up. "Can I use your bathroom?" he said.

"No," I said. "I'm afraid not."

"Why not?" asked my father.

"There's a plumbing problem. The toilet's backed up."

"Maybe I could take a look at it for you," said Officer Brown. He headed for the hallway.

"No. Don't go down there. It's all right. I'll fix it later."

"I don't mind, really. I'm good at things like this."

"No," I said.

Officer Brown ignored me.

"No!" I shouted. "Don't go in there!"

Officer Brown stopped and turned. He rested his hand on his gun holster. "Miss Shea, is Mr. Verhoven in the house?" He looked at me with such frankness and sympathy that I felt I had to be honest.

"Yes, he is."

Officer Brown took his gun from his holster and walked slowly down the hallway.

"Katherine, this is not easy for me," said my father.

I turned and looked him solidly in eyes. "She's here too."

My father looked up at me, not seeming to comprehend what I was saying. We watched each other in tense silence.

The bathroom door creaked open, then there was a moment followed by the thud of Officer Brown's body hitting the floor. My father looked hesitantly at me, then went down the hallway. I followed a few steps behind. Officer Brown had passed out, his arm flung out to the right, the gun a few inches away on the floor. His shoes had blood on the soles. I saw my father peek into the bathroom, then pull back. He covered his face with his hands and looked away. He stayed frozen like that until I went to him and led him by the elbow back into the living room. I helped him to the chair and he sat down.

We sat in silence for maybe five minutes.

My father looked helpless then. I'd never seen him look like that. I always thought I'd wanted to see him like that, but I'd been wrong. I actually felt sorry for him.

"My neglect is criminal," he said.

"You did your best," I said, surprised by the tenderness in my voice.

"Katherine, what are you talking about?"

"There are worse fathers."

He seemed surprised that this was an issue. "And worse husbands, no doubt," he said. "I failed you and your mother."

"She's here," I repeated. "Were you looking for her?"

"Looking for her?" My father's eyebrow's descended and he pulled his head up sharply. "Your mother's dead, almost a year now." I watched him closely. His face hardly moved. "I told that Italian construction worker, your boyfriend." He looked rattled, more confused then scared, as if he suspected me of playing with him. "Petro."

"Pietro," I corrected him.

"I know he told you."

"That's right."

It took me a minute to get up from my chair.

I went down the hall to the bedroom.

I looked in the mirror and saw with mild surprise that I was wearing the dogwood earrings. I was alone and the room was filled with a vacuum of silence, as if someone had been laughing riotously, hysterically, and suddenly stopped.

I packed a few things, without really thinking what they were. My mother was right. I had to escape while I still could.

When I came back to the living room, my father still had not moved.

"I'm leaving now," I said.

My father looked up at me. "You can't leave, Katherine. We'll work something out. Everything will be all right."

"What are you talking about?" I said.

"You killed him in self-defense. He was a murderer anyway. The police will understand."

"Arthur didn't kill Travis," I said. I imagined Arthur sawing off Travis's feet and hands, Travis's head.

My father blew his nose into his handkerchief and I could smell his sweat, I could smell Officer Brown's deodorant, his toothpaste, his laundry detergent and soap from down the hall. Out in the back field I could smell where the deer had come close, then smelling me, taken off. And I knew that it would rain that night, just a little, although it was nowhere in the forecasts. I knew all of this, just as I knew that Arthur would come back after dumping the suitcase, even though he knew I was responsible. He came back because he wanted me to tell him that it wasn't true. I don't know why. Maybe he loved me.

"How did you become this way?" asked my father.

But my father's ingenuousness failed to fool me. How could he claim not to understand my hunger, a hunger that was everywhere—in art, in literature, at the boundaries of our knowledge, in the dark jungles of our planet—the basic hunger in us all? Our civilization, the "America" that was a source of unending pride for him, was not based on the nurturing of the weak but on their calculated demise. He seemed to find my motivations a mystery, that I, because of my particular appetite, was the "other." But here he was wrong. His need for control, for money, for power, was based on the foundation of a populace debilitated by the appetites of the strong. This was his history. My history. The history of the world. My father's horror of me was not one of incomprehension, but fear.

Was I not him?

Were we not all cannibals dispensing with the defenseless, concerned only with our own survival?

"Is there anything you want to tell me?" he asked.

I considered this. I wanted to tell him that the fact that he didn't eat people didn't make him Mr. Wonderful, never had. That he'd never fooled my mother, nor me. But I felt sorry for him, strangely enough, so I kept this to myself.

"I'm going to be all right," I said.

I did want to tell him that Boris was dead, for Ann's sake. It would have been the generous thing to do, but also stupid. Generosity usually was. Ann would sell some large canvas in the next couple of months. She'd have to go out to the storage space in Williamsburg and by then Boris's reek would be more than the cedar chest could handle. She might even figure it out on her own, the fire I'd lit that day to burn the manuscripts, the coincidence of his disappearance. Soon, no doubt, everyone would figure everything out, without my help.

"Dad," I said. "I have to get going. Do you have any cash?"

"What?" he said.

"Do you have any cash?"

"Where are you going?"

I had decided to head to Canada, which was only six hours away. It was time to try my luck in a new country.

"Where are you going?" he repeated.

"I can't tell you that," I said.

My father looked suddenly old, tired beyond belief. His shoulders slumped and from where I was standing, looking down on his head, I could see that his hair had thinned and soon his scalp would be as visible as it had been when he was a baby. He reached into his pocket and pulled out his wallet. He had a couple of hundred dollars in there, and some smaller bills. He looked at the money, than back at me. He said, "You know I loved your mother."

"I know, Dad."

"You know I would have done anything to save her."

"I know that." I went to squat by him and placed my hands on his knees. "Don't worry. Everything will work out."

My father looked up at me, utterly defeated, and handed over the cash. He said, "Somehow I think I will never see you again."

31

The night of the big snowstorm my father managed to call home before the lines went dead.

"I need you to be a big girl," my father said to me. I was ten years old. "I'm going to have to spend the night in a hotel in Boston." He gave me the phone number. "Now listen closely. You should get some wood, a lot, before it gets dark. There's a good chance that you'll lose power. You and your mother should sleep in the living room."

"Yes, Dad," I said.

"And most importantly, make sure she takes her medicine. Promise me."

"I promise."

My mother was napping on the couch. Her feet were pulled up under a wool blanket and her black hair spread over the pillow. Her skin was pale, translucent, and I could see her eyes twitching in a dream. Her lips pulled up for a moment over her teeth and her breathing quickened. For a moment I was stopped by her beauty. She looked like Snow White in her glass coffin, somehow alive but more dead. I had the pill and a glass of water for her to take it with. I'd stacked a pile of wood beside the fireplace but the power was still on, the house bright and humming with it.

"Mommy," I said. And she woke up and smiled. "I have your medicine."

She propped herself up on an elbow and took the pill. She looked at it. "These pills make me so sleepy," she said. She leaned over to the potted palm and dug a small hole with her index finger into which she dropped the pill. She covered it over with soil then took the glass of water and poured into the pot. "Maybe it will grow into a big medicine tree," she said. "This is our secret."

Then she got up from the couch, wrapping the blanket around her shoulders like a shawl. My father never let her drink—he said it interacted badly with her pills—but she liked to drink and I remember her opening a bottle of wine. "What shall we do tonight?" she said. "Maybe there's something inappropriate for you on TV."

We started watching a movie, something I found quite dull—especially the bedroom scenes—but soon the power quit and I was saved.

"Now what?" she said.

"I'll light a fire," I replied.

We took the cushions off the couch and arranged some sort of pallet on the floor. I brought down comforters and pillows from upstairs. Outside, the wind howled and all the doors in our old house rattled in response. My mother and I sat on the cushions, warm and happy, staring into the fire. She was halfway through the bottle of wine.

"Katherine," she said, placing her hand on my shoulder and then on my face and then on my hair, "what do you want to be when you grow up?"

"I want to be you," I said.

"Me? No. Be something better."

I thought again. "I want to be famous."

"For what?"

"Does it matter?" I asked with complete sincerity.

"I don't know," she responded.

"I suppose I will have to be successful."

"Maybe not. I think success is overrated. Think of your father." And we laughed.

"Sometimes," she said sadly, "you can be famous for being a magnificent failure."

"Really?"

She nodded. The snow was drifting up against the house, two feet high against the back sliders. I could see it piling up on the windowsills, sealing us in. "Think of the Donner Party. Do you know of any of the other parties that made it across the Sierras with no problems?"

"No," I said.

"We remember them because they didn't make it. Only a few did. The rest died. And they're famous."

"I don't want to die like that," I said. "Maybe I could be one of the people who made it out. Who else is famous for failing?"

"Do you know who Franklin is?" she asked.

"Benjamin Franklin?"

"He was successful," she said disparagingly. "I meant Sir John Franklin, the explorer. He was a magnificent failure. He died in the ice trying to find the Northwest Passage. He took all his men with him."

"What's the Northwest Passage?"

"Franklin was trying to find a way to get from the Atlantic Ocean to the Pacific Ocean by going north, rather than south around the bottom of South America. He was with two steamships. They disappeared into the ice and were only found ten years later, on King William Island."

"Where's that?"

"Up, up, up north. Somewhere between Greenland and Canada."

"Tell me about Franklin."

"Franklin's first failure was in Canada. He had a plan to go up the Snare River and then down the Coppermine. He was going to find the western entrance of the Northwest Passage, but he really didn't know what he was doing. He had voyageurs with him—mixed-blood French and Chippewa Indian—to hunt and navigate. And he had a surgeon to fix people. And some English to be English when they found the entrance to the Northwest Passage. It took him a long time. He went up the Snare River in birchbark canoes, then down the Coppermine. At times the canoes had to be carried. Summers were short and he kept getting stuck in the snow. Sometimes it was sixty degrees below zero. He mapped about three hundred miles of coastline, wanting to go further, but there wasn't enough food to go on. At that point there wasn't enough food to turn back either, but he had no choice. It was the middle of August when his group finally headed north again. There was snow. The voyageurs were sent on hunting parties, but they found little. One voyageur fell ill and had to be tended to. Franklin broke the party up into three groups. The doctor, two Englishmen, and another voyageur, Michel, stayed behind with the sick man. Franklin pushed on with the other men, then he divided that group into two. The fast people he sent ahead to get help while he walked on slowly with some others. But the third group, the one with the sick man . . ."

"What happened to the third group?" I asked.

My mother smiled and she laughed a little. "It's a little gruesome and it might scare you."

"I'm not scared," I said, but I was and liked it.

"The sick voyageur died and they left him. The doctor and the other two men were starving, as was Michel, but he went out hunting. He said he'd found the carcass of a wolf torn by a deer's horn. He offered them this meat and they ate it up. But there was no wolf. Michel had gone back and carved up the dead man. They ate the dead man's body."

My mother laughed and I giggled nervously.

"Then what happened?"

"The doctor and one of the other Englishmen went out to look for *tripe de roche*, which is some sort of wild mushroom, and while they were digging around, they heard a gunshot. They rushed back and found that Michel had shot the other Englishman, shot him dead. Michel said it was an accident, that his gun went off. But the dead man was wearing a nightcap and that nightcap had gunpowder on it, which meant that Michel had been holding the gun close to the dead man's head."

"So it wasn't an accident?"

"No. The two Englishmen were terrified that Michel was going to shoot them."

"Why?"

"Because he was hungry."

"Oh."

"So the doctor shot Michel." My mother gestured for me to get her cigarettes off the coffee table, and I did. "When the doctor and the other Englishmen finally caught up with Franklin, they were stronger than any of the other men. It was impossible for them to have subsisted only on the mushrooms, but no one talked about how they'd made it out of the snow."

"Why didn't anyone talk about it?"

"I suppose because they were English. The English don't talk about things like that."

The fire snapped and crackled in the grate. The fire shifted and a heavy log fell, throwing sparks onto the carpet. My mother calmly stamped them out with the ashtray. "Franklin went to Tasmania after that, as a governor. Everyone thought his exploring days were over, but then they sent him to find the Northwest Passage from the east, and he died up there, frozen in the ice."

"What did he die from?"

"I think it was the tinned beef, botulism. Not a very spectacular death. But then Franklin was not a very spectacular man. All of his crewmen died, some on the ship from the tinned beef, others trying to find their way to the whaling camps."

"They all died?"

"Imagine it, the snow, the ice, and death breathing over them all, one by one. And then the wind, burying them beneath the snow, preserving all the bodies as if the Arctic Circle was a huge meat locker."

"That's very sad," I said. "They must have been very cold."

My mother stroked my hair. "One man might have made it out."

"Really," I said, a bit cheered.

"His name was Crozier and he was tough, not like Franklin. He knew the Arctic well. He was heading for a river with the stronger men, but they were all dying around him because there was no food. The men started eating the ones that had died. Then they were strong and could go on. Crozier ate whatever was there. He headed south and the men marched with him and they died and he ate them and in the end, he was the only one alive. Some people say he joined up with the Chippewas."

"Is he famous?"

"Crozier? Not as famous as Franklin."

"Because he was successful," I said sadly.

"Perhaps."

I fell asleep shortly after that and awoke maybe an hour later. My mother was fixing the fire and the flames under lit her face, showing her broad cheekbones. Red light reflected in the whites of her eyes.

"Can't you sleep?" she asked me.

"I don't want to. I wish it snowed all the time like this. Then I'd never have to go to school and you'd never have to take your medicine."

My mother sighed. She pulled her blanket around her and looked at me with tenderness.

"What is the most important thing in the world?" I asked.

"What do you think?" she asked.

"Love, probably."

My mother laughed. "Who told you that?"

"I don't know. Someone must have."

"Well it's not," she smiled. "That's what people tell little girls."

"Why?"

My mother stared at a fixed point in the fire. "They tell little girls that so that the little girls will fall in love with handsome men and get married. And the little girls believe them and grow up into old women who take pills and sleep on couches."

"Was Dad handsome?"

"Very. And he still is, only you can't see it."

I thought for a moment, then took up my mother's cigarettes and lit one, puffing a little and coughing. She didn't seem to care.

"So what is the most important thing?" I asked.

Mother nodded to someone, not me, an invisible authoritative someone in the middle of the room and all the darkness left her face.

She smiled that wild smile that she sometimes had, that made my father rush her home when we were out. "The most important thing is hunger."

"Hunger?"

"Persius, who was a writer in ancient Rome, said that the stomach is the teacher of the arts and the dispenser of invention. He was right." My mother looked at me appraisingly and I tilted my head to one side, as always weighing what the grownups told me with appropriate skepticism.

"Know hunger and satisfy it," she said. "That's the key to success."

"But I don't want to be successful."

"Then it's the key to freedom and everyone wants to be free."

But I didn't know what freedom was and when I thought about being free I was left with the image of me standing on the side of the road, alone and deserted.

The next morning I woke up with an icy breeze blowing on my face. The back sliders were wide open. A strong wind had swept the back-yard, pushing the snow into neatly angled drifts up against the fences, obliterating our little rock wall—created by field-clearing pilgrims—at the back. It was not yet dawn but a near-full moon threw off a blue light reflected on every surface and even the trees, weighted with ice, glowed silver.

My mother, stark naked, was running around the yard.

My first instinct was to get her coat, to cover her up and bring her in, but I didn't. Instead I watched her clumsy dancing, leaping, spinning and wondered how she could be barefoot on the ice and snow and not feel the cold at all.

ACKNOWLEDGMENTS

Many books were useful in the writing of this one, especially *The New Golden Land: European Images of America from the Discoveries to the Present Time* (Hugh Honour, Pantheon Books, 1975), for aiding me in my pursuit of Columbus and Vespucci; *The Fatal Shores* (Robert Hughes, Knopf, 1986), for introducing me to Alexander Pearce; *History of the Donner Party* (C. F. McGlashan, Stanford University Press, 1940), for preserving the remains of the Donner Party members; *Iceblink* (Scott Cookman, John Wiley and Sons, 2000), for knowing what happened to Franklin; *Desperate Journeys, Abandoned Souls* (Edward E. Leslie, Mariner Books, 1988), for its canny chronicling of man versus nature; *The Custom of the Sea* (Neil Hanson, John Wiley and Sons, 1999), which reminds us that the concept of civilization can be brought to anything; *Romantic Art* (William Vaughn, Thames and Hudson, 1978), for keeping Gericault and Goya alive; *Man Corn: Cannibalism and Violence in the Prehistoric American Southwest* (Christy G. Turner II and Jacqueline A. Turner, University of Utah Press, 1999), for its perseverance in the face of modern morality; and for the book *Goya* (Keizo Kanki, Ward Lock, 1970), given to my mother for Christmas once when I was small, which has gnawed on my mind for the last twenty-eight years, with special thanks to Gordana, who was from Split and had the inspiration to give it to her.

Also, I would like to thank Esmond Harmsworth, who braved all sorts of tempests and was willful enough to force the multiple revisions. And to Elisabeth Schmitz, who oversaw the final product with care and intelligence.